you're so vain

ANGELA CASELLA

ac

also by angela casella

Babes of Brewing

Best Served Cold

Worst Nanny Ever

Unlucky in Love

The Love Fixers

The Love Bandits

The Love Losers

The Love Destroyers

The Thief Who Saved Christmas

Finding You

You're so Extra

You're so Bad

You're so Basic

You're so Vain

Fairy Godmother Agency

A Borrowed Boyfriend

A Stolen Suit

A Brooding Bodyguard

A Reluctant Roommate

Bringing Down the House (Nicole and Damien's story)

Highland Hills

(co-written with Denise Grover Swank)

Matchmaking a Billionaire

Matchmaking a Single Dad

Matchmaking a Grump

Matchmaking a Roommate

Bad Luck Club

(co-written with Denise Grover Swank)

Love at First Hate

Jingle Bell Hell

Fraudulently Ever After

Matchmaking Mischief

Asheville Brewing

(co-written with Denise Grover Swank)

Any Luck at All

Better Luck Next Time

Getting Lucky

Bad Luck Club

Luck of the Draw (novella)

All the Luck You Need (prequel novella) by Angela Casella

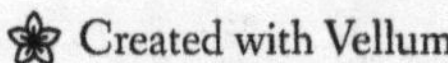 Created with Vellum

For my sister, Jennifer, who's a kickass single mom like Ruthie. May that slender flame burn bright.

And for Flour, the corgi. You are an absolute and utter pain in the butt, but I adore you anyway. Kind of like Shane in this book. (And oh, how he would loathe being compared to a dog.)

SHANE

"I'M NOT GOING to get the job, am I?" I ask the balding man sitting in front of me, who very distinctly wants me out of his office. He's been fidgeting in his chair and eyeing the paper bag sitting on the corner of his desk since I first sat down across from him. I've been staring at the birthmark or mole on his bald pate, barely hidden by his combover, and wondering if it's cancerous.

Maybe I've made an overly straight-forward remark, but then again, I'm tired. It's a couple of weeks into the new year, and this is approximately the thirtieth job I'm not going to get after quitting my old firm on Thanksgiving Day. My former boss, Fred Myles, warned me I wouldn't get a legal job within thirty miles of Asheville if I quit.

But he didn't leave me much of a choice. He'd agreed to defend two people I knew to be guilty. That's not the kind of thing that would normally stand in my way—everyone deserves good defense —but the two people in question are the parents of one of my best friends, Lucas Burke. And he's the one who turned them in.

We're something like family, me and Burke and our friends Leonard, Drew, and Danny. Especially Danny and me. And screwing Burke over would have meant screwing all of them over.

Still, I'd actually considered staying. At one point, I'd felt certain I would stay, personal consequences be damned. I'd worked hard for that job. I wouldn't say I loved it, but I felt a devotion to it that ran deeper than love. When it came down to it, though, I couldn't bring myself to stay. It was either loyalty or weakness that pulled me back, although I suppose some people would call loyalty a weakness.

When I left, I told myself Myles was all bark. He's more fossil than man, and his balls have probably shrunken into his diaphragm by now. But what do you know?

Turns out the old geezer was right about something.

Every good practice in the county has denied me, and so have most of the bad ones. I actually interviewed for a couple of ambulance chasers last week, men who have a billboard with a crying man on it that says, *Someone hit you with your car? We'll turn you into a star*.

It felt like the bottom of the barrel, the job I wanted so little I'd get it by default. But Fred Myles was a godparent to one of the guy's sons, so the interview lasted all of five minutes. I got the sense he'd asked me in just to get an adrenaline rush from crushing me.

The man sitting across from me, whose name I couldn't pull out of my pudding of a brain if I tried, frowns at me and says, "Well, no. You came in here reeking of whiskey, and you don't even seem to know what this firm does."

Guilty.

"But the reason I'm not getting it is Myles, isn't it?" I press. "You know Fred Myles?"

He frowns at me, his features pinching together. "I've never heard of the man."

Huh. Well at least I lost this one honestly. That's almost a relief.

I salute him and get up, a little unsteady on my feet, because, yeah, I may have indulged too much last night, or very early this morning.

"Take it easy," I say. "Enjoy the muffin."

"It's a scone," he tells my back.

Perfect. I am officially less interesting than a dry, shriveled puck of a baked good.

I leave the office and wander the streets for a while, feeling the uncomfortable press of having no destination and nowhere to be. Burke and Leonard run a home restoration business, and they've offered to give me work until I find a new job, but I didn't go to law school so I could run around with a hammer. Even so, as the months have crept past, doubt has entered my mind, sticky and cloying and not at all like me.

What if I don't find a job here?

What if I have to move?

What if I can't find a job *anywhere*?

I loathe self-doubt almost as much as I loathe Fred Myles for taking my life away from me.

Because my job *was* my life. I gave everything I was to that asshole's firm, spending nights and weekends there. My mother framed the photo of me getting made partner, and I hung it up on my wall. It's still there, right next to a wooden sign reading *Bless this mess*. Because when your mother has swung from one bout of depression to another for more than twenty years, you hang up any damn thing she gives you.

I walk until I feel warm despite the January chill, then finally duck into a bakery.

"Coffee and a scone," I tell the woman behind the counter, because I hate myself a little right now, and for some reason it seems appropriate to indulge in a baked good I will not enjoy. She's a pretty brunette with blue-green eyes, the kind of woman I'd normally try to charm, but I barely notice or care.

"What kind of scone?" she asks. "We have thirty varieties."

"Surprise me."

"Bad day?" She tips her head, studying me.

"Bad year."

Her lips form a tentative smile. "We're only two weeks into January."

"When you know, you know."

She lifts her eyebrows as she picks out a scone, and I go through the mechanical act of paying for the breakfast I don't want before sitting down at a table by the window and taking out my phone.

I take a sip of coffee as I lift the phone to my face to unlock it. The first thing I see is a text from my buddy Danny:

How'd it go? Should I take out the whiskey in a sad way or a celebratory way?

I snort, then nearly drop the coffee when I see something else in my alerts.

It's an email from Monty Freeman of Freeman & Daniels.

I interviewed with his firm back in December. The interview itself was unremarkable. The offices were dusty, as if the lawyers who worked there had been stuffed inside and forgotten, and Freeman himself was overly friendly. I'd hoped that friendliness meant he was interested in taking me on board. But then I ran into him on Christmas Eve, a few weeks ago now.

It wasn't a promising encounter.

I'd been walking with Danny's little sister, Ruthie, and her daughter, Izzy, because we'd met on the sidewalk and were all headed to the same Christmas party.

Ruthie and I do not get along. When she was a little kid—a toddler, for fuck's sake—she used to pretend she was a dog so she'd have an excuse to bite me. The years haven't improved things between us. She's the kind of woman who excels in driving people crazy, and she seems to have a special interest in driving *me* crazy.

Don't get me wrong, she's my best friend's sister, and I feel protective of her. I've needed to roll out that protectiveness every now and then, because she's a beautiful woman, the kind of woman whom men gravitate toward—including the asshole she was married to for less than six months. But life's better for both of us if there's distance between us.

Of course, Freeman loved her. He fell all over himself asking her dozens of questions about her latest vanity project—a bookmobile she set up in her old camper van. She'd even flashed him photos of it, because *of course* she did.

One of Ruthie's favorite topics is how vain and self-involved I am, but I'll be damned if she doesn't like turning the conversation to herself whenever possible.

And sure, it didn't do much for my ego to get ignored by a prospective employer in favor of a van nicknamed Vanny. But maybe that encounter had actually buttered him up, because now there's this email...

"Don't get your hopes up," I whisper to myself.

I feel someone staring, and look up to see a woman wearing a furry onesie watching me like *I'm* crazy.

A low moment, to be sure.

I click into the email, everything in me concentrated on the phone screen.

I feel beyond pathetic that I'm this desperate for a job at a general practice firm I hadn't heard of a few months ago, but I need this. I need it bad. I'm sick of feeling like a failure.

Mr. Royce,

Excuse me for my late reply. I've been away for an extended holiday vacation with my family. I must tell you what an absolute pleasure it was to meet your wife and daughter on Christmas Eve. You have a beautiful family, and I might add that family is very important to us here at Freeman & Daniels. Some lawyers care more about the job than they do about their lives outside of it, but we know what's truly important. One of the benefits we offer is excellent insurance for our employees and their families.

I would be honored if you'd come in for another interview at your earliest convenience.

Yours truly,
Monty Freeman

Well, shit.

I'm frankly mystified that he'd spend more than two minutes around Ruthie and me and think there's anything between us, let alone that we're married and Izzy's mine. I'd like to know how he got that impression, but at the same time...

He seems enamored with his own misunderstanding.

I can't let this lie, can I?

It's the kind of thing he'd find out quickly enough if I actually took the job. I won't have a family to put on his "excellent insurance" or to bring to company picnics or square dances or whatever it is they like to do. Besides, he may be the sort who likes to do a full background check on his employees.

The truth is that I never intend to get married. Now, I'm no monk. I go out on dates, occasionally. Sometimes I date the same woman for a few weeks or even months. More often, I go to bars or parties, places where I can meet someone else who wants a single-serving relationship. Dinner or drinks, followed by sex and a swift goodbye in the morning. It's the only type of relationship I had the time or inclination for when I was at Myles & Lee, and until I get my shit together, I don't even have the inclination for that.

Plenty of people have told me I'll change my mind when I meet the right woman. Hell, a couple of months ago, a crackpot psychic actually told me to get ready for wedding bells because I was about to get married. They're entitled to their opinions, but they're wrong.

I've seen some truly ugly divorce cases—people who pledged to love and honor their spouse, and just a few short months or years later wanted nothing less than the complete destruction of that same person.

Then there's my dad. He died when I was a teenager, and my mother's never gotten over it. Never even attempted to. Love ruined her life—and it might have ruined his too, only in a different way. It made him think small. He was a school principal, but he had it in him to be a superintendent or head of the school board. But he always said he had everything he needed, and a position with more responsibilities would take him away from my mom and me.

All four of my best friends seem bound and determined to race each other to the altar, but that hasn't convinced me I'm wrong. Marriage is a bad bet. A losing proposition. A sure way for a person to take leave of their senses and hitch themselves to an anchor that'll hold them back. I'm not being sexist—all of that could just as easily be true for a woman as a man.

I wouldn't say I'm vain, the way Ruthie thinks, but I *am* ambitious. I feel driven to succeed. To *do*.

And yet...

I'm reaching the bottom of the Asheville barrel. It's not a huge city, and there are only so many law firms. I've already started sending out feelers to Charlotte, and I have a couple of interviews there next week, but the thing is...

I don't really want to leave.

This is my life, my home, and I don't want to let Myles drive me out.

Which is why I find myself crafting a delicate response to Freeman that neither confirms nor denies that I have a wife and child.

two

SHANE

A WEEK LATER, I'm sitting in Freeman's office, staring into his smiling face. That smile's been fixed on his face for so long it's got to hurt. I feel sweat dripping down my back from the effort of smiling back.

"Just a *delight*," Freeman is saying. "I don't mind telling you that we were thinking of going in a different direction. The first time we met, I was concerned you might not be the right fit for us. But then I saw you and your wife together, and I thought to myself, 'You got him all wrong, Freeman. There's no way a woman like that would marry a man who was all work and no play.' You see, we value balance above all here. It's one of our core principles." He points to the wall to his right, where there's a collection of framed images.

My eyes rest on a cartoon of a beagle with a tie and the words "Monty Freeman, the legal beagle" scrawled below it. It's not the kind of thing I'd choose to frame, particularly since it hammers home his resemblance to a long-faced dog, but I'll write a sonnet about it if it gets this guy to hire me. Still, I'm guessing that's not what he's talking about, so I keep up the perusal until I find the Venn Diagram next to it. Family, law, and community, and in the middle, all of them intersect in Freeman & Donnelly.

Apparently, this middling law firm is the only thing holding our society together. Who knew.

I cough and then nod seriously, as if it's the most insightful doodle I've ever seen. "Yes, I can see that. Family's important to me, too. You know, they're the ones I do it for. No point in working so hard for nothing."

What the fuck am I saying?

Up until now, I've avoided outright lying to the man, but I'm edging in closer and closer to it. The thing is...

It's pretty obvious I wouldn't be here if not for Ruthie. I'm not getting this job unless this guy and his friends think I'm married to her.

Maybe I can convince her to play along. I can pay her a few hundred bucks to show up at a dinner party and talk about what a stand-up husband and stepfather I am. Danny wouldn't like it, but I doubt she'd be any more inclined to tell her brother than I'd be. One dinner. Maybe two. Then I can start making excuses for her. Maybe the best move is to play it off like *she's* the workaholic—too obsessed with Vanny to hang out with the other spouses or go to any events. *Oh, she wishes she could be here, but you know how it goes. Those books won't read themselves.*

If they ask why she and Izzy aren't on my insurance, I can tell them she has better insurance.

Except, no, that obviously wouldn't work. Why would the diner she waitresses at offer better insurance than this family-friendly law firm? And running a bookmobile is obviously not the kind of gig that comes with a health plan.

The question's an interesting one, actually, because I find myself wondering if Ruthie has any health insurance at all...

"Yes, quite," Freeman says.

I've completely lost the thread of what we were talking about, but I nod sagely. "Indeed."

Freeman leans back in his chair, still smiling at me like he's forgotten there are any other facial expressions. Does he smile like this in court?

I can't imagine that would go over well. Then again, from what I've gleaned, the majority of their cases don't go to court.

This is *not* a job I want. Six months ago, I would have laughed off the idea of working with the smile-happy legal beagle. It's obvious the people at this firm spend all their time pushing paper. They probably have office parties with supermarket sheet cakes and white elephant Christmas parties.

I've defended a lot of guilty assholes, but at least it always came with a bit of a thrill. I was playing a high-stakes game, and I knew it.

This place isn't like that.

This place is a joke.

But if I get a job here, then I might be able to get a different job after Myles & Lee loses the case that compelled me to quit. People will realize I was intelligent for having left a sinking ship—the first rat smart enough to run.

I'm glad you've realized you're a rat, I hear Ruthie telling me. Her voice likes to pop into my head now and then to let me know when I'm being a tool.

Mentally shaking the thought off, I have to acknowledge an alarming possibility: Myles & Lee might *not* lose the case.

Myles is a mummy, but his conscience is smaller than Jiminy Cricket's dick, and that's basically a superpower when it comes to crafting a cutting defense for someone who is very obviously guilty.

Even so, it'll probably be easier for me to get another job once Myles's ire cools down—or he gives up the ghost and retires. Then I can move on or, hell, maybe I can conquer this firm and make it my pet project.

Freeman is still studying me, his perusal making me a little uncomfortable. Finally, he says, "Why don't you wear your wedding ring?"

Well, shit. That's the kind of direct question it's hard to duck or banter your way out of.

I grin back at him, my mind working the problem. Then I open my mouth, hoping like hell the right words fall out. "Lost it down the sink a month ago. Truth is, I'm not much of a plumber. I tried to get it out and sprayed the whole bathroom full of water. Ruthie wasn't too pleased with me. Started keeping her rings off in protest."

There it is...the actual lie. I should feel guilty for letting it slip—for doubling down when I should be backing off—but I don't. Maybe my conscience isn't much bigger than Myles's at this point.

Freeman chuckles, "Oh, I know how that goes. Reminds me of when I was first married. Except my wife's the one who lost her engagement ring. I searched the whole house for it, top to bottom, spent *hours* looking, and it turned out she'd left it at work."

I give a little chuckle—the chuckle of a man who knows, even though I haven't got the first clue. That sweat continues its descent down my back, and my expensive white shirt probably has pit stains.

Freeman gives his desk a little slap. "Well, Shane, I'm pleased as punch you're interested in joining this firm. Donnelly's on vacation, but I've got his blessing to invite you on board. What do you say?"

There's a moment when I can do the rational thing and back down. I'm relieved by his offer—*massively* relieved—but the fact remains that I don't really want this job, and if he knew the truth, he wouldn't want to give it to me. Lying about something like this is, objectively, wrong.

But that doesn't stop me.

"I'd be honored to join the team."

What do you know? It's another lie.

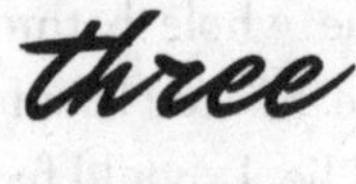

three

RUTHIE

"COME ON, COME ON, COME ON," I say, trying to turn the engine over again. It gives a dying growl. "Dammit, you piece of shit, asshole, dick-licking—"

My neighbor walks by on the sidewalk, lifting a hand in greeting. Her face is not friendly, which isn't surprising for three reasons. Reason Number One: She probably thinks I'm an unfit mother because she saw me carrying a bag full of empty fast food containers to the dumpster last week. Reason Number Two: She's a sour old woman who survives only on nicotine and finding fault in everyone around her, and Izzy and I just so happen to live directly across from her in this crappy apartment complex. Reason Number Three: She could hear everything I just said. Vanny's driver's side window stopped closing all the way last week, and now I have to wear mittens every time I bring him anywhere.

"Hello, Mrs. Longhorn," I say in a syrupy sweet voice. "Lovely to see you."

Her answer is a snort so loud it causes a couple of crows to fly off.

"You had another Amazon package waiting outside your door this morning," she adds, pausing. It's phrased as an accusation.

12

"Yes," I say, my fingers flexing around the keys. Maybe my desire to run her over will make them magically work this time.

"Awful lot of packages you're ordering for a single mother with a child to take care of."

"They're gifts from my wishlist," I say. "I guess I have a secret admirer or something."

Her hand lifts to the collar of her coat as if she's warding off evil. "You have men buying you things? Didn't your mother teach you anything?"

"No, she didn't, actually."

I could tell her they're not from a man, but I don't know if that's strictly true. No one will admit to being my benefactor. My best guess is that my friends have all banded up to make sure I have the things I need. A new backpack for Izzy. Larger clothes for her. An industrial-sized jug of soap. A new thermometer. Simple things that I can't really afford. I shouldn't accept the gifts, and I definitely shouldn't keep adding to the list. But those little gifts, those signs that someone is looking out for me, are food for a starved soul. So I keep adding things to the list, and I keep accepting them with a grateful heart.

Damn her for making me feel bad about it.

"Well, she should have," Mrs. Longhorn harrumphs, then passes by, pulling out a packet of cigarettes as she goes.

I'm tempted to say her mother should have taught her not to smoke, but that would only prolong an unpleasant conversation. Instead, I give her back the finger once she's passed me, then try the keys again. Nothing.

So I do what I always do when I have car trouble. I take off my gloves so I can call my best friend, Tank.

Tank runs an auto repair shop, and if not for him, Vanny would have been relegated to a scrap heap years ago. Literally. He gave the van to me as a Christmas gift several years ago after I sent him a blog post about the growth potential of mobile businesses.

Then again, it seems like my old camper van is still headed that way. Every week something new goes wrong. Maybe cars are like people and there's only so long they can last, regardless of how well you care for them.

Tank picks up on the second ring. "Are you okay?"

No. "Why is that the first question everyone always asks me?"

"You're supposed to be working at the diner right now."

"Thank you, Captain Obvious," I say, being a bit prickly, because even *I* know it's not professional to call in sick so you can devote time to what is essentially a hobby.

Especially if you have a child to support on your own.

Especially if you just learned that you need to get expensive ear tube surgery for your child—surgery you will probably be paying for in installments for the rest of your natural life.

You're getting paid for the event today, I reassure myself. *More than if you worked your shift, probably.* But it doesn't make me feel less guilty. The payment still won't be large enough to cover the time and expenses I've already put into this enterprise, and I'm not going to get paid at all if I can't get Vanny moving.

Breathe in, breathe out.

I close my eyes tightly, shutting everything out, my hands gripping the steering wheel like it's a life preserver. I lean forward, resting my forehead against the cool, peeling leather, the phone still pressed to my ear.

I need this to work out. I need it bad.

If only ear surgery were something I could add to my Amazon wishlist.

My brother would help me cover the cost, but I hate asking him for money.

"Something's wrong with Vanny," Tank says with the confidence of someone who knows me well.

"He won't start," I say, feeling my heart speed up in my chest.

"I'm supposed to run a bookmobile event at Buchanan Brewery's southside location in half an hour, and he won't start."

Getting the gig at Buchanan had felt like a big deal. Buchanan Brewery is one of the biggest breweries in town, and sure, I don't expect that many people on a Monday afternoon, but then again, this town runs on tourists. Local kids might be in school, but rich people pull their kids out of school all the time so they can go on vacation. They probably have nannies or au pairs who come with them and teach their children French while they sip on craft beers and talk about the shitty economy.

I wish *I* were a rich person.

Instead, I'm a hustler always trying to make something happen. It really feels like I have an idea that might grow legs this time...

Whenever I open up the back of Vanny, I feel a magical tingle that I've only previously experienced while watching Izzy leave her room on Christmas morning. Or, let's be honest, when I'm falling in love with a terrible man. I built bookshelves into her sides and stacked them full of thousands of storybooks. Little fairy lights line the interior, and on the exterior of the van there's a beautiful mural that Tank's friend painted for me, designed based on one of Izzy's drawings. There are poofs and stuffed animals and drawing pages, and it's basically the best place on earth for little people to hang out while their parents watch them from a short distance away and drink.

I've also formed a partnership with Dog is Love, a local animal shelter, and they're bringing an adoptable dog today for the kids to read to. I mean, who wouldn't want to do that? And, yes, the only reason Buchanan Brewery took my call is because the owner of the shelter is married to the events director, but you've got to take your breaks when you get them.

Izzy begged me to let her stay home from Kindergarten so she could come, because the one thing she wants more than a functional household is a dog. I couldn't let her skip school, but I *did* promise to take pictures.

But if I don't show up, then that sad, unadopted dog's fate will also be on my conscience.

Shit, shit, shit.

"I'm already on my way," Tank tells me, and I feel a softening of my jaw and shoulders, because Tank never says things he doesn't mean. He's always been good to me, ever since we were five, which is probably why I've never wanted to be anything but his friend.

I only seem to fall in love with men who use me and then throw me away, like a piece of gum that's lost its flavor.

I breathe in deep, then release the breath.

"Thank you. I owe you, like, a dozen beers."

"I'll settle for your first-born child," he says, and I can tell he's grinning.

"No can do, I promised Izzy I wouldn't give her away for a penny less than a billion dollars."

He laughs. "I'll be there in ten."

I stick the phone in my coat pocket. Needing to feel like I'm doing something productive, I try the keys again. Vanny makes a rude noise. I'd look under the hood, but even though Tank has taught me some basics, I'm no expert—I can check the level and color of my oil but not replace it.

My phone buzzes with a text, and I remove it from my coat pocket again. I flinch a little when I see it's a text from Dustin at Dog is Love. He sent me a photo of a little, big-headed, short-legged mutt with the cutest overbite that ever made a dentist cringe, along with a message:

> Flower is ready for her bookmobile debut!

Guilt digs in its nails. Because of me, Flower's going to miss out on going home with a family of rich tourists who don't have the sense to say no.

"This can't be happening," I mutter to myself.

Just then, because apparently the mounting feeling of—*too much, too much, mayday, mayday!*—needs a boost, my phone buzzes with another text, this one from "Vain," the nickname I set for my brother's best friend, Shane Royce.

Shane's the kind of guy who can't walk past a reflective surface without looking in, and can't take part in a conversation without bending it toward his own purposes. Other than the way he looks, which is, admittedly, *quite* pleasing, the only thing I like about him is that he loves my brother Danny, but even that he seems to do half-heartedly, like he'd rather not. Like he's bound to Danny by history but wishes he were instead best friends with someone *important*.

I'm not particularly interested in anything he has to say, but I *am* curious about why he felt compelled to say anything at all.

I click through, and my brow furrows.

Hey, Ruthie. Can we meet? I have something important to discuss with you.

My heart starts racing. I can't think of any good reason why he'd ask to meet. Despite our inescapable presence in each other's lives, he has as much disdain for me as I do for him. Does Danny have terminal cancer, and he doesn't know how to tell me? Maybe it says dark things about me that my mind goes there, but I do have an addiction to Lifetime movies. Mostly because I can watch them on my laptop for the price of viewing glitchy ads.

I type out a response.

Just tell me now. What's wrong?

I'd rather discuss this in person.

Stop being difficult and tell me. This is about Danny, isn't it? Is he okay? What happened? Or is it Mira?

It's not about Danny or his girlfriend. I'll tell you when I see you. Can I swing by your apartment after Izzy goes to bed?

I make a face, because I can think of a dozen other things I'd rather do with my night.

Please? I wouldn't ask if it weren't important.

And, I repeat, Danny and his girlfriend are both fine. This doesn't have anything to do with them.

I'm baffled. It's probably the only time I've ever seen or heard the word "please" from him. What could possibly have motivated the great Shane Royce to use that word, and to me, no less? That and nosiness can be the only explanation for my answer:

Fine. I'll text you when she's asleep. Bring me a pastry and something to drink.

Alcoholic, in case that wasn't clear.

Seriously?

I know you enjoy pointless arguments, but I'm not in the mood for one right now. Consider it the price of doing business.

A few dots appear, but I decide I'm done with him and pocket the phone again so I can put my gloves back on.

I try to stay peppy and excited, but there's a sinking sensation in my chest that Shane's messages have hooked into.

It feels like everything is falling apart. Again.

This isn't the first time I've tried to make a mobile business happen. There've been other iterations of Vanny that took months for me to plan and only weeks to fall apart.

A pet clothes boutique. A mobile store selling only unicorn toys...I mean who wouldn't want that?

Everyone, apparently.

Maybe it's time to give up and accept that I'll be waiting tables and selling shit on eBay until I'm seventy.

Shouldn't it be enough for me to be Izzy's mother? There are other moms at her kindergarten who send their kids in with charcuterie lunch boards accompanied by homemade pickles and bread. Moms who volunteer every time a message goes out over ParentSquare and walk their kids to school without looking like they're on the verge of having a stress-induced heart attack at twenty-eight. Maybe I could be that kind of a mother if I tried hard enough. Maybe being that kind of mom would be enough to satisfy me.

I sigh, and then my mouth drops open as I glance in the rearview mirror and see Tank driving in with his tow truck. It doesn't speak much toward his faith in reviving Vanny, but I guess he's as aware of the time crunch as I am.

He parks, then gets out, and I do the same.

"Why's your window open, Ruthie?" he asks with a frown.

It's a good question. It was supposed to be warmer today—high forties, they were saying—but it's probably in the thirties. "I wanted some fresh air?"

He frowns. "Why didn't you tell me it stopped rolling all the way up?"

Because it's one thing to ask for help when your van won't start, and it's another to constantly request small favors.

Tank's just my friend—not my boyfriend or partner—and I can't go treating him differently.

"There were more pressing matters," I say. "Like the fact that he won't turn on." I try not to pout as I add, "How unprofessional am I going to look if I get towed in?"

A corner of his mouth lifts. "Less unprofessional than if you didn't show. I don't have time to figure out what the problem is if you've got to be there in twenty minutes."

I submit with a stoic nod, and he spends the next ten minutes getting Vanny hooked up. The last ten minutes before I'm supposed to show are spent on backroads, since no one wants this beast on the highway.

Finally, we pull into the back of the Buchanan lot, which is more empty than it is full.

I glance at my phone. There are half a dozen alerts, including messages about a school Parent Team meeting I won't be attending, a text from my estranged mother, and a SPAM notice that my Facebook Page for Vanny is scheduled for deletion.

The first time I got one of those, I called Danny in a blind panic, and he explained that it was a phishing scam. Of course, he ended the conversation with a five-minute lecture on Facebook being a massive security risk. "What are they going to steal?" I finally asked. "My debt? They can have it. Maybe I'll start using 1-2-3 for all of my passwords."

That shut him up.

Now, I breath out a sigh, because at least the numbers on the top of the phone tell me what I'd like to see. We made it, with just a minute to spare.

Maybe luck hasn't forsaken me yet—a thought that immediately has me reaching for the fake wood of the dash to give it a knock.

RUTHIE

MY HEART STARTS to soar again, even though my van's still attached to a tow truck. We beat the odds. We're here. Then I see my contact from Dog is Love through the front window, talking to Jack Durand, the events coordinator from the brewery. They're standing on the sidewalk attached to the parking lot.

They both turn to look at the tow truck pulling Vanny, and the events coordinator takes a step back—as if so surprised he can barely keep his feet.

I glance at Tank, who nods. "Get on out and see what's shaking."

So I do, sidling up to them like it's perfectly normal for me to have shown up this way.

Jack greets me. "Hey, Ruthie. Engine trouble?"

"Yeah," I say. "But what's in the back is all that matters, right?"

His smile is tight, though, and Dustin's running his hands through his white beard like he wants to pull it clean off.

"I guess you didn't get my text either?" Jack asks. He has an aw-shucks expression that promises nothing good.

"No," I say, feeling a jolting sensation in my chest.

"Sorry," he says, gesturing to the tow truck—"especially since you went to all this trouble. But we've cancelled the event. I would've texted you sooner, but one of our pipes sprang a leak, and it was a madhouse. It was supposed to be a warm day, but—" he gestures to the cold air as if it's a color that can be seen, "—it's not. Looks like it's only going to get colder. We'd love to have you back in the spring, though." He glances at the tow truck again, and Tank gives him a cheerful wave. "Might give you time to iron out a few wrinkles."

Shame wraps around me like a discarded Christmas ribbon.

Not good enough.

Not smart enough.

Not enough, period.

I feel a tell-tale sting in my nose, a sign that tears are trying to betray me, and I cough, trying to choke them down. "Of course. That makes sense."

I'm about to ask Dustin about Flower—poor Flower who was supposed to be the star of the show, but will now never know what happens in *Llama, Llama Red Pajama*, when a woman I recognize bustles up to us. It's Josie, a psychic who knows my brother, distinct from other psychics because she seems to get off on telling people things they don't want to hear. Including Shane.

She crashed Thanksgiving dinner, which my brother and his girlfriend hosted, and then told Shane he'd be getting married soon. It was hilarious, but also total bullshit.

She's wearing a fluffy coat over a bright red dress and has a black veil pulled over her face. A multi-colored carpet bag is clutched in both hands.

"Oh, you're giving her the bad news," she says. "I was hoping I'd be here for that."

Her meaning hits me like a truck. My mouth drops open, and for the first time during this encounter I am genuinely offended. Turning to Jack, I say, "You're cancelling me, but you're paying *her* to entertain people? She's a hack. She told my brother's friend he's going to get married soon, and anyone who's met that man knows he'd cut off his own finger before he puts a ring on it."

"A week," she says. "It'll happen in a week. Might want to order a cake." She laughs. "Or tell him to get a bonesaw. I guess it's his choice."

I give Jack a pointed look.

He shrugs and shifts a little on his feet. "She can do her act indoors." His gaze finds Tank and the tow truck again, and I can hear him silently adding, *And she doesn't make my brewery look like a used car lot.*

"It's okay," Josie says, turning to me. "This is what's supposed to happen."

"Tell that to the dog in the back of Dustin's van," I snap, because Flower's cute underbite is seared into my memory.

Josie's quiet for a moment, staring up at the sky, or maybe the clouds moving in, which look suspiciously like they might contain frozen white stuff. "Unfortunately, you're right to be worried about her. She'll never get adopted if she stays at the shelter," she says at last, her gaze meeting mine. "She'll spend the rest of her life there, miserable and alone, wanting something she can't have, and her only friend will be a hedgehog." She shrugs, making the veil rustle. "Bummer."

Maybe I'm an easy mark—Shane would certainly say so—but tears rise in my eyes.

Dustin snorts. "Well, now. That's the one animal we don't have."

"Save it for the guests, Josie," Jack grumbles. He tugs on the belt loops of his jeans and stares longingly at the door leading back into the brewery.

Josie shifts her attention to him. "The remote you lost is wedged under your couch."

He flinches, then tries to shake it off. "My wife just told you it was missing to mess with me. If it's under there, she's the one who put it there."

Josie gives him a look she probably thinks is mystical and then shrugs. "Some people choose not to see beyond the obvious, even if life tries to open their eyes."

"You really want her to do this for your paying customers?" I plead, fixing my stare on him. I don't know why I care about getting him to pull the plug on her when it's obvious a bookmobile event would be a bust today, but I do. "People don't want to be messed with or told they're going to die alone. They want to be reassured everything is going to be okay."

Josie gives me a steady look. "Some people like hearing the truth. But you're not one of them, are you, Ruthie? That's why you wouldn't let me do a reading for you at Thanksgiving."

"Maybe I just didn't want you to spout your B.S. at me in front of my daughter," I snap, irrationally angry. Because she's right, of course. I told myself there was no point in getting a reading because she was full of it. But part of me worried she'd tell me something I really don't want to hear.

That none of my schemes are ever going to work out.

That I'll live a small life, barely noticed by anyone except for my brother and my daughter.

That I'll die alone, and not just in the cosmic sense that we all die alone.

That I'll never fall in love with a man who loves me back.

"Your daughter's not here," Josie says with a smile. "So I guess I can tell you that your—"

"Can I meet Flower?" I ask Dustin, turning my back on Josie.

Maybe I'm a coward, but I don't want to see the knowing expression in her eyes.

"Surely can," Dustin says, brightening.

I take a deep breath, because I know I have to look back. While

I don't care about being rude to Josie, who is rude to everyone, I *do* want Jack to think well of me. He said he'd have me back in the spring—if Vanny's working—and I'm clutching onto that not-really-a-promise with both hands. After letting the breath out, I turn to him and say, "Goodbye, Jack. Thanks for..."

I trail off, because I'm honestly not sure what I should be thankful for. Certainly nothing that's happened today.

He nods. "I'll be in touch."

Then, because I can't help myself, I glance at Josie. I guess I'm half expecting her to say, "*He won't,*" which would be embarrassing for everyone other than her.

Instead, she gives me a knowing smile and says, "I wouldn't mind an invite to the wedding. Let Shane know, huh?"

There are a dozen things I could say in response to that, such as *What wedding?* And, *If you're talking about Shane's theoretical wedding, you should know that I'm one of the last people he'd invite. He may have come to my wedding, but that's only because my brother chose to misunderstand that his plus one was supposed to be for a date.*

But an uncomfortable tingle goes down my spine, because Shane *did* send me those cryptic text messages.

Is there a chance he's actually getting married?

I mean, it's not as if it matters to me. Shane could get married to a whole harem of women for all I care. I mean, it would be weird, obviously, and he'd probably have to move to another country to make his multiple marriages legal, but at least it would take him away from here. It's just...

It would be weird, is all. Shane's always made such a big deal about how the institution of marriage is just a trap and blah, blah, blah.

You're letting her mess with you.

The voice in my head is correct, so I nod a final time and turn back to Dustin. We get a few steps away before he shakes his head and says, "Don't you worry, Ruthie. I've met Josie a time or two, and she's a woman who likes causing a fuss."

"How many adoption applications have you gotten for Flower?" I ask, still feeling that uncomfortable pressure in my chest.

He scrunches his mouth to the side, his gaze on the Dog is Love van, parked on the other side of the lot from the tow truck. God bless Tank. He's been waiting in there for at least ten minutes.

"None," Dustin finally says. At my gasp, he adds, "Some dogs don't have much pep when they're in the shelter. She's cute as a bug, but she's been with us a year."

"A year?" I ask in horror. "Tell me the truth, Dustin, do you have any hedgehogs at the shelter?"

This time his laugh is more self-assured. "No, we do not. Can't say I've ever seen a hedgehog other than on Instagram."

That's a relief, at least, but I can't shake my uneasiness.

"Now, mind you don't make any loud noises," he says as we reach the back of the van. He starts pulling on his beard again. "She shies away from loud noise."

"And you thought it was a good idea to have kids read to her?" I ask, caught off-guard.

"She likes kids." He rocks on his feet and puts a hand on the door handle. Then he opens the back, and there she is, in a wire cage much too big for her. A little stuffed toy that's seen better days is caught between her front legs, which look too short for a dog with such a big head. She's cowering, her big head near her legs, her wide eyes fixed on us. My chest feels both gooey and broken.

"We think pitbull and corgi," Dustin comments without being ask. "Don't ask me how that happened, because I don't want to know. All I know is those legs can move awful fast for being so short."

I reach out a hand slowly, but she edges away from me, as if she's been hurt before and has come to expect it—as if any open hand is a hand that might hit her.

Something inside of me quakes. Then my gaze lands on that stuffed toy.

I lift a quivering finger to point at it. "What's that?"

"You know," he says, bemused, "most of our dogs tear through toys. Give 'em one, and it's gone in five minutes, but she won't let go of that thing. Brings it everywhere."

It's old and tattered, but it's distinctly... "It's a *hedgehog*," I say in a shaky voice.

"Is it?" he asks, his voice stunned. He pulls out his phone, does some Googling, and then whistles through his teeth. "Well, I'll be." He gives the brewery a glance before turning back to me. "She must've heard about it from my boss. Jack's wife. That woman would resort to guerrilla tactics to get a dog adopted." He says it with admiration.

Maybe he's right. But my aching conscience insists I can't take chances with Flower's life.

"I want her," I say, even though I'm aware of three things. Thing one: I'm slightly allergic to dogs. Thing two: I can't have a dog in my apartment until I pay the animal fee, and I don't have enough money to do that. And if I can't afford that, do I really have the money to feed and shelter a dog? Thing three: I'm being impulsive again, and it never works out for me.

At the same time...

I know what it's like to feel alone and abandoned with nothing but a hedgehog, in Flower's case, and a van, in mine, to hang your hopes on. I can't let this dog wither away in the shelter. I can't. And if I bring her home, Izzy will have that Christmas morning look for weeks...

"You really want her?" Dustin asks in wonder.

Yes, no, maybe.

I nod, my heart thumping, feeling a sneeze building. "What do I have to do?"

"Well..." He pauses to scratch his beard. "There's paperwork you need to fill out, and a fee to be paid." Another scratch. "But I'll let the fee slide because you're our partner."

At this point, I've done nothing other than help them accrue gas fees. I'm already feeling emotional, and tears try to gather in my eyes. I sneeze, then wipe my nose on the sleeve of my coat. I promise myself I'll clean it later, but the dusty hue of the fabric suggests it's a lie.

"Thank you, Dustin."

"Thank *you*," he says, sounding a little surprised again. "I didn't want to say so earlier, because I didn't want you to feel pressured, but I was beginning to think this little girl would never find a home."

Maybe I should be worried about whatever behavior traits caused this worry, but resolve has steeled my spine. I've decided to do this, and I'm going through with it. Izzy's going to get her dog, dammit.

"Well, she has a home now," I say, "and no one's taking her away from me."

I'll just need to keep her hidden from Mrs. Longhorn. And building management, until I raise enough money for that fee.

"Well, all right, then. Now, if you want to take her and send me that paperwork later, that would be just fine. I can give you some food and a few toys, too. What do you say?"

I'd say he's pretty eager to get rid of Flower. Somehow it only makes me want her more. My nose itches; I wipe it. Another sneeze escapes.

"You allergic to dogs?" Dustin asks with a concerned look.

"No, of course not. It's this dry cold that does it to me."

He nods as if I've said something sensible.

"Thank you," I add. "This is great."

Which is how I end up returning to the tow truck with a wire dog crate with a canine passenger and a big plastic bag.

Tank shakes his head as I open the door. "Leave it to you to be gone ten minutes and come back with a dog, Ruthie."

He's right.

"I'm guessing you didn't tell him you're allergic?"

Let no one say my friend doesn't know me well.

SHANE

If you still want to come over, you can do it now.

Be forewarned, I'm in a bad mood.

When are you in a good mood?

That's not helping.

I'M STANDING in front of a bakery case, feeling my eye twitch. Is that a tic? It feels like a tic.

What's a pastry, anyway? Would any kind of baked good qualify, or is this supposed to be some *British Bake Off* bullshit? I could text my mother to ask, but she'd probably ask me who the pastry's for, and I don't want to set her off on a tangent of, *Oh, please, settle down, Shane, and give me some grandchildren.*

Scowling, I cut my losses and stuff the bag full of cookies and dried-hockey-puck scones. But after I've done that, I see the refrigerated case next to where I'm standing, and there's a frosted minicake, shaped like a heart. Should I get one for her for the irony? Ruthie might be a pill, but she's capable of finding irony funny. So I

30

add that to the basket, and then another one. Because even if Izzy's asleep, I should still get her something.

I don't know what Ruthie likes to drink, other than that she's not a fan of whiskey. So I grab some pink shit that passes for wine, then a six pack of cider in case that won't do. I need to show her that I'm a man capable of conciliatory gestures.

Sucking up. I already know you can do that when it suits you, suggests Ruthie's voice in my head. I dislike the way she keeps popping in there. Like she's my conscience the same way Jiminy Cricket's dick is Myles's. But that's Ruthie—edging her way into every situation.

She just had to charm the pants off the legal beagle, and now here we are...

Except that's unfair, and I know it. This was my doing, pure and simple.

I sigh as I head to the register. The checkout clerk, a teenage boy with braces and a fresh batch of acne, gives me a sidelong look as he rings up my purchases. Then, as if he's worked himself up to it, he asks, "Are you bringing these to a sorority party?"

A laugh escapes me. Because it *does* look like I've shopped for multiple women—not one, infuriating, difficult-to-please one. "Something like that."

He nods four times. "*Legend.*"

I felt like one once. Now, I'm sucking up to a woman who drives me crazy so I can get a job for a lawyer I don't respect.

"How do you do it, man?" he asks as he finishes bagging the last baked item. "I can't even get one girl to look at me."

I glance at him, taking in the acne and the braces. It's like looking through a periscope into a past I didn't like. Sighing, I say, "Confidence. Women like a confident man." I nod at the huge bag of baked goods and alcohol. "And listen to her hints. She says she likes pastries, you buy her ten of them. The bigger the gesture, the better it'll go down."

Or at least that's true of most women. It occurs to me now, with this bag of crap, that it's never been true of Ruthie.

"So it's just for one woman?" I can see his spirits sinking.

I grin at him. "Today, it's just for one woman, but I've been invited to sorority parties back in the day. Give it time, my friend." Then I collect the bag and head out to my car, feeling a little better for cheering the kid up.

When I get to Ruthie's, I park, scowling a little to myself. I've stopped by here before with Danny, and it's always struck me as a very insufficient sort of neighborhood for them. The buildings are old and ill-kept, with siding that looks like it could be pulled off like a fruit by the foot. Ruthie must make peanuts at the diner, though, and even less from her little schemes. Danny helps her when he can, but she doesn't let him do much.

I'm feeling contemplative as I get out with the bag and approach the external door of their unit, knocking twice.

There's a strangled yelp that makes me frown, followed by a muffled curse, and the door to the apartment directly across from Ruthie's cracks open. I turn toward it and see an older woman. Her gray hair is in curlers, and she has beady eyes that remind me of the hamster Danny adopted last Christmas. She's got to be cold in her pink, long-sleeved nightdress, but she doesn't flinch.

"Was that a *dog*?" she asks in a voice that sounds like an exhaled cigarette.

"No, ma'am," I say, even though it sounded an awful lot like a dog. What the hell is Ruthie up to now? Whatever it is, I feel like I have no choice but to be complicit, since I came here with half a grocery store in hand to ask for a favor. "I jammed my foot against the step."

"*You* made that sound, young man?" She gives me a measuring look, taking in my suit and peacoat. The bag in my hand.

"Yes, it was me."

Her gaze narrows. "Awful late to be paying a visit to a young mother, don't you think?"

Awful nosy is what I think. Then again, I've cracked harder nuts. This woman has nothing on me.

"She's my best friend's little sister. I like to keep an eye on her and her girl." It might be my imagination, but I could swear I hear Ruthie snorting behind the door.

"There's no need for that," the woman says as if I've offended her. Her expression shrivels like an old lime lost at the back of a fridge. "I keep an eye on everything in this neighborhood, particularly those girls."

Yes, I'm sure she does.

"It reassures me to know that," I tell her with a respectful nod, and the old biddy retreats inside her apartment and closes the door behind her. Something tells me she's got her eye glued to the spyglass, though, and I resist the urge to salute. Barely.

Another beat passes, and Ruthie opens the door to her apartment. She has a single slender finger pressed to her full lips. Maybe it's the power of suggestion, but I'm struck silent by the sight of her thick, wavy mass of dark brown hair and light blue eyes, currently fixed on me with a scowl. And even though it's cold as a witch's titties out here, or so my friend Leonard would say, she's got on an oversized sweatshirt and lycra shorts so small a microscope would be needed to locate them. I've seen these particular shorts before— they're a favorite, I guess—so I'm familiar with the way they cup her ass, and how it's nearly impossible to look away.

The realization that Ruthie's beautiful crept up on me. It was like one day she was an aggravating kid, always trying to grab attention from anyone who'd give it to her, all elbows and knees and messy hair, and the next she'd become a woman. And not just any woman—the kind of woman who'd stop men in their tracks.

I've learned to steel myself against reacting to Ruthie as a woman, though. It's what I call my own, personal Rule Number One: pretend you're not attracted to Ruthie Traeger.

Swallowing back my reaction, I roll my eyes and lift the bag. "You asked, and I delivered."

"Come in," she mouths, forcefully waving me inside.

I follow her in, and she hastens to shut the door behind me as I take off my coat.

"What was that all about?" I ask, glancing around for somewhere to put the coat. The corners of my mouth lift when I notice the two coats already slung over the side of the sofa, and I add mine to the pile.

Ruthie glances at the door, frowning, then gestures me farther inward. I shrug and follow her into the kitchen. It's an open floor plan and only seven or eight paces from the door.

Tucked under the little round kitchen table is a wire crate with a little big-headed, small-legged dog in it, chowing down on some chew stick that's probably the desiccated body part of an animal.

I groan. "Well, will you look at that, I hadn't even walked in yet before you made a liar of me."

I set the bag down on the table and cross my arms. It's the lawyer in me—the man trained by Fred Myles—but it crosses my mind that she'll be more willing to see things my way because I have some leverage.

"I'm going to tell the front office," she says, her tone annoyed. "We're *allowed* to have pets. I just haven't gotten around to it yet."

"Why'd you get a dog, anyway?" I ask, amused. "Danny told me about the reading-to-dogs thing, but I didn't realize you planned on kidnapping one. Don't you think you're taking the big white van thing a little too seriously?"

She stomps one of her feet, which makes me grin, and then the neckline of her oversized sweatshirt slips over her shoulder. I look away from the slope of her neck and the sight of a bright red bra strap as she bends to examine the contents of the bag. "You're such an ass," she says. "The event got cancelled earlier. Josie the Great says hello, by the way."

"What?" I ask, jolting to attention. It's been weeks since I've given any real thought to my buddy's psychic...

Well, friend feels like it would be a stretch. But she did tell me that I was going to get married, and I'm here because I need to convince Ruthie to pretend she's my wife. I'm the last person to be taken in by hacks and liars, but it...

It makes me a little uncomfortable, is all.

Ruthie hoots and pulls out one of the heart-shaped cakes. Looking up at me with shining eyes, she lifts the box. "She was very concerned about making sure you had cake for your wedding, and look, you bought some."

She must see the frozen look on my face, because she shakes her head and smirks, then saunters over to a drawer and pulls out a couple of forks. "Don't worry, Romeo. I told her you're a player, and you'd sooner cut off your finger than put a ring on it."

"What'd she say to that?" I ask woodenly as she sits at the table. The little dog in the crate stops attacking her snack for long enough to sniff Ruthie's toes and then give them a lick. Ruthie grins so big it wrinkles her nose. It reminds me of the hundreds of times I've seen her do it before, and I feel a gush of reluctant fondness—and of regret.

Because she's never grinned like that for me.

She shoves a fork at me. "Sit. Enjoy my bounty."

Shaking my head, I say, "They're for you and Izzy."

"I *insist*," she says, holding her fork in the air like it's a weapon. "You don't get to throw calorie bombs at me without letting one catch you."

I lift my hands up, palms out. "Do I get to choose?"

Her smile turns crafty and she nods to the chair across from her. "Sit." I have to sit facing sideways, my legs having nowhere to go under the table. But I wedge myself in, and she pushes the cake in between us with a smile of victory. "You've got to eat your own cake."

"So, I can tell you're dying for me to ask. Why'd you see Josie, and what does that have to do with you kidnapping the mutt?"

She opens a can of cider and presents me with a second one. I'd planned on hitting the whiskey at home, but I don't say no. Maybe she'll be in a more congenial mood if I drink with her and eat the cake. I don't particularly want grocery store cake, but I guess that's my fault for not getting the good stuff. "They cancelled the reading-books-with-dogs event and brought Josie in instead. Because she can do her schtick inside." She lifts the can, wielding it like it's a weapon she can clobber me with. "Now, I know what you're going to say, so I'm going to beat you to it. I never should have tried to get the book-mobile off the ground in the winter. It was stupid and short-sighted and exactly like me."

I watch her, my eyes taking in that red bra strap while my mind remembers the way the bottom of her sweatshirt almost covers those shorts, as if she's got nothing on underneath it but panties.

I pop the top of the cider for something to do, and also because I need to remember Rule Number One. "Sure, I might have been thinking all of that, but I'm too well-mannered say it."

Laughter spurts out of her. "Fuck you. And I'll have you know the dog's name is Flower. She will also answer to Flo if you ask nicely."

I cough, then say, "Did you name her Flower, or was that her name at the shelter?"

She studies me over the top of her cider can. "You figure I did, right? Silly, knows-nothing Ruthie with her fairy lights and bookmobile."

"So she came to you with the name you would have chosen," I surmise, smirking at her. Because I may have come here to charm her, but I do enjoy this game we play, which has only one established rule on my side. "I'm guessing you saw that as a sign from the heavens."

"Could you blame me? Josie the Great had just told me Flower would spend her whole life alone in the shelter with only a hedgehog as her friend. Then I went to meet her in the van, and guess what she was holding between her paws?"

"If it was a dead hedgehog, I question your logic in bringing her home."

She shakes her head, a smile playing at the edges of her lips. Then she pops the lid on her cake. "It was a stuffed hedgehog."

I shake my head ruefully. "They played your bleeding heart like a fiddle. I'm jealous of the hustle."

"You would be." She waves her fork at me, then spears it into the middle of the heart cake, which feels like bad news for my plan.

"You're starting in the middle?" I ask.

"Just to mess with you?" she asks, spearing out some cake. "Absolutely." Then she sticks the fork in her mouth and makes a sound that isn't helping me form an immunity to her sweatshirt and shorts.

"Ruthie, for God's sake."

"It's *good*."

"It's shitty grocery store cake. It can't be that good."

"Yeah, speaking of which, thanks for the awesome gift, *Vain*." She lifts her eyebrows. "Now what, pray tell, brings you here? We can dance around it all night, but we both know you want something. You *always* want something."

"Why, Ruthie, I'm hurt."

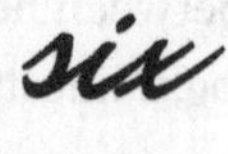

six

RUTHIE

AS IF I'M frivolous enough to think *I* have the power to hurt him. Shane and my brother are five years older than me. When I look back at the photos of Shane from when they were teenagers, I see a gangly kid with acne. At the time, though, he seemed larger than life —as if he already knew he'd grow into this impressive swan of a man, dark-haired and muscular, with the kind of forearms that inspire sonnets. It's because he's always had this air of confidence. Of *everything I see belongs to me.*

He also seemed noble back then, particularly because of how he looked out for my brother. My brother is on the autism spectrum, or at least we're pretty sure he is. His diagnostic appointment is later this year. But when we were kids, no one talked about that kind of thing. Danny was just the smart, weird kid who couldn't ride a bike well. My parents talked about him in the third person as if he were deficient in understanding...right up until the school asked to test him, and they were informed he was a genius. After that, they expected his genius to pay. He was basically the money maker of the household from his late teens onward.

But kids didn't care about his genius status. They cared about his differences and enjoyed informing him of all of them, as if he

38

didn't already know. My parents didn't protect him, but Shane did. He'd cut down the kids who hurt him with his words or, occasionally, his fists. He was like a knight, riding in to the defense of the person I valued most in the world.

I'd seen him engage in other acts of kindness too. One time, he found a bird's nest that had tumbled from a tree in our yard. My mother said the baby birds were as good as dead and told Danny to throw them in the trash, but Shane insisted on taking it home so his mother could bring them to a conservation center.

Did I ever have a crush on Shane?

Yes, an excruciating one, but it lasted only until I was ten, nearly eleven, when I overheard him asking Danny why he kept letting his little sister tag along. That's when my rose-colored glasses shattered. My hurt feelings sharpened to dislike every time he called me "kid" or "kiddo," a practice he continues to this day.

To my dissatisfaction, I worshipped him for just long enough to carve our initials into the bench in safe space, the overlook in the mountains where Danny used to bring me to get away from our parents when they were shouting at each other or on one of their drunken benders. Our initials are still there—R&S with a heart around it—mocking me.

Because Shane Royce has grown up to be a vain, self-important dick, and there's not a single doubt in my mind that he's here because he wants something. For some reason, he thinks I can and will give it to him.

Flower licks my toes again. So far, she's been an angel—and Izzy is so deeply in love with her that she drew five pictures of her before bed and begged me to let Flower sleep in her room. The only way I could actually get her to go to sleep was by encouraging her to imagine multiple Flowers jumping over a fence—*look, this Flower has a red bow around her neck; ooh, that one's wearing a studded collar, Izz!*

The only real downside is that my nose is itchy and running, and my eyes are bloodshot, but allergy medication was created for a reason, right?

Shane clears his throat and glances off in the distance. He looks like an orator who's about to say something important, but appearances can be deceiving.

For example, I have to admit that a person would struggle to find anything wrong with Shane's appearance. Sometimes I can't help but notice his defined jaw, always with the slightest bit of stubble. He's the sort of man who's fastidious enough to shave every morning, even in the middle of a personal crisis, but a razor can't quite take care of the job. My destructive imagination has wondered what it might feel like. Then there are his eyes, an uncertain shade of hazel whose appearance can be influenced by the color of his suits and ties.

Yes, there's no denying Shane Royce is a good-looking man. It's one of the things I dislike most about him, because he *knows* he's a beautiful bastard—and he wields that knowledge like it's another weapon in his arsenal.

He glances back at me, his eyes more green than brown or blue today, because his tie is a light purple. The shop probably gave it some fancy-ass name like lavender haze or aubergine, because he definitely doesn't go to the Goodwill like I do. He looks like he just stepped out of a Gucci ad.

"Why are you wearing a suit?" I ask in a burst of annoyance. "Were you trying to impress me? Because it's about twenty-eight years too late for that."

He lifts his eyebrows, his mouth tilting up wryly. "Maybe I was trying to impress your neighbor. You really think you're going to get that dog past her? She probably sleeps next to the door, propped up in her chair, one eye pressed to the glass."

I toy with my fork. "I have a plan."

"Oh?"

It's an invitation I won't be taking him up on. He seems to revel in hearing about my plans and ideas so he can shoot them down. My hopes *amuse* him. And, sure, my plan comprises of a large tote bag I have that would easily fit Flower—if she stays silent and doesn't move.

It's a terrible plan.

"You know, Mrs. Longhorn would probably be more impressed if you'd shown up in your tighty-whities," I say, shifting the subject. "Seriously, why the suit? You don't have a job."

"Thanks," he says drily. "The no-job thing is part of why I'm here."

"Sorry," I say, grabbing another forkful of cake. "I'm not hiring at the bookmobile."

A corner of his mouth ticks up. "Cute. Actually, I *have* been offered a job. You met a partner at the firm before Christmas. Monty Freeman?"

A memory of a long-faced man with apple cheeks and sweet, warm eyes flashes through my head. We ran into him outside of Danny's girlfriend's bar on Christmas Eve. He was such a *nice* man —full of stories about his wife, Hilda. He'd asked me encouraging questions about the bookmobile that had made me hope my idea might lead somewhere other than a ditch. But I'd felt Shane darting annoyed looks at me the whole time.

"I remember him," I say. "He's a very sweet man, and I could tell how devoted he is to Hilda."

"Who's Hilda?"

I roll my eyes. "You wanted a job with this guy, and you didn't even pay attention to his wife's name?"

A cunning look lights his eyes. I *know* that look. I've seen it often enough. When I was a kid, it usually preceded him convincing my brother to do something potentially dangerous in pursuit of one of his grandiose plans. *Screw lemonade stands, let's run a computer repair business. Why not pay someone to buy us lottery tickets? If we win, it'll be worth it.*

"I *didn't* want the job," he says, running a hand over his stubbled jaw. I can't help it, my eyes follow the movement. "But my exboss has stonewalled me, and this guy's the only lawyer in the county who'll take me on. You know, he really liked you."

"So I helped you get this job you don't want?" I ask, smiling at him.

"Yeah," he says. "You and Izzy did. You know...he thought we were a family."

Laughter bursts out of me, cut off when Flower lets out one resonant, very clear bark.

Crap. Hopefully, Mrs. Longhorn gave up the ghost and went to bed. How a woman her age has hearing like that I'll never know...

"Shhh, baby," I say, getting down on my knees in front of her wire crate. She licks my hand.

I sneeze.

I eye Shane, who's watching me with an expression I can't interpret. Was he checking out my ass? Deviant excitement fills me, because I enjoy catching the glances he probably thinks are so subtle.

He lifts his eyebrows.

"I'm going to let her out of her crate," I say. "We'll see if she can sense evil."

But the second I open the wire door, she passes me and goes to Shane, her little tail wagging.

He shocks me by getting down to her level to pet her. Something in my chest...eases, like hard candy turning to caramel. This is why Dog is Love has a yearly calendar of men posing shirtless with dogs—there's something sweet about a big, strong man showing love to a dog. No doubt Shane knows it, and this is another piece of him trying to butter me up.

"You're not worried about your suit?" I ask, reclaiming my chair. My eyes are riveted on him.

"I like dogs. I had one when I was a kid."

I notice he didn't answer the question, but I'm too hung up on being surprised to say so. I don't remember him having a dog. Then again, I never went to his house—only Danny did. In fact, they spent much more time there than they did at our house. Shane's an only child, and he lived alone with his mother after his dad died when he was fifteen. My brother probably welcomed the chance to get away from our parents. Shane made it pretty clear he welcomed the chance to get away from me.

Flower licks Shane's hand and then climbs into his lap, no joke. And instead of putting her down like a hot potato, he lifts her and sits in the chair like that—my little dog curled up on top of him.

"Fuck, you must really want something," I say.

He has the good grace to laugh. So do I. In fact, I laugh so hard I sneeze again.

"Yeah," he finally admits. "I do. But I also really like dogs. Maybe you can put it down to another piece of kismet since you seem determined to believe in signs."

"Go on." I pick up my fork, trying to signal a disinterest I don't feel.

"Freeman only offered me the job because he thought I was a family man. I'm not going to dance around it, Ruthie. I let him think you were my wife. I want to pay you to go to a few events with me to keep up the ruse." He gestures to the dog cradled in his lap. "Dogs are expensive, and I'm guessing the reason you're waiting to report her is because even an apartment complex this crappy has a pet deposit. Plus, I know you're trying to get your bookmobile off the ground. This could be good for both of us."

My mouth gapes open, and shock curls through me. The fork drops from my hand.

He's being manipulative, but I see no need to point out what we both must already know. My head is swimming—Josie was so certain he'd be getting married, and now he's here asking me to pose as his wife. Also...he's not wrong. I could use the money, more than he knows.

But I dislike dishonesty, especially to a sweet man like Mr. Freeman. If Mr. Freeman wants a family man at his company—one who's going to stay for the long haul—he certainly hasn't found one in Shane. It would be a dick thing for me to help Shane fool him into thinking otherwise.

Desperate as Shane is, he shouldn't have done this. I'm guessing this sort of dishonesty might even be serious enough to see him disbarred, not that I'm a tattle tale. While he may not be my favorite person on the face of the planet, he's important to Danny and Izzy, who insists on calling him Uncle Shane even though I've told her a dozen times he's not her uncle.

And a little voice inside of me insists that maybe this is my chance to finally rise up—to achieve things that *too expensive* or *no time* have made impossible.

But for some reason, the first thing that comes out is, "But I'd have to pretend I like you."

For a second, he looks almost...hurt, but then he barks a laugh. "I think you could manage it. You pretended to like that drink Mira made you a few weeks ago."

It's funny that he noticed, and also that we're having this conversation as if it's perfectly normal for two people who barely tolerate each other to pretend they're married. Then again, from what I've witnessed, plenty of marriages devolve into a state of unhappy toleration. I'll certainly never get married again for real.

Don't get me wrong, I don't dislike marriage for the same reasons Shane does. I've already been Googling engagement rings so I'll be prepared to act the instant my brother says he's ready to propose to his girlfriend. And if he doesn't get with the program, I may have to be the one to introduce the idea, because there's no way I'm letting her go. It's just...

I don't trust myself to pick the right person, and the last thing I want is for Izzy believe in a dream that will never become her reality. I'd allow myself to fall in love with the wrong man, but I won't let her do it.

"Yes, I know how to pretend." I say slowly, then pick up the fork again and dig out a huge bite of the heart cake. Because my mind is whirring, and maybe the sugar will help it whir faster. With any luck, it'll make me forget my itchy nose while it's at it.

Shane pets Flower and then gives his defined jaw another swipe. "There's a not insubstantial chance Freeman will figure it out," he says. "Because I won't have anyone to put on his *excellent* insurance, but I figure I only have to keep him fooled for a few months. If I put some time in, people will forget about the mess with Myles. Hell, if there's any justice, he'll lose the Burkes' case, and people will realize I did the smart thing, walking out on him. Then I can get a job that actually challenges me, we can pretend we got divorced, and all will be right in the world."

It's a pompous thing to say, but my mind is stuck on two of the words he dropped. *Excellent insurance*.

Ear tubes. *Ear tubes*.

My heart is beating so loudly, I'm surprised Mrs. Longhorn doesn't bang on the door to complain.

But Shane's not the only one who knows how to work a conversation to his advantage. If I let him know how much his insurance interests me, I'll be handing him an advantage. Better to hold it back for now.

"What if someone from the firm sees you out with another woman?" I almost laugh at the image of poor, sweet Mr. Freeman thinking he's caught Shane in the act. What would he do? Invite him into his office for a brandy and a chastisement? No, I'd like to think that nice, well-mannered man would douse him with a glass of water for my benefit.

He frowns. "Well, while this is going on, we'd both have to hold off on dating." He pauses, then adds, "Unless it's somewhere outside of Asheville, I guess."

"Let me guess, do you have a favorite prostitute who lives just outside of the city limits?" I ask with a snort.

His frown deepens. "I'm insulted that you think I'd have to pay for it."

I don't. From what I can tell, he always seems to have someone on the hook—sometimes multiple someones. Not that I care, obviously, but I don't want people to think my fake husband is stepping out on me, so I say, "There's zero chance I'll have time to date someone outside of city limits. And you don't get to step out on our hypothetical fake marriage if I don't, so no dating for either of us."

That particular rule won't be a problem for me. I've gone on dates since my ex-husband, Rand, signed the divorce papers and the ones relinquishing his paternal rights, but none of them have gone anywhere. I haven't wanted them to. Because I'm smart enough to recognize a pattern. To know that the same man who's telling me that I'm lovely and smart and my ideas for Vanny are revolutionary will shift the discourse soon enough. The compliments will bleed into remarks about how I'm naïve and foolish and exhausting. How I couldn't even manage to open a tin can if it weren't for him. And it will happen so slowly I won't notice until it's too late, and I'm under his control.

Rand wasn't the first man like that in my life, so I must keep attracting them or unintentionally seeking them out.

No thank you. Might as well quit while I'm behind.

"Sure," Shane says carelessly. "I'll be busy anyway."

It's not exactly flattering, but I'd prefer not to be flattered by him.

"How much would you pay me?"

His gaze narrows. "I was thinking we could do it by event."

I shake my head, pursing my lips. "No can do, Romeo. If I'm not allowed to date anyone else, then I get paid by the month. A thousand bucks." My pulse revs up. "And I want in on that sweet insurance."

He tilts his head, more of a tell than he'd usually give, and I know I've surprised him. Then he swears and jumps up, my little dog clutched in his hands. I'm tempted to tell him he's overreacting, but then I see the pee still dribbling from her.

And I can't help it. I burst out laughing.

seven

SHANE

"IT'S NOT FUNNY, RUTHIE," I grind out as I put the little gremlin on the ground. The dog wags her tail as if she expects a treat for covering me in urine. "Do you know how much this suit cost?"

She rolls her eyes. "No, and you'd better not tell me. If it costs more than my rent, I'm going to get salty." She gets up and grabs a roll of paper towels off the counter. For half a second, I wonder if she's going to dab at my dick; for half a second, I'd like her to. Instead, she hands over the whole roll, and I begin the thankless task myself.

"You know..." she says, watching me. I'm conscious of her eyes on me while I rub the area over my dick with paper towels. It's easily the least sexy thing a woman's ever watched me do, but I can't deny I have a strange awareness of Ruthie tonight. "Maybe this is a sign that you shouldn't wear expensive suits to casual events. You should invest in some white T-shirts. Get wild and buy a pair of jeans or two."

"I have jeans. And white T-shirts. Multiples of each."

"I haven't seen evidence of it for years."

"It's not as though we spend lots of quality time together," I say, sighing because the paper towels haven't done anything about the stench, and I'd rather not walk out of here looking and smelling like I went into this woman's home and pissed myself.

"I know, thank God," she says, but she's grinning at me. She takes the pee-soaked towels from me and tosses them in the trash before washing her hands in the sink.

The little dog has retrieved her shitty hedgehog toy, which saved her from the shelter, and retreated into the living room. She's gnawing on the toy half-heartedly while lying on the rug.

I follow Ruthie to the sink, and she squirts soap into my hands. Her fingers glance off mine, and an electric heat floods me. It's the way she's still grinning, I decide, like that dog pissing on me is the highlight of her day, or maybe even her month. It occurs to me that my rule might be harder to follow tonight because Danny's not here. Because it's just the two of us, Ruthie and me, for the first time in... well, maybe for the first time ever.

"It's not funny," I tell her. I may have told her I didn't wear this suit to impress her, but I haven't been wearing it all day. After I got back from Freeman & Daniels, I went to the gym for a couple of hours and then ran some errands for my mother. The suit was for Ruthie—because I figured if you're going to show up and ask a woman to marry you, even if it's fake, you'd better look good doing it.

It was for Ruthie, and now it's covered in piss.

Maybe that's appropriate, actually.

"You have a very restrictive sense of humor," she says. "I feel sorry for you. Also, do you want something to change into?"

I lift my eyebrows as I scrub my hands. "You want to put me in a pair of bootie shorts too?"

Her gaze drifts down to her legs. I expect her to scowl at me, and I'm not disappointed. "You a puritan, suddenly? Or does your attitude only apply to women you don't want to sleep with?"

I'm about to say *who says I don't want to sleep with you?*, because the rhythm of our banter seems to demand it, but something stops me. Maybe the truth that I *do* want to sleep with her. That anyone attracted to women would. Instead, I settle for, "I didn't say I don't like them."

This surprises her. I see it in the almost quizzical look in her eyes. Ah, Ruthie has convinced herself I'm incapable of anything approaching kindness toward her. Fantastic.

"I wasn't thinking bootie shorts," she says, handing me a dishtowel with a gingerbread man on it—clearly a relic of the holidays. "I have an old pair of Rand's sweatpants that I used to wear when I was pregnant with Izzy."

"No," I say, almost before she finishes. "No, thanks."

Her eyebrows lift. "You'd prefer for people to think you pissed yourself?"

"Than to wear something that belonged to him? Yes." I've worked with some terrible people, defended worse ones, but there are few of them I dislike as much as Rand Callaghan. Of course, Ruthie doesn't know everything about my history with him, and I'm not going to tell her. I'm also not going to wear the fucking pants.

She shakes her head slightly as if I'm being unreasonable. Then swipes at her nose. I've noticed her do that a couple of times tonight. Is she sick?

"Sometimes clothes are just clothes."

"Can't do it," I insist, even though I smell like the bathroom at a truck stop.

Sighing, she says, "I have some pajamas I forgot to give Danny for Christmas. You can wear those."

"You got him pajamas?" I ask, unable to keep the hint of amusement out of my voice.

She rolls her eyes and motions for me to follow her. "Have *you* tried to shop for him?"

She has a point. Danny's a guy who doesn't want very much,

something that's hard for me to understand. I've always wanted more than I have. Always. It's what keeps me on top of my game.

I follow her down the hallway, trying to ignore the perfect round globes of her ass in those shorts. Then I pause, because she's leading me toward what is obviously her bedroom. Maybe it's foolish to start drawing arbitrary lines, but I don't think I can go in there with her right now. My mind isn't quite right, and being around a bed, particularly *her* bed, isn't going to help me wrestle it back into control.

She glances back at me, her eyes teasing, and I feel a strange thrumming inside of me. "You being a puritan again, not wanting to go into an unmarried woman's bedroom?"

"Get the pajamas, please, and then we'll talk." Because I haven't forgotten what she said before the dog pissed on me. *I want in on that sweet insurance.*

But there are small lies and big ones...

Ruthie goes inside and emerges a couple of seconds later with some blue checkered plaid pajamas that would have made Danny a perfectly boring gift.

"Remind me never to do a white elephant exchange with you," I say, earning myself another scowl.

"Go put them on before I change my mind."

So I do, my mind still working.

Sweet insurance. Sweet, sweet insurance.

I emerge, my soiled suit slung over my arm, feeling like a class-A douchebag in a pair of matching PJs. "I should be in a Christmas ad for Sears," I complain as I walk into the kitchen. She's sitting at the table again, taking a bite of cake, and there's the slightest bit of frosting on her top lip.

Her gaze lingers on me for a second, and she smiles, "Why am I surprised you object to looking normal for a change?"

"There's nothing abnormal about a man who enjoys looking sharp."

"You could stand to loosen your tie sometimes."

She wouldn't be the first to say so, but she is always the one who says it the longest and loudest.

I sit down across from her and grab the cider she set out for me. "Is this your way of admitting that you purposefully had your dog urinate on me? You know, I'm impressed that you managed to teach her that command in a single afternoon. How did you signal to her? Snap your fingers? Suck your lip?"

Shit. The words tumbled out of me because that's where my attention is focused—on that little bit of frosting on her upper lip, just asking to be licked. As if the power of suggestion has commanded her, she sucks it in and tilts her head when she finds the frosting.

"Way to drop a hint. And the boring pajamas suit you."

"Because I'm boring," I say, smiling. "Nicely done, Traeger."

"You said we'd talk." She pushes the plate away, suddenly nervous. I see it in the way she's holding herself.

"Yeah. You told me you want to get on my insurance. I can't lie in the paperwork, Ruthie. If I got caught, I'd be disbarred. I'm okay with skirting the line, but I can't vault across it."

"So you're saying no." She exhales and then takes a long sip of her cider.

"Is there a reason you need it?"

She doesn't say Izzy's name, but I notice the way she glances at the hallway leading to the bedrooms. Worry infiltrates me. Izzy's just a kid, but you read about kids getting cancer or other diseases. Needing brain surgery or chemo.

It's not that bad, I reassure myself. *If it were, Ruthie wouldn't have kept it to herself.*

Still, the worry weaves in deeper.

"Izzy needs it," I press. "Why?"

She shakes her head ruefully. "You and your lawyer ways. I'd like to think I can keep secrets from you."

"It's easier not to. Why does she need it?"

"Ear tube surgery. She's had six ear infections in the past four months. They make her so uncomfortable."

I let myself accept the relief. This is a problem that can be fixed. "Your insurance won't cover it?"

"Barely. It would still be thousands of dollars."

Shit. I don't need to take a good look around this place to know everything is from discount bins. "Danny would help you. No questions asked."

"He doesn't have that kind of money lying around. Besides, you know I can't accept that kind of help from him. Not after everything."

Everything goes something like this: Danny spent the last ten years chained to her ex-boyfriend's company. Jarrod Travis is a piece of shit, but he's lucky enough to run a multi-million-dollar web security company, Safe-T Net. He tricked a barely legal Ruthie into having an affair with him. After it ended badly, Danny, who has mad computer skills, hacked into Safe-T Net's system and crashed it—for a week. Jarrod knew he had him over a barrel, so he gave him an ultimatum: work for him and pay restitution or go to jail and take his chances with the court system. He didn't have a decent lawyer, so he took option A.

That's why I decided to become a lawyer. I figured Danny deserved better than to get the runaround, but I doubt Ruthie would believe me if I told her that. She'd point out that the defendants who hired my old firm weren't desperate kids in need of a break, but rich and usually guilty people who'd been raised to expect breaks. To be angry when they didn't get them.

It's true, but here's another truth: you don't always end up where you meant to go. Sometimes you start in one direction and find yourself in another without any idea how to get back, and no memory of why it was important to keep trying.

Danny was only recently able to quit his job at Safe-T Net,

because he sold a computer game that he and our other friend had developed in their free time.

Ruthie didn't ask Danny to intervene in the Jarrod Travis situation, but she's always felt like it's her fault. So she doesn't ask him for help unless she's desperate.

"Ruthie," I say, reaching across the table to touch her hand. It's warm and soft, and it's been a while since I've felt a woman's hand. That must be why my thumb instinctively starts moving back and forth across her skin. I pull away as if I'd been burned. "I'm not opposed. You know I care about Izzy. She's like a niece to me."

"She's not your niece," she responds quickly—a rote response.

I know Izzy's not my niece; she knows Izzy's not my niece. But I have no sisters or brothers, and my mother was an only child. My father had a brother, but they didn't like each other in life, and my uncle didn't feel the need to keep up with my mom and me after he died. So it's just the two of us, and I'm probably never having any kids. So sometimes I hang out with Danny when he's watching Izzy and pretend she's family because he is. I get her birthday presents, Christmas gifts, and sometimes we take her out to puppet shows and other kid shit that I don't enjoy other than to see the smile it puts on her face.

"You know what I mean," I say.

She nods, giving me that justice. "You're good to her. I've always appreciated it."

I care about Izzy, and now I'll be in a position to make sure she gets what she needs without bankrupting Ruthie. My lie can be twisted into something good. All it will take is...

Breaking a promise I made to myself.

Sweat beads on my brow, and I grip the side of the table. What I'm about to say is insane, but it also feels strangely right—as if everything that's happened today has led up to this moment. Clearing my throat, I say, "I can tell it cost you to admit that. It's just... Like I said, I'm willing to do it, but we'd have to get legally married."

SHANE

RUTHIE'S FACE drains of color, and I have to laugh. "You look like you're the one who just got pissed on."

She blinks at me and then takes another swipe at her nose. "I feel like I am."

"You're not doing great things for my ego right now."

Giving me a smile that looks forced, she says, "You don't need help with that. I'm guessing you're talking about a marriage in name only. You'd stick to your life, and I'd stick to mine, except for work gatherings. No hanky-panky, no moving in together, no—" she waves a hand in the air, "—marriage shit."

"You guess correctly," I say, feeling a moment of relief, because it doesn't sound so big when she says it that way. It doesn't sound like a step that will change everything. "It would be a mutually beneficial arrangement that only lasts for as long as is mutually beneficial. You get the insurance, and I get the peace of mind that comes from only having partially lied to my boss."

She thinks this over for a moment, then shoves at her ruined cake with the fork, pushing it toward me. "Have some."

"No thanks."

"It's symbolic."

I have to grin. "You're sharing your broken heart with me?"

Something flickers in her light blue eyes, and I feel like an asshole, because I *know* her heart has been broken. More than once. "Fuck, I'm—"

"Eat my broken heart and choke on it," she says, but she's still smiling slightly.

So I do, because I'd like that smile to stay.

After choking down a forkful, I nod as if it's the chef's finest caviar. Not that I like caviar. Myles can have his private chef dress it up any way he likes, but there's no ducking the fact that you're stuffing your face with fish eggs. Still. I know how to impress people who don't want to be impressed.

For some reason, maybe just the sheer amount of time we've known each other, I've never tried that with Ruthie. Maybe not even when I should have.

I look up at her from over my fork, and when our eyes meet, I feel an electric current running between us—perfect understanding, or as close to perfect as the two of us are ever likely to get. Then I grin at her and say, "Huh. Turns out a broken heart tastes like shitty grocery store cake. I'll bet mine would be more like champagne."

She balls up a napkin and throws it at me. I catch it, and see her studying me. It goes on for several seconds, and that current snaps between us, filling me with a sensation I couldn't put a name to. Finally, she nods, and the moment ends. "Okay, asshole," she says with a sharp smile. "I honestly can't believe I'm saying this, but I *will* marry you. Even if it means Josie is right, which is frankly terrifying."

Hearing her say that, I feel my pulse race, my hands get clammy. They're words I never intended to hear from anyone. And they're particularly jarring from this woman who enjoys thinking the worst of me.

Her smile turns knowing. "Oh, don't get your panties into a twist, Vain. It'll be a purely platonic arrangement. Like you said, it'll be for our mutual benefit. Sounds exactly like the kind of thing you'd get off on."

"What about you?" I ask, lifting my eyebrows. "You're not looking for your happily ever after?"

Ruthie snorts, her nose crinkling, then forks up more of the substandard cake. "No. We both know marriage doesn't last forever, right?" There's a wry twist to her mouth, like she's making fun of herself. Like she's remembering all that time she spent getting her hair done for her wedding day, for a relationship that would only last a matter of months. I feel like I should acknowledge the past, but the moment passes like sand through an hourglass. There; gone. She takes another forkful of cake, then adds, "It would only be for a few months, until Izzy gets her surgery and you quit."

"What are you going to tell Izzy?"

"As little as possible. You'll tell your boss she's your step-child. But I'll leave her with Danny or one of my friends whenever you need me to go somewhere with you."

I nod, because I don't want to confuse Izzy or mess with her in any way. "Speaking of Danny..." I say, my heart working faster. "What do we tell him?"

"The truth," she says, conviction in her eyes. "But we're going to do it after the fact."

"Better to ask for forgiveness than permission," I say, grinning, because we're thinking the same thoughts again, and there's something thrilling about being on the same wavelength as her. We're building something together, even if it's a lie, rather than tearing each other down.

"Who will our witnesses be?" I ask.

Her smile stretches wider. "Josie, of course." Then she shrugs. "We can ask her to bring her boyfriend, or my friend Tank could do it."

"Tank?" I ask with a snort. "Is that his real name?"

She gives me an unamused look. "As if Shane is any better?"

It is, but I don't say so. I don't ask who Tank is to her, either, even though I'd like to know. Maybe I'll ask her later, when I have that right.

When she's your wife?

It's a fucked-up thought, and a reflection on how fucked up my life has become. But if I can get a job *and* help Ruthie and Izzy, what's the harm? Who would we be hurting? It's a lie, and some would argue that any lie is by nature despicable, but we're going to make it the truth.

"You've seen Tank before. He's been my friend since I was a little kid."

I vaguely remember her palling around with other children, but the last thing you care about as a kid is what kids five years younger than you are doing. "Okay."

She gives me the flat look of someone who knows I've drawn a blank. "Tank's the one who gave me Vanny."

"Oh, so we have a lot to be grateful to him for."

"We do," she says in a dangerous tone.

I lift my hands. "I mean it."

I don't. Tank hasn't done Ruthie any favors by giving her that crappy van. The problem is that it's just mobile enough that it lets her keep changing course. If you want to open a business, you need to seize one idea and run with it—not change your mind every time something doesn't go as planned. My dad always said if you're going to win, you need to learn how to lose, but Ruthie mustn't agree, because a hint of failure is enough to shut her down.

I don't like losing. I loathe it with every fiber of my being. But I don't let it shut me down. I don't throw in the towel and say oh well. I figure out how to win next time.

Ruthie needs to pick one of her ideas and run with it—to find her way around failures instead of letting them crush her before her plans have had a chance to crystallize.

But if I tried to tell her that, she'd say I'm being unfair, an asshole. Or she'd tell me this idea is the one she's been working toward all along—the one that's *right*. But she probably would have said the same thing about whatever idea she was chasing down last month. Because that's Ruthie's thing.

It drives me crazy to see someone who's so smart and driven keep driving themselves toward the wrong things.

She scrutinizes me, then says, "We need a prenup."

I laugh. "Did you think I'd try to take Flower from you? Or is it these pajamas you're so protective of?"

Her eyes are molten, and I feel a little shiver of excitement that probably marks me as a sick bastard. "I was just saying what you were inevitably going to say," she says, her tone tight with contempt. "I figured you'd want to cover your bases. But fuck you for implying I don't have anything valuable."

I nod, because it was a shit thing to say, and I own it. "Okay, but who's going to draw it up? It wouldn't be ethical if I did."

"Surely you have a friend or two?"

The words bring my mind back to Danny. How pissed is he going to be about all of this? Probably very. Then again, I know he'd do anything to protect Izzy, and I'll be helping her. I tell myself that'll be enough. I nearly broke my friendship with Burke last year. That was hard enough. I can't stomach the thought of losing Danny.

He's like a brother to me.

But she's not like a sister, a voice whispers in my head.

That's true. There was a time when I only saw her as *his* annoying little sister, back when she was growling and barking at me, or following me around asking dozens of questions, but that time has long since passed.

She's not a friend, not a sister, and yet...not nothing.

She annoys the hell out of me, but I have this strange yearning to see her when it's been a while. Maybe it's because she always challenges me, and I've been spending most of my time in a world where no one truly says what they mean or means what they says.

She's my barometer for how I'm doing as a person, and from the look on her face, today hasn't been a banner day.

I nod tightly. "I'll see that it gets done."

"We keep all of our own stuff once this is over. What's mine is mine and what's yours is yours."

I don't say anything—I don't even smile—but Ruthie swats me with her hand, which *does* make me smile.

"I really did want Flower," I say. Hearing her name, the little terror wags her tail, unnaturally long for a creature her size, and comes scampering over. "You here for Round Two?"

At this, Ruthie starts laughing so hard she bends over from the force of it, nearly face-planting in the shitty cake. Then she sneezes again.

"What?" I ask, rolling my eyes.

"Round Two. I was just...I was imagining her taking a..."

"Taking a shit on these pajamas? She should. They look like the kind of pajamas you'd give your grandpa so he could shit in them."

Ruthie laughs harder, leading to two more sneezes, and I smile and shake my head.

"You're allergic to this dog, aren't you?" I ask. Because of course Ruthie has a big enough bleeding heart to bring home a dog she's allergic to without having a plan for addressing said allergies. That's Ruthie for you.

"No," she says, scowling but still laughing. Then she rolls her eyes and amends her answer. "Only a little. It's nothing allergy medication won't resolve."

"Do you have any?"

"I'll get some."

Sure she will. Something tells me she'll pick up another shitty pair of pajamas for Danny first. Everyone else always comes first, which is the kind of thing that doesn't end well for anyone.

"What about the pajamas? Do you want me to launder and return them? Send a selfie to Danny and ask if Mira's into plaid?"

She makes a face, studying me through her laughter. "Keep them." She starts laughing again in bursts, sneezing every now and then. "They...they...suit you."

"This is a new low," I say in a murmur. "Insulting me to my face like that." I want to see her laugh harder so she'll squirm in her seat, that oversized sweatshirt trying its damnedest to cling on. Fuck, I'd like to watch it fall down, but that's my dick talking—and I've given my dick plenty of lectures on what it is and isn't allowed to react to.

Ruthie Traeger is at the top of the list. She doesn't make it easy to follow Rule Number One, but I'm not a man who's intimidated by a challenge.

"You've...got to leave...I'm going to pee my pants."

"Maybe I want you to. It would feel like justice for what Flower did to me."

She laughs harder, one hand clutching the table—and I have a traitorous mental picture of her clutching that table with both hands, her ass lifted up in those little bootie shorts.

I get up ungracefully, the chair nearly falling back behind me, and Ruthie manages a scowl through her gales of laughter, lifting a shaking finger to her lips.

"As if I'd wake Izzy, but you won't," I say. "Can I have a shopping bag for my piss-covered suit?"

Still laughing, she points a shaking finger toward a cabinet, and I go to it, rolling my eyes to myself when a dozen bags fling themselves out like an inflatable snake the instant I open the door, because there must be two hundred of them crammed into the space. "Why do you keep all of these?" I mutter as I claim one of them.

"Don't..." Ruthie says, finally getting control over herself. "I feel guilty about that. I just always forget the reusable ones. I save them so I can reuse them or bring them back to the grocery store someday, but I always forget."

"So you keep them to make yourself miserable."

She sobers and nods, and I find myself thinking about those sweatpants of Rand's. I wonder if she keeps those for the same reason. I don't like the thought, but I like the thought of them being sentimental even less. That fucker doesn't deserve to lick the questionably clean floor of this apartment, much less have his ring on her finger.

I get the suit squared away while she watches me.

"Well, what happens now?" she finally asks.

"I'll get my friend to draw up the prenup, then we can get a marriage license and go through with it. The sooner, the better, so we can get Izzy on the insurance from the beginning."

She thinks this over for a second and then nods. Tilting her head to the side, she asks, "Do you think Josie's really psychic?"

"No," I say, laughing with genuine humor. "She probably tells two thirds of the people she meets they're getting married. She got lucky. I'd prefer if you don't ask her to be one of the witnesses, but I have a feeling you're going to do the exact opposite of whatever I say, so I'll leave it up to you."

She smiles at me as I pack up, and Flower pads over to sit at her feet, her doggy face seeming to grin at me. Of course she's grinning—she's marked her territory, and her territory is apparently me.

"I'll be in touch," I say, and Ruthie pulls off a smart salute that makes me roll my eyes again. "Say hello to the tyke for me, kid."

Her scowl is like a balm to my soul—I've always called her that, and she's always hated it.

As I put my coat back on and turn to leave, I remember the very particular lie I told the legal beagle. "I need to get you a ring," I say. "Me too, I guess."

She laughs, but this time without humor. "I have a ring."

I'm already shaking my head before she finishes. "I'm not going to let him think I bought you that rinky-dink thing."

Her chin firms. I know I've stepped my foot in shit again, but I don't care. She didn't pick out the rinky-dink ring—her asshole ex did, and I refuse to apologize for insulting him.

"You're a snob."

"I am," I agree. "I'll handle it."

"Let me," she argues. "I'll pick out the biggest Cubic Zirconia at Walmart."

She looks like she actually enjoys the prospect, but I shake my head. "I'll handle it."

This may be a sham marriage, a lie, but I'm not going to have my wife, fake or not, wandering around with something that's obviously a Wal-Mart special.

"Fine," she says, sounding done with me. She starts in on the cake again, then pokes the bag and says, "Take some of this stuff with you."

"I got it for you and Izzy," I remind her.

"First rule of fake parenting—don't douse your child in sugar."

I give her a half a smile. "I'll have to remember that. Talk to you soon, Ruthie."

But before I can to the front door, I hear a little voice saying, "Mama?"

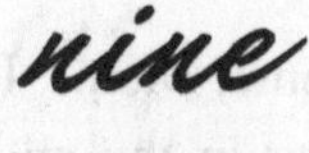

SHANE

IZZY APPEARS from the back hallway, her hair in a frizzy dark halo around her head. She's wearing *Frozen* pajamas, and it's impossible not to smile, especially when she catches sight of the sugar buffet set out in front of her mother, who looks like she's throwing a bunch of mental f-bombs. "Did you get this for me, Mama? Can I have some?"

"It's not for right now, honey," Ruthie says, snapping the plastic box shut over the broken heart cake. "It's for...breakfast."

"We're having cake for breakfast?"

"We are now." Her gaze travels to me and then the door. It's obviously a silent plea for me to get out, but it's too late. Izzy's eyes follow hers, widening when she sees me.

"Uncle Shane, what *on Earth* are you doing here? And why are you wearing pajamas? Are you and Mom having a sleepover, like that time Uncle Tank stayed over?"

An ugly feeling swells in my chest, and I glance at Ruthie to see how she reacts. Is there something between her and this man with the stupid name? She said they've been friends since they were kids. That's an awfully long time to be friends with someone like Ruthie without trying anything. I've known her for longer, probably, but I'm also five years older. I didn't need to institute Rule Number One until much later.

"No, honey," she tells Izzy without hesitation. "Shane was just leaving. And he tried on Uncle Danny's pajamas to see if they'd fit."

"That doesn't make sense, Mom," Izzy says, rubbing her eyes. "Why would he come over in the middle of the night to try on Uncle Danny's pajamas? They're not even the same size. Uncle Danny's at least two inches taller than him."

"I'm plenty tall," I can't help but say.

"Yes," Ruthie says with obvious amusement at my expense. "You're very big and strong." She wraps an arm around her daughter's shoulders. "You need to go back to bed, sweetheart. You have school in the morning."

Izzy's face puckers into a pout. "I don't want to go to school. Goldie told me her Polly Pocket was prettier than mine. We're in a fight."

"Why did either of you have your Polly Pockets at school?" Ruthie asks, at the same time I ask, "Is Goldie a person's name?"

"We had Show & Tell this morning, Mom," Izzy says, sounding a little peeved. "I told you yesterday."

Ruthie sighs and lifts one hand from Izzy to rub her own forehead. "And you brought a Polly Pocket?"

"We talked about this already," Izzy continues.

Ruthie looks guilty, as if her failure to remember the toy thing is a profound personal mistake she'll be remembering on her death bed. Someone needs to tell her to chill the fuck out, but it wouldn't be me—I have too much respect for my balls.

"I'm sorry, honey," Ruthie says. "I don't remember."

Izzy sighs. "I *knew* you weren't listening. You had that look on your face you always get when you're not listening."

"You mean when she stares off into the distance?" I say, because

I can't avoid the temptation to get involved in this game. "She's been doing that since she was a little girl."

"You're still here?" Ruthie says, giving me a look that would wither a lesser man's balls.

"So it would seem."

"Bedtime," she says as she squeezes Izzy to her. She bends to kiss the fuzzy top of her head, and there's a warm feeling in my chest, as if I just had a fine pour of whiskey. I might not want a family of my own, but any asshole would see they're cute together. Seeing them is like seeing a baby animal. Even if you don't want a pet, baby animals are, by nature's design, adorable, and it's hard not feel moved by their big eyes and soft fur. "You need to get some sleep. You and Goldie can talk it out in the morning. Remind her that two things can be pretty without making each other less pretty."

"But I want to pet Flower," Izzy says, her gaze zeroing in on the little dog, who gives a flop of her tail at the sound of her name but doesn't get up. Now that she's pissed on me, she's feeling positively restful.

"Okay, go pet Flower, then time for bed."

Izzy doesn't wait—she scampers over to the dog and bends down next to her, worshipping at her feet as if she's a golden god instead of a little mutt with incontinence issues.

Even so, that warmth in my chest is spreading. I can't afford to be soft, though. If I want to carry through with this lie, I need to be calculated. I need to be strong. So I swallow the feeling and clear my throat. "All right, ladies, I'll leave you to it."

"Are you taking Uncle Danny's pajamas?" Izzy asks, glancing up at me.

"Yes," I say. "Your mom showed them to me, and I had to have them for myself." I grin at Ruthie. She's actually smiling at me, which is an interesting change. "What do you think? Maybe you can get him a Polly Pocket instead?"

Izzy laughs and shakes her head. "I don't think Uncle Danny would play with it. He told me he doesn't see the point of them."

I don't know what the fuck a Polly Pocket is, to be honest, but I'm guessing I'd side with Danny on this one. So I just grin at her. "Goodnight, sweetie. Hope you figure it out with Goldenrod. It's no good to be on the outs with friends."

I feel a pang of guilt, because I don't imagine Danny's going to be thrilled with me when all is said and done. It's a shitty thing to do to a friend—something I know he wouldn't do to me. If I had a sister.

"Her name is Marigold," Izzy corrects, "not Goldenrod." Not much better. "But I want *you* to read to me, Uncle Shane. I don't think I can get back to sleep after all this excitement unless you read to me."

I glance over her head at Ruthie, grinning, because I know a Grade-A manipulation when I see one. Truth be told, I'm proud of the tyke. "I'm okay with it if your mom says it's all right."

Ruthie's annoyed glance tells me I've left her no choice if she doesn't want to become the bad guy, and I suppose she's right. "One book," she says.

"Okay," Izzy agrees brightly, giving Flower a hug that looks like it's half-throttling her. I take off my coat again, laying it back over the arm of the couch. Then Izzy leads me to her bedroom, her steps so spritely I'm guessing Ruthie isn't going to get much sleep tonight.

"I'm going to have you read my favorite unicorn story," she tells me. "It's about Bo the unicorn and her friends. They go to school, but it's not like my school. It's a fun school."

"School doesn't have to be fun," I say. "It's where you go to learn stuff so you can get a job and make enough money to buy all the Polly Pockets you want."

"Don't indoctrinate my child about capitalism," Ruthie calls out as Izzy opens the door to her bedroom.

I think but don't say, *Someone needs to indoctrinate* you *about capitalism.*

I've heard enough about her bookmobile scheme from Danny to know it's not going to make her squat unless she makes some changes, but she always accuses me of being overbearing and holier than thou art, and after a while a guy knows when he's beat. Still, I'm smiling as I pad into the little room after Izzy, taking in the glow lights strung up around the canopy of the bed and the framed drawings on the wall—Izzy's work. They're probably better than anything I could sketch, and I say so.

"That's not really true, Uncle Shane. You don't have to treat me like a baby."

"I'd never."

She climbs into bed and points to the book on her night stand, which looks like it's at least a hundred pages long. "There it is. Mom lies next to me and uses that lamp to read. Can you do that?"

There's definitely not room for a six-foot-tall man to lie down in her bed, so I say, "How about I sit on the ground next to you?"

"That wouldn't be comfortable," she says reasonably. "It's kind of a long book. Why don't you sit on my rainbow poof?"

She points to a puffy bag that looks like a rainbow swallowed a dog, so I pull it over and sit on it. The book is ninety percent pictures, thank God, but it still takes me fifteen or maybe twenty minutes to read it. By the time I'm done, Izzy's eyes are heavy, and the sight of her snuggled up in bed brings back that warm feeling. "You get to sleep now, sweetheart," I say, leaning in to kiss her forehead.

"Why'd you really come here tonight, Uncle Shane?"

"Because I wanted to see you and your momma." It may not be the truth, the full truth, and nothing but the truth, so help me God, but it's not altogether false. Danny and Ruthie are grounding to me. They remind me of who I was—not an altogether comfortable reminder, but occasionally a necessary one.

"Goodnight," Izzy says sweetly, and I shut off the lamp and leave her room to find Ruthie pacing the living room.

"Is she going to sleep?" she asks in a low voice. Her whole body seems to be humming with nerves, and without thinking about it, I reach out and run a hand down her arm. It's an unconscious gesture, but it gives me a heightened awareness of her. Of her surprised look and the way her breath is coming out more quickly than usually. Of the softness of the sweatshirt and how much softer her skin would be beneath if I peeled it off. I shake off the thought. I may be physically drawn to her, and possibly her to me, but a physical connection can be found between any two people who find each other pleasing to look at.

"Yes," I say, "her eyes were heavy. She's probably already out."

"*Thank you,* Shane."

She hasn't said that to me for years, maybe even decades, and the way she's looking at me makes me feel like pulling her closer. Something weird is going on with me, no question. So I decide I'd better get the fuck out of here before things go farther south.

"You're welcome. Well." I clap my hands, and immediately feel like a blowhard. It would have tracked better if I were still wearing my suit and not these Brady Bunch pajamas. I clear my throat. "I'm going to go."

She blinks at me, then nods. "Yeah, that's probably for the best." Flower, lying by the couch, gives a little whine like she'd prefer it if I could stay for more torment.

I slide my coat on and take the bag with the soiled suit. "I'll be talking to you soon, Ruthie. Flower."

"Can't wait," Ruthie jabs, but the words lack any of her usual heat.

I smile at her, then say, "Take it easy, kid," because she'll love that. Before she can do more than scowl, I head out the door for real. I feel a little lighter than I did when I arrived, which is ludicrous since my very expensive suit is covered in dog urine, and I'm wearing pajamas and a peacoat. Then again, I've solved my little problem, *and* I have a job.

A *job*.

The past couple of months have been interminable. Unacceptable. But I've finally found an escape, a way to turn the path ahead in the direction I need it to go.

Working for the legal beagle isn't a permanent solution, but it's something, and something is a hell of a lot better than nothing. It's a stepping stone on the way to being myself again.

It doesn't surprise me the slightest bit when the door to the apartment across the way opens the second I exit Ruthie's place.

"There's a dog in there," Mrs. Longhorn says, pointing a withered finger at me. "I know a bark when I hear it."

I make a mental note to call the apartment complex in the morning and settle the dog issue for Ruthie. She may think she can buy herself time by disguising the dog as a child or stuffing it into a bag or whatever plan she's come up with, but she's only fooling herself.

The old lady's eyes widen as she takes in the sight of my-slash-Danny's pajamas. "You went in there on a mission of sin."

Interestingly enough, her tone is not disapproving.

I hold back an "I wish" and instead lift the bag holding my sodden suit. "Actually, ma'am, I'm embarrassed to admit that I made that sound when I pissed myself. Ruthie was kind enough to give me some pajamas she'd bought for her brother so I wouldn't be embarrassed. But you caught me in the lie. I've had an overactive bladder since I was a kid. Can't help myself. I'd appreciate it if you didn't say anything to anyone."

I fully expect she'll say something to everyone. But I could give a shit what the other people in this apartment complex think about me. Better for her to believe I'm a nutjob than that Ruthie is hiding a dog.

The look on Mrs. Longhorn's face tells me I've shocked her speechless, proving there's a first for everything.

I leave the apartment, whistling a tune.

I feel pretty damn good.

The only thing bugging me, although I couldn't say why, is Izzy saying, *It's like that time Uncle Tank stayed over.*

Ruthie's not mine, so it shouldn't matter, but all the same, I'd like to meet this Tank.

ten

RUTHIE

"YOU'RE DOING *WHAT*, BABY GIRL?"

I'm standing at the back of the diner with my boss, Eden, who's looking at me as if I just announced that I'd doused the diner with gasoline and have a pocketful of matches. Then again, I *did* just tell her I need to take tomorrow afternoon off so I can get married.

Shane works fast. He told me about this whole thing last Thursday, a week ago today, and now it's happening tomorrow. We've signed the simple prenup his friend put together, and yesterday we picked up our marriage license in the short window of time between the end of my shift at the diner and Izzy's school pickup.

73

It was a surreal experience, because the last time I'd been there was with Rand.

Remembering the excitement I'd felt that day was like swallowing a spoonful of ash. I'd been so certain I was in love—that Rand was the wealthy, handsome prince who'd stepped into the chaos of my life and pulled me out of it. But it had fallen apart so quickly that I'd barely had time to notice it was happening before it was over. I'm glad he's gone, glad Izzy doesn't have to find out the truth about the man who fathered her, but I also mourn the loss of the innocence and hope I'd felt.

Shane was in a bad mood at the Register of Deeds. *I* was also in a bad mood, made worse by the fact that there was no coat rack and someone had turned up the heat in the office to a good seventy-five degrees. We spent the whole time bickering—so much so that the clerk raised her eyebrows and wished us good luck.

So it surprised me, maybe even shocked me, when Shane handed me a big bottle of Zyrtec before defecting to his car. "For you, kid. Consider it an engagement present."

It made me smile, and I found myself watching his back as he retreated, taking in the way the muscles bunched beneath his shirt, because he'd pulled off his jacket in the office and hadn't put it back on yet.

Eden's still giving me that look, and who can blame her?

I glance around, making sure no one's paying attention to us. No one is. We're hanging out near the back of the diner so we can keep an eye on our tables. One of them is occupied by an older man named Ralph who comes in every morning and orders only coffee. He spends more time ogling Eden and me than he does drinking his beverage and always complains it's too cold or hot, criticisms that seem to have nothing to do with the actual temperature of the coffee.

Turning back to Eden, I say in a hushed voice, "This isn't a big deal. It's not a *real* marriage."

She lifts her eyebrows. "I don't claim to be an expert, baby girl, but from my understanding, most fake marriages don't happen at city hall."

"Seriously," I insist, wishing I'd told her I had a gynecologist appointment instead. I probably should have, but Eden has always been important to me. She's like the mother I wish I'd had. Speaking of which: my mother has texted again and left a voice message—as if she knows I'm going through a period of weakness and might actually accept one of her calls.

I won't. True, I may be bursting to talk about the Shane situation, but she's the last person I'd confide in. When I was a kid, my brother was the only one who ever made me feel loved. My parents had used him for parenting as much as money making. Now, my mother says she's found Jesus and changed her ways, but I can tell when a person's drunk—and she's several drinks in on most of the messages she leaves. She may want forgiveness, but she hasn't changed. She won't. She'll always be the woman who took advantage of my brother and preferred a bottle to either of us.

Speaking of my brother. I almost gave everything away over the weekend, when he stopped over with some toothpaste from the bulk pack he'd bought at Sam's Club.

He's constantly buying shit in bulk because he hates going grocery shopping, and probably also because he knows Izzy and I have needs that I struggle to meet.

Flower met him at the door with a few little flower clips in her hair from Izzy's "beauty salon." After Izzy told him the whole story about Flower in a quick burst of information, he looked at me, eyebrows raised. I expected him to remind me that I'm allergic to dogs or maybe even to point out that he could tell I was allergic to this one. Instead, he said, "Huh, will you look at that. It just so happens that I have some bulk dog food at home too. Can't do much with it. Turns out you can't give it to hamsters."

It was his way of making a joke—and *helping*—and I hugged him so hard I probably gave him a hernia.

I wanted to tell him about the marriage plan. The words were on my lips. But I'd already told Shane we shouldn't. Still, I have to wonder if Danny will be hurt.

He walked me down the aisle at my wedding to Rand. Maybe he'd want to do it again. After all, it may not be a real wedding, but it's the last one I'm likely to have.

A dark feeling fills my gut, because that innocent little girl who wanted to love and be loved isn't altogether dead. She'd like me to know this is madness, and I shouldn't get married and divorced again unless it's because I've fallen in love with another blowhard.

I realize Eden's still watching me, waiting for an explanation she must know is forthcoming sometime this century. So I add, "This guy's Danny's childhood friend. I'm just doing him a favor. No big deal."

"A favor with *your coochie?*"

Laughter bursts out of me, because it's impossible not to laugh at the word "coochie."

Across the dining room, Ralph wiggles his ass in his seat, his mouth pouching into a frown, and I know we're about a minute away from a complaint about the temperature of the coffee.

"You think it's a too-hot day or a too-cold day?" I ask Eden in a whisper.

She tugs one of her locs and rolls her eyes. "I'll give that man a coffee enema. See what he has to say about it then. Never mind Ralph, I want to hear about this man you're 'not really' marrying. When you first told me, I figured you had to be talking about Tank."

I grimace, because I haven't told Tank about the marriage plan yet either. Last week, I told Shane that my friend could be one of the witnesses, but the more I think about it, the more certain I am he's going to disapprove. He would tell me I'm being hasty, which is obviously true. I'm guessing he would also say there are easier ways to make a buck, which feels less true. More palatable, yes. Easier? No.

I'd suggested using Josie as other witness, but I haven't gotten around to doing that either. That one's down to pure cowardice, probably.

She still hasn't told me about whatever she's seen for me, and she was clearly been right about Shane, so...

"Tank's just a friend," I murmur. "You know that. We've been friends forever."

"And this other man?"

Sighing, I say, "I've known him forever too." My eyes linger on Ralph like he's been transformed into the most interesting person in the universe. "This isn't a romantic thing. It's a legal arrangement. Shane wants his boss to think he's a family man, and I need better health insurance. So he's paying me to go to a few events with him, and he's going to put me and Izzy on his insurance. Simple."

She flinches as if a bee stung her in the ass, and I bump her with my hip. "The insurance I get through the marketplace is fine, Eden. You have no reason to feel guilty." I think but don't add: *We both know you're barely turning a profit anymore.*

Or maybe not at all.

She and her husband Charlie, the chef, started Loving Diner two decades ago, their nod to Loving v. Virginia, the Supreme Court Case that struck down state laws banning marriages like theirs. It used to do well...before the town got so gentrified every restaurant needs to have unpronounceable items on the menu to stand out. Their rent's too high, and the décor is on the dumpy side, because Eden flat-out refuses to let me change it.

My comment about the insurance earns a snort. "That's bullshit, and we both know it." Her sharp gaze meets mine. "I'm guessing the legal arrangement thing is bullshit too. You do know every marriage is a legal arrangement, right?"

Don't I ever.

"Sure, but this time it's a legal arrangement that's not going to bite me in the ass. There are no feelings involved."

Her eyebrows hike up higher. "So you're marrying this man, but you don't intend to sleep with him."

This time, I'm the one who flinches. Because I can't help but think of Shane in those pajamas the other night. I can't possibly give them to my brother now, and not just because someone else wore them.

You don't want to see your brother wearing something you wanted to tear off someone.

The thing is...

You don't travel in the same orbit as someone like Shane Royce without wondering if he has the moves and equipment to back up his swagger. I'll never test that personally, but that doesn't keep me from thinking about it. And I'm pretty sure I'm not the only one who occasionally has thoughts. I've noticed him checking out things he shouldn't—the line of my bra or the dip of my V-neck. My ass. It's become an unspoken game to see if I can get him to look. It's a dangerous game, but all games worth playing are dangerous.

The other night, when he was changing out of his suit in my apartment, I had a pounding awareness of what he was doing on the other side of the bathroom door, in a space that's supposed to be mine.

Now, he's probably taking his pants off. His underwear.

I wanted to see what my sink was seeing. My mirror. There's no denying part of me would really like to know what he looks like under all those layers of expensive fabric.

You could probably bounce a quarter off of his abs, and part of me would like to try, for the pure pleasure of throwing something at him.

Except...I have to admit it was decent of him to step in to help with Izzy. Usually, she only spends time with Shane when Danny's babysitting, so I haven't seen them together much. It was...sweet. I can't deny part of me craves seeing her with a father figure because she's never met her father. If I have my way, she never will.

Rand found out I was pregnant and chose that exact moment to tell me that he'd *never* wanted children. We'd discussed kids before getting married of course, and he'd told me he wanted a family. A big family. But he'd back-peddled so quickly he could have won a cycling contest. According to him, he'd only said that because he'd figured I'd change my mind after seeing how easy and fun it would be, just the two of us, no one holding us back or down. He hadn't thought it would be an issue, and certainly not an issue this soon, and didn't I realize that I was ruining *everything*? I must have been taking my birth control pills wrong. I'd never been good at following instructions, and here was the proof.

It had blindsided me and opened my eyes to the other lies he'd told. That his parents loved me (maybe he'd meant loathed). That I didn't need a job if I was going to be his wife (I felt purposeless without one). That it wasn't appropriate for me to hang out with Tank alone because he was a man (to my shame, I'd listened). I'd given up so much to try to please Rand, because I'd thought he was better than me. Richer. Smarter. More important. But I wasn't giving up my daughter. *He* may have never wanted a family, but I did.

He gave me an ultimatum: keep him or the baby, and because he'd asked, it was the easiest choice I'd ever made.

The divorce gave me a small financial settlement—*very* small, since his parents had made us sign a prenup—and he'd readily agreed to sign the form renouncing his paternal rights. If I hadn't asked him to sign it, I could have gotten child support from him, but he would have had the ability to ask for shared custody. He didn't want Izzy, he'd made that perfectly clear, but I wasn't willing to risk that he'd decide he cared more about appearances than his free time. Once the form was signed, the divorce finalized, he found a job in a different town. It was my fault, of course. I'd ruined his life, and he didn't want to live in the fallout.

I don't know what he told his parents, but the first time I saw his mother after Rand left, she marched up to me and told me I was a little slut who'd driven her son out of town. I told her she was an emotionally stunted bitch who'd raised a boy who had the emotional integrity of a box of cereal.

I've seen them around town several times since then, twice this past month. The last time we passed them on the street, Mrs. Callaghan looked like she had tears in her eyes. Her gaze was hooked on Izzy's unicorn hat and Elsa braids. Maybe she saw the Callaghan family resemblance—the shape of Izzy's lips, her eyes. Maybe it made her feel ashamed that she has one granddaughter, the only grandchild she'll ever have, and she doesn't and won't know her. But I'm probably projecting. She could have just been upset because her favorite clothing line got discontinued. Or one of the nails in her gel manicure got chipped.

They've never once approached us, and I prefer it that way.

When Izzy asks about her dad, I tell her that he had to move away for work, and sometimes parents aren't really parents but just the people who gave us life. It's something she shouldn't have to understand but does, because my parents were the same way.

I shake off the intrusive thoughts and find Eden watching me with a knowing expression on her face.

"I'm *not* going to sleep with Shane," I insist, and my other table, a couple of tourists who mustn't set much stock by online reviews, glance up at me. One of them was eating a pancake that flops down from his fork, as flaccid as a drunk dick. I nod and smile. They're midway through their meal, their mouths full, so this would be the perfect time to check on them for maximum annoyance, another game I play to kill boredom.

"Sure, girl. Is he ugly?"

I look at Ralph, whose expression continues to sour as he plays with the coffee mug in front of him. It's a too-cold day, I decide. I can tell because of the way he occasionally tugs on the sleeves of his sweater, like they're not long enough to protect him from our coffee.

"It's not like you to avoid a simple question," Eden observes.

"No," I say with a sigh. "He's not ugly, but he's one of those guys who *knows* he's not ugly."

"Ain't nothing wrong with a man who knows how to use a mirror," she says with a smile. "Better that than a man who doesn't know how to comb his hair. Or a man who has no hair to comb."

It's hard not to grin back—Eden has one of those smiles you just fall into, from the gap between her teeth to her dimples—but I have a feeling of unease. All of this happened so quickly, before I could even process it. Just like with Flower, I leapt in with both feet without knowing where or if I'd land.

The pee smell that won't leave my carpet, and my three pairs of fucked-up shoes say adopting Flower was a mistake. But it's one I can't regret too much. Izzy loves the little dog so much that she taped a picture on the wall over a spot Flower had been gnawing on to make sure she "didn't get in trouble." Besides, the Zyrtec has worked wonders.

I lift a hand to my throat, thinking of Shane handing me that bottle and the muscles bunching in his back as he walked away.

"Do you think it's immoral to marry someone you don't really like for financial gain?" I ask, my voice distant. "I mean, I genuinely dislike this man."

Even as I say it, I feel the wrongness of the statement. My feelings for Shane are more complex than simple dislike. He annoys me, confounds me, and is also capable of surprising goodness.

Of course, it's goodness that's delivered on his terms.

Case and point, he inserted himself into the dog situation last Friday by calling my building manager and paying the pet fee. I have to admit I was grateful because Mrs. Longhorn caught me carrying Flower outside in my tote bag that afternoon. The tote wasn't as big as I'd remembered, and I started blathering about Flower being an animatronic stuffed animal before Mrs. Longhorn gave me a hard look and said, "I don't know what you're playing at, Ruthie Traeger, pretending you don't have a dog when you've already paid the fee for that flea-bitten animal. Maybe you think it's funny, playing games with an old woman."

She'd given me a look that would have made Elsa from *Frozen* jealous and walked off without a backward glance.

So it was definitely a good thing that everything had already been settled.

On the other hand, Shane took care of the situation behind my back, treating me as if I were still the little girl in pigtails who kept trying to tag along with him and Danny on my bike with training wheels.

It had crushed me to find out what he really thought of me. I can still hear him asking Danny, "Why does your kid sister always want to tag along? Doesn't she have any friends of her own?"

Asshole.

My lips tighten with the memory. Admittedly, I'm being a little unfair—he was only fifteen when he said that, but still...

Eden snorts, bringing me back to the present again, to the wall at my back and Ralph frowning at his coffee like it's a woman who did him wrong. Except I'm guessing *I'm* the woman who did him wrong.

"Financial gain, huh? How much money are we talking?" Eden asks, giving me a sidelong glance. "Is this guy rich?"

I pause, then say, "Yeah, I think so. He's a lawyer. He's always wearing really nice suits, and his car probably costs more than everything I own put together. But that's his money, other than what he's agreed to pay me. We already signed a prenup."

She shakes her head, her eyes telling me I'm too stupid to live. "What are you still doing here? Even without this rich not-a-husband, you make more money on eBay than you do at the diner. We've never had a lot of people during the day, and it just keeps getting worse. If you want to make something happen, you've got to give yourself the time to do it. You're not a damn wizard. You can't make time out of nothing."

I puff my lips out, considering it. She's right. I *know* she's right. The "eBay shit" is another side hustle. I get things from Goodwill and estate sales and shine them up, then resell them on eBay. When I crunched the numbers before Christmas, I discovered the "eBay shit" is where I make seventy percent of my income. The diner is thirty-five. Vanny is negative five.

Now, my job as Shane's wife will be contributing almost as much as eBay. I can give up the diner and focus my attention on getting my Vanny events to turn a profit. But the thought of leaving punches a hole in my chest. This is my safe space, the same way that bench in the woods was when I was a little kid. But the way Eden's looking at me tells me it might not be mine for much longer.

"*Eden,*" I say, the word coming out intense, "Are you and Charlie..."

"Ma'am," Ralph says aggressively, lifting up his cup. "*Ma'am.*"

Eden gives me a tight smile and pats me on the back. "He's playing your song."

"What about tomorrow?

"You can have it off," she says. "The whole day. In fact, the diner's going to be closed. And you'll need to tell Charlie and me where to come for the ceremony. You know that man could get himself lost inside of a paper bag." She pauses, her eyes widening. "What are you going to wear, girl? Tell me you have a dress."

I'm an idiot, because tears are welling in my eyes. She's so good to me, and it's hard to feel I deserve it.

"I was going to wear—"

"I'm going to stop you right there, honey. You go get Ralph his hot or cold coffee and tell him he's getting cut off in an hour. We're going shopping, my treat."

Before I can tell her there's no need—I'll wear a sweater dress or something I have lying around the house, because only a real marriage requires a real dress—she gives me a hard look. "I'm not taking no for an answer, so you might as well save us both the trouble."

eleven

SHANE

IT'S a piece of irony that Danny asks me to look at engagement rings with him the afternoon before my wedding to his sister. I say, "Sure, why not?" and hold back the, *Hey, great timing, I'm getting married tomorrow, and I still need to pick up rings. I haven't been able to get away this week, because Mom's depressed again and all of her friends are out of town.*

It's been twenty-two years since my father died, and she still can't get out of bed every morning, but she's not interested in putting away the photos that make her house feel like a tomb. She doesn't want to make any changes at all, really. What can you do?

I took it out on Ruthie the other day, when we were picking up the marriage license, and I felt like a real dick because *I know* it couldn't have been easy for her. She's gotten married for real, after all. There must be memories attached to that, and given that she was married to Rand, I'm guessing they're shit memories.

I won't be able to get the rings while Danny's with me, obviously, since that would lead to questions such as *Who the hell are you marrying?*, but I could grab them after he leaves.

Grab them, like I'm swinging by a coffee shop to get a latte.

For the hundredth time today, I ask myself what the hell I'm doing. Danny's the oldest friend I have and one of the only people I fully trust. I might not intend to fuck his sister, but he still deserves to know about the fake marriage. In all honesty, I don't really understand my own hesitation—I'm doing this for the job, sure, but Izzy's going to benefit from it, and Danny would do anything to help his niece. So he might even be on board with the plan.

There's an easy feeling in my gut, though, like I know it's not going to go down nice and easy like a shot of Macallan.

Still, I can't back down now.

My first day at Freeman & Daniels is Monday, and Freeman is already arranging a celebration for next Friday night to officially welcome Ruthie and me into the "pack"—a pack of legal beagles, one can only assume. I've also been given the go-ahead to start interviewing for assistants next week, so this is really happening. It's a go.

That's a relief, and also not.

Freeman's a good man, but working at his firm will be like getting a job at a Wendy's after working at a Michelin Star restaurant. At least it's still a restaurant, or so I keep telling myself.

I suck it up and meet Danny in the lot of the jewelry store I picked out based on the fact that they've been around thirty years and no one's ever gotten pissed enough to sue them.

He's only been with Mira since November, but that's Danny for you. Once he's certain of something, there's no swaying him, and in this case I'm not so sure he's wrong. Mira's good for him. He has a tendency to dig in his heels, but when he gets dug in too deep, she can help pull him out.

His Subaru is already in the lot when I arrive, not that I'm surprised—he has an uncanny ability to judge when he has to leave anywhere in order to arrive five minutes early. I pull in next to him and get out at the same time he does.

I have to smile a little at the sight of his peacoat and the blue-checkered shirt beneath it. Both Mira picks, I'm guessing.

"Isn't this the kind of thing you should be doing with Ruthie?" I ask as I clap him on the back. "Or someone who believes in marrying for love?"

He gives me a dubious look. "Why else would someone get married?"

I feel like fessing up, but I won't break my deal with Ruthie. So I just shrug. "People do things for a lot of messed-up reasons."

"I asked you because you always know if someone's trying to screw me over. I'd prefer to know before it happens."

"Leonard or Burke would probably know too," I say, because our friends are fellow members of Cupid's cult. Burke is already engaged, and Leonard is halfway there.

Danny gives me a sidelong look. "But you've been looking out for me since we were six."

Emotion tries to make a ball in my throat and choke me, but I swallow it down with as much enthusiasm as if it were grocery store cake.

"You don't need me for that anymore."

"No," he says, tapping his fingertips against the top of my car. "I suppose not."

"What about your sister?" I ask, because my mind is on her. "She'd love to do this with you."

"I don't know, man. You care about being stylish." He motions to my suit as if it's evidence A. "You know I don't give a shit about stuff like that, but Mira does."

"And Ruthie doesn't?" I ask, amused, thinking of those pajamas she bought for him.

"She always looks nice," he says in a pained tone, because he hates admitting anything is less than perfect about his sister. In this instance, he's right. She's on a shoestring budget, but she always *does* look nice. So does Izzy. I'm guessing she has a list of a dozens of things she'd like to buy for her brother, but she probably only had enough extra cash to get him the five-dollar pajama special at Wal-

Mart. She still insists on getting him gifts, though, even though it costs her and probably doesn't bring him much pleasure. I can't decide whether that's noble or just stupid.

Danny rubs the spot between his eyes, like he's getting a headache. "Mira hated the reading glasses Ruthie got for me. So I figured I shouldn't go to her for ring advice."

I'm not sure what possesses me, but I look at him and say, "You should still ask. Ruthie would like to be asked. Maybe narrow it down to a few options and send some photos to get her take. It'll help her feel involved."

He gives me a half smile. "See, this is why I needed to bring you. You're much better at manipulating people than I am."

He's mostly messing with me, but I really do think he means it as a compliment. Maybe I'd take it as one, if I didn't have Ruthie in my head, frowning at me.

I nod to him. "Don't let anyone talk you into buying something you can't afford. You don't want the kind of woman who'll only agree to marry you if the rock's big enough."

"Mira's not like that," he says immediately.

"I know, she'd marry you even if you let Ruthie pick the ring."

"You think?"

"You're not one of the people I'm paid to lie to. And despite the fact that you've only been dating her for three months, I'm not going to tell you it's a mistake. I like Mira. She doesn't have the vibe of a woman who's going to drag you to court in a few years so she can take half of your computer shit and then destroy it on camera."

He smile returns. "I take it that really happened. Who'd you represent?"

"They were golf clubs," I say, nodding to the front of the store to signal it's time to get moving. "And that's confidential."

Danny laughs, but by the time we reach the front of the store, he's quiet again. I know it's not just nerves about the proposal. He hates shopping in general. He can't handle the lights and noise, not to mention the overly friendly strangers trying to sell him something. A salesperson is already staring straight at us—a man with dyed blond hair and a knowing gleam in his eyes.

"We could always shop online," I suggest, lifting my eyebrows.

"And here I thought you had exacting standards," Danny says. Then he takes a deep breath and pushes the door inward; I follow him in. I must feel nervous for him, because my palms are slick, my tie more confining than usual.

I can imagine Ruthie giving me a saucy look, her hand on your hip. *Serves you right. Did you really have to wear a suit to visit your mother and go ring shopping with my brother?*

Yes, because I'm getting one for you too.

There I go again, talking to Ruthie in my head.

I adjust my tie and clear my throat just as the over-eager blond guy scurries around the case to approach us.

He steps in close, beaming, and says, "What can I do for you, friends?"

There are a couple of other people browsing, but none of them have the look of men or women who are here against their will and inclination, the way Danny does. He must come off as fresh meat, an easy sale. A man who is only here because the power of true love bit him in the ass.

It's bright as hell in here, the better to make those gems glitter, and I can already see it getting to Danny. The pop song filtering in over the speakers mounted in every corner probably isn't helping.

Time to move things along.

I clap my buddy on the back. "My friend here has decided to pop the question to his girl. He needs a ring."

"Wonderful," the guy says, beaming. "I'm Michael, and I'm honored to help you find forever."

I choke on a laugh and glance at Danny, because I already know I'm going to want to frame the look on his face. His brows are lifted, his mouth flat. "I'm looking for a ring for a woman who would laugh at that statement."

I choke on more laughter, but Michael has been at this a while. He claps his hands as if this is good news and says, "Ah, a ring for a skeptic. My favorite. Why don't you tell me what she likes, and I'll put together a board of rings for you."

"Uh," Danny messes with the pockets of his jeans, as if he might have stuffed answers in there. "She likes bright and colorful stuff. I'm not really the best judge of what she'd want because I prefer..." He glances around, decides he doesn't personally like anything in here, and waves a hand to allow Michael to draw his own conclusions.

"Is that enough for you to work with?" I ask. My mind's whirring though. I'm thinking of what Ruthie would choose for herself if money were no object.

"Of course," Michael says. "We have something for every taste and budget. I can't wait to find you the perfect ring for your perfect woman. Make yourselves comfortable, and I'll put together some options."

"Yeah," Danny says, messing with his pockets again. "I'm going to sit down." There are a couple of chairs arranged against the wall —leather and comfortable-looking, with an antique-looking table between them. They're probably kept specifically for schmucks who come here to blow their load on a rock.

"Yes, make yourselves comfortable. What can I get for you? Some champagne?" He pauses, then adds, "Scotch, perhaps?"

"Scotch," I say. "Scotch would be great."

Danny nods in agreement and heads for the chairs like he's a Corgi with an ankle in its sights. I start to follow him, then turn toward the attendant. "Hey," I say in an undertone. "Is there any way we can turn down the music? My friend doesn't like to advertise it, but he has some sensory sensitivities, and it's kind of—"

Blaring.

Loud.

Annoying as fuck.

He nods, a flicker of something passing over his face. "You're doing us all a favor by asking. I'm only allowed to turn it down if someone asks."

"Thanks, man. And can you pick out a few rings with red stones? It's her favorite color."

Ruthie's favorite, actually, but I'm hoping that won't come out.

"No problem."

I head back over to the chairs, guilt burning a hole in my gut even though my mission wasn't an entirely selfish one. "Ring shopping's looking up," I comment. "They're gonna turn down the crap music." Might as well tell him. Sometimes he's sensitive to other people intervening on his behalf, but there's no way he's not going to notice the change.

Mira has obviously chilled Danny out, though, because he just nods and says, "I'm not sure how much more of this I can take."

"Hopefully your forever will be on the first board."

"Hopefully, because Michael's... I mean, he's nice, but he's really enthusiastic. People can be too enthusiastic."

His girlfriend and soon-to-be fiancée is one of them, but he doesn't seem to mind when it comes from her. I guess that's what being in love does to a man.

"Yeah, I know what you mean," I say, watching a woman try on a necklace so ugly she should be paid to wear it. She glances into the mirror arranged on the counter and beams at her reflection. "My new boss is too enthusiastic. I don't understand how he survived law school."

"I'm glad you got the job," he says, smiling at me. "I knew something would work out."

I let out a gruff laugh, feeling like shit on the bottom of someone's shoe. "I didn't share your confidence."

"But you still left the firm. I know Burke's grateful for it."

He's right about that. But I almost stayed, even though Burke's been my friend for more than half my life. What does that say about me?

What does it say about me that I *regret* leaving?

Or that I'm willing to move forward with this marriage?

Nothing good, obviously.

"Have they set a trial date, yet?" he asks.

I squirm a little in the chair, even though it is, as advertised, very comfortable. "No. My old paralegal said she'd let me know."

Rachel is sixty and takes no shit from anyone, myself included. Even though I palled around with the other guys at the firm, and we always got scotch and cigars together after winning a case, none of them have kept in touch. Fear of Myles has them quaking in their boots, but Rachel couldn't give a shit. She was reassigned to work with one of the other guys, who doesn't know his ass from his elbow by her assessment, and she's kept me updated on the goings-on. She believes the Burkes will lose their case, so that's something.

Danny nods several times, then rubs his forehead. There are a couple of Band-aids around his fingers. He sees me glancing at them and sighs. "That hamster's an asshole, but he seems to like Mira most of the time."

I laugh. "Well, your sister's dog pissed on me, so you're in good company."

He gives me a weird look as Michael comes by with a tray. He gave us heavy pours on the scotch, which is both good policy on his part—a drunk man won't hold onto his wallet too carefully—and also a relief.

I just messed up.

Michael serves us the scotch, beaming, and says, "I'll be right out with the first board. I have a feeling you're going to like one of these."

"Probably not me," Danny mutters, "but I'm not the one who needs to like it."

"Of course, of course," Michael says, backing away and bowing as if Danny's a king or mafia don who might shoot him in the back.

"When were you at Ruthie's?" Danny asks. "I just found out about the dog over the weekend."

I take a sip of the scotch, find it good, and think as fast as my neurons will fire. I can't tell him the full truth, but I won't flat-out lie.

"Ruthie and I are helping each other with something. She doesn't want to talk about it yet, so I can't say much more. But we'll tell you everything this weekend."

He looks as surprised as if I'd actually admitted his sister and I are getting married tomorrow. "You're working on something together? Willingly? Does this have to do with Vanny?"

"Not directly," I admit. "But I do want to help her with that."

It's not a lie, and I *will* help her if she'll let me. I hate that she's given so little thought to her bottom line.

A lesser man would push me for details, but Danny slowly nods. "Okay, man. I'm glad you two are getting along."

More laughter bursts from me. "I wouldn't go that far, but I think this will be mutually beneficial from a business standpoint."

"So I'm guessing her dog pissed on one of your suits?" he asks with a slight smile.

"Yes, my second best."

I'd saved my best for the wedding, figuring it would be good luck to hold out, which is as far as I'm willing to venture down the path of superstition.

"Tough break." He shakes his head slightly. "You know she's a bit allergic to dogs, right?"

I can't help but smile at that. "She admitted to it after the fifth time she sneezed. Leave it to Ruthie to adopt a dog she's allergic to."

He watches me for a moment, and I can feel the hairs rise on the back of my neck. "She's got a big heart," he finally says. "It gets her into trouble."

I think he's talking about Rand, or maybe Jarrod Travis, but there's no knowing with Danny. He's more perceptive than he seems by half.

When I found out Ruthie was seeing Rand, I warned Danny about him. He lived on my street, growing up, although he was a few years younger. His parents were wealthy, and he was a little shit—the kind of kid who burned the wings off flies, chased toddlers, and got in trouble and blamed it on the poor kid. He looked out for one person, and one person only: Rand Callaghan. He was exactly the sort of asshole Ruthie always accuses me of being.

Danny told me he'd talk to her, but it didn't help. So I'd taken it upon myself to warn Ruthie too—once before she got engaged to Rand, and then again at her rehearsal dinner. She told me to fuck off, not that I was surprised.

I could tell from the look in her eyes that he had her on the hook, just like Michael knows he caught a live one with Danny. But I'd owed it to Danny to keep trying.

I nod slowly. I'm trying to pluck something to say out of the ether when Michael comes running back with a board the size of an elephant's ass.

"Looks like a murder board," Danny mumbles under his breath. Michael has connected different groups of rings with little pieces of red string, probably because I made such a point of 'her' liking red. I get the concept; if she likes this ring, then she might also like these five other ones.

Danny takes a gulp of scotch that drains half his glass, then gives Michael his attention.

"Here we are, here we are," Michael says, setting the board down.

"Are any of these blood diamonds?" Danny asks, and Michael stiffens.

"We use only the most ethical sources." He glances around

before saying in an undertone, "But something tells me these might not be to your liking." He points to three of the sparklers.

So Michael's honest, or he thinks it benefits him to come off as such. Either way, the precaution is appreciated. So was his help with the music. It's become slightly less miserable to be in here.

One of the rings catches my eye. It's a red stone, square cut, with small diamonds to either side. Elegant but kind of flashy. Saucy, like someone I know. I point to it. "Is that a ruby?"

Michael nods.

"It's not bad," Danny says, studying it. "But Mira's iffy on red things unless it's Christmas." He sighs. "And then *everything* has to be red. But I don't think she'd want a red ring."

Michael's a good salesman. Unless he has the memory of a goldfish, he remembers me telling him red is her favorite color. It happened less than twenty minutes ago. The only reaction I notice in him is a slight glance in my direction, but it lasts for maybe a quarter of a second. Danny doesn't seem to notice.

My buddy turns to me. "What do you think? They all look the same to me."

The only sign this horrifies Michael is the slightest pinching of his lips. While I didn't think much of his salesmanship at first glance, I'm not ashamed to admit I was wrong—this man would make a killing at poker.

I help Danny narrow it down to half a dozen choices, with some input from Michael. It's noticed and appreciated that he's not pushing the most expensive rings.

Once we have the selection narrowed down, Danny texts a photo of the remaining contenders to Ruthie. His phone immediately rings, which makes me smile. She'll be excited, I'm guessing. Knowing her, she'll feely guilty, too, and wonder if we're screwing up by not leveling with Danny.

By now, I've convinced myself waiting is better. I don't want to mess up his proposal. While this thing with Ruthie and me is a business arrangement that has a sell-by, Danny intends for his marriage to last forever.

"I'd better take this outside," my buddy says, lifting the phone. And I'd bet all the money in my bank account that he's grateful for a few minutes of peace—even if it's just relative peace since the jewelry shop is off Patton Ave, which is always loud and busy, even in late January when the tourists haven't started filtering back in like a cloud of locusts.

Michael watches him walk out of the shop, then turns to me with a shrewd look. "You're not trying to propose to his woman first, are you? Because, if so, I'd feel honor-bound to tell him. That guy's in love. I've seen it a thousand times. You..." He gives a *jury's out* shrug.

I laugh. "You've seen something like that happen, huh?"

He gives me a real smile. "I've seen everything happen." He shrugs again. "You're looking for a ring, too, but you don't want your friend to know. You can't blame a guy for wondering."

I don't. If anything, I'm impressed.

I point to the ruby. "That one. And I'll need a couple of simple wedding bands. Nothing to take away from the ring itself. I'll buy them after my friend leaves."

"The ruby's the most expensive one," he says, giving me a weighing look as he quotes the price.

I whistle, because it *is* expensive, but I think of Ruthie, of the way her face will light up when she opens the box. It's illogical to care, since she'll only wear it a few times, but maybe she can have it resized for a different finger after this is over. It can be a memento of our short-lived marriage.

Besides, I'd die before I'd admit this to anyone, but it speaks to me of Ruthie's fire. Her sparkle. I needs to be hers.

"That's fine."

He nods and doesn't ask any follow-up questions. Discreet, I appreciate that too.

"Say, do you like your job?" I ask, tipping my head. I see him prepping a canned answer, one that will probably be delivered convincingly. "The real answer, not the bullshit they feed you here."

He laughs. "I like taking care of people, but my boyfriend of five years broke up with me a month ago, and I hawk blood diamonds. What do you think?"

"Ever consider working in the legal field?"

twelve

RUTHIE

"I LOOK STUPID," I mutter to Eden, gesturing to the other people scurrying up the stairs to the courthouse. They're all wearing pantsuits and coats, and I have on a long, cream-colored dress elevated from looking plain by gold embroidery and little beads and sequins at the bust and feet. It's covered by my crappy puffer coat—a pretty blue-gray once, called dove, it's now a brownish-gray no washing machine can cure. The combination makes me feel an idiot, but I wasn't about to take Eden up on her offer to buy me a coat too. The dress already costs more than what I'd make in multiple shifts at the diner, but when I objected to the extravagance, she told me to hush up.

I shouldn't have let her take care of me like that. I shouldn't have soaked it in like hot cement. But it felt so good to be loved up, and I have to wonder if it was her way of giving me a send-off. I can tell she's working up to telling me they're closing the diner. I'm not ready to hear it, though, and she seems to understand that.

Eden gives me a withering look. "I just spent a good half hour helping you get ready, and you're telling me you look stupid?"

"Oh, you've done it now," Charlie says with a grin. He's

wearing one of his beanies. He must have a hundred because he's always wearing one, and it always seems to be a different color.

"I didn't mean it like that," I say, feeling guilty and ungrateful. "The dress is beautiful. It's just...none of this is real. I don't want to act like it's something it's not."

"There's nothing wrong with looking fabulous," Eden says, putting a hand on her hip. "Who cares what anyone else thinks?"

I do, I suppose. I'm wearing a beautiful dress with an ugly coat over it, and Shane will probably take one look at me and laugh. My outfit—half beautiful, half ragged—makes me feel like I can't do anything right. I certainly don't know how to get married the right way.

"You look beautiful, Ruthie," Charlie says, his ears going pink.

"Thank you," I say, feeling a swell of fondness for both of them. "I'm so grateful to both of you." I glance back and forth between them, trying to take in a little more of their goodness.

Charlie and Eden have been married for at least thirty years but still look at each other like it's their wedding day. In all honesty, I think I've only ever heard Charlie say a thousand words, but they must be the right words, because Eden adores him.

The last time I got married, it only lasted for four months, and although Shane and I haven't established a timeline yet, I'm guessing I'm on my second four-month marriage. This one isn't supposed to last, but it's still a statistic that makes my stomach churn.

It won't be like that for Danny and Mira. I know my brother and his girlfriend are the real deal. I couldn't be happier for them, although it boggles my mind that Danny decided to go ring-shopping the day before my sham of a wedding. And Shane, who went with him, didn't say a word to me.

After I got off the phone with Danny yesterday, I texted Shane:

You're terrible fiancé. You were going to get an F, but now you get an F-.

He sent me back the middle finger emoji, then asked if I'd rounded up two witnesses. Honestly.

I told him yes but didn't clarify that I'd be bringing Charlie and Eden and not Josie and Tank. I figured he deserved it for being less than generous with information.

"You can still change your mind, doll," Eden tells me, and I realize we've been standing at the bottom of the stairs for at least a solid minute.

That means we're probably going to be a minute or two late, and I already know Shane is one of those *you're early or you're late* people.

Danny is too, and he raised me to be the same way, but I've never quite managed to pull it off. My brain is always throwing out ideas like it's a shirt cannon at a sports game—usually at exactly the wrong time, or it bequeaths a small shirt to someone who needs a large. Time has a habit of slipping away, so much so that I have an alarm on my phone to remind myself of when I have to leave to pick up Izzy.

Izzy.

I have to remember that I'm doing this mostly for my daughter, so she can have her surgery.

"No," I say, firming my lips. "I'm ready."

When we make it inside, the grey-haired woman sitting behind the desk in the lobby takes one look at me, grins, and says, "Your man's already upstairs, sweetheart." She fans herself. "Got yourself a *fine* man."

"He's okay," I say woodenly as I pull off my coat. I wish I had somewhere to stow it, but I have to carry it in my arms. My comment earns me a frown, then I ask for directions to the courtroom where it's going to happen. I can't bring myself to think of it as the courtroom where I'm going to get married.

I get on the elevator with Eden and Charlie, and I'd be lying if I didn't admit a piece of me wants it to stop so I can rethink all of this. My brother and Mira got stuck in an elevator—twice, actually—and it worked out for them.

But it arrives the way it's supposed to. I sigh, and Eden watches me closely as we get off. She clucks her tongue. "You're clutching that dirty-ass coat like it's a stuffed animal. Give it to me."

I don't object, but as I hand it over, I say, "This is good. Everything's going to be great."

This time, Charlie gives Eden a significant look before shifting his gaze to me. "Ruthie, you don't need to do this because we're closing the diner, we—"

Eden gives him a shove. "I hadn't gotten around to telling her yet, you dolt."

"Then what in tarnation did you talk about for two hours yesterday afternoon?" he asks, giving his hat a little aggravated shove as if it's offended him.

Apparently, even always-happy couples bicker, but my attention is fixed on the message, not the way it was delivered. "You're really closing Loving?"

I'd known it would happen soon—empty seats don't pay the rent or an employee's salary—but it still feels like my safety blanket is being ripped from me again.

Purple and white, with unicorns and shiny silver stars.

Someone spilled beer on the floor at one of my parents' late-night parties, and all of the towels were dirty, so my mother stumbled into my room and took the blanket. Danny was staying over at Shane's house that night, so no one was there to stop her. He washed it when he came home, but afterward I always imagined it smelled like beer. So I didn't mind so much when it disappeared altogether.

"Yes, honey," Eden says, taking my hand and squeezing it. "But you don't need the diner."

It's not the diner I need, but it's not Eden's fault that I've started thinking of her as something she's not. It's these dark spots inside of me, these caverns I've tried fill with different things. With Vanny. With Eden and Tank. With men who don't love me.

Suddenly my eyes are filling with tears, so I turn from her and start walking. "You're right," I say, not looking at her. "It's fine. Obviously, it's fine. Are you going to retire somewhere warm?"

"*Ruthie*," she says, but I speed up my steps.

"You've always liked warmer weather. I understand—"

I turn the corner, and bump into someone—

Someone tall and broad and firm and warm.

Someone who smells so familiar and safe that I'm wrapping my arms around him before I realize what I'm doing. Before I realize it's *him*—the man I'm here to marry.

"Ruthie?" Shane says, as if he's wondering whether a stranger just wrapped her arms around him. The rumble of his voice vibrates through me, deep and soothing, even though it shouldn't be. I can feel his heart beating steadily, though rapidly, beneath my ear. Whatever other flaws he has, there's not one single thing wrong with the way he looks. Or smells. Or *feels*. Despite myself, I already feel a little better—stronger—as if I sucked in some of his confidence and made it my own.

I pull back and stare at him, and for a second I'm seeing him as a stranger would—the firm jaw covered in stubble, the dark hair, cut with precision, the pretty hazel eyes. He's wearing a suit that's even sharper than the one my dog pissed on—gray with pinstripes and perfectly cut for his body. His tie is light green, and it does an even better job of bringing out the flecks of green in his eyes, clustered around the pupils.

There's no denying he's a beautiful man, or that I feel a little turned on by the thought that he will, in name, be mine. For however long this lasts, no other woman will be able to touch him.

He stares at me for a moment, his eyes wide. His mouth opens as if he wants to say something but closes again without issuing a single word. Surprise and something else, something warmer, plays on his face. His gaze flicks back to Eden and Charlie, and he frowns.

There's the Shane I know.

"Josie just showed," he says. "I thought—"

"*Josie's in there?*" I ask in horrified fascination. "But I didn't invite her."

His eyes narrow. "Maybe you told her and forgot?"

"No, I didn't forget. I'm not eighty, Vain." I give his chest a small shove, pretending it's not only because I want to check if it's still solid.

It is, and I drop my hands like they're suddenly stone.

Shane's gaze lands on Charlie, and he frowns. "Are you... Tank?"

Honestly. He knows Tank's been my best friend since I was a little kid. Does he really think I was palling around with an adult?

"Charlie and Eden run the diner," I say, waving a hand from them to Shane and back. "Shane's marrying me so he can pretend—"

He tugs my arm. "Lovely to meet you," he tells them with one of his wide, shit-eating grins.

Then he pulls me back around the corner I just rounded.

"Change your mind?" I ask, raising my eyebrows in defiance. My heart's beating fast now, and my skin's so sensitive I'd feel it if a fly landed on the ceiling.

I tell myself I'm not turned on.

He backs me into the corner, away from prying ears and eyes. I'm pressed up against the wall, his arm bracketing me on one side, and he's leaning in close so he can speak for my ears alone. There's no denying it anymore. I'm *definitely* turned on.

"If you go around telling everyone it's fake, then what's the fucking point?" he asks, his eyes hooded. He's obviously pissed about Eden and Charlie—maybe about Josie, too, although her presence isn't my doing. He's crowding me, and even in that suit, he looks like a prowling animal. Maybe especially in that suit.

"They're not going to tell anyone," I say, rolling my eyes and forcing myself to act unaffected. "They go to bed at eight-thirty every night." I shrug and add, to myself more than him, "That's probably why they need to close the diner."

"You're out of a job?" he asks.

"And into a new one." I reach out and tap his nose. He captures my hand in his, the contact buzzing through me. With his other hand, he reaches into his pocket and pulls out a little velvet box.

"Do you want me to get down on one knee, Ruthie?" he asks, his voice throaty and amused, and I'm embarrassed by how much I feel it between my legs. I'm thrumming there. As if a couple of strokes of his fingers is all it would take to...

I clear my throat and consider whether to yank my hand back, then don't. "You got the fake rings yesterday? Did you do it while Danny was in the bathroom? How positively diabolical of you."

He flips the box open, and a gasp escapes me. I feel tears in my eyes again, and an overpowering blend of emotions—confusion and joy and deep, deep sadness. Because it's a good fake. It's a beautiful ring, actually, exactly the kind of ring I would have chosen for myself. But he didn't buy it because he cares about me. He only did it because he wants to look good in front of his boss.

"It's beautiful," I admit, staring up into his eyes. Emotion flickers in his gaze as he studies me, and it sends a shiver down my spine. Neither of us saying anything else for a long moment—we just stare at each other, our eyes locked, as if I'd challenged him to a stare-off.

To my shock, he's the one who looks away first. "Good," he says, clearing his throat. "I wasn't sure about the size, but Mira doesn't seem to have particularly big hands either, so I went with the same size Danny got. You know he probably measured her finger in her sleep."

A laugh escapes me, and it's just on the edge of a sob. "You really are diabolical."

He doesn't comment, just releases my hand so he can slide the ring out of its casing and put it on my finger—a finger that's been bare for five and a half years. I can feel the whisper of movement as he slides it on, the slight tingle of his flesh moving against mine, his fingers marking me with this ring—*his* ring. A ring that's beautiful but fake, just like us.

It's the strangest moment of my life, I think.

The box goes back into his pocket, and a ragged sound escapes me.

He seeks out my gaze, and there's something like concern in his eyes—concern for me, though, or concern for his plan? If he noticed the tears, he might be worried I'm on the verge of backing out.

"How'd Josie know?" I ask, not because it's my foremost worry or thought, but because it's strange. I wouldn't willingly admit it, but I'm a little wary of Josie the Great. I might even be afraid of her.

"We're about to find out," he says gruffly. "But let's wait to talk to her until after the ceremony. I don't like that we've kept the justice of the peace waiting."

"Because you might have to deal with them some other time, in a professional capacity, and they'll think badly of you?"

He gives his head a wry shake. "You think I have a secondary motive for everything, don't you?"

Yes. Maybe it's easier that way, because a lot of the time he *does* have a secondary motive. I've learned how dangerous it is to trust the wrong people.

"You definitely have a secondary motive for *this*," I say, gesturing between us. It's then I realize we're still standing too close, less than a foot between me and that firm, warm chest. I inch back.

"No, I'd say that's my primary motive," he says with a smirk, then clears his throat and takes my hand, leading me away from the wall. "But I have no ulterior motive in saying you look beautiful this morning, Ruthie."

"Well, I figured you'd want photos for your office to really drive the farce home," I say, trying to feel unaffected by his comment. I don't want to desire his approval, but I do. In some ways, I'm still that little girl who used to follow him around—who mooned after a teenage Shane so much that I counted his zits like they were stars in the sky. But I would rather die than let him know that.

"Good thinking," he says. He glances at me as we round the corner. "Why didn't you bring the G.I. Joe guy?"

A snort escapes me. "Tank?

"Do you know several adult men named after G.I. Joes?"

There's no sign of Charlie and Eden, so presumably they continued on to the courtroom to give us some privacy.

"I haven't gotten around to telling him yet," I mutter.

"You think Romeo's going to get upset?"

I roll my eyes. "I told you he's just a friend."

He's quiet for a step, then he says, "You ask all your friends over for slumber parties?"

I almost laugh, because I'd hoped he'd forgotten that, but of course he didn't. Shane is like Mrs. Longhorn—he picks up on damn near everything I'd prefer for him not to notice.

Since it's none of his business what happened that night, I deflect. "You don't get to control my life or my friendships, Vain." There's more venom behind it than I meant to add—venom more rightly directed toward Rand, who hurt my friendship with Tank. "This is a business deal."

Shane gives me another sidelong look, his gaze beating into me in a way that makes my blood boil. I can't tell whether it's because I'm angry or...something else. "Sure," he finally comments. "But no more sleepovers. We need to maintain appearances."

I could point out that we don't live together, which will undoubtedly look stranger than me spending time with an old friend, but it's not worth the wasted breath. "Fine," I say. "No dating and no sleepovers for *either* of us."

There's an edge of amusement to his smile as he nods. "Jealous?"

"As if. You're the one who has your panties in a twist about someone I've known since kindergarten."

"Speaking of people we've known since kindergarten. When are we going to 'get around' to telling Danny?" he asks. "It felt shitty, lying to him."

I don't like the way he said that—like he only kept quiet because of me, because *I'm* dishonest.

"I didn't stop you from telling him," I say. "If you'd asked me yesterday, I would have told you to go for it."

We bickered all our way through getting the marriage license, so I suppose it tracks that we're bickering on our way down the aisle.

His jaw tightens. "He's not going to get mad at *you*."

"Are you kidding me?" I ask as we turn another corner. I can see it at the end of the hall—the door of the room in which my legal status will change, once again, from single to married. For the brief months it lasts. A pulse of sadness moves through me, settling around my heart. I try to shake it off, but it's as persistent as Flower when she gets ahold of one of my shoes. "He gets mad at me all the time."

"But if he gets mad at you, he'll forgive you. He may not forgive me."

I'm taken aback, because there appears to be real vulnerability behind the comment—as if he's afraid he might lose Danny. I've always figured he sees my brother as a chain, holding him back. But maybe I got it wrong, or just didn't get it entirely right. Relationships are complex. You can love someone and resent them. Want them in your life and feel desperate for them to leave.

You can be desperate for them to like you even if you don't like *them*.

"He'll forgive you," I say as we come to a stop in front of the door. My heart is pumping faster again, adrenaline threading through my veins, because we're doing something wrong. Even though I still feel conflicted about it, it's kind of...fun.

There, I said it. I feel like a naughty high school student skipping classes so I can smoke with the older kids behind the bleachers. And yes, I *was* that naughty high school kid.

"I'll make sure he does," I add.

He smiles at me, and if there's a hint of condescension in it—of, *sure you will*—then I'm not going to call him on it at this precise moment.

"Let's get married, kid," he says.

I roll my eyes at him as he reaches for the door, but I can't totally hold back a smile.

thirteen

SHANE

I COULD PROBABLY WRITE a briefing about the fifty ways in which this is an error in judgement.

There's the questionable wisdom of lying to my boss before I even start working for him, followed by lying to my best friend, and then there's this truth...

Ruthie, whom I've been training myself to ignore for years, looks absolutely fucking gorgeous. She's in a cream-colored dress with a simple cut that hugs her tits and hips and ass, with sequins and embellishments designed to bring a man's attention everywhere it would naturally be inclined to go. Her dark hair is down around her shoulders, wavy, as if from being compressed in my fist, and her lips are painted a bright red, her eyes as blue as the Carolina sky.

Rule Number One. Rule Number One. Rule Number One.

She's a dream in that dress, and I can lie to everyone else but not myself. When I backed her into that corner, it wasn't because I wanted to scold her or was looking for an opening to give her the ring she should have already had. It was because I wanted an excuse to touch her. Because a fucked-up part of me wanted to lay claim to her right there in the courthouse. That same part of me took pleasure in putting my ring on her finger even though I'd promised myself that I'd never do any such thing with any woman, ever.

I'm usually not the kind of man who changes his mind.

It's these last few months. They've been like a truck that keeps mowing me down and backing up so it can do it again. My impulses aren't as controlled as usual, because they're not in service to a greater cause. I'm a man in need of a purpose, and five minutes ago, my dick thought breaking Rule Number One might be the very thing.

I'm in trouble.

But I've backed myself into a corner as surely as I just backed Ruthie into one, and sometimes the only way out is through. Freeman needs me to have a wife, *this* wife, and if I lose Freeman, then I don't have a Plan B other than to wait for the shit to hit the fan with the Burkes' case. That could take months, though, and months of inactivity is unacceptable.

If you're not growing, you're withering, and I don't want to sit at home doing nothing, letting depression seep in and try to tug me down. So I open the door to the courtroom, Ruthie beside me, my awareness of her blistering through me, throbbing and real and undeniable.

The officiant, Dena Rothschild, is at the front, looking at her watch. Shit.

Ruthie wasn't wrong about me. I don't care to make bad impressions on people I might have to work with in the future. Or, at the very least, am liable to run into.

We walk past Ruthie's friends and also Josie, who's scrolling on her phone and ignoring us. She's wearing an off-white dress—a disrespectful choice for a wedding, or so I gathered from a former client whose mother-in-law wore off-white to *her* wedding. She said it should have been her first sign something fucked up was happening, but he'd proposed on Mother's Day because he figured it would be the ultimate present to his mother, so I'm guessing there were red flags snapping through the air right along.

A weird sensation rocks me as we walk past Josie. It's what my mother would call a goose walking over your grave.

While I don't believe some psychic woo-woo led this woman to the courtroom at the right place and time, something did. She has unspecified plans and information she shouldn't have. That's a dangerous combination. And, fine, I don't like that she told me I was going to get married months ago, and here I am, about to sign a license legally binding my life to someone else's. Sure, it's not a real wedding, and most psychics probably tell *everyone* they're going to get married. But it's undeniably strange, and I dislike things I can neither understand nor predict. It's in those zones of uncertainty that bad things happen.

Without warning, I get a flash of the worst moment of my life. I can smell the overturned sauce pot, see my father's look of surprise as he slumped over. My mother's screams ring in my ears.

My teeth are pressed together as we approach the front of the court room. Dena gives me a suspicious look.

I nod and force a smile. "Let's get going."

I hear Ruthie snort beside me. "This is everything I've ever dreamed of."

"I knew your imagination was lacking," I snipe back. Shit, I shouldn't have said that.

Dena clears her throat. Her eyes on Ruthie, she asks, "Are you *sure* you're ready to move forward?"

I can imagine what this must look like to her, and it's not good. I nod. "We're ready."

"Yes," Ruthie says, her mouth curling into a red-lipped smile that promises I'm going to suffer. "I can't wait to strip that suit off him. You know, he insisted on saving himself for marriage. Nothing I could say or do would persuade him."

I give her a flat look. She wants to embarrass me? Fine, two can play that game. I'm tempted to say something equally outrageous, like *Most people still consider anal sex to be sex,* but I'll have to see Dena again, so I don't want to go too far down that road. "We wrote our own vows," I offer instead.

"Uh, okay," Dena says, her gaze darting from us to Josie the Great in her veil, to the elderly couple Ruthie has befriended despite her terrible pay at the diner. "Will anyone else be joining us? Your parents, perhaps, Mr. Royce?"

I have another flash of that dinner, of my father—talking one second, telling one of his stories, and the next...

Wincing, I grind out, "No."

Ruthie doesn't correct the supposition that Eden and Charlie are her parents, not that I blame her. Her parents are drunks, her father is who-knows-where, and I've helped her mother out of legal trouble a couple of times as a favor to Danny.

Ruthie's giving me a sharp look, as if to say, *you may think you got me good, but I'll prove how wrong you are.* I hope she does. This feels like an extension of our game, and I need that now. I didn't realize this experience would be so...unsettling.

In theory, our plan had seemed simple. Make the agreement, get the legal documentation, and boom—suddenly, I'm not a liar, or not much of one. Every marriage is a lie, if you ask me. No one knows what they're going to want in two years, five, ten. To bind your life to someone else's is a hollow promise. A promise made for the person you'll become, not the one you are. I'm not the same person I was ten years ago. I certainly am not the same person I was twenty years ago—zit-faced and obsessed with Dungeons & Dragons. People grow, and they outgrow each other.

A voice in my head suggests that I still haven't outgrown the friends I had at thirteen. I'd thought I would, but I can't seem to shake them. I don't *want* to shake them. Because it's only with them that I feel...

Dena clears her throat, and I realize she's been saying some shit.

"Sorry," I say, "I was lost in my lady's eyes. Who could blame me, right?"

Ruthie snorts. Dena looks like she's seriously rethinking her career choices, then she asks, "Are you ready to get started?"

"I am," I say, taking Ruthie's hand. The ruby ring is sharp, but her hands are warm and soft. A strange sensation skates across my skin—almost like Ruthie's got an electric charge and it's passing from her to me.

"Go ahead and say your vows," Dena says, sounding slightly interested, like she has no idea what's coming but suspects it'll be entertaining.

I squeeze Ruthie's hand, trying to squelch the electricity down so small it's like an ant. "Ruthie, who would have thought I'd marry the little brat who used to follow me around pretending she was a dog? For a while there, I thought I was going to have to report you for stalking, but you made me come around eventually, huh? I used to think you were the last woman I'd ever marry, but you've made me realize personality isn't everything. I guess there's something to be said for persistence."

There, let her run with that. I'm actually exited to hear what she comes back with...

Her eyes spark, and I feel it all over. My dick particularly feels it. I need to shrink my desire for her, but unlike most of the things I try to battle into submission, it's not listening. Especially not when she's looking at me like that.

She clears her throat, licks her lips, and if this is her revenge, I'm fucking toast. I don't think she knows how she affects me, and if I have my way, she never will.

"Oh, Shane. You do have an excellent memory. Do you remember the time you and my brother got drunk on my parent's stash, and you peed in the coat closet? I put up that sign saying 'Not a Bathroom' to help you avoid making that little mistake again. That's what a married couple should do—find little ways to help each other. I pledge to keep you from pissing in coat closets for the rest of this marriage."

"You're thoughtful like that," I murmur, smiling at her. She has the spirit of a contender—and so do I. I could go ten rounds with Ruthie and never get tired of it.

Of her, an intrusive voice suggests, but that's clearly bullshit.

"Well, this is certainly unconventional," Dena mutters under her breath. "You can exchange the rings if you still care to do so."

So I slide the other ring around Ruthie's finger and then give her the one I bought for myself.

She lowers it onto my finger, and a shiver makes its way down my spine, because this is a moment I told myself would never happen, and even if it's unfolding in an unconventional way—here it is, happening, nonetheless.

"And do you, Ruthie Traeger take this man to be your lawful husband?"

There's a moment's pause, and for a second, I think she's going to say no. But she sighs and says, "Yeah, fine. I do."

Dena looks to the ceiling, as if hoping it'll tell her how she came to be here, marrying two people who dislike each other the majority of the time. Then she says, "And do you, Shane Royce take this woman to be your lawful wife?"

"I do," I say, Ruthie's hand still in mine.

"Then you may kiss the bride."

Ruthie's breath hitches like she'd forgotten about this part. Truthfully, I've been thinking about what her smart mouth would feel like against mine, and this is my opportunity to kiss her without it meaning anything. Because we'd agreed to the wedding, and this is part of it.

Ruthie gives me the stink-eye, but when I give her a slight nod, she presses her hand, still encased in mine, against my chest and gets up on her toes. I lower to her, and suddenly it's like all the oxygen has been sucked out of my lungs.

Despite what I said, I'm very aware that this woman is no longer the little girl who followed me around barking and snapping like an ill-tempered Jack Russell—even if she's still the kind of person who'd find that funny. And now her lips are brushing against mine, her hand hot against my chest.

Fuck, in that moment, I want her to open to me. I want her to offer herself up like a flower lifting to the sun. She'd say that analogy's a sign of my vanity, but I don't see myself as the sun—more like the bee that would buzz in and take what's not mine.

She opens her lips slightly, and I suck in her bottom lip and let my tongue roam over it. My other hand lifts into her hair, feeling its silkiness against my skin. I want to gather it up in my fist, but I have some self-control left, because I stop there.

She makes a surprised sound, the kind you might make when you open a present that surprises you by not being a profound disappointment, and I consume it like the greedy bastard I am. The kiss deepens, and it ignites something feral in me. I want more, and I aim to take it. So does she, judging by the way her mouth moves against mine, seeking more.

Then a wolf whistle reminds me of where I am—the courthouse, in front of a woman I'll have to encounter again. I don't have to look to guess the wolf whistler was none other than Josie the Great.

When I pull away, Ruthie is watching me with sharp eyes. As I return her gaze, she lifts her hand and wipes her mouth. It shouldn't wound me—she's posturing, and I know it—but it does nonetheless.

Dena seems bemused. "Have fun," she says, then gestures Eden and Charlie forward to sign the papers as our witnesses. Because this is a legal arrangement, after all. Even if it's messing with my head.

"Excuse me for a moment," I say to Ruthie and the others, because I see Josie the Great standing at the exit as if she's a one-woman roadblock.

"Actually, we need to clear this courtroom," Dena says, glancing up from the papers after Charlie hesitates, messes with his hat, and then signs his name with a sigh. "Why don't you all go celebrate somewhere?"

Otherwise known as *get the hell out*.

"I know just the place," Eden says pointedly. She gives me an appraising look of someone who doesn't think much of what she's seeing. Fantastic, another woman who'd like to wear my balls as earrings. Usually, I'm known for my ability to charm women, but I have a feeling I won't be charming anyone today.

"Will there be cake?" Josie pipes up for the first time since I entered this room.

RUTHIE

I JUST GOT MARRIED.

I just got fucking married.

Shane Royce is my husband, and he kissed me.

And now, I'm sitting in the diner with Shane, Eden, and Josie, as if it's any other day. The diner is empty, of course, but that's not so different from usual. Charlie's not with us because he insisted on heading into the back to get some food for us—although I suspect he's also ready for some alone time after the trip to the courthouse.

I am too, truthfully.

That kiss...

My lips are still tingling from it, even though I made a show of wiping it off to signal to Shane that he couldn't rattle me if he tried.

To pretend that I won't be thinking of it late at night, when I'm alone and it's harder to remember why that's the way it's supposed to be.

Dammit. Dammit. *Dammit.*

I take a big sip of sweet tea, watching across the table while Shane pushes the straw around in his drink with an expression bordering on disgust. This isn't the sort of place he'd go. He may have grown up in Asheville, same as me, but he's part of the gentrification problem. He probably has power lunches at the kind of restaurants that serve multiple tiny courses that are pushed around on their plates and ignored. I scowl at him. So does Eden.

Shane mixes thing up and scowls at Josie. "You still haven't explained why you were there."

She cocks her head, studying him. "You told me you'd never get married. You don't like being wrong, do you?"

Laughter escapes me. Shane shifts his stink-eye to me, and I laugh harder. "No, he can't handle it."

"I'm never wrong," he blusters, which makes me laugh harder. His jaw flexes. "I didn't mean it like that. But I'm not wrong about this. You weren't there because you sensed we'd be getting married at the courthouse on that day and time. Who told you?"

Josie gives him a look that's as transparent as plaster, then says, "No one told me. I was at the courthouse for another matter, and I saw you come in. But the universe intended for it to happen. I can see that very clearly."

"So you *didn't* intentionally wear white to another woman's wedding?" Eden asks, as if this was a stumbling block for her. Maybe I would have minded if it had been a real wedding, but truthfully, I'd barely noticed. My attention had been on Shane.

"Why would that be a problem?" Josie asks. "You're not one of those women who tells other women what to wear, are you?"

Eden gives her an incredulous look, but Josie continues, "As I was saying, the universe arranged all of this to help me."

Shane's focus swivels to me, and I feel a twitch in my fingers, the errant need to reach out and touch his tie. "And you say I'm self-involved," he says.

"You *are* self-involved," I retort, then point at Josie. "So is she. More than one person can be self-involved."

"I'm going to go see about that cake," Eden adds, apparently tiring of our conversational hoops.

"Chocolate cake wreaks havoc on my chakras," Josie calls after her.

I wonder if she even knows what a chakra is. Maybe she's just one of those rare, unfortunate souls who doesn't like chocolate.

"*Why* did the universe arrange all of this to protect you?" I ask. Shane's giving me one of his classic *Oh Ruthie* looks, like he thinks I'm unwise to engage her.

Josie takes a swallow of sweet tea, grimaces, then pushes it away. "I've fallen into a little legal...misunderstanding. A small-minded man thinks it's my fault his wife decided to leave him for his best friend. It's not his limp dick or refusal to go down on her that's to blame, no, of course not. It was all me. He's saying I 'alienated her affections.'" She makes a sound of disgust. "As if she had any affections left to alienate. He took care of that years before she started coming to me for weekly readings."

Weekly?

"What did you say to her?" Shane asks, surprising me with his interest.

"Only the truth. That his best friend has been in love with her since before the wedding, and *he* has no objection to making a woman come. She made the obvious choice—a choice she would have made at some point whether or not she'd come to speak to me. I'm only a cipher. My job is to pass on what I see. To pass on the *truth.*"

"And what happened?" I ask, drawn in despite myself.

"My boyfriend was going to represent me in court—he still has his license—but he got into a verbal altercation with the plaintiff at the farmer's market last week." She sniffs. "He didn't say anything that isn't true—the plaintiff *is* an asshole. He's a Scorpio. Very sly. And the moon was in Virgo. Never get with someone who has that combination. Anyway, my boyfriend was really upset with himself, so he said I should probably find another lawyer. I was at the courthouse this morning asking for a continuance because the trial was supposed to be this week. I was leaving when I saw you."

Shane laughs, looking genuinely amused by this, but if he can't see the train barreling down at him through the tunnel, then *I* can.

She wants Shane to represent her, which he finds funny, but the real gift the universe gave her is knowledge of our secret.

Josie hikes her glasses higher with her middle finger—a creative way of telling Shane to go fuck himself that I add to my mental list for when it's bright enough to warrant sunglasses.

"It's interesting to me that you just got married to your best friend's sister after you were so adamant about never getting married," she tells him. "Did *love* change your mind?"

And there it is. I guess she'd need to be a hustler to make it as a psychic, especially in this town, where you don't need to stumble very far before falling into a storefront promising a psychic reading.

Shane's expression hardens. "You're threatening to tell Danny? We're going to tell him, although we'd appreciate it if you let us do it first."

"I can see that he's not the only one who'd be interested. Yes, that's very clear to me."

The dawning horror on Shane's face tells me he's finally clued in, and I can't deny I'm kind of enjoying this. Shane needs someone to challenge him, and it's nice to sit back and watch for a change instead of having to be in the driver's seat.

"Do you bug people's cars?" he asks, his tone harsh. "Follow them? That's fucked up."

She huffs a laugh. "Says the man who used to have a private investigator on retainer." She shakes her head. "No, the universe didn't tell me that. Mira did. Your brother's girlfriend." She adds this with a glance at me, as if I might not remember the name of Danny's future fiancée. "But no, I don't usually follow people around. The universe led me to you. It was a favor, you could say, for being its spokesperson."

"Not a favor to me," he grumbles.

"You're going to represent me," she says confidently. "The trial is a month from now."

"You'll have to pay," he says, meeting her gaze. "I'm not doing it pro bono. I wouldn't have any way of explaining the situation to Freeman."

"Not a problem," she says, which surprises me. Maybe I should add 'psychic' to my list of possible business ideas, since I haven't had a single bite on Vanny since the cancellation last week. It's not surprising since the weather has been cold and cloudy and not at all inviting. I should have opened a hot chocolate truck, probably, but my imagination never stops to consider things like weather. It's a curse, having plenty of ideas but not being any good at executing them. Admittedly, I've been distracted and busy, not at my best.

Shane sighs, then fishes a business card out of his pocket and hands it to her. "I start on Monday."

"And you already have business cards?" I ask, immediately wishing I hadn't said it. It makes me sound like a child and I know it.

He gives me a smirk. "I hired an assistant too, yesterday at the jewelry shop."

No one could say Vain isn't efficient.

"A couple of months ago you didn't have business cards or a family. You work fast," Josie adds. "That's good. You'll get this settled quickly for me."

He watches her for a moment and then says, "Maybe not too quickly. Did it occur to you that this might be fantastic publicity for you if you play it right?"

I have to smile. He may not believe Josie's psychic, but he loves solving problems. He can't help himself.

It's then Eden walks out with a tray and three slices of cake. Chocolate cake with chocolate frosting, my favorite.

Josie points an accusatory finger at it. "I told you chocolate messes with my chakras."

"And that's why the third slice is for me, sweetie. From what I can tell, you weren't invited to the wedding anyway. But you go on and have yourself a nice afternoon."

I have to smile at that. Eden has a rare ability to cut people in two without being rude about it.

Josie lifts her chin. "The cake's probably better at the café across the street."

"I won't argue with you there," Eden says as she sets the tray on the table. "I'm guessing there's a reason we don't have any business. Either way, you've got places to be, and this isn't one of them."

Shane nods to Josie. "Call me this weekend to set up an appointment."

"I will." Something flashes in her eyes, and she smirks at us. "Enjoy the wedding night. I can tell it's going to be *quite* interesting."

"I hope your third eye didn't tell you that," I mutter. I don't like the way she's looking at me, like she can see the dirty thoughts that have been pinging around in my head.

Josie gives us a mysterious smile as she gets up and beats her retreat, Eden lowering into her chair after she vacates it. The bell rings as Josie steps through the door, and it nearly bangs her in the ass on her way out because she pauses to give us a significant glance over her shoulder. She's probably hoping to add an extra layer of mystery to whether or not Shane and I are going to fuck tonight.

We're not, obviously, and I feel another surge of relief—both because she's leaving and because I never took her up on her offer of a reading. If I'm this fazed by a prediction that's obviously wrong, how would I feel if she got something else right?

A hand lands on my arm, big and broad and hot, and a shiver runs the full length of my spine, from my neck down to my ass. I turn to look at Shane, my whole body rigid with shock, because I've always been reluctantly attracted to him, but that kiss made it ten times worse. No, not just the kiss. It was hearing him ask if I wanted to see him on his knees before me.

I *do*.

"She's full of shit, Ruthie," Shane says.

I flinch but don't move his arm. I can't bring myself to, not when I'd prefer for it to stroke up and down my body like I'm a cat he's petting.

"But you're going to represent her?" I ask, lifting my eyebrows.

"She didn't leave me much of a choice," he says, his voice thick with annoyance. "Besides, it's a frivolous lawsuit. The plaintiff deserves to lose and reimburse her for her legal fees."

"So he's the one who'll be paying your salary while his best friend fucks his wife. That's a hard pill to swallow." I don't know why I'm being antagonistic—everything Josie said suggests this guy's a real piece of work—but I feel off-kilter. Bickering with Shane is familiar, and familiar things are soothing when your world has been upended.

"Want to spoon-feed that pill to him, Ruthie?" he asks, his eyes on mine, his hand still splayed over my arm as if he wants to pin it. That thought's all it takes to make me squirm uncomfortably on the booth seat.

So, naturally, I claim one of the slices of cake from the tray and take a bite, slowly licking the frosting off the fork. The way Shane's pupils dilate makes satisfaction pump through my veins—just like when his eyes dipped to my bare shoulder the other night. This game we're playing may only exist in my head, but I enjoy dominating in it.

"You'll be paying my girl monthly?" Eden interjects.

Shane, still watching me instead of her, nods.

"She'll need half upfront," Eden continues. "That'll be enough to help her get Vanny off to a real start."

"It would help more if you didn't fire her," he says pointedly as he raps his fingers on the side of the table.

"She's not," I say, just as Eden gives him a look that would wither a succulent.

"Our landlord hiked the rent by thirty percent, hotshot," Eden says. "We were barely coming out even as it was."

"Let me take a look at your lease agreement." He says this with the officiousness of a man who's used to getting his way.

Eden snorts and shoves his cake toward him. "Not every problem needs to be solved, let alone by you. It was another sign telling us what we already knew. When it's your time, there's no point fighting it."

Josie would probably say it was a message from the universe, but Shane flinches at her words. The look in his eyes, almost as if he'd seen a ghost, is unexpected.

Then *I* flinch, because my phone is buzzing in my pocket. My first thought is that it's Danny—that Josie the Great lasted all of five minutes before calling him and confessing everything. But it's Izzy's school.

SHANE

EVERYTHING in me is on high alert as Ruthie listens to whoever's on the other line.

She started by asking if it was another ear infection, but the woman's response, while negative, obviously was not comforting. Something worse than an ear infection, then.

Her lips are pressed into a tight line, her color pale. Her cake fork drops onto the plate, forgotten. And if Ruthie is forgetting chocolate, something is definitely fucking wrong.

"I'd like to pick her up early," she says quickly. "I'll be right there."

There's a tightening in my gut, because nothing can be allowed to happen to Izzy. She's sweet and innocent and everything that's missing from my day-to-day life.

I push out of my seat, then watch, numb, as Ruthie pockets her phone and stands. Eden, who was sitting next to her in the outside seat, gets out, giving her room to leave.

"Ruthie, what happened?" I ask, trying not to sound worried. Failing, probably.

"My mother showed up at the school at recess," she says, her voice shaky. "She found Izzy. I don't know how she knew—"

"She looks just like you, that's how. Did she try to take her?" My voice is quavering with rage, so I take a deep breath and stuff it down. I need my poker face. I need to be the cool, collected lawyer who stares down witnesses—the one who doesn't appear to have any emotions other than the drive for justice.

I don't need to be the lawyer who secretly pukes in the bathroom before every closing statement because the pressure is too much.

Danny and Ruthie's mother is a pestilence. She and her ex-husband made my friend's childhood a living hell, first by convincing him something's wrong with him because he's different, and then by using him to support the whole family so they could spend all of their time drinking and pretending to be twenty. I've kept her out of jail for Danny—getting her free and clear of a couple of Drunk and Disorderlies—and in return she was to leave her children alone, just like they want. But apparently she's pickled herself enough to forget her promises.

I fully intend to help remind her of them.

She will not bother Ruthie or Izzy if I have anything to say about it, and it turns out I have plenty to say.

"I don't know," Ruthie finally responds. "I don't think so, but she's been trying to call me for weeks now. Maybe months. I haven't answered, so maybe..."

Her voice is small, her expression frightened. This isn't Ruthie the Ballbuster. She's vulnerable and scared, and something inside of me cracks. I feel the need to wrap her up, to keep her and Izzy safe, to *do* something.

"It seems like she's trying to get your attention in a different way. Well, she has it. Let's go."

"Together?" she asks, lifting her eyebrows.

"Yes, I want to hear what happened. I can help you."

She gives me a dubious look that hits like a fucking stab wound to the gut. "Why would you want to help me?"

"You're my wife," I say, my tone glib. She doesn't need to know about this protectiveness unfurling in my gut. She doesn't need to know that I've felt it before, almost always for her and Izzy. For Danny. They're the only real family I have left, because my mother checked out years ago, and my father is dead. We may not always see eye to eye, we may dislike each other half the time, but Ruthie is mine to protect. She always has been.

"Lucky me," she says sarcastically, but she doesn't ask me not to come. Thank fuck, because I would have had to do it anyway, and then I never would have heard the end of it.

"You go see to that little girl," Eden says, nodding.

Ruthie nods back. "Can you tell Charlie—"

"Don't you worry about Charlie, he's a grown-ass man."

We're out in the parking lot before I realize Ruthie left her coat behind—a dirty puffer that's seen better days.

I shrug off my peacoat and wrap it around her shoulders.

"I don't need it," she says. "And what will Izzy think?"

"What will she think when she sees us dressed up like this?" I ask, leading the way to my Range Rover. "She's going to know we were up to something."

"We're taking my car," she insists.

"Ruthie..."

"My car."

She's letting me come, so I can be generous. Even if her car looks like it would be lucky to make it a few miles before falling apart. I nod and follow her to the jalopy Subaru, holding back a smile as she says, "You need to wait for me to open the passenger side door. The handle doesn't work on the outside anymore."

"I thought you said your friend was a car guy," I comment after she gets in and opens the door for me.

She rolls her eyes as I get seated and close the door. My nose twitches. It smells like fast food and looks like it's gone its whole life without a single cleaning. I'd prefer to be in a dozen other places, but my wish to get the fuck out of this car is smaller than my need to be there for her.

"He is," she comments, not waiting for me to get my belt fastened before starting to back up. "But what you don't seem to understand is that I can take care of myself."

"The door begs to differ," I say.

She ignores me. "Izzy won't think anything of you wearing a suit," she says, returning to my earlier remark, "but I guess this dress is a little...fancy. I'll tell her we were at a fancy dress party."

"At noon?"

"Adults do weird shit," she says, waving at the front windshield.

"Or so you've been told."

I'm gifted with another eyeroll. It comforts me more than it should, but it's good to see her feeling more like herself, her panic winnowing down to annoyance.

"Still, you'd better take off the ring," I tell her.

She gasps and says, "You're right. Shit. I'm bad at this lying thing."

"It's a good thing I'm good at it."

We've reached a traffic light, and she glances at me, her gaze beating into me. "Is it?"

I feel a bit disquieted, but I clear my throat. "Yes, and in this particular situation it's to your benefit too."

"I can't deny that," she says as she starts driving again. We're mostly quiet for the rest of the drive, but I notice that Ruthie takes the ring off at the stoplight, putting it in the drink opening next to the wheel—as if a ring that costs multiple thousands is no big deal and won't be stolen from a car that doesn't have doors that operate appropriately. I guess there are downsides to letting her think it's fake. But I make a note to move it or ask her to before we get out.

Ten minutes later, we're in the principal's office with Izzy, who looks no worse for the close encounter with her crappy relative. Her hair is in two ponytails and she's sucking on a lollipop someone must have given her. I figured they wouldn't give kids lollipops in school, but then again, I haven't darkened the door of a school since I was in one.

"Can I have a word?" the principal asks Ruthie.

"Can you—" Ruthie starts, turning toward me.

I nod before she has to finish. "Come on, Izz."

We leave the office and settle into two chairs in the hallway outside, situated across from a *Hang in there* poster with a monkey on a branch that probably has been there since my childhood. "Why's Mom wearing that dress, Uncle Shane?" Izzy asks around the lollipop.

"You'll have to ask your mom," I deflect.

"But she has your coat on. Why does she have your coat on?"

"It went better with the dress than her old puffer."

She makes a face. "That coat has seen better days, and it *is* a dazzling dress. She looks like a princess. You think she'll give it to me when I'm old enough for it to fit?"

"I think she would." I tap my hand against the chair arm. "Someone approached you in the playground today?"

I'm not going to confirm that woman was her grandmother. It's not my place. But I always prefer to have as much information as possible—and it seems especially important in this situation.

"Yeah," she says contemplatively, leaning back. "I think it was my grandmother. She said so, and Mom's shown me pictures. I told her that if she really is my grandmother I don't like her very much. She was really mean to Uncle Danny and to Mom."

I sigh and lean back in my chair too. "I'm sorry that happened, Izz. Were you scared?"

She gives me a look meant to level. "No, don't be silly. She's a little old woman. I'll bet she couldn't even arm wrestle me."

Maybe not, but that's not to say she couldn't whisk her into a little white van—or find someone else who could.

"She have anything else to say?"

"She said she had some friends she wants to introduce me to, but I'm not dumb. Mom tells me never to go off with strangers, and even if she is my grandmother, she's still a stranger."

Well, damn. I don't like that one bit, but I don't let it show on my face. Instead, I distract her by telling her that I'm going to be representing a psychic at court—and, in turn, she fills me in on the latest Polly Pocket drama.

A few minutes later, Ruthie emerges, and the sight of her in that dress, again, nearly makes me fall out of my chair. I like that my coat is still layered over it, because it means her scent will attach to it—and mine will attach to her.

She seems to feel better, more confident, and she says, "Let's go get ice cream."

It's about thirty degrees outside and it's lunchtime, but I shut my mouth and nod. Because if they want ice cream, we're going to get some fucking ice cream. I'm also going to stick around until I can talk to Ruthie in private, because I need answers before I can figure out how to handle this situation.

sixteen

RUTHIE

THE NERVE OF THAT WOMAN...

My mother didn't show the slightest interest in me when I was a child, and now she thinks she can lay some sort of claim on my daughter.

I was practically shuddering with rage by the time I left the principal's office. She assured me that the conversation between Izzy and my mother only lasted a minute, maybe two, before they ushered Izzy inside and asked my mother to leave school grounds. But a minute or two is a minute or two too much. It makes my skin crawl to think about Izzy being alone with her.

Maybe Shane knows all of that, because I keep expecting him to leave, and he keeps not leaving.

True: we did take my piece of shit car, but he's an industrious man, and I have a feeling he has a passing acquaintance with Uber Black. Plus four friends who'd probably drop whatever they're doing to help him out.

We get ice cream, a decision I can tell he judges me for—but when I order him a banana hammock to mess with him, *he eats it.*

We go back to the apartment and find the hell that Flower has wrought. Apparently, she's the kind of soul who can't be contained by a crate, whether it be zip-up or steel, and I can't find it in myself to try harder to keep her imprisoned. I keep thinking about that year she spent in the shelter with nothing but a dirty hedgehog toy for company. And, sure, logically I know Josie and the owner of Dog is Love might have concocted all of that to make a "hard sell," but it still tugs at my heart.

What doesn't tug at my heart?

Coming home to step in a pile of shit, thoughtfully placed just inside the door, while Flower wags her tail like a maniac. There are also two torn-up books, a broken vase, and three shredded wires.

Shane offers to clean up the mess, his face pinched in a way that normally would have made me laugh. But I don't. He's giving me the chance to have a sit-down conversation with Izzy about my mother, and I'll have to take it. That's no laughing matter. I didn't mention my mother in the ice cream shop because I wasn't mentally ready to talk about her.

Truthfully, I'm still not.

"You can just leave," I tell him, pulling off the soiled shoe with a grimace. "Izz and I will clean it up."

Mrs. Longhorn opens the door across the way, her face instantly pinching when she sees the mess just inside my door. She opens her mouth to say something, but Shane shuts my door before the words can get out, essentially slamming it on her.

Surprised laughter gushes from me.

"Don't get used to me cleaning," Shane says, taking his suit jacket off. My laughter dries up, because I can see his muscles flexing under his shirt, and it's a sight that's dissonant with laughter. Then he has the nerve to roll up his sleeves and flash his perfect forearms. "I'm not going to be your Mrs. Doubtfire, but I'm staying."

"I think you should let him," Izzy says as she gives Flower some love. "I really don't like picking up poop, Mom. It's my least favorite part of having a dog."

Preach.

Sighing, I say, "Fine, you can stay if you insist." I pause, watching with something like disbelief as he grabs one of the thousands of plastic bags from their spot and prepares to clean. Then I remember my manners and say, "Thank you."

I can feel his smile rather than see it.

Grabbing Izzy's little shoulder, I say, "Why don't we go to my room so I can change out of this dress while we talk?"

"Okay, Mom," she says as she follows me. "Can I leave school early every day?"

"No." I smile, thinking of when I was her age. There were always a million things I wanted to do, and school didn't encompass half of them. There was a right way of learning and a wrong way, and my mind has never been able to compartmentalize like that. "Today was a special day. An ice cream for lunch day."

"What were you celebrating, Mom?" she asks as I open the door to my bedroom. A sigh of relief escapes me, because at least Flower hasn't developed opposable thumbs.

There's a sound of footfalls behind me, and I can feel Shane at my back. For a second, I have an insane impulse to lean back and soak in his warmth, but even though today has been a messed up day, I have enough presence of mind to hold back.

"Huh, sorry, Ruthie," he says. "Looks like she got to your room too."

I turn on him with a glower. He looks surprised for an instant and then like he's about to burst into ill-advised laughter. "You're telling me it always looks like this?" he asks.

"On a good day," says Izzy matter-of-factly. "Mom spends all of her time making the rest of the apartment look nice. She forgets to spend time on herself. Except you didn't forget today, Mom. You look like a princess."

My heart feels like it's taken up residence in my trachea, because when the hell did she get so grown up? She shouldn't have to have these adult thoughts. She should only need to have kid thoughts about unicorns and ice cream for lunch. I was never allowed to be a kid, which makes me want it for her even more.

"Oh, Izzy," I choke out. "You don't have to worry about me, honey. You don't ever have to worry about me. It's my job to worry about you, not the other way around."

Izzy rolls her eyes. "Mom, *of course* I worry about you. I worry about everyone I love. That's what people do."

There she goes again, being much too wise.

Shane surprises me by squeezing my shoulder, his grip hot and firm, and I feel it course through my body, as if it's infusing me with strength for the conversation ahead. Given it's Shane, I'm surprised he doesn't follow us into the room and demand to lead the conversation, but instead he steps back to clean up after my disaster-area dog.

I feel unmoored by the day, by *him*, by my mother.

But I take my little girl's hand and lead her past a pile of washed clothes I have yet to fold to sit on the bed. Which I made by pulling up the covers, thank you very much, Shane. Izzy sits down beside me.

"So, my mother came to speak to you at the playground, Izz? Was it definitely her?"

She scrunches her face. "I think so. She looked like those pictures you showed me, only her face was more like that apple that we found in the back of the refrigerator door. And she smelled like Uncle Tank did the morning he slept over at the apartment."

So she was loaded. So much for the new leaf she's turned over, not that I'm surprised. This is who my mother is—the kind of person who'd get drunk and approach her grandchild on a playground.

"I'm sorry that happened. What did she say to you?"

My heart thumps in my ears as she tells me. It thumps harder when she says my mother wanted to introduce her to someone.

Thank God Izzy's okay. *Thank God.*

"Principal Smuthers says they're going to keep better watch

when you're on the playground, okay?" I say, running a hand over her hair, needing to reassure myself again that she's okay.

"Mom, why are you really wearing that dress? You don't go to any dressy parties."

"Uncle Shane invited me to one," I say. "We're going to be spending a bit more time with him over the next few weeks, if that's okay."

"It's more than okay," she says, bouncing a little on the bed. "Uncle Shane's cool. When he read the Unicorn Diaries to me the other night, he gave all of the characters different voices. Can you do that for me, Mom?"

My feel choked up again, but this time for different reasons. Damn him for being such a confusing mix of parts. For being this wonderful person with my daughter and so insufferable with me most of the time.

But he wasn't insufferable today, a voice in my head whispers. That's not entirely true, but he *has* made himself useful. He's stood up for me and also stood by my side. Maybe he did it for Danny, or for Izzy, but I'd like to believe that our relationship is as complicated for him as it is for me.

"I can try, sweetheart."

That's all I ever do, but most of the time I feel like I'm failing. Still, if I'm good at anything it's getting back up, pulling on my big-girl pants, and trying again. So I stand and hold a hand out to my sweet, wise daughter. "What do you say you help me fold clothes volcano? Someone very wise recently told me that I'm not as good at taking care of myself as I am other people."

She lets me lift her up. "First you should change out of that dress, Mom. It's not really a working-around-the-house kind of dress. You have a lot of clothes that would be more appropriate for that."

Indeed, I do.

seventeen

SHANE

THIS PLACE IS A DUMP, with peeling paint and a carpet that smells like pee from dogs who haunted these rooms before Flower was a glimmer in her parents' eyes. Sure, Ruthie's tried to spruce it up by painting the walls and putting out flowers and some of Izzy's drawings dressed up in frames, but there's no disguising that essential fact.

I don't like that they live here. I like it even less than I did last week, because if Rita Traeger's poking around, she'd be able to weasel her way into this place, no problem.

I pace in the living room after I finish cleaning, the little dog pacing with me. "What are we going to do about this, Flower?" I find myself asking the dog in an undertone.

Representing psychics. Talking to dogs. Getting married. I'm really going for the *new year, new you* bullshit. But the dog answers me, no joke, giving a little whine followed by a bark—which is a passing of the buck if I've ever witnessed one.

"Yeah, you're right. I guess I can't expect a dog to do anything about it." She wags her tail and then licks my hand, which would be more exciting if she hadn't just eaten a mushroom that probably rolled under the fridge before Christmas.

The dog's kind of a pain in the ass, but I still like her. She reminds me a bit of Ruthie—she'll ruin your life but wag her tail and look cute as hell while doing it. Of course, if Ruthie knew I was mentally comparing her to a dog, she'd flip a shit—a thought that makes me want to smile, but I can't stick the landing right now.

"You're a good dog," I say, scratching her behind the ears.

A throat clears, and I glance into the hallway. There's Ruthie in those barely-there shorts, a different sweatshirt over them. Damn, she looked good in that dress, beyond good, but this combination makes me even crazier. Those shorts are the bane of my existence and also the cherry on top of a shit sundae.

"Are you talking to my dog?" she asks with a little smile.

"What's the point of wearing a sweatshirt if you're wearing those shorts with it?" I ask, because her shorts are messing with me. From the satisfied expression on her face, maybe they're meant to.

"Mom likes this look," Izzy says, appearing from behind her with a stack of dish towels that she puts away in the kitchen. "It's her usual around-the-house look. I think it's because Uncle Tank told her that she has nice legs."

This fucking guy.

"Interesting," I say, glancing at Ruthie's muscular thighs and tapered calves. She *does* have spectacular legs, but he's a small-minded man if he doesn't find plenty to admire elsewhere.

"Tank's an old friend," Ruthie says dismissively.

"So am I. Does that mean I get to tell you which parts of your body I like best?"

I didn't mean to say it. I particularly didn't mean to say it around Izzy, but this is a day of firsts and fuckups.

"No," Ruthie says pointedly, "because you're Danny's friend, not mine."

I grab my chest as if wounded, even though what we have couldn't properly be called a friendship. It's not nothing, though, and she's lying to herself if she thinks otherwise.

"That wasn't very nice, Mom," Izzy says. "You should apologize and ask Uncle Shane to stay for dinner."

I grin and reach out my hand for a high five. Izzy steps in and gives it to me, the little dog dancing around her feet.

My mood lifts. Other than seeing Danny last week, I've spent most of my time fixing up my mother's house, trying to motivate her to eat something other than cereal for dinner and stop looking at old photo albums. To get a new therapist who won't serve her platitudes with cheese sprinkled on top.

That's gotten me nowhere, but at least I know her refrigerator is full of food and the friends who have stuck by her have returned from their vacation and are aware of the problem.

Truthfully, despite Ruthie's shitty apartment and nosy neighbor, it's nice being here.

Ruthie grins at Izzy. "At least I've taught you right, daughter of mine." Turning to me, she says, "Shane, what do you say, will you stay for dinner?" She puts a hand on her hip, bringing my focus there. "There's pasta and tomato sauce and frozen vegetables. You're welcome."

"How about I order takeout for all of us?"

Her eyes glimmer, and she shakes her head. "Pasta and frozen vegetables or I rescind the invitation."

"What does rescind mean?" Izzy asks, a furrow in her little brow.

"It's something only rude people do," I say, giving Ruthie an arch look. "So I guess your mom must have been joking."

Ruthie wins, of course. She makes the pasta, and I eat the pasta, but I also win—because I use Uber Eats to order cake from a bakery downtown. When it shows up, Izzy doesn't get the significance, but Ruthie gives me a *point to you* look over the white cardboard box. I have the pleasure of having surprised her. Of having both displeased and pleased her with the same action.

It's obvious she expects me to leave after the cake, but I have no intention of going anywhere until Izzy is in bed so we can talk privately about Rita—and the dangers of staying in this apartment.

Maybe they can move in with Danny and Mira for a couple of months, until we're certain Rita stopping by the school was a drunken fluke.

"Well," Ruthie says after we finish cleaning the dishes. "I have to get Izzy to bed soon, so..."

"Mom," Izzy interjects, her eyes full of excitement. "Can Uncle Shane stay a bit longer so he can read the Unicorn Diaries? He does the funniest voice for the teacher."

"Who? Mr. Rumptwinkle?" I say in my best unicorn bray.

"Yes!" she laugh-screams, and I'd cover my ears if it weren't so damn cute.

"It's up to *Uncle Shane*," Ruthie says, giving me a look saying she knows my game. I've decided to stay, and she won't prevent it, but she's not happy.

That's fine. She'll be even less happy after I've spoken with her.

We play a round of Candyland, and then Ruthie gives me a sly grin. "Honey," she says to Izzy. "Why don't we play Pretty Pretty Princess Unicorn?"

"Yes!" Izzy shrieks, running off to grab the box.

Ruthie's smug expression suggests she thinks she's getting away with something.

"Dare I ask what Pretty Pretty Princess Unicorn is?"

"Oh," she says, giving me a glance that shivers through me and settles in my dick. "You're about to find out, Vain." Then she reaches out and taps my nose, the same way she did the other night. Goddamn, it's like that small contact radiates outward and lights me up from within. It *awakens* me.

Izzy comes traipsing back in, holding a bright pink and purple box. "It's so fun, Uncle Shane," she says in a rush. "We each get to pick a color of jewelry, and there's a spinboard and a cursed ring and a unicorn headband. And by the end we're all going to look so pretty."

I give Ruthie a flat look. "Well-played."

Then, because I'll do this for Izzy and no one else, I help unpack the game.

I'm the winner, rah, rah, me, and by the time we're finished, I have on a necklace that doesn't fit and had to rest on my hair like a headband, clip-on earrings, a bracelet that doesn't fit and had to be woven around my finger as a ring, a ring that barely clings to the top joint of my pinky, and a unicorn crown. I look like an idiot, and Ruthie's grin is blinding. I'm amused, and dear God, I am so turned on by her. It may have been the dress that started it, earlier, but whatever it unleashed is still throbbing through me.

"I think we need a photo," she says with a clap of her hands. She's got the bracelet on too, and a necklace and earrings. Izzy's got them all except for the crown.

"We should take one," Izzy says, "but I'll admit I'm disappointed that I didn't get the crown."

"Here, you take it," I say, because I'd really like to get it off my head. I had to jam it on to get it to fit.

"No, no, you were the winner," Izzy insists, tugging on one of her ponytails. "It wouldn't be right if I wore it when you were the winner. *I* just wanted to be the winner."

"You are the best sport in all of sportdom," Ruthie says to her with an even wider grin. "I'm proud of you."

"So am I," I say with a grimace, because I came so close to being able to ditch the crown. But being close to winning is still being a loser. "But sportdom isn't a thing."

Ruthie raises her eyebrows. "Come over here, Mr. Rumptwinkle. Time for photos."

She's a sadist, because she makes me take the selfies since "I have longer arms." Flower gets in on the action too—Ruthie holding the squirming dog in her arms so she can be in the photos.

I'm certain they'll make their way to Danny at some point. And once that happens, surely the rest of my friends will see them too. But I can't quite find the energy to be mad about Ruthie thinking she's getting away with something. I tell myself it's just because she'll be more liable to see things my way in the conversation that's about to come, but I don't fully believe it.

Afterward, while Ruthie's getting Izzy ready for bed, I find myself looking at the photo. Ruthie's mischievous grin makes me smile, and Izzy looks overjoyed. But it's the look in my own eyes that's a bit disarming. I look satisfied. Happy. Nothing at all like a man whose arm has been twisted into wearing a unicorn crown. For the first time, I understand why Freeman might have gotten things so wrong about us, because we almost look like a family. It reminds me of the photos lining the hallway in my mother's house. The thought makes me click away from the photo and pull up my messaging app to send a quick text to my mother.

> Was today a good day?

> I'm fine, Shane. You don't need to worry about me.

Except we both know that's not true. It hasn't been true since my dad died. It may never be true again, a thought that makes me feel like an elephant and its best friend sat on my chest and decided to have a tea party there.

I'm still feeling that pounding sense of dread when Ruthie emerges and tells me that I'm being called to duty. I read Izzy her story, then tuck her into her little pink bed.

I thought she was asleep, but before I go, she blinks open her bright blue eyes. "I love you, Uncle Shane," she says, which fills me with raw emotion and shame.

"I love you too, honey," I say, then head out into the living room to have a come-to-Jesus moment with my wife.

She's sitting at the kitchen table, Flower at her feet and a glass of whiskey in front of her. There's another glass of amber fluid at the seat across from her—my seat, I'm guessing. Interesting. I've never known her to like the hard stuff.

"Did you poison it?" I ask as I cross the distance between us and sit in front of it.

"There's only one way to find out," she tells me with a saucy smile that makes me feel like Rule Number One is one of those dry-as-fuck scones, crumbling to pieces.

I lift the glass and gulp, because I need the raw heat of it in my gut. It's been a strange day—the kind of day that makes a mark on a man's soul. If I have a soul, it's made a mark on mine.

"Why'd you insist on staying, Shane?" Ruthie asks, leaning forward a little. The sweatshirt gapes, giving me a glimpse of her silky black bra, which gets the enviable job of cupping her tits.

I clear my throat and look up, quick enough to catch the sly smile on her face. "You enjoy toying with me, Ruthie?" I ask. Not what I'd intended to say, but my self-control hasn't slipped back into place.

"So, you've noticed, huh?" she asks. There's a flush on her cheeks, but something tells me it's not embarrassment. It's the same feeling that's coursing through me.

Fuck. *Fuck.*

I take another gulp of whiskey. "Yeah. I've noticed."

Her smile stretches wider. "It's not every day a woman gets to marry a pretty, pretty princess. Can you blame me for wanting to commemorate it?"

I clear my throat and straighten on the chair, trying to stuff down the need frothing inside of me—urging me to pull down those inadequate little shorts and show her what her games do to me.

"I stayed because I wanted to talk to you about Rita."

Her face creases into a scowl. "What do you have to do with it? She's my cross to bear."

"Not entirely true," I say, rapping my fingers against the table, needing something to do with them so I don't give in to the urge to touch her, to take her.

"What do you mean, Shane?"

"Just that I've helped Danny in the past. She's gotten pulled in for Drunk and Disorderlies, and I've helped her stay out of jail."

"You did what?" she asks crisply, her flush now all anger. This, at least, is familiar. Ruthie mad at me. Ruthie telling me I've overstepped. Ruthie thinking I'm selfish and small-minded. This, I know how to navigate.

"He didn't want her in jail. He figured... Well, I guess he figured you'd feel the same way."

"And neither of you thought to ask me?" she asks, her hand curling into a fist on the tabletop. "I'm just a kid, right? At twenty-eight, with a kid of my own. I don't deserve a say. If she went to jail, it would be because she deserves it."

My gaze is on that fist, because part of me wants her to pound it against me, or open it and spear it through my hair. "Drunk and Disorderlies are usually bullshit," I tell her, my voice thick. "A way to keep poor people in prison and away from the rich people who don't like seeing them. I thought you'd be averse to that kind of thing."

"Maybe if it wasn't *her*," she says with an acrimony that surprises me.

"We should have talked to you," I confirm. "But Danny and I figured she'd be better at sticking to the rules we set if we gave her something in return."

"You were bribing her not to reach out to me?" she asks, her eyes alive with fire.

"Yes," I say with no remorse. She gets up off her chair so suddenly it falls, and the little dog goes scurrying into the connected living room, probably sensing a grenade has gone off. I get up too, because I'm a man who would rather face my fate standing up.

She backs me into the wall behind me. It's not appropriate, it's not good, but there's no denying the truth: I'm so fucking hard it hurts.

"You're still wearing your crown, your majesty," she says, smirking at me even though her eyes are furious.

"It's about time you realized who I am to you," I say, mostly because I want to see how she'll react.

"My queen?" She crowds my space, her body nearly pressed to mine. There's only a whisper of space between us, and my dick throbs and demands.

Touch her, take her. Claim her.

"Your lord and fucking master." I grin at her, challenging her. *Your play, Ruthie.*

She takes another step closer, and I nearly hiss at the press of her bare thighs against my suit. I want to run my hands over them, to cup her ass. To switch positions with her so I can push *her* against this wall. Rule Number One is the slightest whisper in my ears at this point, and it's hard to remember why it once seemed so important.

"Why did you stay, pretty, *pretty* princess?" she asks, her head angled up to me, just inches away—a distance I could span in an instant.

"I think you and Izzy should stay somewhere else until we can figure out the Rita situation. Maybe with Danny. We'll go talk to him tomorrow anyway. Tell him about all of this."

She laughs in my face. "Look at you, trying to control me. You think that paper we signed today gives you the right? It's a lie. It's not even a lie that holds water because we aren't in a relationship."

"I care about Izzy's safety," I say, because I know she won't believe me if I tell her I care about her, too, in my way.

"So do I, you sanctimonious dick," she says, pushing me into the wall, her hands hot brands against my chest. "Why would staying with Danny make me the slightest bit safer?"

"He has an alarm system," I say. "And an attack hamster."

"I have Flower," she says, gesturing to the living room. I don't look away from her, but I already know the only thing that dog's dangerous to is my suit. She's probably less threatening than Danny's hamster, given the cuts on his fingers. "And Mrs. Longhorn. You think she'd let anyone break into my apartment?"

"She might not always be there," I say, even though that's probably not true. But it would be foolish to count on a busybody old neighbor as an alarm system. Nosy Mrs. Longhorn may be, but she wouldn't be a deterrent to a person with bad intentions.

"If you think my mother's truly dangerous, then you were a fool to help her."

"Dangerous people have dangerous friends. She said she wanted to introduce Izzy to someone. I don't like that."

"Do you think *I* like it?" she asks, giving me another shove.

"There's nowhere for me to go, Ruthie," I say thickly. "You already have me up against a wall." I leave off the—and *now what are you going to do with me?* But I'm thinking it. It would take a stronger man than me to not be thinking it.

Her breathing catches, her hand wraps in a fist around my tie, the slight pressure a fault line leading straight to my dick. "I'm going to call her to tell her to back off," she says. "And I'll put in a security system. I'll pay for it too."

"With what?" I ask as she keeps tugging on the tie. My heart is racing, everything inside of me revved up and wanting.

"With the deposit you're going to give me, just like Eden said."

"How about you let me buy it with the deposit?" I ask, because any system good enough to keep them safe will cost more than five hundred dollars.

There's a flash of frustration in her eyes—of rage—because I'm sure she knows it. "You love manipulating me, Vain. If you had your way, you'd be in control of everyone. The lord and master of the world."

"I'm trying to keep you and Izzy safe, dammit." I want to touch her. I *need* to touch her—it's pounding in my veins like a curse. Like a blessing. But if I let myself fully break Rule Number One, I don't know if I'll be able to find my way back. I'll be lost in the woods. In her. I curl my hands at my sides, digging my fingers into my palms hard enough that my short nails are probably leaving marks on the skin.

"That's my job," she says scornfully. "I'll take care of us. I'll provide for us. I have a long-term plan."

"With Vanny?" I sound dubious because I *am* dubious. I know enough about the bookmobile to have gathered that she doesn't have a plan for making steady money off of it, or adapting her setup to account for changes in weather and circumstance.

"You're an asshole," she says heatedly, hatred flashing in her eyes. "You love nothing better than putting me down."

"I don't love putting you down," I say, my voice rising slightly. I remember Izzy, hopefully asleep down the hall, and lower my voice. "I never have."

"It amuses you to watch me fail." Her eyes are glistening as she says it, but if they're tears, I doubt she'll let them fall in front of me. Regret digs into me.

"Never. I'd like to help you, if you'd let me. Your ideas aren't bad—"

She lets out an incredulous laugh, her hand tightening around my tie, as if she'd like nothing better than to squeeze the very life out of me.

"But you don't spend enough time planning out any of your projects," I continue, determined to say this much, because unless someone tells her, she's going to keep doing the same thing again and again. I know all about vicious cycles. My mother's caught in one, and I doubt she'll ever find an out. "You're always so excited in the beginning, but you don't think through how you're going to make a sustainable income, and then you give up without even really trying. You give up the second it doesn't work out the way you wanted it to. I've always wondered why, Ruthie. I've wanted to talk to you about it, to help—"

Her grip tightens until it hurts a little. And that also makes me harder. "You think you know me?" she seethes. "You think you have the solution to all of the problems in my life? What about you? You're so far up your own ass you've nearly made it to your trachea. Do you honestly think you're too good for Mr. Freeman and his firm? It only took a five minute conversation for me to know he's a better man than you'll ever be. You could take lessons from him."

Fuck. She goes for the jugular. I grab her hand on my tie but don't attempt to loosen her hold. A twisted part of me likes it. Likes it too that she doesn't speak in platitudes and praise. She tells me like she sees it. Even if I wished she saw something more in me than a funhouse reflection. A voice in my head says that's all I've let her see—purposefully. Maybe that's true. Maybe it was one more way I've kept my attraction buried.

"Sure," I say, my hand moving over hers, engulfing it. "You're right. He's a good man, a regular Mr. Rogers, and he'll get fucked over twice a day until he dies because of it. I don't apologize for taking care of myself. You should take care of yourself too. You have a good head, Ruthie. Use it. One-time fees from venues aren't going to carry you. Why aren't you selling books or merch? What services can you offer in the winter? How are *you* capitalizing off your association with the animal shelter, or are you just letting your own heart be bled dry?"

"I hate you," she says, her eyes glistening. Her hand pulls harder on my tie, enough that it almost hurts.

"You want to punish me, Ruthie? To hurt me?"

"*Yes*," she says, her voice shaking. "You're trying to hurt *me*."

"I'm not. I'm trying to talk straight to you, the way you always do to me. I'm treating you as an equal."

She swallows, my eyes tracking the movement in her slender throat. Sweet fuck, she's beautiful.

"Why are you really here, Shane? Tell me the truth."

"I told you," I say, swallowing. "You're Danny's sister. He's my best friend, so it's my job to protect you."

She tugs on the tie again. "You listen to me, and you listen good. It's my job to protect myself. I'm a grown woman."

"There's no mistaking that," I say, my voice low and husky. "You must realize I've noticed."

"Then why persist in using that horrible nickname?"

I can't help but smile a little. "Because I've tried to keep thinking of you that way. You haven't made it easy. I'm guessing that's why you're always wearing those shorts around me."

She lets out a harsh laugh. "You assume everything is about you." Her hand flexes on the tie again, although she's eased up. Her chin tips up to me. Her lips are still painted as red as a cherry, lush and soft. Now that I've tasted them, it's hard to hold back my hunger for all of her. She releases the tie, and I instantly miss the soft pressure—the implication that she wants to lead me by my tie to her bed. "You heard Izzy. I do it because Tank told me I have nice legs."

A growl issues from the back of my throat. I'd told myself I wouldn't touch her, but I'm almost rabid with the need to shift our positions and press her into the wall. She needs to feel like she's in control right now, though, and I won't take that away from her. Even if I suspect neither of us are in control. Still, I find myself reaching for her chin, tilting it further up so our eyes meet and hold.

"Are you lying to me, Ruthie?" I ask, my voice holding a note of danger. I'd never hurt her. I'd die before hurting her. But there's something to be said for punching a wall in a fit of rage. I've done it before, and the feeling of the drywall crumbling around my fist, my knuckles bloody, made me feel better. For five minutes.

"Yes," she says, and licks her lips. My thumb reaches up to chase her tongue, following its path and feeling the plump red lip.

A gasp escapes her. "Do you wear those little shorts for me?" I ask, feeling a pounding in my veins, my cock, my whole being.

"No, you narcissist. I like them." My thumb is still on her bottom lip, and I keep it there.

"Did you wear them for me *today*?"

"Yes," she hisses, as if the word costs her, and she's going to be sending me the bill.

"Did you want me to give you a spanking, like the bad girl you are?"

She makes a sound that tries to be laughter. "I'm the one who has you backed into a wall. It's time you noticed." She pushes my thumb from her mouth but moves in closer, rubbing against me to let me know she's noticed my hard-on and doesn't object to it. My whole body is attuned to hers, from the way she's breathing to the feel of her through the fabric.

"What are you going to do about it?" I ask, my voice a stranger's voice. I don't think I've ever felt this far gone, as if control were a foreign concept and not something that's become so easy for me it's like breathing.

"Maybe I'll give *you* a spanking."

Maybe I'd let her.

Her hand finds my tie again, and a breath of relief escapes me, because I liked it there. This time she pulls it down. I recognize the movement for the welcome invitation it is and lower my head to claim her red lips.

I'm so hungry for her, starved. I suck on that bottom lip as if it's the answer of life, and if I release her, I'll never learn it again. Her tongue finds mine, her hand still wrapped around my tie, pulling me down, directing me like I'm the damn dog. And I can't say I don't like it. I shift the angle so I have more of her, my hand lifting to her hair, fisting around it like I wanted to do earlier, in the courtroom.

Its soft silken weight in my hand is a boon, a prize, a revelation. She releases a little sound into my mouth, and my dick pounds commands to me. But I won't rush this moment, because I already know it's not going to last.

There's some madness driving us tonight. Madness that feels better than sanity. Maybe it'll ruin everything, but right now I don't have the ability to think of anything but the feeling of this woman in my arms, of her lips consuming mine, her teeth nipping at me, her body pressing closer like the only thing she needs in this world is my cock.

I know better than to believe it, but maybe I'll allow myself this one moment of vanity. Because I've never wanted someone so much in my life.

My other hand drifts down from her back to her ass, the soft globe fitting perfectly in my hand. It's round and firm, and I want to explore it for hours. I've spent years trying to ignore the way my body reacts to Ruthie, but I haven't succeeded. I've memorized this maddening woman in bits and pieces, a flash of flesh here, a brush of the hand, a scent captured and remembered. All those stolen pieces are coming together now, forming a map that's still incomplete. I want to complete it—to be an explorer and to form a map so thorough future generations will marvel at my genius, but no one will be allowed to see that map except for *me*.

It's a stupid thought, but maybe that's only appropriate because I'm being stupid. Sudden panic licks through me, because this wasn't supposed to happen. It was *never* supposed to happen.

When Danny asks me if I've ever touched his sister or intend to touch her, I will no longer be able to honestly tell him no. If he wants to punch me, that'll be his right. Maybe that's the real reason I haven't told him about the marriage yet—because I knew I wanted her. Because I've wanted her for a long time.

Then there's Ruthie herself—she'll regret this. She already

dislikes me the majority of the time, and if we add another layer of complication...

I pull away from her mouth, but I can't get my hand to leave her hair or her ass. It's like they've been super-glued there.

"I've wondered what it would be like," she says with eyes that glimmer. They remind me of that ruby in her ring, bright and dangerous. That's why I had to get it for her. It only felt right for her to have a ring that fit her soul.

"To kiss someone you hate?"

"To kiss *you*."

"*I* knew what it would be like," I admit, my hand moving over her ass, because I'm no longer control of it. It's decided that my mind has worse ideas than my dick.

"So why didn't you do it sooner?" she asks.

"You know why."

"Because you don't like me," she says to my lips.

"Does it feel like I don't like you, Ruthie?" I ask, placing a kiss on her top lip, her nose.

"You want to fuck me, but that doesn't mean you like me, Shane. We both know they're different things."

"You aggravate the hell out of me," I say.

"How *romantic*," she tells me, her tone sarcastic but playful. Then she gets on her toes and bites the lobe of my ear, sending a shot of electric pain right to where I'm hard for her. I push her ass closer, needing the feeling of her grinding against me again, because I'm so hard I may pass out from blood loss to the other parts of my body.

"You drive me crazy," I say, my voice shaking. I take my hand from her hair and cup her jaw again. I'm nearly shaking with the need to kiss her. "You make me feel like I *want* to be crazy."

She licks her lips slowly and says, "Maybe you should let yourself. Tonight. You know, it's not a legal marriage if we don't consummate it."

She's not strictly correct, but a lack of consummation would be grounds for divorce or annulment. Then again, we'd always planned on getting divorced.

Still, I don't correct her. My cock likes the way she's thinking. My cock has banished all thoughts of Rule Number One and its importance to my sanity.

"You want me to fuck you?" I ask in a rough whisper as she grinds against me again. I claim her mouth before she can answer, wanting to show her how good it's going to be between us, how hot. This time, she's the one who pulls away.

"Once," she says. "Only once."

"You think once will be enough for us to get it out of our systems?" I ask, lifting my eyebrows. "It won't be for me," I admit. "A thousand times wouldn't be enough. It's only going to make me want you more."

She looks stunned for a moment, as if she hasn't realized the effect she has on me—the effect I've been doing my damnedest to ignore.

"*Why?*"

"I don't know," I say, which is half honest, half not. I know that she's gorgeous in a way that's painful—with those long muscular legs, her nearly black hair and blue eyes, and the confident way she moves her body. I'm sick of the practiced slickness of my world—of women who move artfully because they know someone's eyes are on them. Ruthie's not like that. She's self-possessed. Sexy. And then there's her saucy as fuck attitude, always directed my way. I'm used to women trying to impress me, to please me, but Ruthie always presents me with a laundry list of my faults. It makes me want to hear her scream my name...

So, yes, I know why I want to fuck her—anyone would—but I don't know why I *need* it. I've never let myself need something like that before, and I don't like it. When you need something, or someone, you lose control. You lose power.

As if she can hear my thoughts, she reaches down and wraps her hand on my straining dick through my pants. "Tonight, Vain. Only once. That's the rule."

If I accept her rule I'm breaking mine. I'm shattering it and cutting my feet on the broken pieces. But I already know how I'm going to answer. With her hand moving over me like that, there's only one way I could possibly answer.

"One night," I say. "But not only once."

"Always negotiating." There's no heat to her tone, though—the heat's all in her eyes. In her hand, caressing the head of my dick through two layers of fabric. I feel it as intensely as if she had her mouth on it. My teeth are pressed together, every bit of my body tense. "Okay," she says, "but you need to be gone before Izzy gets up in the morning. How many times do you think you can go, Romeo?"

"I intend to find out. Do you have protection, or am I going to have to make a trip to the store like this?"

Her smile lifts in a partial smirk. "I'd like to see that, but yes, I have something. They're in my room."

I don't like thinking about what that means. About Tank liking the look of her legs. Jealousy is not a usual emotion for me, and I don't care for it. Logically, though, I know that if she were really with him, she wouldn't be doing this with me.

I put my other hand on her ass and lift her up, hoisting her over my shoulder. She squeaks in protest and then presses a hand over her mouth because she doesn't want to wake Izzy, and I carry her into her bedroom.

RUTHIE

"YOU FUCKER," I say as Shane practically throws me down onto the bed. "You couldn't have princess carried me?"

I'm posturing, mostly. I've never been more turned on in my life. All this time, I've been attracted to him, however unwillingly, and despite my little game, I had no idea he wanted me this much. It's surprising, exciting, and a little terrifying too.

He takes his tie and starts loosening it with one hand, and I have to practically squirm against the intense sensation between my legs. "I thought *I* was the princess," he says.

He still has that damn crown on his head, but instead of making him look stupid or silly, it reminds me of how patiently he played the game—how perfectly unselfconscious he was as he clipped on the earrings or found a way to wear the necklace and bracelet. He did it to make Izzy happy, and even though it made me gleeful to see him fully decked out in his Pretty Pretty Princess attire, it also put a lump in my throat. An uncomfortable rush of emotion in my chest. Seeing it on him now...it makes him sexier, and not just because he's a man who has the confidence to put a unicorn crown on his head without whining.

Rand never would have.

In a rare moment of fondness toward Shane, I say, "You still have the crown on, you know."

"Good," he says, throwing the tie. I take note of where it goes, because I've decided I'll have use for it later. He stands at the foot of the bed and starts unbuttoning his shirt. I go to pull my shorts off, but he shakes my head. "You gave me one night, and I'm going to make the most of it. That's mine to do."

I could complain or dissent, but I want him to pull them down. I want him to do wicked, wicked things to me.

"The crown?" I ask haughtily, my eyes tracking those buttons as he reveals more of himself. He's wearing an undershirt, and I promise myself I'll be the one to remove that. He can trouble himself with the buttons.

His grin wicked, he says, "You can pull it off when my head's between your legs. I won't need it anymore, because I'll feel like I have a crown on when I hear you calling out my name."

"You're such an insufferable dick," I say, getting up onto my knees on the mattress to sweep the unbuttoned shirt off his shoulders. It falls to the floor, and I slide my hands under the undershirt, reveling in the feel of him, hard beneath my fingers. Danny mentioned Shane's been spending a lot of time at the gym lately—that he doesn't know what to do with himself when he's not working, and here's the evidence. He's hard and muscular, and I want this so much, I'm probably going to come the first time he touches me between the legs, even if his dick is nowhere as big as it felt through his pants and his BDE energy advertises.

"You *want* my dick," he says, his voice full of confidence I want to puncture, except it's hard to tell him he's wrong when we both know he's right.

So I settle for saying, "That's all I want. No one told you to talk. You always talk too much."

I see a flash of his white-toothed grin as I pull the sleeveless shirt over his head. The crown must really be lodged in his hair because it stays on. And Shane Royce is standing in front of me in nothing but a unicorn crown, suit pants, a belt, and socks. There's nothing for it—I have to kiss him. So I do, kneeling on my bed, his muscular body pressed up against me. His lips are as confident as the words that come out of them, and they make me feel like I'm melting into a puddle.

I want to whisper platitudes to my past self, to the little ten-year-old girl who wanted him so badly, even though she didn't understand what the wanting meant. *I'm going to have him, for one night I'm going to have him, and then I'm going to show him that women can take what they want too, then turn their backs with no remorse.*

Because I might want to sleep with Shane, but there's no way I'm going to let him control my life. All I want is to sate my curiosity about whether he has any bite to go along with that bark. It would feel wrong never to find out, when he's always hanging around in the background of my life—a sexy phantom.

"Take off your socks," I say through a mouth full of cotton. "I can't sleep with a man who's wearing socks."

"But the pants aren't a problem?" he asks, cocking his brow as he deals with the socks.

"They're my problem. I'm going to take them off."

I reach for his belt, my hand shaking slightly.

"I get to take something off of you first," he says, nodding to me.

"Okay," I say, because I have every intention of being naked too, of feeling him against all of me.

His hands slide beneath my oversized sweatshirt, and the slight pressure of them against my flesh sends a rush of sensation through me—almost too strong—and then he's lifting it over my head, leaving me in the bootie shorts. He makes a sound like a hiss when he sees my bra—black silk with mesh cutouts.

"Did you wear that for me too?"

"Arrogant much?" I ask. "I wore it for *me*." I like wearing pretty lingerie. It's like a secret between myself and the world—yes, I may look like a hot mess mom. Yes, I *am* a hot mess mom, but on my terms.

"I'm glad," he says, and for a second I'm thrown—he's glad I did it for myself or he's just glad I wore it? But then I don't care anymore because his mouth has lowered to the mesh cutouts, and I can feel his tongue slide over my nipple. I'm grateful for that mesh, because if I felt him against my bare nipple, I'd probably do something ridiculous like squeal.

I start attacking his belt. That's the best word for it. It needs to come off—now—and I *will* be its executioner. He watches me do it without helping, his eyes hooded, an aggravating smirk on his face as if he's accusing me of not even being able to belt properly. Finally, I get the buckle loosened, and seconds later his pants and boxer briefs are pushed down.

My hand finds his cock, sweeping up and down it, because I need to touch it to believe this is actually happening—also because it turns out his BDE has plenty to back it up, not that I'd expected otherwise.

"Fuck, Ruthie," he says, "you can't touch me right now. Give me a minute."

A rush of power leaves me almost giddy. My touch makes Shane Royce feel like he's going to lose it? Well, hallelujah. I guess something would have to do the trick.

I release him, and I don't have time to make a smart remark before he leans in again to kiss me, his hand finding my hair and fisting in it the way he did in the living room. The nerve endings light up, and I feel like the Christmas tree I only took down last week. The man has mad skills, too, because with his other hand he manages to unclasp my bra on the first go—something that takes more effort for me, and I do it every day.

His mouth moves to my jaw to the place at my neck that's a hotline to the rest of my body, and then down to my breasts, my hand finding the back of his hair as he kisses them and then runs his tongue over my nipple before capturing it in his mouth. Something flashes in his eyes and he pushes me back onto the bed and tugs me to the edge, his hands already working on my shorts and panties. They're form-fitting, but they don't hold out for more than half a second against Shane Royce, who's spent the last two months haunting the gym.

Seconds later, I'm splayed open for him at the bottom of the mattress. He stands between my legs and looks down at me for a long moment—his gaze intense, varying between green and blue and brown now that he doesn't have a tie to tell them which color to favor. His chest is defined and covered in a sprinkling of dark hair, and he looks nothing like the boy in my memory. We're reflected in the large vanity mirror behind us, so I can see his bare muscular ass, the long muscled slope of his back.

A laugh escapes me, because I am absolutely the kind of person who laughs at moments like this—when I'm so keyed up and full of wanting, it has to escape some way.

"What's so funny?" he asks, his hands blazing twin paths up and down my thighs. I have a pulse of self-consciousness, because I don't think I've shaved for a few days—I honestly don't remember—but he doesn't seem to give a shit or even notice.

"It's just—there's a big vanity mirror behind us. It seems appropriate because of your nickname."

He glances back, just for a moment, and then smiles at me—it's a sinful smile, and I feel it right between my legs, even before he gets down on his knees. "Then you'll be able to watch me two ways when I have my head buried between your legs," he says, pulling my legs even farther apart, baring me to him.

I feel another pulse of self-consciousness, but it's obliterated when he breathes out a swear and starts kissing a blazing path up my thigh and to my center. He glances up at me, that stupid, adorable crown still on his head, and says, "You're so wet for me,

Ruthie." He looks like he's announcing he just built the Empire State Building himself, by hand, and I feel a swell of annoyance.

"Why do you assume it's for you? Maybe I'm just insatiable."

He growls and sucks in my clit, making my hips buck up. As he pulls them to his face, feasting on me, I pluck the crown off his head. Even though I love Pretty Pretty Princess as much as the next girl, I want to weave my hand in his short hair, to pull it. Then I put the crown on my own head because I feel like the queen of the universe. "I'm your queen," I say, earning another growl that vibrates through me and gives me the first quakes of my orgasm. I spiral further when I look in the mirror and see him on his knees, his back bare, his face at my core. Shane must feel it coming, because he curls one finger inside me, two, finding the bundle of nerves and igniting them while he sucks my clit—and I'm gone. I'm toast. I'm a puddle. In this one, brief moment, I'm his.

"The condoms," he says, his voice rough. "Where?"

Taking off the crown and setting it on my bedside table, I wave to the top drawer of my dresser, beneath the mirror. I don't even think about all of my pairs of old and period underwear until after he's stepped over and opened the drawer. But he clearly doesn't care. He's a man on a mission, swiping through until he finds the row of condoms. It takes him only half a second to roll one on, although watching him do it, his reflection in the mirror offering a second show, will be burned into my brain forever. He's so impossibly beautiful, and in this moment, I don't hold it against him. I'm glad for it.

He returns to me, still a puddle, my legs hanging over the side of the bed, because I've decided I'm not ready to move yet, particularly if he's coming over here to give me that cock.

"I need to be inside of you," he says, stroking his big hands down my legs. I wrap them around his waist, because I need him too, even if I can't bring myself to say it. "I've never needed anything as much."

He stares me in the eyes as he says it, and I feel an uncomfortable twist of emotion—of wanting to believe him but knowing he can lie when it suits him. He must be lying now.

"So do it," I say, lifting my hips up, because I may have just come, but I know he can give me another. And maybe more.

He reaches down to position himself, an almost pained look on his face, then slowly slides in—giving me time to adjust to the *very* welcome invasion. I know I can take it—my body gave birth to a baby and is therefore capable of anything—but I still feel an almost painful but very pleasurable stretch, leading to a sensation of complete fullness and the desperate need for friction.

He swears loudly, leaning his head back as if he's worshipping at my altar, my hips lifted to him, his hard cock seated inside me, and this, too, is a moment I'll remember forever.

I don't like the way I'm memorizing these moments—I want to live them—so I push into his thrust, pulling another swear from him. "Don't be gentle with me, Vain."

"I hadn't planned on it," he says, pulling out and using my thighs for leverage as he thrusts back in again. "Touch yourself, Ruthie. Touch yourself while I fuck you."

Because his hands are busy, and he can't reach my clit. Probably also because he wants to watch. So I do, and the look on his face, worshipful, is as intoxicating as what he's doing to me. Then he leans over me and takes my nipple in his mouth, sucking while he continues to move inside of me, my legs pulling him closer because they don't seem to want to let him go. One of my hands finds his muscular ass, the other his hair, holding him in place because I feel greedy, and the way he's sucking my nipple is sending more pleasure spiraling to where I need it. I'm starting to clench around him already, as if every part of me wants him closer. He shifts to the other nipple, pausing to place a kiss between my breasts. A muffled cry escapes me—muffled because he presses his palm over my mouth. He knows Izzy is down the hall.

I'm an insane woman, because his hand on my mouth makes my desire spike. I kiss his hand, then bite it.

"God, I'm sorry," he groans, thrusting in again, deeper, so deep I feel like my body has consumed him, and then holds for a moment. "I'm already close."

"Hold off," I squeal. "Think of Fred Myles."

He gives a surprise laugh, followed by a growl as I pull out from under him. He lets me, though, looking to me for direction, and I say, "Lie on your back."

"Are you going to take control?" he asks, appearing amused and hopefully fired up by the thought.

"*Yes*. I'm going to own you, Shane Royce, and you're going to like it."

I've been thinking about this all night—turned on by that tie and wanting to touch it, to use it to tug him closer. It's not the first day I've had that intrusive thought, but it's the only day I'll ever be able to do anything about it.

I retrieve it as he gets onto his back, his cock jutting up for me.

He gives me a wicked smile and puts his hands behind his head. I climb onto him, the thumping of my heart matching the feeling between my legs, and tie his hands together, using one of the knots I learned in Girl Scouts. Let's see him try to get out of that before I let him.

There's a scar on his forearm, small and blotchy, and I run my finger over it. "What's this from? I've always wondered."

Something passes through his eyes, but it's too fast for me to follow and tug it out. "I'd rather not talk about that right now. I'd prefer to keep the focus on you, me, and my favorite tie."

I don't call him out on it, because I want to be lost in this moment too.

"It *should* be your favorite," I say, reaching down and lining him up. I play with him, rubbing against him without giving him what he wants, but he doesn't move. He just stares at me, taking his punishment and silently telling me what he wants from me.

"Am I driving you crazy?" I ask, placing my palms on his chest and sitting on him just beneath his cock.

"You always drive me crazy." His smile widens. "I see no reason why you shouldn't drive both of us crazy for a change."

He's right. My body is demanding more of that thick cock. I don't want to make either of us wait any longer, so when I rub myself against him this time, I slowly sink down, taking all of him in. The look of satisfaction and raw need on Shane's face, paired with the feeling of him stretching me and my sensitive clit rubbing against him, his cock captured inside my body, is nearly enough to make me come on the spot.

I take his tied wrists in one hand while I ride him. "You're mine to do with as I like."

I'm prepared for him to roll over and prove me wrong—his wrists are tied together, not secured to anything else, and he is very strong and capable. Maybe I even slightly want him to do that. But instead he smiles and lifts his head to kiss my breast. "Yes, I am." Then he repeats what I said earlier. "Don't be gentle."

I'm not. I grind down on him hard, holding his wrists, and he bucks up to meet me, seeking more, because I'm pretty sure neither of us can get enough right now.

"You're driving me wild," he confirms.

"That's the idea," I say, throwing my head back as I sink down onto him again, feeling every thick, delicious inch, my hand still holding his as they flex under my touch. I've never felt so powerful, so beautiful, and so needy.

I hear him swearing under his breath, and I look down and meet his eyes. They're heated, and he says, "You're fucking gorgeous," as he slams up into me, his hands twitching again under my touch.

"So are you," I admit, and I lean down and kiss him as I keep moving my hips. Slower, though. It's a deep, dirty kiss, our mouths locked together, our tongues moving, and it's then that I feel my body tightening around him again.

"Shane," I whisper into his mouth.

"I feel you," he says, his voice strained. "Oh, God, you feel so good. Ruthie, I need..."

"I know what you need."

Still moving over him, on the edge, my whole body ready to fall, I untie his hands.

With a fevered sigh of relief, he strokes them down my body. Then he finds my ass and presses it down as he thrusts up, bringing our connection even deeper—and it's happening, I feel myself cresting over the edge into a pleasure so deep I might drown in it. A gasp escapes me, and he meets my eyes, his gaze intense and greedy, and thrusts in hard and deep. Sounds I didn't realize I was capable of making pour out of my mouth, and he captures them in a kiss that he only breaks because he's groaning and jerking against me in a fast thrust that suggests his control is utterly broken. And the look of joy on his face as he comes seems to break something inside of me— while at the same time building something new.

He keeps his hand on my back, but moves us onto our sides, and we lay like that for a moment, panting, staring at each other in what can only be called wonder. "*Ruthie*," he finally says with an emphasis that makes me laugh.

"*Shane*."

He grins at me, shaking his head slightly, then kisses me on the neck before getting up to dispose of the condom.

When he comes back, I'm still lying there, shocked, pleased, and frankly a little terrified—because it was the kind of experience that changes a person, and I don't know if I want to be changed that way.

"Come take a shower with me," he says, leaning in to kiss me. And I honestly can't think of anything I'd rather do. Of course, we don't just take a shower. He takes me from behind against the wall, because he says he can't go all night without taking me this way—those shorts have given him *an imagination*. Minutes later, he tells me the reality is better than anything he came up with in his mind.

I have to say he's right.

It's late, and he should go. I *know* he should go, but when he climbs back into bed with me, both of us still not completely dry from the shower, I don't stop him. And I don't stop him when he pulls the covers up over us and holds me to him as if I matter. As if this weren't just about fucking out the energy that's been zinging between us for years.

"You're so beautiful," he murmurs to me. "Do you know how hard it's been to pretend not to notice?"

"Yes," I admit, unable to stop myself from smiling at him. "Why do you think I taunt you?"

He runs a hand over my jaw, cupping it, and then kisses me—a soft kiss from a hard man, and I feel it all the way down to my toes, the tingle coursing through me and reminding me how good he feels, how unexpectedly right.

Just tonight.

Then he pulls back, smiling, and says, "I thought you taunted me because you're a little brat, and you can't help yourself."

I scowl and pinch his arm. He tickles my side, and just when I'm on the verge of getting up to stomp my foot, he wraps his arm around me, his body spooning mine with warmth. It feels...nice.

But it shouldn't feel nice with *him*.

"You can't stay, Shane," I say, almost sad about it.

I expect him to object, or maybe to insist he'd never wanted to stay, but he surprises me. "I know. But I'd like to lie here with you for a little longer. Get the most out of my one night. You know I like to capitalize on my wins."

"Okay," I say, my throat thick.

"I need to go talk to Danny tomorrow," he says into my ear, making me flinch.

"You're going to tell him about *this*?" I ask, alarmed.

He laughs, but there's an edge to it. "No, I don't plan on telling him I fucked his sister until my dick felt raw, but I need to tell him about our agreement and your mother. Unless you'd prefer to do it first."

He says it like someone who feels a deep-seated need to do it first but is struggling to be polite. Fine by me. I'd prefer to go second, and if that makes me a coward, so be it.

"You can do it," I say. "You like taking control of things."

"So do you, Ruthie." One side of his mouth lifts in a delicious smirk that I don't want to like. I don't want to like him either. I remind myself of earlier, of his attitude about Vanny and his super-ciliousness about my mother.

He kisses the side of my neck, then peers into my eyes. His eyes are wells of color. Intense. Is this what it feels like to be on the jury in one of his cases? No wonder he's had so many wins. "You know," he finally says. "I'm not sorry."

Neither am I.

I feel good. I feel *great*. I feel like I could climb a mountain. Or succeed at something, *anything*, I set my mind to.

Because if I can conquer Shane Royce, I can conquer the world.

When I wake up, my first impression is that the bed is empty. It's cold, and I have a flash of loneliness. Of wishing he'd stayed, even though it had been my intention to kick him out and leave him to the questionable mercies of Mrs. Longhorn.

But then I notice it, winking up at me from the pillow—my red engagement ring.

It shouldn't make me feel anything. It's as fake and meaningless as the marriage license I signed, and the fact that Shane and I had some fun doesn't change that. But there's no denying the ache in my chest. It's because of what happened before, I decide. Because of Rand and the way he walked out on me. Because marriage is so often a hollow shell.

Still, I put it on a chain and slip it around my neck before I leave the room to make my coffee. It'll be a little secret, just for me.

I check my phone, and there's a single message from Shane—

> I'm still not sorry. I'm going to go see Danny this morning. I'll let you know when I've left his place.

I'm playing with the necklace, my eyes fixed on the coffee machine but not really seeing it, when it occurs to me that Josie the Great was right.

It really was one hell of a wedding night.

nineteen

SHANE

I'M A SCREWUP, and now I have to go to my best friend and tell him...what? That I slept with his sister and felt happy for the first time in who knows how long? That I married her because of a business opportunity?

That she confuses the hell out of me?

That I'm never going to be around her now without feeling a persistent need to sink into her?

Those aren't the kinds of things you can say to a man if you ever want to see him again without getting a fist to the face. But I do have to tell him something. And he needs to know his mother's been coming around. I owe him that much.

So I spend a few mostly sleepless hours in bed and then get dressed without showering. I can't bring myself to wash her off of me, not yet.

Ruthie said just once, and she was right—even though it's a travesty not to repeat something so mind-blowing, we can't. Because if we repeat it, it'll become a habit. There will be the compulsion to make it mean something. And that would create complications I can't even begin to imagine.

Which means I have to avoid seeing Ruthie as much as possible.

I don't put on a suit, because I remember Ruthie telling me she's barely seen me in anything else for years. Then I text Danny asking if I can come over. He says yes, and adds that Mira has requested pastries.

What is it about women and pastries?

So I stop by the grocery store to grab a similar haul to the one I brought over to Ruthie's a couple of weeks ago. My buddy with the zit problem is back.

"My man," he says when he sees me, making me grin. He offers his fist for a bump, and I give it to him. He takes in my bounty, then glances up, his eyes wide. "You're getting more. Does this mean it worked?"

Not in the way he's thinking, but I nod. "You treat a lady nicely, and things will work out better for you."

It's not necessarily true in my case, but it should have been.

As I watch him scan my purchases, I reflect that I told Ruthie some messed-up shit last night about Vanny, or at least I didn't phrase myself well. I've never been good at saying things gently, in the way people want to hear them. When I'm talking in front of a jury, I have a silver tongue, but I try not to treat the people I know well the same way I would a stranger I want to fool and trick. It slips out sometimes, of course, the way bad habits do.

Should I apologize again? Send her flowers?

But I throw both ideas out, because I don't want to send the wrong kind of message.

I want Ruthie again. I want her so badly, it's physically painful. But she's a woman who wants a real husband—or at least the fact that she got married once, on purpose, suggests as much. I can't give her that, and I don't want to fool either of us into thinking otherwise.

So I can't apologize with flowers, or in any way that will give both of us ideas.

But there's another way I can say sorry, one she won't ascribe to me.

"I'll remember the pastry thing," the kid says. "Anything else you can tell me?"

"Listen to what she has to say," I tell him. "I'm told that's important." I obviously need some improvement on that front, but that doesn't mean it's not good advice. Besides, the kid's already proven he's a better listener than I am.

I take the things and leave, making my way to Danny's building.

Mira buzzes me up, and I head upstairs, my mind buzzing with a thousand different thoughts and worries—and with the leftover high of my night with Ruthie.

Mira answers the door with an expectant look, then actually gives me a round of applause when I lift up the bag of pastries. Her hair is pulled back in a colorful bandana, and she's dressed in a fuzzy sweater that makes her look like she's gearing up for a trek through the tundra. The clapping gives me a good look at her hands. There's no ring on her finger, so I'm guessing Danny's still figuring out how he'd like to pop the question.

Now I'm going to have to tell him I technically beat him to the altar.

"Come on in," Mira says brightly. "You cracked the code. We only welcome people who come with acceptable offerings."

I step inside and shut the door behind me. "You're going to give me a bigger ego if you applaud me for something so simple. I'm told my ego doesn't need any help."

"You underestimate how much I hate being cold," she says, making a grab for the bag. I hand it over immediately. "My ankle still throbs like a motherfucker when it's cold."

She broke it several months back and only got her cast off a few weeks ago.

"Who said that to you, anyway?" she adds. "Was it Ruthie?"

The corners of my mouth tip up without any conscious effort on my part. "How'd you guess?"

"Danny told me about your *super* mysterious collaboration with her." Speaking of Danny, my buddy steps into view from the back of the apartment. He's wearing his reading glasses and has the squint-eyed look of someone who's already been on the computer for a couple of hours. "I told him you were—"

Danny gives her a significant glance, and she cuts herself off and mimes zipping her lips. He smiles slightly and shakes his head. "Nope, I don't believe you."

She shrugs, uncaring. "You probably shouldn't. You know I'm terrible at keeping my mouth shut. Anyway, who wants pastries? I'll make more coffee too. You can never have too much coffee."

"You did," Danny insists, wrapping an arm around her hips before releasing her.

"Yes, but I'm going to have more."

"I'll have some," I say. Because I'm working on maybe two hours of sleep. I felt a strange compulsion to stay awake at Ruthie's house, probably because I knew that if I fell asleep I might not wake up in time to leave. Or at least that's all I'm willing to admit to. It would be more disturbing to my peace to consider the possibility that I'd done it purposefully, so I could memorize the feeling of her curled up next to me, her hand on my chest.

"Thank you," Danny says with a grin at his girlfriend. "Otherwise Mira's going to drink it all, and she'll decide we have to go ice skating or something."

"Ice skating?" Mira repeats. She leans over and gives him a hug. "Look at you giving me great ideas."

"I fell into that," he says with a half-smile, but he doesn't seem at all sorry for it. That's interesting given that I've been ice skating with him before, and he hated everything about the experience, from the slickness of the ice to the way the skates fit his feet.

It strikes me, not for the first time, that he's a different man with her. More confident. More at peace.

I feel an uncomfortable wriggling sensation inside of me, because I'm going to have to break that peace.

Better to pull it off like a Band-Aid, advice I've always believed in but haven't always followed.

"Can we talk for a minute, bud?" I ask Danny.

"Aren't you talking now?" Mira asks, then laughs and waves a hand at my imagined objection. "I get it, you want to talk privately. I'm cool with that. Why don't you go out on the deck and sit near the space heater."

"Thanks." Danny leads the way, and I follow him, my heart thumping erratically in my chest.

He switches on the space heater, and we settle in the chairs we've occupied hundreds of times, maybe thousands.

The feeling of *I fucked up* is getting more powerful—a throbbing that overtakes even the euphoria of last night. Of the feeling of happiness it lit deep in my chest, in a place most things don't touch.

We're quiet for a moment, and then my friend turns to me, eyebrows raised. "I'm guessing you didn't come over here to ask me if I have a plan for the proposal yet."

"No," I admit, "but you can tell me if you want."

His mouth twitches. "I'm going to do it in the elevator, obviously."

Obvious, because he and Mira got stuck in an elevator together for two hours last fall, and are probably together because of it.

"Appropriate," I say with a laugh. "You going to arrange for it to stop too?"

"You're not the only one who can make things happen," he says, messing with the arm of his chair. "I told the building super, and he gave me the green light to use the stop button as long as we're the only two people on it. As if I'd propose in a full elevator." He angles his head. "So, what's up? I could tell something was on your mind the other afternoon, but I figured you'd tell me in your own time."

He had? That means my poker face is off, and if my poker face is fried, I'm fried with it. A lawyer is only as good as their ability to hide emotion—or at least that's what Myles told me. Given he's such a successful asshole, I have to imagine he was correct. Then again, I'm going to be defending a psychic and probably helping with some property deals, so I'm guessing it's unnecessary for me to be on my A-game immediately at Freeman & Daniels. Maybe the poker face is something I can reclaim, just like the dignity I lost in my old job.

Sighing, I force myself to sit upright and turn toward him. "This is about my collaboration with Ruthie."

He nods. "I figured it might be. She's been weird too, like when she's about to unfold a new business idea and isn't ready to tell anyone yet."

"Well..." I pause. "It's kind of a business idea." I think about launching into this by telling him that Ruthie lost her job at the diner, but it's a shitty tactic and I won't stoop to it. Maybe I would if we were in the courtroom, but we're not. I owe him more than that. "This isn't easy for me to say..."

But say it I do. I launch into a story about Freeman's misunderstanding, and how Ruthie wanted health insurance for Izzy. He's stone-faced through it all—as unreadable as the most hard-to-woo jurors, and I feel sweat beading on my hairline despite the cold.

"So you're getting married?" he says flatly.

This is where I really screwed up. I steel myself to tell the truth and nothing but—and accept all the pain it brings. "We already did. Yesterday."

We sit in silence for a few minutes, this time not at all comfortable, looking out at the view. Finally, he says, "I thought you didn't like Ruthie. The two of you have never seemed to get along, even when we were kids. You could barely handle being in the same room as each other. But Mira sees something different."

"What?" I ask, so taken aback, I nearly fall off the edge of the chair I'm sitting on.

"You should have told me the other day, at the ring shop. It's fucked up that you didn't say anything."

I feel like I have whiplash, but this obviously isn't the moment to interrogate him about what Mira thinks she's seen. "It is," I acknowledge. "I've felt bad about that."

"Not bad enough to be honest with me."

"That's true."

He finally turns to look at me, and I see the banked anger in his stare. Maybe he's not just pissed about this—maybe it's a hundred little things that I've done. How I'm the one who wanted to stop the weekly D&D games we'd had with our friends since middle school. How, before I quit my job, I'd pared back on the time we spent together, including our morning bike rides. The truth is, I don't understand why I did any of those things.

"You got my sister to lie for you."

I don't try to defend myself. He's right. I was desperate, and I did a desperate thing. I wasn't thinking about Danny or how he would react or whether it would destroy a friendship I had already undervalued. I was thinking about myself and my need to have some sort of meaning. To have a purpose that went beyond the mechanics of taking care of my body.

"I would have taken care of Izzy's operation," he continues. "I would have found a way."

I nod, but I can't help but add, "Ruthie wouldn't have let you. This way she feels like she's doing something for the money. She wouldn't have let you—or me—just give it to her."

He considers this for a moment, then gives me a tight nod. "You're still an asshole. If I'd known, I would've...I would've at least gone there to support her *and* you. You took that away from me." He doesn't look pissed anymore, but I can feel it radiating from him. I can see it in the way he's pulling splinters out of the arm of that chair. He probably doesn't even realize it, but later his fingers will be raw, maybe even bloody.

If only he knew...

Guilt claws at me. But I meant what I said to Ruthie. Even if Danny finds out, even if he is livid, it's hard to be sorry for that stolen night.

"I'm going to leave," I say, "but there's something else I need to tell you first."

I fill him in on the situation with his mom and the school and my plan to get a security system installed at the apartment.

He shakes his head. "I should have let her get put away for the Drunk and Disorderlies."

"They wouldn't have given her much jail time for that," I say. "I figure you bought yourself some time. Some goodwill. Ruthie says Rita has been leaving her voice messages for weeks or maybe months. This is her amping up her behavior. Ruthie's going to give her a call. Tell her to back down. I told her to make a police report, too, but you know they won't do much, particularly not since it's a family member. An old woman."

He swears and runs his hands through his hair. Sighing, he adds, "I'll call her too."

"I don't like that she said she wanted to introduce Izzy to some-one," I say. "Do you think she could have been talking about Rand?" I didn't mention that particular fear to Ruthie last night because I'd already done a good job of inciting rage in her.

But he's already shaking his head. "My mother doesn't know Rand. Not personally. Ruthie stopped talking to her way before she and Rand started dating. And he never would have struck up a friendship with my mother. Ruthie's family was a source of embar-rassment to him." He says this with no self-consciousness. His parents are a source of embarrassment to him too, of course, and he has no ego I've ever seen evidence of. He wouldn't have cared if Rand found him embarrassing, because he'd strongly disliked the tool even before I'd cautioned him. "If he wanted to see Izzy, he'd tell Ruthie directly, but he's never shown any interest. I doubt that's going to change. He got re-married last year to some eighteen-year-old debutante."

If anyone would know, it's him. Danny's good at finding information other people don't want him to, and I'm guessing Rand didn't see fit to hide that. He's probably proud.

"Fucker," I say, growling it out.

"You think the new wife knows he got a vasectomy?" he asks.

"The better question is how you know."

He gives a slight shrug, a smile on his lips.

"Did you perform it yourself?"

His lips hike up higher for a second, an almost laugh. "I wish. But my point is that it's not him. Maybe my dad's back in town, and he and my mom decided to give it another go. Or maybe she wants to bring Izzy to a church service or something." He runs a hand along his chin, thinking. "But you're right. I don't like it. I don't like any of it."

"If she doesn't back down, we can have Deacon check her out," I say, referencing the private investigator who used to work for Myles & Lee but quit after they took on the Burkes' case. Unlike me, he quit immediately. Because, unlike me, he put his integrity over personal gain.

Danny actually laughs at that, shaking his head as he looks out at the view and then at me. "Mira treats Deacon like he's her long-lost grandfather, but I think he probably should have retired ten years ago. He's an incompetent private investigator, and I think he's deaf in one ear. Last week I asked him if he wanted a beer, and he launched into a five-minute monologue about deer season."

"Huh," I say, because this is bad news. How many people have I recommended Deacon to? Enough that it's embarrassing.

"If my mother doesn't back off, I'll talk to Burke. He's not using Deacon anymore. I think he hired the couple he worked with last summer, the husband and wife team who helped him find evidence against his parents. They were tied up with some personal business for a while, I guess, but they're back in town, and they've already found some more dirt on the Burkes. Maybe we can hire them to keep an eye on Rita."

It feels like he just took a bat to me, because Burke didn't tell me any of that. In fact, I can't think of the last time I talked to Burke, one on one. Or hung out with our whole group of friends. Everything in me has been focused on finding a job—on recapturing my sense of purpose. But maybe the distance isn't only my doing. Maybe Burke hasn't totally forgiven me for how long it took me to quit Myles & Lee. Maybe he doesn't trust me, especially not with information about his parents and their case. Maybe he's not so certain I wouldn't go running to Fred Myles and prostrate myself at his feet, offering up information about these new private investigators.

Maybe he shouldn't trust you, a voice in my head suggests. *Maybe no one should.* It's Ruthie's voice, of course. I'm starting to think she's my conscience, and if so, maybe it's not the worst thing to ever happen to me. She's a powerful force, much bigger than Jiminy Cricket's dick.

"Okay." I nod, trying to sound like I'm not fazed by any of this. "What evidence have they found?"

His expression is almost pitying. "You'd know if you'd come last Saturday."

"Last Saturday?" I ask, the words ashen in my mouth. What did I miss last Saturday?

"All of us guys got together for a D&D game. You didn't answer any of our messages. I tried calling you, too."

And Danny hates calling people, always has.

Last Saturday was the day my mother's neighbor had called me to say she hadn't seen my mom leave the house for four days, and she was getting worried.

She wasn't getting worried of course—I'll bet she was hoping something 'interesting' would happen so she could tell all of her friends she was the one who'd noticed.

I run a hand over my face. "I'm sorry, man. I completely blanked. I didn't even see the messages." He knows about my mother's off-and-on depression, but I haven't told her she's slipping again. If I did, I'd feel like I was doing it to earn his sympathy and distract him from what I did. And seeing as he doesn't know the half of what I've done, it would feel wrong to let him offer his support.

At least this assures me that Burke didn't purposefully shut me out. But I have the sinking feeling that I've created a rift there nonetheless, much like I've finally done the job of creating one between myself and Danny. It's my job to fix things for people, but it's always easier to fix things for other people than to pull out the glue and look at the shards of your own life.

"You've been doing a lot of that lately," he says, but he doesn't sound pissed anymore. "But you got the job." He gives me a smile as if to acknowledge that we are both well aware that I didn't do it through my charm or capabilities. "So everything's going to be all right now, huh?"

"Yeah," I say, the word ringing hollowly in my ears. "I'm sure you're right."

"The guys and I will take you out for a drink next week," he adds, "to celebrate your new job."

Shock beats a tune in my ears. "But you're pissed at me."

"And I'll still be pissed next week," he says, giving me a look that guarantees it. "But I realize this wasn't entirely self-motivated. You wouldn't have gone through with it if you didn't want to help Ruthie with her insurance."

"Oh," I say, because it's the only thing I can think to say. I'd figured this might be it, the moment he'd finally tell me that I don't have the same blood pounding through my veins, so there's no reason for him to keep putting up with my bullshit. "I thought…"

I can't bring myself to say it. To lay open my chest like that.

"I know what you thought," he says, watching me now. Danny has trouble reading people sometimes, but he's never had trouble reading me. After my dad died, he was the only one who'd talk to me in the way I needed to be talked to. Other than my mom, he was the only who'd felt bothered to talk to me about it at all.

I feel choked up but don't want to let it show, so I just nod.

"Well, let's spread the good news," he says flatly, making it clear he's still upset and maybe will be for a while.

"You want to call the guys?" I ask, surprised. Then I nod, because he's right. If I feel left out, it's because I've cut myself out. There's a solution for that.

"Leonard can install the security system," he says.

I nod, and he sets up a group call on his phone. It's still early enough for a Saturday, but they all pick up. Burke, Leonard, and even Drew, our buddy who moved out to Puerto Rico with his fiancée.

"What's popping?" Leonard asks.

Danny turns to me with a half-smile. Wry as ever, he says, "There's no contest the great Shane Royce can bear to lose, so he got married before any of us."

twenty

RUTHIE

I TALKED to my mother this morning for the first time in years. She was unrepentant about sidling up to Izzy at school, because if I'd done my job as a parent and child, she wouldn't have needed to resort to such extreme measures. I asked her why she suddenly gave a shit, and she claimed that religion had opened her heart.

I don't buy it. Not from her. She wants something, and it's not selfless. So I told her to back down or else I'd involve the police.

Her response was, "What did I do wrong, Ruthie, for you to wind up like this?"

"Would you like me to text you a list?" I asked.

She bit into me for being a surly, ungrateful child. For siding with Danny and turning my back on family, for which the good lord would definitely smite me.

Leave it to my mother to mold the teachings of religion to best serve herself.

She said she'd stay away from Izzy but asked me to give serious thought to officially introducing them. I lied and said I'd think about it, and that was that.

Afterward, I asked Tank if he could grab coffee, because I suddenly felt a powerful need to get out of the house. He agreed, and we're here now, Tank sitting across from me at a table much too small for him. I've just told him the whole story about Shane—minus the sex—and he's watching me with the concern you'd show someone who's suddenly starts hearing voices.

This particular coffee shop thoughtfully added a little play area for young kids, so Izzy's coloring a unicorn at the kids' table, a small hot chocolate in front of her, while we discuss my poor life decisions. A couple of college-age girls at a table near us keep darting glances at Tank, like he's a fish they can reel in if they stare hard enough.

"You *married* him?" Tank asks, his voice gruff.

I have the inane urge to quote Charlotte Brontë—"Reader, I married him," but that probably wouldn't improve Tank's opinion of my sanity. It hits me that Shane is probably with my brother right now, spilling the news to him. Last night, our stolen night, was...

It was incredible, but today's like the morning after the kind of night out where you drink excessively and say "that's tomorrow's problem!"

Yeah, I've done that too.

"It's no big deal," I insist, messing with the top of my hot chocolate as if it—and not me—might be the problem. The sore throbbing between my legs and the cold jewel trapped beneath my shirt both insist I'm a liar. "It's a purely platonic, logical arrangement."

He gives me a look that sees more than I'd like. "That's bullshit, Ruth. You've known him your whole life and disliked him for most of it. Why would you give him this kind of power over you? You've always said he's manipulative. A jerk."

Despite myself, I lift a hand to the slight lump under my sweater, feeling the ring through the fabric. There's the strange urge to defend Shane, but I deny it.

"I didn't give him anything," I lie, thinking of last night, of the way Shane looked up at me after I tied his wrists together and how it felt to move on top of him. Like I really was a queen. But power is a give and take thing. Sometimes you're giving it away without even realizing until it's all trickled out of you, and you're empty of the ability to do anything but *survive*. Maybe Tank's right, and I've already started down that path. Maybe I'm a fool to think I can play a game with Shane Royce and win.

"I don't like this," Tank says with frustration, running a hand back through his hair—light brown and not long enough for a pony-tail but getting there. "If you needed help with insurance, you could have come to me. *I* would have married you."

"I know," I say softly. "And that's why I couldn't."

Because on the night Tank stayed over, he told me he was in love with me, complimented my muscular thighs, and then fell asleep in a drunken stupor on my couch.

I love Tank too, but I'm not in love with him. I wish I could be. He's a man any woman would be lucky to love—a man who opens doors and remembers birthdays, who wants to celebrate just because, and who always, always is concerned about other people's feelings. But I've always had a wild heart, one that doesn't know what's good for it. You can't bridle a heart like mine into submission, however much you try.

My friend may have slept that night away, drawn into it by the alcohol, but I spent every excruciating minute awake—attacking myself. Because if I were any kind of mother or friend, I'd find it in myself to fall in love with this man who wants so badly to take care of me and my daughter. This man who'd love us the way I've always dreamed of being loved. But my fool heart wouldn't listen, and I couldn't lie to him.

So I told him the truth in the morning: I love him, but not like *that*.

That was eight months ago now. I want him to move on—to find someone who'll deserve his sweet cinnamon roll of a heart. I worry that I'm selfish for still wanting him in my life. But he's stuck by me like the steadfast man he is, and I can't find it in myself to push him away for his own good.

He fidgets in his chair, his cheeks flushing slightly, because we're both thinking about the same thing. "I wouldn't have expected it to mean anything, Ruthie. I would have done it just to help."

"I know, and I accept too much of your help as it is. With Shane, it's just a financial arrangement. I don't feel like I'm taking advantage of him. And it's happening at a good time." I pause, then add, "Eden and Charlie are finally giving up the ghost."

His mouth scrunches to one side in sympathy, but he's obviously not surprised.

"You knew this would happen."

He shrugs. "I'd guessed, but maybe it's a good thing. No one was making much money there."

I can't deny that, but the thought of losing my safe space and my friends still puts a hole in my chest. I probably won't see Eden and Charlie much anymore, after they close Loving. They'll talk about staying in touch, the way co-workers always do before someone leaves a job, and maybe in the beginning they'll mean it. But as time passes they'll find other things to notice. Even if they do stay in touch, it won't be the same. It won't be like they're family anymore.

I guess it's the things you've never had that bring about the deepest kind of wanting.

I swallow it down like Izzy swallowing her vitamins and say, "I'm going to really throw myself into Vanny this time."

"Okay," he says, obviously humoring me. He *always* humors me. "But if you want to try something different, maybe you can come work at the shop with me. I'll get you a bandana and everything. Hell, we can go to one of the shops on Haywood and get you a 'Van Life' tattoo."

"What about your current assistant?" I ask, surprised.

"He sucks," he tells me with an easy smile. " I'll fire him and hire you, problem solved."

Only it wouldn't be problem solved for me. I don't want to work at an auto shop, and I especially don't want to work for Tank. He'd be doing it just for me, not because he thinks I'm particularly good at it. Maybe I'm stubborn, the way I've been told by everyone I know since birth, but that makes a difference to me. I also want to believe that I have the ability to stick with something and make it work.

I want Shane to be wrong about me, even if I have to admit he's right about the holes in my plan. There's the weather problem with Vanny's current iteration, but there must be a way around it. A collapsible tent? Space heaters? Jugs of hot chocolate?

I take a sip of my hot chocolate and find it delicious and warm. Maybe this coffee shop would be willing to partner with me. That could help me get around some of the food prep restrictions.

Shane could help you figure this out, a traitorous voice in my head suggests. *He offered, and he's good at talking things out.*

It's tempting, but the more alluring possibility is to do it all myself to prove that I can. To show him that I'm not some little girl with ideas too big for her, but a capable woman who can solve her own problems without his help, thank you very much. Why, I'll bet I could even solve *his* problems for him, and I'm tempted to try just on spite, and...

Tank's still looking at me, waiting for an answer about the job.

"No," I finally say, messing with the top of my cocoa cup again, my gaze lifting to Izzy. I have to smile as I watch her hand hover over a bin of overused markers, searching for the perfect color. She's like me—always trying to get it right—but at least she has me to assure her that it's okay to fail. Even if I don't think it's okay when *I* fail.

"Why'd I know you were going to say that?" Tank asks, still smiling, because I'm not sure he knows how *not* to smile. It's one of the things I love about him. He's like an angel perched on my shoulder, encouraging me with smiles and grins and candy. Shane's my devil, fanning my ambition and lust. I sigh, because the thought of Shane holding a devil's pitchfork makes me hot with need.

There's no denying I want him more now that I've had him—but I'll be stubborn about this. I decided one night was all we'd have, and I intend to stick to it. Nothing good can come of giving a single more drop of my power to Shane Royce.

"So," Tank adds, pausing to take a sip of his latte. "Do you have a registry for this fake marriage?"

"No," I say with a grin. "But if you decide to send a Kitchen-Aide mixer, I'm not going to return it."

"Add it to your wishlist," he says, grinning back. "Maybe your wishlist angel will send it."

"Is this your way of finally outing yourself as my benefactor?"

He lifts his hands, palms out. "It's not me. You know how I feel about ordering shit online."

That it's never how it looks in the pictures. He claims this is also why he will never online date, but I can't help but think I might have something to do with that. It's something else to feel guilty about it, and that's another list that's always getting longer.

When Izzy and I get back to the apartment, hand in hand, there's a welcoming party waiting on my stoop that consists of my brother, Mira, who's holding a potted poinsettia, and Danny's friend Leonard. Leonard has a plastic bag with him, weighted down by whatever's inside.

My eyes meet my brother's, and fierce emotion fills my chest. He knows. Or at least he knows something. I should have been the one to tell him, and shame coats me like a dirty sweatshirt.

"Mom," Izzy says, dancing in place. "Uncle Danny brought a party! Can I go give everyone hugs?"

"Yes, sweetheart," I say as I run a hand over her hair.

I let her skip over to them, my heart still pounding in my chest, my eyes on Danny, even as he catches my daughter in a one-armed hug.

Danny means so much to me...

He's my brother, but he's so much more. At one time, it felt like he was the only anchor holding me to this earth. Without him, I might have floated up into the air and gotten lost in the storm clouds forever.

I follow Izzy, who's moved on to Mira and is exclaiming over the poinsettia, and Danny wraps me into a tight hug. Leonard stands off to the side, giving us space, but if he's the slightest bit uncomfortable it doesn't show.

"I guess I should say congratulations," Danny says in my ear, his tone wry. "But I'll admit I'm a little hurt that Josie the Great got to be there and not me."

"I should have invited you." I pull away, feeling the crush of conflicting emotions in my chest. "I'm sorry. I hate disappointing you."

His mouth lifts a little. "Who said you're the one I'm disappointed in?"

Oh. *Oh.* To my shock, I feel the urge to defend Shane again.

"Is that why he's not here?"

"He said he was giving us some space to talk. I...I talked to our mother. I guess you'd already given her a call." His mouth tips into a smile. "She didn't seem pleased to hear from me."

"Or me," I admit. "But you don't have to be upset with Shane, Danny. It was my idea...the not telling you until after, I mean. I...I knew you'd want to pay..."

I feel Izzy watching me, her gaze curious, and I can practically *feel* Mrs. Longhorn with her eye pressed up against the glass, so I ask, "Can we talk about this later?"

"Of course."

I hear a door opening just as I turn to open my own door.

It's Mrs. Longhorn, of course. She's holding a little tote bag over her shoulder as if to signal she's going somewhere, but there's nothing inside of it. "Ah, there you are," she tells me. "I heard noise outside of your apartment last night. Four in the morning. I looked at my clock, and I said to myself, 'Nothing good happens at four in the morning, Ethel.'"

I could beg to differ, but my face feels like a heated brick. I can't possibly look at Izzy, because if I do, she might offer up the information that "Uncle Shane" was still around when she went to bed last night.

Leonard lifts the bag in his hand. "Then it's a good thing we're here to install a security camera and some bells and whistles. We'll make sure the rodents and perverts stay away, huh?"

"I had to bring the dog out," I mutter.

"Did you?" Mrs. Longhorn asks. The way she says it suggests she saw more than she's letting on. But why would she offer me an out? She must want something. I am honestly curious about what someone like Mrs. Longhorn could possibly want, but I have a feeling I'm not going to like it.

"Yes. She's still getting used to apartment living," I say.

"Did you also bring her out at five a.m.?" she asks.

Now I genuinely have no idea what she's talking about, and I say so. I was dead to the world at five a.m. Was someone actually out here, or did a couple of squirrels wake her up?

The possibility that it might have been a person sends a shiver down my spine, but at least she's proven she really is nosy enough to notice an intruder.

She turns from me with a sniff and returns to her apartment, the empty tote bag still over her shoulder. Standing in the doorway, she swivels to look at me again. "I should hope your camera won't be directed at my door. I *do* enjoy my privacy. But if you'd like to come over sometime this weekend, Ruthie, I can tell you a thing or two about training your mutt. I've had many dogs in my day."

I wouldn't be surprised if she stores their skeletons in a closet. I have less than zero desire to go to her apartment, but I nod because she's clearly waiting for me to.

The door shuts behind her, and I finish opening my door, feeling a buzzing in my ears. Shit. What if the whole apartment smells like sex? Izzy wouldn't have understood what it meant, earlier; *they* will.

But Flower has provided me with a good cover by peeing all over the carpet. I'm going to pretend that's because she understood the problem and not because she clearly isn't potty trained at three years old.

"Guess that four a.m. walkabout didn't do the trick, huh?" Leonard says, getting on his haunches to say hello to Flower.

Izzy joins him, wrapping her arms around her in a hug that can't possibly feel good for Flower, who wags her tail anyway. "Doesn't she have the cutest little face, Leonard?"

"That she does, Little Bit, that she does."

Danny helps me clean up, even though pee has always grossed him out, and I announce that Flower's going to spend the next couple of hours in my bedroom.

"I'm going to help Leonard with the security system," Danny says, having washed his hands for a second time. "But maybe we can go for a walk later."

Just him and me, I'm guessing. He'll want to talk about our mother. I'd prefer to continue pretending she doesn't exist, but I guess the problem is that she's remembered *I* exist.

"Can I stay?" Izzy asks, giving the front door a serious look. "I'm pretty sure I can help."

A glance passes between Danny and Mira, and she says brightly, "I'll come with you, Ruthie. You might need to keep the poinsettia in your room."

I glance around the apartment with new eyes, a visitor's eyes, and I can see why she'd think so. Every surface is covered with...

something. Izzy's art, or handouts they helpfully sent home from school that will go unread until I have a fit of guilt and spend two hours reading them all while downing a glass of wine. Books that I ordered for Vanny but haven't arranged inside yet. *Running a Business for Idiots*, which hasn't been as helpful as the title would suggest. Still, Danny and Mira have clearly decided she should try talking to me alone—because I might say to a future sister-in-law what I wouldn't to a brother.

Maybe they'd be right, except I already know Mira's personal filter is as effective as Swiss cheese. Annoyance pokes at me, because as much as I love my brother and Mira, I don't need them showing up and treating me like a kid in my own home, peeking into corners to make sure I haven't been up to no good.

Still, I find myself leading the way into my bedroom.

Mira shuts the door behind her, confirming that she's not here to discuss poinsettias, and sets the plant down on my dresser. It's reflected back at me in the mirror, and memories of last night shiver through me. I'll never be able to look at that mirror again without seeing Shane's reflection in it, probably.

The thought reminds me of the possibility of a sex smell, so I try to sniff the air without looking like I'm sniffing the air. I sprayed a little air freshener in here earlier, but there's still an underlayer of—

"The poinsettia was a ruse, obviously," Mira says.

"Does that mean I don't have to take care of it?" I ask. "Because there's a ninety percent chance it's going to die if you leave it here."

She grins at me. "This is why I like you. You're like me—you cut straight to the point."

"I hope it's not the only reason you like me."

"The fact that you keep a unicorn crown on your bedside table doesn't hurt." Her nostrils flare, and panic floods my system. "What's that sm—"

I grab a perfume bottle from the dresser and spray it in the air between us, as aggressive as one of the perfume ladies in a department store.

"DKNY Apple," I blurt.

She coughs, and rubs at her eyes. "Uh, nice. But that's not what I was talking about, I—"

Her gaze narrows as she studies the cheap crown on the bedside table.

Oh, shit. I see it too—a tiny piece of a metallic wrapper. Last night, there were condom wrappers strewn around the room like candy wrappers next to a pumpkin bucket after Halloween. I must have missed this piece.

She takes a step toward the table. Annoyance prickles my skin again, even though I know Mira better than to think she's capable of *not* invading my privacy right now.

I'm tempted to run past her and grab the partial wrapper, but that would be more of a tip-off than spraying her in the face with a bottle of old perfume. "Oh, yeah," I say, trying to play it cool. "I raided Izz's leftover stocking candy last night. Oops. You caught me. Please don't tell her, she'd be pissed."

And she'd also offer up the information that she finished her candy two weeks ago.

"Soooo...you thought it would be fun to wear a unicorn crown while you were eating your kid's old candy in bed?" Mira asks, pausing as she glances around the room. The bed was made hastily, and there are very obvious puckers from where my fingers balled the cover so hard they made indentations.

"Yeah. Yup," I say, avoiding the impulse to run my hand over the comforter. "When you put it that way, it sounds pathetic, but let me tell you, a good time was had."

"I believe that part, at least," she says, a smile playing on her lips.

Fuck. It's definitely not noon, but I really need a drink. Maybe two.

I shrug. "It's not that strange. I'll bet you do all kinds of weird shit when you're alone."

She gives me the look of a woman who knows a partial condom wrapper when she sees one. "Ruthie, I'm going to pretend I believe you stayed up until four in the morning with your dog, eating old candy and spritzing yourself with a bottle of perfume that had dust on it. Because I'm not going to tell Danny anything you're not ready for him to know." She gives a dramatic pause, watching for a reaction I struggle not to give. "But I want you to know that you're basically killing me right now. I mean it. You have no idea how much this is costing me."

"They were Twix bars," I blurt. "Twix bars are delicious. Anyone would have gone for them. I defy you to find a person who doesn't like Twix bars."

She lets out a small sound of amusement that doesn't quite reach laugh status. "Next time, presuming this exact scenario repeats itself, you might want to say they were 3 Musketeers. The wrapper's silver."

Dammit, she's right, but I don't want anyone to think I'm a person who salivates over 3 Musketeers bars. So I settle for not saying anything.

There's a twinkle in her eye as she says, "I have to admit I'm curious about how the unicorn crown figured into this."

"No comment." I swallow. "And you're making me a drink after this. A strong one."

"Will you tell me eventually?" She sweeps some hair that fell out of her bun behind her ear. "I'm not a person who can go around comfortably not knowing things."

"Presuming there were something to tell, I imagine I'd tell you eventually," I say, ignoring the little voice inside that suggests I sound as politic as a tie-wearing lawyer. I take a deep breath, trying to calm myself, and say, "Now, what did Danny want you to ask me?"

Her lips twitch. "He wanted me to make sure Shane didn't back you into anything. But I'm guessing the only thing he backed you into was a wall."

I have a visceral memory of crowding him into that wall. I swallow. "He *is* a bossy bastard."

Her eyebrows lift. "Good thing you like bossy bastards, huh?"

"Well, I don't like this one." But I can't say it with the usual conviction. "He thinks he knows better than everyone, especially better than me." There, that I can say without a quaver in my voice. I can even summon some righteous indignation.

She laughs and shakes her head slightly. "Well, I can believe that. All men think they know better. Even your brother."

She's got me there.

"Well, anyway," she continues. "There was no coercion, so..."

I cough. "No, nope. No coercion whatsoever."

She puts a hand on her hip and eyes the door. "You know, I doubt your mother is going to whimper and go away. I wouldn't be surprised if she just showed up on your doorstep someday. Or ours."

My heart instantly start thumping faster, because my gut tells me she's right. When my mother wants something, she won't stop until it's hers...or every possibility of getting it has been so thoroughly obliterated there's nothing left but dust falling through her fingers.

I haven't seen my mother in years. The last time was at a coffee shop, when I was seven months pregnant with Izzy. It wasn't planned, or at least not by me. My eyes were dull from crying, and I could barely register where I was, let alone why I was there. I was desperate. Tired. Lonely. And so deeply, deeply sad. I'd thought Rand would change his mind in the beginning...and then hated myself for wanting that. Because only a bad person would turn his back on his wife and child.

So when my mother approached me in the coffee shop, I agreed to bring my peppermint tea over to the table and sit with her.

"Rand left you," she said. "That's what happens when you reach for the sun, Ruthie. You get burned. Anyone could see that man was too good for you. A man like that was never going to stay with a girl who went to community college. No matter. You were smart to get pregnant. He'll be paying child support for eighteen years. You won't need to get a job."

When I told her that I'd had Rand sign papers forsaking his rights to Izzy, she'd called me stupid and shortsighted. A fool. She'd claimed I was taking something away from my daughter before she was even born. When I explained that I didn't want to risk that he'd ask for half custody just so he could pay me less, she said I *should* let Rand have her half the time—he had plenty of money to hire nannies.

I'd told her I wasn't taking parenting advice from someone who barely knew how to be a person, let alone a parent, and that was that.

"You may be right," I tell Mira through numb lips. I know what my mother would say if she found out about Shane—*you got your-self another big fish, Ruthie. Now what are you going to do about it?*

"Maybe it'll make you feel better to have it all out with her, you know?"

I swallow, then add, "I know you're the type of person who likes to face everything head on, Mira, but my mother is never going to understand what she did to Danny and me. She's never going to care."

"But *you* care," she says, giving me an uncharacteristically serious look. "Danny does. Maybe it's time to air your grievances and then shut that door forever."

It's the caring that pulls us all down in the end. If I didn't care so damn much, none of it would hurt the way it does. That's what I'm thinking when my phone buzzes. I pull it out, and it's an alert from my bank—a transfer of five hundred bucks. I sent Shane my bank info earlier, and he hasn't hesitated to make use of it. Another buzz, a message from him.

> Guess what? Leonard and Burke happened to have some extra equipment lying around, and Danny's going to set up the security system and monitor it. They're doing it for free, so I transferred the agreed-upon amount.

Well, will you look at that. He found a workaround. There's a reluctant smile on my face as I hustle Mira out of the bedroom, and I can feel that ring against my chest as if it's making an imprint on me.

twenty-one

SHANE

"DANIELS COULDN'T BELIEVE it when I told him you'd already brought in a client for the firm," Freeman says with a chuckle, clapping me on the back. "We're not used to that kind of hustle around here."

Obviously not, I think but don't say. The near-mythical Daniels is apparently still on some never-ending vacation. Then again, there really is an excellent benefits package.

I had a corner office at Myles & Lee, with plate glass windows overlooking the city, and I've been reduced to the windowless closet Freeman and I are standing in with my new assistant. It smells of mildew and my disappointed hopes. Michael's cubicle desk is outside—a dull setup with a potted poinsettia on one side that someone probably bought for Christmas and decided they'd rather not keep alive. The leaves are edged with brown.

Maybe he'll decide he doesn't prefer this place to the jewelry store after all. If he likes being surrounded by shiny things, he won't find much of that here.

I force a smile. "It's an....interesting case," I hedge. That much is true. It'll be easily resolved, at least. All we have to do is create a seed of doubt—and if the plaintiff's best buddy was interested in his wife before the wife ever met Josie? Well, there's your seed. Let it sprout.

Freeman gives me an indulgent grin that feels familiar yet not. Heartburn webs through my chest. I've felt off all weekend—as if the ground I'm standing on has turned to gelatin, and I'm the only one who's noticed.

At least Danny and Leonard got a security system installed at Ruthie's. According to Ruthie, the cameras have picked up nothing other than a couple of amorous squirrels.

That's been the limit of our interaction over the weekend. I asked about the cameras; she told me about the squirrels.

I wrote out a few other messages and deleted them without sending. I paced my apartment. I cleaned. I worked out. I checked on my mother. Through it all, there was a sense of unease, of something not quite being right. Of something *missing*.

I told myself it was ludicrous. I've gone months without seeing Ruthie. On a couple of occasions, a full year. It never felt like this... like I'd been hollowed out.

Still, we'd agreed to only one night.

So I've kept my distance, and she's kept hers.

Maybe it's good that we've stayed away from each other. I'm not sure I know how to forget the Ruthie from Friday night. The taste of her, the touch of her, the sound of my name when she moaned it—and surely she'd have something to say if I admitted *that*.

It's not my pussy you're hung up on, Shane, it's the sound of someone orgasming out your name.

She'd be wrong—it's both.

I get another back pat, then Freeman glances at my hand and beams. "I see you found your ring."

"Got a new one," I say, pleased that I don't have to lie. My mind flashes back to the ruby ring I laid on the pillow next to Ruthie. Awake, she's always flashing fire and trying to metaphorically—and sometimes literally—knee me in the balls. Asleep, she looked like an angel, her hair splayed out over the pillow.

Clearing my throat, I nod to Michael, whose bemusement doesn't show in his eyes. "That's where I found Michael. Best salesman I'd ever had. Turned out he was looking for a job."

"Oh, you don't say." Freeman seems so thrilled, he'd probably float right out of the window if there were one. "You know, I truly believe in fate."

If you ask me, it's no attitude for a lawyer to have—we should seek to control fate, not bow to its commands. But I nod as if he's said something brilliant.

He waves a hand around the depressing space. "Feel free to make it your own. And we encourage everyone to add photos of their loved ones to our family board in the conference room. We're all excited to see Ruthie on Friday evening," he adds, his smile indulgent. "Wendy is arranging a special experience for all of us."

I'll bet. If that candy bowl on her desk in the lobby is any indication we'll be sidling up to a buffet somewhere. "Wonderful," I say. "We can't wait."

"Do you have a dog? We have a pet appreciation day once a month. Wendy puts together little treat bundles for them."

I nearly asphyxiate on my own spit. At Myles & Lee we had a dart board with the DA's face on it. We took bets on whether the jury would swing someone's way. And, on one memorable occasion, a couple of the other attorneys and I got drunk at the office late at night and played pin the tail on the ass with a photo of Myles. But we were intelligent enough to destroy the evidence.

This is *not* Myles & Lee.

It's like the Disneyland of lawyers' offices—if Disneyland were beige and the candy handed out looked like it came from the discount bin or your grandmother's basement.

I clear my throat. "Thank you, sir," I say, which isn't an answer to anything. Although I could lay claim to Flower, who would surely enjoy the treats, I won't put Ruthie's and Izzy's photos out for anyone to see. It doesn't feel safe, which is a stupid thought, because I doubt anyone's going to take one look at them and turn stalker. Still, there's no denying the impulse. "Do you have any other cases for me to get started on? I'm a quick study."

He pats me on the back again. "No, no," Freeman says, "we believe in giving people time to get settled in. You said your client is coming in this morning?"

I nod, because Josie should be here soon. She called me yesterday to arrange it.

"Work on your new case and getting oriented to the office. More work will come."

I'm not sure what the fuck there is to get oriented with—he just gave me the grand tour—five offices, a cubicle farm, and a front desk where the office manager keeps her huge tub of candy. I'm guessing she doesn't only offer it up to children, because I've already had it lifted toward me three times.

"Thanks," I say, holding my hand out for a shake.

Freeman pumps it enthusiastically, then adds, "And thank you for getting all of your paperwork filled out for HR."

There is no HR—it's another hat worn by Wendy of the candy bowl, but I smile at him.

"Of course."

At Freeman & Daniels, coverage begins on the first day of the next month after employment. Tomorrow is February 1, so it begins tomorrow. Izzy can get her surgery. I'll be able to help her *and* ease Ruthie's mind, which is only fair, since she's helping me.

Thinking about that, I feel a swell of warmth. Hell, I feel down-right gracious toward Freeman, even though there's something about him that makes me uncomfortable. Maybe I just think someone this nice must be playing at something. That's what life has taught me to believe.

Freeman pats me on the back one final time, proceeds to pat

Michael on the back, and then heads for the door. He pauses in the frame and turns with a big grin.

Does the legal beagle ever frown? The ornery part of me would like to test the theory—and another part of me, the part that I buried nearly twenty years ago, doesn't ever want to find out. That's the side of me that likes Freeman and wants, begrudgingly, for him to like me.

"Say, everyone enjoys going to a psychic. Why don't you see if your client will come to the dinner on Friday evening and do a team-building exercise for us?"

"I don't believe she's known for giving...pleasant fortunes, sir."

"Oh, that's neither here nor there, son," he dismisses with a wave of his hand. "I'm not someone who likes getting smoke blown up my behind. It would help everyone unwind from the work week."

"I'll talk to her," I say, although I hope I can avoid doing any such thing. She's already infiltrated my life to an alarming degree.

He nods, smiles, and then leaves.

Neither Michael nor I say anything for a solid minute.

Finally, he gives me a pointed look and says, "I'm surprised you hired me. I could get you into trouble."

The fact that he is capable of both bullshitting and cutting directly to the point is one of the reasons I value him. I nod. "But we're going to work together, and I'd rather you knew the score going in." I give him a woeful smile. "Although if you've changed your mind, I won't hold it against you. This place is... It's like what you'd get if there were a lawyer's office in Candyland and people paid in licorice sticks."

He laughs. "I've got no problem with people being nice to me. It's a refreshing change."

"You don't think people can be too nice?" I ask, thinking of my conversation with Danny.

"I guess we're both about to find out." He shakes his head. It's obvious he thinks I'm crazy, and maybe he's onto something. I definitely have an attitude about this place—a chip on my shoulder about Freeman.

Michael lifts his eyebrows, two shades darker than his hair. "Did she like the ruby?"

"Look," I say. "You're going to meet Ruthie sooner or later, so I'm going to tell you right now that she doesn't know the ring is real. I'd prefer it if you weren't the one to tell her."

His eyebrows lift higher, like they have a mind to disappear into his hair. He gives a whistle, then says, "She thinks *that* stone is fake?"

His affront is real, and I have to laugh. "Not everyone's a gemologist. I'm guessing she hasn't given it a second thought because she wouldn't think I'd get a real ring for..." I shrug.

He studies me, his gaze shrewd. "So why did you? My old bosses would fillet me for saying so, but there are fakes that look the same. No one would question you, and you'd have saved yourself thousands."

I can't tell him what I don't know. The only explanation I have is that it seemed important for Ruthie to have a ring that was special and real. It's a dangerous thought about a dangerous woman, and I shrug it off. "She's helping me out. I figured she could keep it. Have something nice for herself."

He watches me for a second before saying, "There's not much you can do with an engagement ring if you're not engaged or married. If she hawks it, she'll get less than half its value." He angles his head. "But you'd know all of that."

I clear my throat, trying to ignore the way my skin is prickling. Like he's said something worthy of notice. "Why don't you go out there and figure out whether there's any coffee? Our client's going to be here in less than an hour, and I'm warning you right now, she'll make this place seem normal."

His gaze is almost pitying as he says, "Shane, with all due respect, I think it *is* normal."

~

Michael probably wants to take that back half an hour later, when Josie and her boyfriend are seated across from us in my cramped office. I have a notebook out, but I have yet to write anything down.

"You want us to get you off by proving you're psychic?" I ask incredulously.

"Well, she is," says the boyfriend. His name's Poe, although I'm not sure if that's the name he was given at birth or one he's bestowed on himself. "She knew you were going to get married, didn't she?"

"We're not supposed to talk about that," Josie says. It's a surprisingly cooperative thing to say, so I'm already on high alert when she shifts her gaze to meet mine. "But he's right. I *did* know that."

"I'm sure you tell dozens of people the same thing. For many of them it will be eventually correct—for a while."

"But I was right about the wedding night, too, wasn't I?" she asks, giving me a knowing look. I don't like that she's thinking about what happened between Ruthie and me. Sure, she was right, but maybe that wasn't so hard to predict either—there's always been an energy between us. A combustibility. Josie the Great is less psychic than she is observant. A useful skill, to be certain, but there's nothing supernatural about it.

I clear my throat, trying to bury the animosity I feel about her taking a shovel to my personal life. "Let's focus on the issue at hand."

Josie and her boyfriend exchange a glance that makes me want to break the desk in half, then Josie says, "You told me this case could get us some great publicity. You were right. Poe and I have decided this is our chance for a TV show. We're going to prove I'm psychic, and when we do, the offers are going to come rolling in. It's time to level up." She says this with complete confidence, as if thousands of other people haven't tried to prove they were psychic and failed.

"If it were possible to prove the supernatural, it would already have been done," I say flatly, resisting the very strong temptation to add, *by someone other than you.* "There's always another possible explanation. If anything, the people in the courtroom might think you've looked into their backgrounds. They might take it personally if you know things you shouldn't."

"Ah, but she doesn't need to prove anything," Poe says, leaning in. "She just needs to give the jury enough evidence for them to think there's reasonable doubt. We can put past clients on the stand."

Michael nods in his seat next to me, the traitor.

"Nevertheless, you can't make a mockery of the courtroom," I say slowly, trying to rein myself in. I feel like my fuse is being nipped shorter and shorter.

Poe heaves a sigh. "You're thinking too linearly."

"Good," I say, because fuck me, that's a compliment. "This is what we do—we prove the husband's friend was interested in the wife before she ever went to you. The jury would deliberate for less than five minutes."

Poe leans forward and props his elbows on the desk. "Look, man," he says. "I was like you once."

A laugh nearly escapes me, because I highly doubt it. His hair hasn't seen a pair of scissors in months, and he's wearing a flannel shirt over a band T-shirt.

Poe nods. "Yeah, I was. I worked at a place like this."

Well, that explains it.

"And your girlfriend here showed you the error of your ways?" I guess. I get a flash of Ruthie in my head, giving me her patented *you're being an asshole* look.

"She showed me that I'd placed artificial limits on what was possible. Most people do." He pauses, watching me, and I'll give him this—he has the timing down. Finally, he says, "You have to admit that her way could work."

I glance at Michael, who seems to be enjoying himself. Then again, he's used to pandering to fools out to waste their paycheck. This is at least something different.

"My third eye tells me this is what needs to happen," Josie says, finding my gaze and holding it. I can't deny I feel a little uncomfortable, but I'm not about to look away first. "And it also tells me you're going to get some big news today. When you do, maybe you'll change your mind about me."

"That's such a vague prediction, anything would fit it," I say flatly, unimpressed.

"It's news that'll interest all of your friends."

"Is it that I'm defending you? I've already told them. They've given me their condolences."

She shifts in her chair. "They all like me. I've been incredibly helpful to them."

"If you say so."

"Well, if that doesn't impress you, then how about this? Your wife and her daughter are going to move in with you next week. Her little dog too."

"Now I know you're full of—" *shit* almost comes out, but I hold myself back at the last moment. Still, she is full of it. I may be partial to that little dog, but I don't want her shitting in my shoes. Besides, it would never work. Sure, I'd thought about telling Ruthie that she and Izzy should come stay with me for a while, but that was before we fucked.

There's no way in hell I could stay under the same roof as her now. It would be...I'd feel like Tantalus with that fruit held just out of reach.

Josie lifts her eyebrows. "You wait and see. Both of my predictions are going to come to pass, lawyer man. Then you'll know."

I sigh. "I'll know that you're way more involved in my life than I'd like."

"You're working for her," Poe points out. "Not the other way around."

"That doesn't mean I have to let her build the defense for me," I say, annoyed. "Let me do my job. I do it well."

The dank room this firm has stuffed me in suggests otherwise, so I feel compelled to add, "I was made partner at thirty-three."

"Here?" Poe asks, glancing around at what is patently not a partner's office.

"No," I have to admit.

"The other place fire you?" he asks conversationally.

"He quit," Josie says, staring at me. "Because he has more integrity than he'd like to believe." She's staring me down again, and maybe this is her real talent, but I don't budge and I don't look away. "He was grateful to marry Ruthie because that meant he wasn't really lying to his boss." She pauses, staring some more, staring until my eyes start to water, and then adds, "You didn't want to really lie to Freeman, because he reminds you of *him*."

And suddenly I'm frozen in my chair as if pinned by a phantom weight on my chest, my breath coming in fast puffs.

"You can text or email me," she says. "We'll send you a list of witnesses. You can talk to them, see what you think."

Poe nods to her, and they rise from their chairs. Michael gives me a pointed glance, silently telling me to do what I know I must, but I can't seem to get up or even say anything. So he offers to escort them out. He's back what feels like seconds later. When he says my name, the ice is broken, and I shake my head as if waking from a dream.

"The boyfriend's right," Michael says. "I know I'm no lawyer, but I think this could work. It would definitely make headlines. Isn't that what you want?"

He's right, and he's wrong.

I want to make headlines, but not for winning a case by arguing that the defendant is psychic.

Still, this is the defense she wants, and I wouldn't put it past her to fire me in the courtroom if I attempt to do things my way. A public firing wouldn't be a great look for my first case at Freeman & Daniels, or my dying career.

Besides, Michael has a point—it would attract attention if I won this case using *that* argument. It would be a mark of a lawyer who's flexible enough to try something unconventional and good enough to pull it off. A lawyer like that could win *anything*.

I let out a sigh so deep it makes the pages in my notebook gust. "I guess we're doing it. Shit. Who would've thought?"

The corners of Michael's lips rise. "Her, maybe." He pauses. "What did she mean earlier, when she said Freeman reminds you of *him?*"

"I don't know what she meant," I say slowly. I don't intend to say more than that, but I find myself continuing anyway. Michael's easy to talk to. It's one of the reasons I hired him, so I can't resent him for that quality now. "But something clicked when she said that. He reminds me of my father."

He gives me a knowing look. "And your father's dead."

Is everyone around here psychic suddenly?

"Sorry," he says, flinching. "I shouldn't have said that. But you wouldn't have frozen in your chair like that if he were alive. We were trained at the jewelry store to look out for emotional tells. It's how you make a sale."

I'd been taught to look out for them too. And trained never to give them. I feel like I'm cracking at the seams. Like all the things I'm supposed to hide are seeping out of me.

My phone buzzes, and I check it so I can have a moment to collect myself. It's a message from Rachel, my old assistant from Myles & Lee.

The Burkes' trial date has been set for April 19th.

That's two and a half months from now. Add in a month for the trial, though it may well be less, and I'll be here at Freeman & Daniels for at least three and half to four months.

I guess the Burkes and I are both facing down sentences.

Still, I don't feel horrified by the prospect of being married to Ruthie for that long. If anything, it's a relief. That should give her plenty of time to schedule Izzy's surgery.

Then it hits me.

Motherfucker, I really *did* get big news this afternoon.

RUTHIE

CONVERSATION WITH SHANE

We're meeting for the work thing on Friday night. Seven o'clock. You should come to my house beforehand.

No, thanks. I'll meet you there. Just tell me where it's being held.

I was being polite. I need you to come to my house first.

You, polite?

I know, right? It surprised me too.

Are you trying to seduce me? Because I meant what I said. One night was all you get.

Yes, I understood you perfectly. It would look strange if we showed up separately.

So why don't you come here?

Your apartment has associations for me now.

Wear the ring.

Yes, sir. (She says with sarcasm.)

That's yes, lord and master to you.

Yes, Princess Peach.

CONVERSATION WITH MIRA

Are we still pretending that you were eating
Christmas candy you stole from your child the
other night?

I'm just saying…it would make you seem like less
of a loser if you were actually banging a hot guy in
a suit.

You know, speaking hypothetically.

Candy's delicious. There's a reason children go
feral for it.

Sighhhhh. Still pretending. Don't worry, I'll check
in with you every day for the rest of your life.

I'VE BARELY HEARD from Shane, except for his texts about Friday night and also the insurance.

This distance from him is what I wanted, so it's ridiculous of me to be disappointed. At the same time, I can't forget what it felt like to tie his hands together and take him. Or watch him in that mirror while he made me come with his mouth, the muscles in back flexing as he added his fingers to the game. Or...

Or what it felt like to fall asleep in his arms, his familiar scent hanging around me like that unicorn safety blanket that was lost to me all those years ago. The thing that was so precious to me is probably sitting in a landfill somewhere, wrapped around someone else's plastic baby doll.

Of course, there's nothing about Shane that's safe—and as each day passes, I build my walls higher.

Friday will be a performance, a show, but he'll probably want to touch me so he can come off as a doting husband, and if I don't have a spine of steel and walls of brick, I might do something I'll regret.

So I remind myself of all the things I dislike about him. I repeat them in my head like a mantra. *Shane is vain. Shane is condescending. Shane doesn't believe in me.*

It's that last one that leaves scores in my flesh. Shane sees me as a quitter, someone who can't stick the landing and doesn't really try. Someone who has ideas but lacks drive, which is clearly a quality he holds in the highest regard.

I shouldn't care what he thinks, but I want him to grovel at my feet. To tell me that I am what I'd like to be: a strong, independent woman who doesn't have any use for a man except in bed.

I work at the diner on Monday and Tuesday, but there aren't many customers beyond Ralph of the too-hot or too-cold coffee, and I don't like the thought that Eden and Charlie might only be keeping it open for me. So before I leave on Tuesday, I sit Eden down for some of Charlie's subpar sweet tea and a serious talk. She admits they're on the verge of running at a loss and would prefer to close sooner than later. "But baby, I want to do it with a bang, not a whimper." She tells me to spend the rest of this week and all of next working on Vanny and my eBay hustle, but next Sunday we're going to have a closeout party that will make the angels weep. Her words.

"But are you really sure?" I ask. "Should we be trying to do something to save the diner, instead? I can start a petition or maybe try to go viral on social media."

She shakes her head. "No, our days of service are over. Let someone else step up and give Ralph his cold coffee."

"But Eden," I say, the tremble in my voice giving me away as I soak in the cheap plastic tables, cracked booth upholstery, and crappy overhead lighting, "this place means so much to so many people."

"It means so much to *us*, you mean. To you and me and Charlie, and it'll be with us just the same after it closes, because the important things aren't enclosed by brick and mortar, my girl."

But her words don't totally soothe me. When I don't respond, she hugs me tightly and says, "Now, I know what you're thinking because I know you, but I meant what I said. You're not going to get rid of us. I'm going to be seeing you, Ruthie, whether you're working here or not. You're family."

"Thank you" is all I manage to get out, but the words feel insufficient. I'm not sure any words would do the job, actually. I worked here back when business was brisker, before I met Rand. It was my placeholder job, the one that brought in steady money while I tried to figure out my big idea, but he'd convinced me to quit. To stop looking for any ideas other than to be his wife. I came back after I left him, and Eden took one look at me and wrapped her arms around me. She said, "You came to the right place," and she's spent the past five or so years showing me how true that is.

I feel my eyes well with tears, because I love her. Because I hate that this place is going to become something else soon. Probably the city's eight hundredth CBD store, or a shop selling Keep Asheville Weird bumper stickers.

Then Eden grabs my face, her thumbs soothing down my cheeks. "You listen good. You're going to talk the hell out of Vanny at this party we're having. You're going to make damn sure everyone knows your name and what you're up to. That's why we're doing it."

"I love you, Eden," I manage to say, which is at least better than "thank you."

"I love you too, baby girl. Now scram."

She's wearing her serious face, so I listen.

I do a pretty admirable job of pretending I'm not going to bawl, right up until I sit down in the driver's seat of my car and start bawling. It doesn't feel fair that Eden isn't my mother, but at least I have her anyway.

I spend the next day helping Eden get word out about the party, and then I pour myself into preparing a hard sell for Vanny.

I get a couple of space heaters and make a list of other things I'll need to acquire over the next week: collapsible and moveable book cases, plus a collapsible table. I already have a few beanbag chairs that I can add to the ones I've been stowing in the van.

Once I have everything, I can move Vanny events inside.

There's something else that asshole Shane was right about: one-time payouts from the venues aren't going to be enough to finance my business. I need other sources of income. I decide not to put all of the books for sale, but I make book bundles and price them out. The work is done on the dining room table, where Izzy does her crafting, and a few of her works in progress fire up another idea. I can put together book-making kits too—and even lead a class on how to do it.

Then I contact the coffee shop Tank and I met at the other day and ask about stocking their hot chocolate. They're all about the idea. Better yet, the manager tells me he wants to have me hold an event at the coffee shop, so long as Danny is now fully mobile.

I make another phone call, this time to Dog is Love. After discussing the ins and outs of potty training an older dog, Dusty and I get down to business. He seems excited about the possibility of creating a joint logo we can plaster over merch, especially when I assure him a percentage of the proceeds would go back to the shelter.

I'm proud of myself. I feel strong. I feel capable. I feel like I could kick Shane Royce's ass.

I want to tell him about everything I've done, and I dislike myself for caring so much.

There's been no more trouble with my mother, other than a rambling voice message she left on my phone. She says she got the message "loud and clear" from both me and Danny. She's going to keep her distance, but there *is* something she needs to talk to me about first. Something important she should have mentioned on the phone but didn't.

No thanks.

She's trying to reel me back in, same as always.

Then there's Mrs. Longhorn. I've done a pretty decent job of avoiding her, if I do say so myself, but I know it's only a matter of time before she catches me at a weak moment.

On Friday, I drop Izzy off at Danny and Mira's apartment for a sleepover, along with Flower the dog, who takes up residence next to their hamster's cage and starts barking at it. From the way she's going at it, I expect it'll go on for some time.

"Is this okay?" I ask my brother, who's scratching his head as he watches them.

"What? You think she's going to eat him?" he asks. "I honestly wouldn't mind that much, but Mira might be upset."

"Uncle Danny!" Izzy shriek-laughs, and I don't miss his wince. He loves Izzy, but the joyful screams of a child, mixed with the persistent barking of a dog, is enough to drive anyone up a wall. How much worse must it be for someone with sensory sensitivities?

Mira shows up with his noise-cancelling earphones a few seconds later without being asked.

He smiles as he takes them. "I knew I loved you for a reason."

"Yes, we've established there are hundreds of them," she says, giving him a quick kiss.

God, I'm so happy for them. But there's also a feeling of...well, I guess it must be jealousy.

"We'll be fine here," Mira assures me, then gives me a hip check. "Well, don't you look like a hot little piece?"

I roll my eyes. "I'm wearing a coat."

"But it's a *new* coat." She's right about that. I was embarrassed of my dirty stuffed-animal-esque coat, so I added a coat to my wishlist.

It wasn't expensive or anything, but I still felt guilty when it showed up on my doorstep two days later. Guilty and a little euphoric.

Mira waggles her eyebrows. "Let me guess, you're going to have another candy fest later?"

I frown at her. She gives the shrug of a woman who's waited too long for a scoop.

"When did you have candy, Mom?" Izzy asks, her eyes fixed on me. "You've always said you don't like the way it feels on your teeth."

"I don't," I say, bending to kiss her forehead. "But sometimes any sugar will do."

Mira waggles her eyebrows. Thank God Danny's busy watching the dog-and-hamster show, but honestly, she's becoming a liability.

"Okay," Izzy says, "but I'm disappointed that you ate it without me. We'll talk about it later, though. Say hi to Uncle Shane. I'll see you in the morning." She gives me a kiss and then skips down the hallway.

I hold back the requisite, *he's not your uncle*.

"Let me walk you out," Danny offers. I'm hoping it's just because he wants an excuse to leave for a few minutes. He still hasn't put on the headphones, and Flower is letting her presence be known.

"Okay," I agree.

When the door closes behind us, I give him a look. "I see Mira's not wearing her ring yet."

He gives me a half-smile. "It's not enough for one of us to be married?"

"Oh," I say, feeling a solar-plexus punch of guilt. "You're waiting because of me."

He takes a step toward the stairs, and I follow him.

"It's not because of you," he reassures me. "Mira's planning a

Valentine's Day party at her bar. She gets wound up when she has an event coming up, so I figured it would be better to wait."

"Oh, that sounds like fun."

He gives me a wry look as we reach the top of the stairs. "If you say so. She gave me the green light to skip it. We're going for a hike the next day to celebrate." He watches me for a second. "Why don't you go to the party, Ruthie? Izzy can stay here with me. You don't do enough for yourself. Maybe Tank could come."

"I'll think about it," I tell him, a lump in my throat. Because Tank isn't the person I'd like to go with, even if he should be. I don't let myself acknowledge who I'd really like to go with. "I should leave."

He nods, then adjusts his glasses. "Say hi to your husband for me, huh?"

I shove his shoulder. "Very funny."

"You look beautiful, Ruthie." He smiles at me, his eyes filled with warmth, and that lump lodges itself in my throat.

"Danny, am I quitter?" I ask, the question coming from nowhere, or at least it feels like it is. Maybe it's been eating away at me since Shane and I faced off last Friday.

"What makes you say that?" he asks, frowning. Then his expression hardens. "Did Shane say that to you?"

He sounds seriously pissed, and I can't let that stand. Even though Shane is the person who made me question myself and my approach to the bookmobile, I've realized I *needed* to question myself. I was throwing my efforts at a wall, waiting for it to break, rather than trying to build a door. He opened my eyes, even if I didn't like hearing what he had to say or how he chose to say it.

"No, it's just something I've been thinking about."

He smiles at me and places a hand on my shoulder, steadying me the same way he's always done. "Ruthie, I'm going to tell you something you've told me often enough. You need to stop getting in your own way. You have what it takes. You've *always* had what it takes. You just need to believe in yourself like I believe in you."

"Mom thought Rand was too good for me."

"And she pickled her brain long before you came along," he says, his tone harsh. "If you believe her about that, then do you believe all the sweet things she and our father had to say about me? Do you think there's something wrong with me for being the way I am?"

"No, of course not," I say, my hand lifting to my chest. I find myself holding the ring, something I've done a few times this week. I release it like it's a burning coal.

"So why the hell would you believe anything she has to say about you?"

"Because I'm not good at finishing things," I tell him, feeling tears prickling. "I always feel like I'm barely getting by. Maybe I'm a leech. One of those people who feeds off of more successful people, you know?"

I think of the wishlist gifts. Of the dress from Eden. Of Tank fixing Vanny.

Of Shane giving me the ring...

Danny puts his hands on my arms and looks me in the eye. Sustained eye contact usually makes him uncomfortable, but he doesn't look away. "You stop that. You're a wonderful mother and person, and if you can't see all of the things you give everyone around you, then you need to know that *I* see them. So do other people. I'm lucky you're my sister."

Tears well in my eyes and start falling. "Not as lucky as I am that you're my brother," I say, wrapping my arms around him. He hugs me back hard, because he can probably tell that I need it. I thank him. I hug him. I tell him again that I love him and am so damn lucky to have him in my life.

Still, that lump stays firmly lodged in my throat all the way to Shane's house, which I've never visited before. What an odd thing, to be married to a man whose house you've never been inside. It's blue and tidy, and the clapboard shutters are painted a bright white.

I sit in the driveway for half a minute, thinking, wondering if I should just drive off. But if I leave, I'll be guilty of what Shane accused me of the other day. I'll be a quitter. Someone who's *afraid*.

The truth is, I *am* afraid. My hands are trembling, and my heart is beating faster than it should. Last week, I felt confident that I could sleep with him and shake off any feelings it might create, but that was foolish. Because here I am, afraid to go inside. Afraid of how it will feel at the restaurant when he slips an arm around my waist and acts casually fond toward me.

This is pretend, I remind myself. *It's not real.*

But my heart beats even faster as I take the ring off the chain around my neck and slip it onto my finger. Then I take a deep breath and get out of the car.

Shane meets me at the front door of the house. He's wearing a suit, because *of course*, and the green tie I wove around his hands the other night. His eyes take me in, dilating a little as they move down my new coat to the bottom half of my dress and then up again. His jaw works, and I know he's not immune to me.

Heat pumps between my legs, because I have a visceral memory of how that tie felt against my hand, of how heady it was to have my way with him. To sink down onto his big, deliciously thick cock while I was holding his wrists.

There is something deeply wrong with me—and him, I guess, because he looked at his collection of dozens of ties this morning and decided to put this one on.

"Is that tie your version of my bootie shorts?" I ask, cocking my brow.

He smiles. "Good to see you too, kid. You got a new coat."

Talk about mixed messages.

He's wearing that tie, but he's gone back to calling me kid, a nickname he admitted he used to keep me at a distance. He insisted on having a security system installed in my apartment but has barely been in touch all week. I probably shouldn't be surprised we're still playing a game. This is what we do—we play with each other the way a cat toys with its prey.

He tries to step forward, to leave the house and keep me from entering, and my stubbornness kicks into high gear. I'm going into that house. He's been in my apartment, after all. It's only fair.

"Aren't you going to invite me inside?" I ask as I duck under his arm and enter the foyer. It's small and compact, but it must be the tidiest house in Asheville, not that I expected anything different. In the front room, there's a leather futon on the wall next to the door, along with an oversized coffee table with nothing on it. Seriously, nothing, not even a coaster. Across the room, a flat-screen TV is anchored to the wall. There are a couple of uncomfortable looking armchairs, and the whole place has the look of being unused. As if Shane had wondered into a model house and decided to stick around.

I'm not surprised, really—Danny told me he used to practically live at his office, and here's the evidence. It's a house that's barely been lived in by a man who doesn't want a home. I should remember that.

He follows me in, sighing, like my expectation for him to fulfill this basic piece of social decency is unacceptable.

"I'd like a tour, I think," I say.

He dips his head to look at his watch. "We're going to be late."

"I arrived exactly when you asked me to," I say loftily. "If you didn't schedule in time for a tour, then that's your own rudeness biting you in the ass."

He grumbles something, then says, "This is the living room."

I walk around, mostly to annoy him by eating into his schedule, and take note of the lack of decoration on the walls—other than a framed photo of him and the partners from Myles & Lee.

I give him a pointed glance. "You kept that up?"

He swallows, and my eyes follow the motion, taking in the expanse of his throat and the spot where his green tie begins its journey downward. I feel a swell of pure lust that makes my knees wobble.

"My mother had it framed for me."

My eyebrows wing up, because I get what he's not saying. "You haven't told her you got canned?"

"It's not a good time for that," he insists, looking out the front window, like he'd magically transport us into a car if he could.

"But you'd be able to tell her you have a new job. You don't think Freeman's worthy?" I ask, taking offense for the older man. True, I hardly know Mr. Freeman and I *am* hoodwinking him at Shane's request. But he struck me as a very nice, very genuine person, so I at least have the courtesy to feel bad about it. "I guess you're already planning your next move now that you know the Burkes' trial date."

My brother told me about that, not Shane.

He shakes his head, and annoyance flashes in his eyes. I can tell he's pissed, *genuinely* pissed. "You're always determined to think the worst of me, huh? Nothing I do is with good intentions. Everything is to benefit myself."

"Are you saying you *don't* think you're too good for Freeman?"

"That's not why I didn't tell my mother about the job."

I notice he didn't answer my question, for what are probably obvious reasons, but that's not what I latch on to. "So why didn't you?"

He flexes his hand, then says, "That's her business. She wouldn't want me talking about it."

"Have you told Danny what's going on?" I ask, taken aback.

His eyes meet mine and hold. "No, but he probably wouldn't be surprised." He watches me for another moment, his gaze rising a flush to my skin, and then says, "Can we please just go? There's no way in hell I'm going to show you my bedroom right now."

He says the word in a rumbled growl that shakes me. As if he's barely holding himself back from carrying me in there over his shoulder. My whole body is begging for him to do it. To make me *feel*, the way he did the other night.

But, to my surprise, I want him to open up to me even more. Maybe I'm the vain one to think I could succeed where so many others have failed. I'm foolish to even want to—I've called him vain and conceited a thousand times and meant it. Why would I want a man like that?

"When did your dad—"

"Let's go. I'm driving." He surprises me by reaching for my hand. I give it to him, nearly gasping as it engulfs mine—his grip warm and firm and overwhelming.

When I feel his fingers run over the fake red ring, that gasp does escape me. There's something possessive about the gesture, like he's leaning in toward my ear and whispering, "*Mine.*"

"You didn't show me the kitchen," I object. "The second bedroom."

"Josie told me you're moving in here next week. I'm guessing you'll have another chance to see it."

"Excuse me?" I say, putting my free hand on my hip.

"I didn't say I believed her," he tells me, but there's no hint of a smile on his mouth, wry or otherwise. Having me here has made him uncomfortable, which perversely makes me want to stay.

"I need to use the bathroom."

"I don't keep any prescriptions in there," he says, finally giving me a flicker of a smile. "I regret to inform you that you'll find minimal information from going through my trash."

"What about Rogaine? Are you secretly going bald, Vain?"

"Not yet, but if you really move in, the stress will get to me eventually." The smile is almost fully there now, and I feel a sense of victory for having pulled it from him. No, more than that. I'm glad for it. I wanted him to smile for his sake, which is a worrying development.

"Well?" I say, angling my head.

He waves a hand down the hall. "You're welcome to go smell my shampoo."

"Very funny." I don't really have to use the bathroom, but I go anyway. And I do look around, as if some secret inch of this place will contain the key to fully understanding Shane Royce. I'm surprised by how much I want to find it. But it's a blank slate, even more so than the living room, which at least had that framed photograph as a clue.

So Shane has a weak spot for his mother and an aversion to talking about his father. Duly noted. It's nice to know he has a weak spot at all. Most of the time, I go around feeling like I'm a collection of them, and he comes off as someone who's invincible and knows it.

Again, I have that desire to know him. It's a strange feeling to have toward someone I have, in some way or another, known for most of my life.

twenty-three

SHANE

SITTING in my car next to Ruthie, stuck within a couple of feet of her, is an exercise in self-restraint. I knew it was going to be hard to see her again without begging for a repeat, but I told myself it wouldn't be this hard. It turns out my imagination was lacking again, because my hands seem to keep reaching out for her, wanting to touch her hand, brush against her coat, pinch her ass.

At least I had enough presence of mind to hold back from doing that last thing. I tell myself that part of her power over me is the dress she's wearing. Her coat might cover most of it, but it's her new coat, not the dirty puffer, and I can see enough that my imagination very gamely fills in the rest.

It's a sexy red dress with a thigh slit. She knows her legs are fabulous and brings attention to them—a confidence that's as much of a turn-on as the flash of leg covered in sheer black stockings. They're the kind with the little line up the back. I could stare at Ruthie in those stockings for hours, but I'd prefer to take them off her, to watch the translucent material side down her legs.

I'm in trouble. More so because it's not just sex that I want. After my meeting with Josie, I wanted to call Ruthie and tell her more than I should, because I figured the situation would amuse her. Then I got drinks with the guys on Wednesday and finally had a long talk with Burke, who should resent me but doesn't, and I wanted to tell her about that too. Because I really don't deserve my friends, and she was right to think so. I also wanted to ask about her conversation with her mother and, more distressingly, I wanted to hold her hand while she told me about it. I don't understand what's happening to me, other than that I broke my rule, my most important rule, and now I'm living in the fallout.

I desire my wife...and I also care about her.

I try to swallow the thoughts, but they're in no mood to cooperate.

"Soooo," she says, "Josie the Great, huh? How's that going?"

I don't want to talk about Josie the Great right now. I'd prefer never to talk about Josie the Great again, but the subject has one advantage: I'm much less likely to get hard while sitting in traffic if we're discussing the case.

"She wants me to make the argument that she's actually psychic," I say, giving her a quick look. It's dark, but I can see the outline of her face, the glitter of her eyes in dusk. Her lips are a pop of color. "You want to go on the stand?" I tease. "You're a big fan of hers."

"Are you really doing it?" she asks, ignoring my comment. I can tell she's laughing at me, even though she hasn't let out the sound.

"Yes, she has me in a corner," I admit. "Freeman's taken a shine to her. She bumped into him when she was leaving the office and told him he had purple energy. They both seemed pretty pleased about that, so apparently it's a good thing. I'll give Freeman this, he thinks there are less risky stances we could take in the trial, but he's going to let me do what I think is best."

"Which in this case is what she thinks is best."

"Precisely. So we're all screwed." I give her another side-eye glance. "She's coming tonight. He wants her to give readings for everyone."

Ruthie flinches, lifting her fingers to her painted lips. I understand the impulse—I'd like to touch them too. I'd like to suck them, bite them, and I'd *really* like to see them wrapped around my cock.

"What if she gives us away tonight?" she asks, her fingers moving back and forth.

I train my eyes out of the windshield and tell myself it's because I need to keep us safe, not because I'm too weak to look at her right now without touching. "Like I said, she has me in a corner. She might be full of shit, but she's not stupid. She's observant. If she gives us away, I'd lose my job, and she'd lose her hold over me. There'd be no benefit to her."

"But she could ask Freeman to represent her," Ruthie argues, then pauses and laughs. "You don't think she'll do it because you think you're better than Freeman."

I stop at a stoplight and steal a glance. She's smudged her lipstick a little, but maybe the people in the party will assume I've done it. I like the thought. I *want* them to think she's mine.

She's not yours, and you don't want her.

If I repeat it more, it could start sounding true. I do that sometimes before a trial. *He's innocent. He's innocent. He's innocent.* Because if you don't believe it, the jury won't either.

"I didn't say I was a better man, Ruthie. But a better lawyer, yes."

She rolls her eyes.

"How's Izzy?" I ask. "Is Goldie still insulting her Polly Pockets? I mean, honestly, with a name like that it's pretty rich of her to be insulting anyone."

Her mouth gapes open as the light changes and I start cruising again. "You remembered all of that?"

"Why wouldn't I? When people are important to me, I remember the things they say."

I'm prepared for her to make a comment about all the people I deem forgettable, but she's quiet for a moment, then says, "No more

Polly Pocket-related incidents. No more sightings of her grand-mother either. I guess hearing from both me and Danny helped. For now."

"That's good," I say, although I already knew that. I've asked Danny to keep me updated. If their mother pulls any other shit, we're agreed we'll talk to that private investigator couple Burke knows. There'll be no dicking around with Ruthie's and Izzy's safety on the line.

I pull into the restaurant and park but make no move to get out.

"Huh, I've never been to this place," she says, peering out of her window. "It looks *fan*-cy."

I sigh, then straighten my perfectly straight tie. Is she suffering the way I am? It occurs to me that I'm never going to be able to make it through the night unless we set some boundaries. For years, Rule Number One made it possible for me to keep Ruthie at a distance. Maybe that strategy will work for me again tonight.

"Look," I say, clearing my throat. "We should probably establish some ground rules before we go in."

She turns in her seat, watching me with the bright eyes of a predator. "Are you going to want to touch my ass, Vain?"

I resist the urge to swallow but cannot resist the urge to lean closer. It's cold, even in the car, but sweat is beading on my brow. My skin is crying out for her—a touch, a kiss, a—

"No, Ruthie," I say dryly, my gaze catching on a curl that's tumbled into her face. "I don't want to grope your ass in front of my boss." I give in to the temptation to tuck her hair behind her ear. Tugging in a ragged breath, I say, "But I may hold your hand."

"Or kiss me?" she asks, an anticipation in her voice that isn't helping with the sweat situation. She shuffles in her seat, her arm pressing against mine, and I lean in without intending to.

"Maybe," I say, my voice husky to my own ears. "A husband would kiss his wife. Chastely."

"What would a chaste kiss be like?" she asks, her eyes holding mine. "A depraved woman like me has no idea what chastity means. You might have to show me."

"That won't be easy," I admit, swallowing.

"You pride yourself on you mansplaining ability. I'll bet you can figure it out."

It's the only invitation I'm liable to get from her. I lean in and kiss her softly on the lips. My lips want to linger, to pillage, to *take*, but I leave it as a soft press. A tease. Maybe it's also a question. The tie, I realize, was its own question. *I'm feeling things I shouldn't, how about you?*

Her eyes flutter open, and her face stays where it is—inches from mine, so close I could count the freckles across the bridge of her nose. My heartrate accelerates, but then she pulls back, taking my ability to count with her.

"Let's go," she says.

But I don't move, and neither does she. I take her hand and trace the fingers slowly, feeling the energy snapping between us, demanding we do something about it.

"I've been thinking about you," I admit, because I can't help it. Because that simple, stark truth is exerting itself.

Her eyes widen, but she doesn't pull away. Her gaze holds mine in a challenge. "It hasn't seemed like it."

She doesn't sound upset about it, necessarily, but suddenly I feel like a prick. I told myself I was giving her what she wanted, but I basically ran. In truth, I've done that with a lot of women. In the past, I've told myself it's no big deal—set the expectation, and when you stick to it, you're just being honest. No one could fault a guy for being honest. But it's different with Ruthie. Ruthie is...*Ruthie*.

I'd wanted to do more, but if I'd let myself give in and call her, then last Friday would mean something. I don't know how to *let it* mean something. My whole life has been about making goals and reaching them. My goal this year was to get this job I don't want, then use it as a scaffolding to find a more satisfying position. In no way does pursuing my best friend's sister *for real* fit into that plan.

But she's not just my best friend's sister anymore. She's *my wife*.

I didn't think it was going to mean anything. It shouldn't—it's a piece of paper, and paper can be ripped and burned and destroyed, but somehow it does.

"I know what it's seemed like," I say, then I lift her hand to my mouth and kiss the skin just beneath the ring. "But it's true. I can't stop thinking about you. It's driving me mad. You've been on my mind constantly, every moment. Every day."

She takes a quick breath, her eyes fixed on mine. Their scrutiny is felt in every inch of my body. "Is that why you wore the tie?"

"I've worn it every day since last Friday," I admit. But I have some elf-restraint left. I don't tell her that I've also worn the pajamas she bought for Danny, because she chose them. It's saying something that I've wanted to be in that ramshackle little apartment with her and Izz rather than in my own house.

"*Shane.*"

Our gazes hold, and there's a moment—a pounding, mindfuck of moment—when I almost turn on the car and put it in reverse. Because I don't want to be here with her, putting on a show. I want to finish that tour she backed me into earlier so I can show her my bedroom. I want to have her on my bed, against my wall, in my shower, on my couch. I want to add memories of her all over the house, so that each surface will be full of them. So that being there will mean something.

She swallows, and my hand lifts of its own accord to trace the line of her neck—the places my mouth learned last week. Her mouth opens, closes, and then she says, "Let's go inside."

It feels like she just throttled me, but I force down the wanting and the harsh bite of disappointment. And I get out of the car and circle around to open her door.

"Mrs. Royce?" I hold out my hand.

She goes rigid for a second, then says, "I think I prefer Queen Ruthie."

She laughs as she takes my hand, and I try to laugh with her, but I know, with a sense of clarity that hurts, that I've truly fucked myself over this time.

I won't ever stop wanting her.

SHANE

"HOW DID YOU TWO MEET?" asks Hilda, otherwise known as Mrs. Legal Beagle. She's a nice enough woman, although she errs on the side of saccharine, just like her husband. I wouldn't be surprised if she carries candy in her purse on the off-chance she might come across a crying child.

Freeman rented out a private room in the restaurant. There are high tables and appetizers that get cycled around every five to ten minutes, as well as glasses of champagne brought around on circular trays. By my count, Ruthie's had two, maybe three. I'm guessing she's drinking to drone me out.

She's been snippy with me ever since we got out of the car. Maybe she's mad at me for toeing the line she drew last week. Or maybe it was being called Mrs. Royce she objected to. There's no knowing, because we haven't been able to talk privately, which is inconvenient, because the only thing I really want is to get her alone.

It doesn't help that I can't keep my eyes off her. The dress is even sexier when it's not half covered by a coat. She looks like the queen she called herself in that slinky red dress that has the nerve to cover up a good portion of her body but the good grace to do it in a way that shows more than it hides.

But Josie and her boyfriend haven't shown yet, so we'll likely be here for at least another hour. The other attorneys are present, except Daniels, who's still off living his best life somewhere. Michael greeted Ruthie with interest but thankfully said jack-all about the not-so-fake rings. He's proven to be both competent and discreet. He's also put in the legwork of contacting the first round of Josie's witnesses, several of whom he quickly identified as liabilities.

It's an Italian restaurant, and the whole place smells like tomato sauce, a scent memory that has me on edge. When I mentioned the smell to Ruthie, she shook her head with a small smile and told me I'm probably the only person in the world who objects to sauce. I didn't bother telling her that I used to like it just fine.

"Well," Ruthie says to Hilda, giving me a sidelong look that promises trouble. "As it happens, we do have a funny how we first met story."

"No really," I say, putting an arm around her waist. "I'm her brother's best friend."

Ruthie pouts at me, then turns conspiratorially toward Hilda. "You know, I carved our initials into a bench when I was ten. But he thought I was a pest back then. I heard him talking smack about me to my brother, and it broke my heart." She waves a hand. "But that's how it is when you're young. Your heart gets broken every five minutes."

My heart feels like it stopped beating for a second. Because I can tell from the slight quaver in her voice that it's true. Or at least my gut tells me so.

Distantly, I hear the door opening, but I don't swivel to look at the latest plate of appetizers or champagne. My attention is so utterly Ruthie's that I temporarily forget Hilda exists. Ruthie's lips are parted slightly, and there's a look of remembered hurt in her eyes.

"You never told me that," I say.

She lifts onto her toes and bops my nose with her finger, as if we've been transformed into those children again. Ruthie, the little ten-year-old pest who kept following Danny and me around, when the last thing I wanted to do was take care of anyone else. I was doing enough of that at home. "*You* never asked."

"*Where?*" I ask, my voice ragged. Because even though it shouldn't matter, I want to see the proof that I mattered to her once. That I meant enough to her that she wanted to make the evidence of it permanent. I wouldn't have cared then, if I'd known, but I care now.

"The safe place," she says in a whisper, and that's a real gut punch. I know the safe place. It's a lookout in the mountains where Danny always goes when he needs to get away from everything. He's brought me there before, and I know he used to take Ruthie. To tell her it was a place where their parents' chaos couldn't touch them.

And she wrote my initials there...

"*Ruthie.*" Emotion pounds through my veins.

"Goodness," Hilda breaks in, the interruption nearly making me growl. "How romantic that you found each other again later in life. How did it happen?"

"*Well,*" Ruthie says, turning toward her. "He got so blind drunk he puked on me."

"I don't like where this is going," I comment.

"You wouldn't," she says, angling a glance at me. "I didn't like it either. It was a very nice dress. But then he told me the truth."

"Which was?" asks Hilda, clearly on the hook. Ruthie's good at enthralling an audience. If she'd had a taste for it, she could have been an excellent lawyer.

"That he was the one who'd been sending me a red rose every Valentine's Day since I'd turned eighteen."

Great, now I sound like a serial killer...and one of those creeps who get excited about underage girls' eighteenth birthdays, as if the difference of one day is enough to transform a teenager into a woman.

"Oh, how *romantic*," Hilda says, so at least she doesn't want to have me arrested.

"Yes," Ruthie says, "and then he told me, 'I'm scared of walking out of this room and never feeling the rest of my whole life the way I feel when I'm with you.'"

Hilda tilts her head and frowns. "Isn't that from *Dirty Dancing*?"

"Yes." Ruthie grins at her and leans into me in a show of fondness. "It's our favorite movie. Makes him cry every time."

Before Ruthie can tell the women that I knit sweaters with her discarded hair, I say, "Look, Ruthie, pâté, your favorite," and hustle her toward a waiter with a tray.

She makes a face. "No, thank you. It's like meat mousse."

"You're making me look like an asshole," I say under my breath, pulling her closer so our conversation can go unobserved. The hum of conversation in the room is accompanied by the kind of "easy listening" music that makes going to the grocery store such a thankless chore.

"If the shoe fits..." She says it teasingly, like she's hoping we can both laugh about this, but I don't find it funny. Mrs. Legal Beagle is going to talk to Mr. Legal Beagle, and I've started caring what Freeman thinks about me.

I'd rather castrate myself than admit this to Josie, but it happened because she made me realize that Freeman reminds me of my father. Now seen, the resemblance of character can't be ignored. Ruthie's right about one thing—Freeman is a better man than I'll ever be, and the reminder that I'm here lying to him digs deep.

"C'mon," Ruthie wheedles, her breath champagne sweet against my ear. She's so close that if she leaned forward, her red lips would be on my lobe, and even though I'm still feeling off-center, I wouldn't mind if she sucked on it. Not even if she bit it. "At least I didn't tell her you have a small penis."

"She wouldn't have believed you," I say flatly.

She laughs at this, and I steer her away from a fresh-faced waiter who's approaching us with a tray of full, bubbling flutes.

"You don't want me to have any fun?" she asks, giving me an accusatory glance.

"If downing champagne and making cheap shots at me is your idea of a good time, then maybe I should go back to calling you kid."

Her mouth opens. No doubt something really cutting was on its way out. I probably deserved it this time.

Seconds later, Freeman comes bustling up to us with Josie and her boyfriend, who must've arrived while we were talking to Hilda. She's wearing the same dress she had on at the courthouse the other day, so either she really likes it, or she's playing mind games and reminding me that I'm her legal bitch.

"Our guest of honor has arrived," Freeman says. Leave it to Josie to become the guest of honor at a celebration that was thrown for me.

"Hello, Josie," I say, needing to reach deep for politeness. "Good to see you." I nod to Poe. "And you."

"Oh, it's okay," she says flippantly. "You don't need to lie about it. We're used to people not wanting to see us."

Freeman opens his mouth to speak, but I beat him to it.

"I'm not lying," I lie as I try to silently communicate that Josie should play along if she wants me to play along.

"All right, sure," she says, giving me a thumbs up. "So I'm guessing you and Ruthie wouldn't mind getting your readings first? I have to get my crystal ball set up, but then we'll be ready to go."

She points to an old carpet bag sitting on the ground just inside the door. It looks like the kind of thing that would contain a fucked-up creature in a horror movie.

"Uh, I don't think so," Ruthie says as she leans into my arm. I curl it more tightly around her on reflex. "I'm a little...shy."

"Really?" Freeman asks with interest. "You don't come off as shy."

No, she doesn't...because she's not. So what is this all about?

"Can you give us a minute?" I ask, lifting my eyebrows. "We were just about to call the nanny to check on my stepdaughter."

"Sure," Josie says, rubbing her hands together. "I wanted to get my hands on some of those appetizers. Did you bring the Tupperware, Poe?"

If he had any shame left in him, she's clearly scared it out, because all he says is, "No. Remember? We couldn't find any of the lids. They were all square-shaped lids, but the containers were round."

I tug Ruthie away, leaving Freeman to solve that conundrum. Knowing him, he'll order them appetizers to go instead of reminding them that they're eating here for free, and that should be enough.

We step out into the hallway connected to the private room, and I close the door behind us. The smell of sauce is just as strong out here. Do they pump it into the air?

There are two chairs across from the door, a couple of private bathrooms to the right and the rest of the restaurant is accessible by a long, narrow hallway to the left, ending in a closed door.

"What's wrong?" I ask Ruthie, leading her a few feet away from the door and then leaning in close, one hand on the wall by her head. If someone comes by, they'll think it's an intimate conversation, no more or less. If it's someone other than Josie, they won't be inclined to interrupt us.

She bites her bottom lip, and I restrain the urge to soothe my tongue over it.

"I just...I don't really want to hear what she has to say."

"I can't believe anyone does, but you know most of it is nonsense."

"That's not true," Ruthie says, suddenly looking close to tears. "She knows lots of things she shouldn't. What if..."

"What, honey?" I ask softly, running my free hand over her jaw. I've rarely seen her like this. Ruthie's always ready with a smart remark, a retort. She's not the kind of woman who lets life rock her.

She ruins the effect by laughing.

"You'd prefer your other nickname?" I ask.

"No, sorry, it's just..." Her short-lived humor dies, and I regret being the man who killed it. "I...I...really want to try with Vanny. I've been working hard all week, and Eden's having this big close-out party at the diner next weekend. She wants me to use it to promote my business. I guess I'm..." She swallows. "I'm worried that I'm going to try this time, really try, and I'll still be a failure."

Shit. Fuck. This is my fault. Me and my catastrophically big mouth. I didn't mean to throw her into a spiral of self-doubt.

"Ruthie," I say, tracing her face again. "You are not a failure. I didn't mean for you to walk away thinking that last week. That's not how I feel. You...amaze me. I've never known anyone else with so many ideas and the strength to keep getting up and trying again. You probably won't thank me for saying so, but I've always thought we were a bit alike. We have the same drive. I just...I thought maybe you wouldn't have to try so hard if you stuck with one idea."

She laughs, but tears glimmer in her eyes. "You're going to want to remember this one for posterity, Vain, but you were right. I kept giving up because I couldn't stand the thought of pouring myself into something and failing. I still can't. And I'm too much of a coward to stand it if Josie tells me that's what's going to happen in front of everyone. I know you think I'm dumb for believing her, but I *do*."

"I don't think that at all," I say, leaning in to kiss her forehead, because she hasn't given me the go-ahead to do more, and I *need* to comfort her. "You're one of the bravest people I know. Brave people feel fear, Ruthie. Don't think they don't. Only a dumb person is never afraid. Fear can be useful. Fear can drive people to do great things."

"*You* don't feel fear," she says as she glances up at me. Somehow her hand has found its way to my chest, her fingers playing with my tie.

I layer my hand over hers. "That's not true. I'm afraid you're going to throttle me." But there's disappointment in her eyes, and I know she was hoping for something real. I feel the press to give it to her, even though my heart is beating in my ears and that smell is overwhelming. Maybe the need to unburden myself has been building inside me for a while now, unseen, the way most diseases are. The words burst out, like water from a dam. "I'm afraid I won't create a legacy big enough to be remembered."

"What are you talking about?" she asks, her brow wrinkling.

"It's a vain wish," I admit, my hand flexing slightly over hers, because I don't want her to pull away. I couldn't bear it if she did. "My father wasn't remembered. He...." I pause, swallow, taking in the scent in the air. "I don't know what you know, probably not much, but he died in front of me and my mother. He came into the dining room holding a pot of sauce for dinner, and he dropped it. That's what the burn on my arm is from, and we were cleaning it off the walls and floor for months. After that, he just...collapsed. We called the ambulance, but I knew he was already gone. His eyes were open." My voice is shaking, and I'm full of shame, but I keep going, because now that the words have started they won't stop. "I found out later they call that type of heart attack a widow-maker because so few people survive it."

I don't look at her. I can't. But I feel her burrowing into me, holding me in her arms as if she's the one who's taller and larger. I feel myself needing it. I've never said any of this out loud before.

"Everyone wanted to talk about him at first, Ruthie. They talked about what a good man he was. How much people loved him. But he lived a quiet life. They stopped coming after a few months. It didn't take them long to forget about him. They moved on. Forty-eight years on this earth, and in the end, what did it matter? His own brother didn't come to his funeral. The people who came cried and carried on and said it wasn't fair, and the next day they were doing the same shit they'd always done, without a second thought for him. Like it didn't matter. The only ones who remember are my mother and me, and she can barely get out of bed some days because of it. *Still.* So, yes, I'm afraid of things. I'm afraid I'll fail, and I'll be forgotten too—and the last bit of him that's left, the bit I carry, will be lost forever."

"Shane," she says, her voice shaking slightly. One of her hands travels up my shirt and finds my face. The other stays on my tie, mine layered over it. I meet her eyes and am relieved to find sympathy there but no pity. There's also warmer emotion that hooks into me and makes it impossible to look away. "Oh my God. I thought you were going to say you were scared of spiders or something. I...I remember when it happened, but I didn't know any of that."

"I know," I say, bowing my head. "You were probably about ten. I was a dick. I didn't mind you hanging around with us. I knew what it was like for you at your place. But I..." I swallow. "I didn't have a kind word for anyone back then, not even your brother, but he stuck with me anyway." And part of me has never been able to forgive him for what he knows. For the weakness he's seen in me. "I'm sorry. I guess that kind of set us up for..." I wave, not able to put what we've become into words. Because we're not enemies, but we've acted like it. It's part of the game we've played—one for which we never discussed the rules.

The hand she has around my tie flexes, and she pulls me down to her. I've never been so glad to be partially throttled.

This isn't a gentle kiss, like the one in the car, and it's not at all chaste. She's attacking my mouth, and I'm attacking her back, crowding her into the wall, because the need I've been trying to tamp down—the need that drove me to wear this tie, those stupid pajamas—is spilling out and overcoming me. And all that exists is Ruthie and her sweet mouth and her forceful attitude. Ruthie, *my* Ruthie.

I keep my mouth on her as I lean down to run my hand up that dress, finding the slit that's been driving me mad all evening. She hopefully chose this dress because she *wanted* to drive me mad. I need to feel the rasp of her stockings against the tips of my fingers. All night, I've imagined the pleasure of pushing them down. Of tracing my hand to her core.

I shouldn't have done this last week.

I probably shouldn't be doing it again now.

But Ruthie has a rare talent for making me break the promises I've made to myself—and maybe some of them *should* be broken. I'm beginning to think Rule Number One is at the top on that list.

I'm still concerned this will be the end of my friendship with Danny, which has lasted nearly as long as my life. But I'm not worried enough that I'm ready to step away from her. It feels like stepping away from her would be the end of *me*, or any part of me that's good.

She pulls back, her lips glistening. "We need to find a someplace that has a locking door."

"I can't...you're..." I swallow. "You had three glasses of champagne."

She gives me a wry look. "You think that's enough to make me too tipsy to consent? You're so *old*." She retreats from me, then walks in a straight line, one foot in front of the other, arms splayed out to either side.

She looks like a dancer, a vision. An illusion wrapping a ribbon around my brain. She's easily the most beautiful thing I've ever seen.

"Have I proven to you that I'm fuckable?" she says in an undertone that hopefully doesn't carry.

"I knew that. I'm not an idiot. But you really want to mess around in a supply closet?" I'm partly asking because I want her to repeat it. She always makes such a big point of not wanting to butter up my ego, and then she goes and says a thing like that, implying she can't wait for me.

"Or a bathroom. This looks like a place that has clean bathrooms."

There are two single-stall bathrooms with locking doors just down the hall from us, there for the use of whoever rents the private room. It's a serious risk. Someone might end up waiting outside, and then they'd see us leave together. Or there's a chance those disgusting pate cups will give everyone diarrhea and there'll be a run on the bathrooms. It's an unappealing thought that should sober me, and it might have, if Ruthie's eyes didn't light up when she saw where I was looking. She walks to the closest bathroom with a gleam in her eyes, her ass sashaying, and then glances over her shoulder and beckons me forward with her hand, fingers splaying and un-splaying.

I follow her. Of course I do. I follow her as surely as if she had my dick in her other hand, because she might as well. The bathroom is lowly lit, with a scented candle that finally cuts into the odor of tomato and garlic, and it looks as clean as a bathroom at a restaurant could be.

It'll do. I'm not going any farther than the door.

I close it behind us. Lock it. Back her into it as I look into those crystalline blue eyes. "*Ruthie*," I say in an undertone. "Do you have any idea how much I've wanted to touch you again? You haven't left me alone all week. You've been in my head longer than that, though, always telling me what not to do, like a real pest."

She lets out a laugh that's half-delighted, half-annoyed, and leans up to kiss the underside of my jaw. "I was thinking the other day that you're like my little devil. The one who sits on my shoulder and tells me to do bad shit."

"Who's your angel?" I ask, already internally scowling, because I think I know the answer. Also because I'm not sure how I feel about being her devil, prodding her to do things she shouldn't.

"Tank." She runs a hand over my brow, laughing. "I thought you prided yourself on your poker face."

"It seems to crumple around you. But you said he's just a friend, and I believe you."

"You're still jealous."

So much so, my jaw might break. If I ever actually meet the man, I'll be hard-pressed to say a full sentence to him. But that's my problem—I would never make it hers.

"I don't like that he stayed the night at your apartment, or that he's checking you out in your bootie shorts. Those are my only complaints. He's your friend, and it's important for people to have friends who understand them."

"Were you jealous of Rand?" she asks, catching me off guard. Maybe she's asking less about Rand than about when this protectiveness started. Well, I won't lie, even if I feel inclined to.

"I wanted to kill him," I admit, running my fingers through her hair, gripping it. Need pulses through my veins, my cock. "He may have run off like the little slinking coward is, but I still want to kill him. He didn't deserve you, and he *definitely* doesn't deserve that little girl. I told you as much back then."

"*Shane.*"

"I didn't understand it at the time," I say, my hand still gripping her, because I can't let her go. I lean in to kiss her neck. To breathe her in. "But I felt sick to my stomach at your wedding. It didn't feel right, and it wasn't only because I knew he was an asshole. I wanted to carry you away with me. I thought it was only because you were Danny's sister, because you were both more to me than anyone else in this world, but it wasn't just that..."

"You better touch me right now, or else."

An incredulous laugh escapes me. "You've been trying to get me to talk, and now you want me to shut up?"

"I want you to put that mouth to other uses while we still have time," she says, her eyes bright, "because I need you right now." Her words are forceful, and gratitude glimmers inside of me because her need for me feels like a gift I don't deserve.

"I need *you*." I kiss her hard, using my hand in her hair to draw her closer, and as with everything, she meets me and exceeds me. While we're still consuming each other, I run my hand up beneath the slit in her dress, following the seam of the stockings. Wanting to rip them off and tie her hands with them, the same way she did with me. Wanting *everything*.

I don't have a condom, but that doesn't mean we can't have other kinds of fun.

I get to the top of the stockings, and even though my cock is painfully hard and pounding, I pull them down slowly, bringing her panties with them, wanting to feel the fabric relinquish its territory to me. The look of her creamy skin emerging beneath the dress makes me even harder. Kneeling at her feet, I look up and see her staring down at me—Queen Ruthie, watching her supplicant. "These are sexy as hell," I tell her, "but I'm taking them off."

Her response is to lift one foot, her hand gripping my shoulder. I grin, because she really is acting like royalty. I slip the shoe off, remove the impediments to bliss, and then slide the shoe back on and move to the other side. Once done, I stuff her stockings and underwear into my pants pocket. I'm unsteady as I climb to my feet, already reaching for her.

I flex my fingers in her hair, bringing her close, and she leans in and bites my lip, drawing out a laugh from deep within me, even as I reach down to trace her. She's wet for me, and the sense of accomplishment I feel is more powerful than when Myles told me I'd made partner. There was a hollowness to that moment, a sense of a disappointment because it didn't feel the way I'd thought it would, and this one holds only anticipation. I circle her clit with my finger, then curl it up and into the best place I've ever visited.

The little gusty sound that escapes her is mine—I helped her create it, and by hell, I'm going to keep it. I swallow it through our kiss and then kiss my way down her neck to the tops of her tits, my finger and palm working her. I'm going to make her come in this bathroom. I'm going to remind her how good it is between us, so—

I haven't gotten that far yet, but I've decided I'm not willing to stuff this thing with Ruthie down with everything else I've buried.

"However good you are with your hand," she says, her breath coming in pants as she grips my wrist, stopping my movements, "it's not enough. I'm going to need that dick again."

She's speaking in an undertone, but it's possible we could still be heard through the door. I'm so far gone for her I don't care. I don't even remember why I should.

"As much as I would like to take you up on that," I say, my voice strained, "we don't have a condom." I rub my finger along a spot that's sensitive for her, and am rewarded by her clenching around me. My dick is in torment, but it's worth it. Anything would be worth touching her again.

"*You* don't have a condom," she says, reaching into her bra and pulling one out. I'm so baffled and turned on, I'll probably die on the spot, but I'll die happy.

"You were planning this," I comment. I can imagine her getting ready, pausing over her drawer before tucking one of them into her bra. It's sexy as hell, and I get even harder as the scenario runs through my mind.

"I like to account for any number of possibilities," she says, her voice a mimicry of mine.

"I should have, but I guess I don't need to so long as I have you."

"What you're saying is that you're lucky," she says, giving me the condom wrapper and then immediately getting to work unfastening my belt.

"Right now I feel like I should go out and buy lottery tickets."

Looking up at me with a satisfied smile, she opens my pants and then pushes them down.

"I thought you couldn't have sex with a man who's wearing socks?" I say.

"I'll make an exception just this once, because I don't want your bare feet on this floor."

"Your exception is noted and appreciated," I say, tearing the condom wrapper just as her hand wraps around me—pleasure settling in my lower back and promising I'm not going to last long. This time. I'm going to have another. I *need* it. Now that I've shattered Rule Number One, why not dance on the broken glass?

I get the condom on quickly and silently offer up appreciation to whoever designed the slinky red dress, because in addition to its other attributes, the fabric is stretchy. Lifting Ruthie up by the waist, I press her back into the wall by the door, and she wraps her legs around me without being asked, the spiky heels digging into me in a way I don't dislike.

Staring up at me, pupils dilated, she tells me, "Give it to me, Shane. I want it."

"Say the words," I say, blood pounding in my ears. "Tell me you want my cock."

"I want your cock," she replies, her lips twitching with a smile, "now stop being an insufferable bastard and give it to me."

I'm holding her up to the wall, and I wouldn't risk letting her fall for anything, so I ask, "Line me up so I can fuck you."

The sight of her reaching down to do it, her hand moving my cock so it's in the right position, is the hottest thing I've ever seen— or will ever see.

I slide in, slowly at first, giving her time to adjust, but she's so wet, so ready for me, that my body begs for more. To go back to the place it left last week and has been missing every second since. The breath leaves my lungs as I bottom out—and Ruthie pushes against me as if she still wants more. As if there's no end to how much she wants me, and I'm glad for it, because I want her that much too. "You feel so good, Ruthie."

"If you tell me I'm a good girl...I'm going to throttle you," she says, making me laugh even as I pull out and thrust back in, her back thumping against the wall.

"You assume I don't like it when you throttle me," I say. "You assume wrong, *good girl.*"

Eyes sparkling, she grabs the end of my tie and drags my head to her, kissing me, her hips grinding against me as I push her into the wall with another thrust. We're all over each other, her hands in my hair, her shoes digging into me as she grips me with her legs, our mouths battling to find an angle that will bring us closer. It doesn't take long before I feel her tightening and clenching around me, and my cock pulses with the need to come. I pull my mouth from hers for just an instant, and she bites my bottom lip as if to tell me there'll be a price for leaving, even for an instant.

"I can't hold on much longer."

"*Don't,*" she insists, her voice urgent, and I know she's on the edge too. That's what takes me the rest of the way there—that and another thrust against the wall with her legs wrapped around me, that pretty dress ruched up for me, her hair a beautiful mess against the white walls.

She lets out a single soft cry in my ear as I pulse into her, her body wrapped around me.

"You're incredible," I say into her ear as soon as I'm capable of saying anything.

She kisses my neck. "I'm going to remind you that you said so."

"Under duress," I tease.

Then I help her down, and we clean up. I relinquish her stockings and, regrettably, her underwear.

Miraculously, there's no one waiting when we leave the bathroom. It feels too good to be true, like it always feels when you get away with something you shouldn't.

We walk toward the door to the private room, hand in hand, but before we go in, Ruthie turns to me. "If Josie still wants to give me a reading, I'll do it."

"You don't have to," I insist. "I'm the one who got us into this mess. I'll tell them we have to leave."

"Here you are again, admitting to something," she says with a half-smile. "You keep it up, I might get used to it."

"Maybe I want you to," I say, not totally clear on what I mean other than that I want this to mean something.

Her answer is to kiss me, and I find myself backing her into another wall, the one just beside the door, because I can't seem to get enough. It's like my desire for her has infiltrated my bloodstream, and it's the only thing my body recognizes as being important for survival.

Then the door to the private room swings open, almost hitting me on the ass—all of it happening so quickly I can't pull away from her, not that I'm inclined to. Then I see who's at the door, and I *do* pull away. Slightly. Because it's Mr. and Mrs. Legal Beagle, along with Josie the Great and Poe, who's carrying a plate of appetizers that's so large that I don't need to be psychic to see a to-go box in their future.

"Goodness, they just can't keep their hands off each other," Mrs. Legal Beagle says. She doesn't seem displeased by it. Based on that, her lack of judgment about the weird roses story, and her taste in movies, I'm guessing she's a *romantic*. I feel almost fond of her for it right now.

"Just like us, back in the day," Freeman says fondly, patting her on the back. And I'm in the very uncomfortable situation of having a hard-on in front of my boss. I'm still angled toward the wall, but even so...

"Come on," Josie says, wearing a veil now, which I suppose signals her readiness to get down to business. "We're ready for you."

RUTHIE

"OH, I don't know about that," Shane says, his arm wrapped around me. "We were about to go home. Izzy's having a hard time getting to sleep." The lie unspools from him so naturally, it disarms me.

He knows how to lie, I remind myself, because I can feel something alarming happening. It started in the hallway of this restaurant, where we're standing now. He let me see past his walls to the boy he'd been, giving me a new perspective on the past we'd shared.

I'm falling for my husband, and it's not just because he looks good in a suit and a tie, or because he has a big dick that he knows how to use. It's because he's a stubborn asshole who sees me for the stubborn asshole I am—and cares about me anyway.

Just like I'm starting to care about him. Again.

Maybe it's that thought that turns me stubborn and contrary, but I find myself splaying a hand on his hard chest. "It's okay, Shane. I'll do it. Izzy will want to hear all about it."

He gives me a look of concern that seems genuine before nodding tightly.

"Oh good," Josie says. "I wanted to do you. I already know what's going to happen for Shane."

He gives her the flat look of someone who doesn't intend on asking for the clarification she obviously wants to give.

But *I* want to know.

"What's that?" I ask as we head back through the door to the low music, buzz of conversation, and scent of sauce. I glance at Shane, remembering what he said about the sauce. He usually comes off as so reserved and self-contained, but there was raw agony on his face when he told me about his father. Even now, my heart bleeds for him. I'm filled with the need to protect him, to take care of him, and—

I'm sure he'd be amused to know how badly I want to prove him wrong. I don't care. I need to show him that becoming great in the way the world demands—known, spoken of, feared—isn't the only way to make a lasting impact. And that his father is likely remembered more than he believes. Danny remembers him, at the very least. He talks about him sometimes, how he used to bring both of the boys out on hikes and bike rides when they were little, a tradition they continue to this day. That's a legacy, or a piece of one, and I'll bet there are others.

Maybe it's hypocritical, me wanting to show Shane that, because I've always been eager to make my own mark—to be someone who matters. But if I can prove to him there's more to life, maybe I'll internalize the message myself.

"Well," Josie says, "Shane's going to win my case, obviously." There's a bit of an *or else* attached to that, I think. "I won't reveal the rest of what I've seen for him in front of everyone else unless he asks me to. It's like attorney-client privilege, you know?"

"Thank you for your forbearance," he tells her dryly.

Josie leads the way to a tall, two-person table where she's set up her crystal ball. Waving me toward the high-legged stool opposite her, she sits down, her boyfriend hovering next to her with his enormous plate of appetizers. I lower onto my stool, very aware of my legs and arms and the awkwardness of everyone in the room staring at me. I'm not someone who minds being looked at, necessarily, but I don't like that they're all waiting to hear my fate, same as I am, like I'm at my own sentencing. Then, to my surprise, a warm arm settles around my shoulder—Shane, standing behind me, wrapping his arm around me.

Someone cracks a breadstick, and I flinch as if it were gunfire. "Hm, it's not good if you're already jumpy," Josie says. "Does anyone have smelling salts?"

No one steps forward, so she shrugs. "That's okay, Suit and Tie can catch her if she falls."

"We have to leave soon," Shane says, his tone struggling to be polite. "Can you proceed, please?"

She gives a slow nod and says, "Poe, the lighting."

He sets down the appetizer tray and heads toward the door, squinting at the light fixture, which offers a simple on or off. "Sorry, it's all or nothing, Josie. There's no dimmer."

"Fine," she says with a huff of air. "We'll keep them on, but everyone should know my sight will be hampered by it."

"That's convenient," Shane quips. His hand flexes on my shoulder, and I've never wanted anything as much as I want him to take me away from here. Which is why I'm staying. If he could be brave enough to face his past for me, then I can face my fear of the future. I need to. Because I have to start moving forward without letting doubt hover over me like a rude ghost.

Josie ignores the comment, her gaze trained on the crystal ball, and a shiver runs down my spine. So much of her is fake and obviously intended to cater to the masses' idea of a psychic. But this— the way she's staring into the ball, her eyes going unfocused but intense, *feels* real.

Poe heads back to the table, and I hear him murmur something like, "You've got this, babe," his hand running across the small of her back, but she doesn't react or even seem to notice. Another shiver makes its way down my spine at this hint of the uncanny.

Then Josie glances up, the transition so quick I almost fall back and take my stool with me. Maybe I would've if not for Shane's steady arm around me, holding me in place.

"Congratulations, you're going to get married again. I saw it here in the ball."

"*Excuse* me?" Shane asks, sounding pissed. But his anger has nothing on the agony in my heart, which is twisting and breaking in my chest.

It feels like proof that the only thing that matters about me is who I'm legally bound to.

It feels like she just broke up with me for Shane, like Michael Wolfe's big sister did in the sixth grade.

I knew we were going to get divorced, obviously. Even if we have unresolved feelings for each other, we're *definitely* not at a place where we should be married. Our lives aren't compatible—mine, barely contained chaos; his, strict order. It suits both of us to pretend, for a while, but eventually Shane will get sick of it. He doesn't want a wife, and I won't be the woman who tries to convince him otherwise. I've learned, firsthand, how painful it is to hope a man will change his mind about what he wants.

Still, I feel sick over the idea of doing any of this again with someone else.

"That's what I saw," Josie says. "I can't fake the sight." She grins at Shane over my shoulder, her expression almost feral, and it occurs to me that this may be payback for his attitude. A warning. I hope so. Because even if it makes me stupid and gullible, I believe she does have talent, and I need her to be wrong about this. "But I didn't see the groom. Just Ruthie here in a white dress. I mean, really, Ruthie, who are you kidding at this point?" she adds with a chuckle. "Anyway, my point is, it could have been a vow renewal ceremony. You must be coming up on ten years married, right?"

"Three and a half," Shane says flatly, delivering the answer we'd decided on.

"Still," she says flippantly, "you're the kind of lovebirds who like to celebrate. I'll bet that's what I saw."

"You heard her, honey," Shane says, and I have to wonder if that word is just for me, because it made me laugh earlier. He helps me up off the stool but keeps his arm around me, and I'm grateful for it. I need his support in a way that should make me feel weak but doesn't. "Better send out the invitations."

I glance up at Josie, my heart hoping for something more. Shane always tells me I'm an easy target—a giant heart that others want to squeeze—and I think he must be right. Because I can feel it all flashing in my eyes. My hopes, my fears, my raw need.

Josie clears her throat. "You're going to be okay, Ruthie. It's going to work out for you."

That's all she says. It means nothing. A Magic 8-Ball would say more, but tears fill my eyes, and I find myself thinking again of that silly unicorn blanket, the one that was tainted by the smell of beer.

Somehow, she knew exactly what I needed to hear.

"*Thank you,*" I say, even as Shane tightens his grip on me. He's a harder nut to crack, and Josie the Great doesn't have the tool for the job.

Am I fool for hoping I might?

Freeman gives a chuckle that sounds nervous, like he's no longer sure asking Josie here was a good decision. Or maybe, depending on how much he believes Josie, he's worried his new employee is less of a family man he thought. Then he pats his belly and says, "Thanks for coming, Shane, Ruthie." He grins at me. "Now, I told my friend about your book mobile, and he's mighty interested in seeing it in action. He's the event planner for Big Catch Brewing, and he's also on the school board. When's your next event?"

My breath catches. This might mean something. This might mean quite a bit. Determination steels my spine even as I feel anxiety welling inside of me. Because it could be another swing and miss. All of this could be.

I take a big breath and then tell him about the celebration at Loving next Sunday.

"We'll be there," Freeman says without pause. "I look forward to it."

Shane tightens his arm around me and says, "I can't wait. I'm pretty proud of her."

Maybe it's wishful thinking, but I think he might actually mean it. It's not until we leave the rest of the guests to Josie's questionable mercy that I realize Izzy will be there with us next Sunday. We'll have to tell her something.

I say as much to Shane in the car. He taps on the wheel, then says, "Let's tell her tomorrow, Ruthie. Maybe we can bring her out for breakfast after we pick her up from Danny's. She deserves to know what's going on."

A feather could have tipped me over. "You think we're going over there together? I figured..."

He gives me a sidelong look accompanied by a smile. "I hope so. It would be pretty rude of you not to invite me after I spend all night making you come."

Laughter spurts out of me, but that's not to say I'm not turned on.

"You sure know how to stroke a man's ego, Ruthie," he says.

"You don't need the help. You do plenty of stroking of your own."

He darts a quick glance at me. "Maybe so, but it feels different when someone else does it."

Goddamn.

"Shane," I say, my voice shaking. "If we go over there together, what will Danny think?"

He gives me another sidelong look, his eyes glittering in the low lighting from the streetlights and the moon. A full moon, which isn't surprising, because the next words that come out of his mouth are definitely full moon words. "There's something special between us,

Ruthie. I want to explore it. I realize the marriage thing might fuck that up, but maybe it doesn't have to. I feel like it would be a mistake for us not to figure this out."

I don't like the way he says "figure it out"—like I'm a problem he can solve and then be free of—but my heart feels like a fluttering bird in my chest. "So you want to tell him we're...what, dating? And Izzy?"

Another sidelong look. "We can tell Izzy whatever you'd like. That's your call. But if we're going to try this, we need to be honest with Danny. It was a mistake to keep him in the dark before, and I try not to repeat my mistakes."

"You fucked me again tonight," I point out.

"And that wasn't a mistake," he says, sliding his hand onto my thigh—it feels so warm, I'm surprised it doesn't burn a hand-sized hole right through my stockings.

I take a moment to think about the insanity of trying to date Shane Royce, when I've spent the past several years focusing on everything that's wrong with him. When I know, deep down, that those issues still exist. He's too driven, too ambitious, and for the wrong reasons. He's emotionally closed-off. He's...

He's intense and too smart for his own good and has deep feelings.

He's good with my daughter.

He makes me laugh and moan and feel and *reach higher*.

He's Shane Fucking Royce.

He's the boy whose initial I wrote on that bench; he's the man who's driven me crazy with need and also anger.

He's my husband, hard as that is to believe.

"No," I admit in a quiet voice. "It wasn't."

Still, even as the words come out, I hear Josie the Great telling me that I'm going to get married again.

This probably isn't going to work out. But I have to try anyway.

twenty-six

SHANE

IN THE MORNING, I wake up with a jolt from a dream about Fred Myles, his withered face leering at me as he tells me that I'm nothing. He created me, and that which we create can just as easily be destroyed.

My heart is racing, but when I blink my eyes open, I realize a few things—Ruthie is next to me, wearing one of my long sleeve T-shirts because she gets cold at night. She's the only woman who's ever stayed over at my house, by design, but seeing her in my bed settles me instead of freaking me out.

We spent the night talking and fucking and making a batch of cookies. I had jack all in the refrigerator, but she claimed she could do something with it, and neither of us has ever met a challenge we didn't want to dominate.

They were terrible. No, terrible doesn't cover it. Inedible is a better word.

"You're supposed to tell me they're delicious," Ruthie told me. "I'll bet you could do it convincingly too."

"Oh, because I'm a good liar?"

"The best."

There was a smear of flour on her nose and I wiped it off,

feeling a surge of...it took me a solid ten seconds to identify it as happiness. "As much as I regret to admit it, there are limits to my ability to dissemble."

She shoved my shoulder. I asked if she wanted another cookie, then threatened to bring them over to Danny and Mira's and tell everyone she'd baked them. And we both doubled over laughing.

For the first time in my adult life, I left dirty dishes in the sink at night, and I didn't care. And I don't care now, because Ruthie has agreed to make a go of this with me.

Her hand is splayed beside her head, her ring on display, her eyelashes brushing her cheek, the dark waves of her hair mussed from my hands. Calm satisfaction fills me, an unfamiliar sensation, because for so long my life has been a quest for more, better, *next*.

But disquiet snakes in and wraps around my throat.

I've never wanted to be in a relationship. I've avoided it. Relationships end. They *all* end. Even if both people choose to stay together, to fall in love with each other again and again as life changes them, they will fall apart eventually. It's rare for people to die at the same time, unless it's from an accident or natural disaster. So if a divorce or breakup doesn't claim the relationship, death will. It'll end badly for someone.

I've never wanted to find myself on the other side of divorce court, arguing about frequent flyer miles or my favorite wooden spoon because I'm so pissed and broken that those things suddenly seem important.

I've never wanted to be the person who is left behind with a missing piece, like my mother. But I also can't bear the thought of being responsible for breaking another person that way. My father would have hated what his death did to my mother. *Hated* it.

A voice in my head—Ruthie's—tells me that he would have hated what's become of me too. He would have hated the way I've avoided making real connections. How I've avoided any woman who might make me feel more than passing lust. Until now.

I want this woman in a way that baffles me, and the more I've leaned into that feeling, the more I've realized a surprising truth about myself.

I've wanted her for a while. I've wanted to kiss that smart mouth and slide my hands under her big sweatshirts. I've wanted to help her with her schemes and hold her hand. I've wanted *her*. But I've buried it down, made it into a volcano that spurts out words that push away rather than pull in. Because I'm scared of Ruthie Traeger. Scared, too, of what it will mean if I really try—and fail.

Ruthie and I are more alike than I ever let myself see.

Feel the fear and do it anyway.

I remember seeing that poster in the room of the school counselor they sent me to after my dad died. The counselor didn't say anything useful—I didn't need someone to tell me it was okay to cry, because the tears wouldn't come. In fact, hearing that it was okay to cry made me wonder what was wrong with me for *not* crying. But that poster...it slid under my skin. It became my blueprint, and if I can follow that motto professionally, then I can also follow it with Ruthie.

Still, I'm worried about Danny. He knows how I feel about relationships—and the three most important people in his life are Mira, Ruthie, and Izzy. He'll probably tell me to forget it. To do what I'd promised and no more. To be a friend and stay the hell away from her, because friends don't screw friends' little sisters.

But there's no unscrewing her, and I wouldn't if I could.

Besides, this isn't just about what I want. Ruthie's willing to take a chance on me. I can't throw that away.

We've agreed to tell both Danny and Izzy most of the truth. We'll say that we may have married for convenience, but we've decided to date because we care about each other. And we'll assure Izzy that we both care about her, no matter what happens.

I get up to make coffee, pausing to pull on a T-shirt and sweatpants from the closet. It's an old house, and if it gets cold outside it lets you know it. I smile at the dirty dishes and then decide to add to them by making scrambled eggs.

I'm still standing at the pan when Ruthie comes into the kitchen and wraps her arms around me from behind—and I feel it again, that glimmer of simple happiness, even if it's chased by the feeling that any happiness is going to be temporary, because happiness is always, *always* followed by loss. Her arms are wrapped up in my shirt, my scent, and it unleashes a primal joy inside of me.

"I didn't know you could cook," she comments into my ear, then bites the lobe lightly. "If I'd known, I would have forced *you* to make those cookies."

"So I could be the one to get the blame?" I ask, reaching back to pull her closer.

"Absolutely. Ooh, coffee." She detaches from me, a feeling of cold crowding my back now that she's gone. Without asking, she pours coffee for each of us. "Let me guess," she says, "you're a very serious man who will only drink his coffee black."

"I have flavored creamer in the refrigerator." I glance back, wanting to see her smile.

She opens the fridge with anticipation on her face, then shakes her head, laughing. Because there's only a plain carton of Half & Half.

"It disturbs me that you can lie so easily." She's laughing as she says it, but it's not the first time she's said it, and I know it's not a joke. She worried that I'm like Rand. I aggressively stir the eggs, wishing it were his face, and set down the spatula.

"I try not to lie in my personal life, Ruthie." I incline my head toward the refrigerator. "Except when it's fun."

"But who gets to decide whether it's fun?"

"Me, I guess. But you'd make a joke like that too. I don't lie about important things."

She holds my gaze for a long moment before nodding. "Okay."

"Okay, what?"

"Okay, I believe you." She lifts a finger. "But don't get too excited. I'm a sucker. I believe a lot of things I shouldn't."

She turns her back to me to carry our coffee to the small circular table in the kitchen. There's a dining room, but I don't often have guests, so I've made it into a home office, with a large desk and my computer. A treadmill.

This is a house used by one person. Empty. Quiet. I've always thought I liked it that way, but I prefer having her here. Her presence makes it feel less like a storage facility—with me as the one thing it stores—and more like a place you might want to stick around for a while.

I carry the plates to the table and we sit next to each other, Ruthie lifting her coffee cup to mine for a clink.

"I don't think you're a sucker," I say after a moment.

"Yes, you do," she says with a nose-wrinkling laugh. "You've as good as told me so dozens of times."

"You believe in people even though the world's given you plenty of reasons not to. A lot of people would say that's a gift. My mother would."

"Not you," she says pointedly, then takes a forkful of eggs and moans in a way that radiates through me.

"No, not me," I admit. I drink some of the coffee, watching her. "But I still like you that way. We can't all be cynical bastards."

She's studying me as if I'm an equation she'd like to figure out. If she finds the answer, I hope she'll let me know.

Then my phone buzzes on the kitchen counter. I get up to check it, because most of my friends wouldn't text this early, and find a message from my mother.

> I'm sorry to bother you, honey, but the fire alarm is going off. There's no fire (ha!). I think the batteries need to be changed, but I'm too short to reach it without the ladder, and I can't find the ladder.

She can't find the damn ladder because I hid it. She's constantly trying to do stuff like this herself, even though her doctor has told her a dozen times she shouldn't be climbing up ladders with her hip. Especially not when she's alone in that old house.

Sometimes, in dark moments, I think she does these things because she's hoping something shitty will happen. That she'll fall, and that'll be it. She won't have to go through any of it anymore. She won't have to get better only to get worse again. She won't have to hang on just for me and her friends.

I text back.

I'll be right there.

Then I glance at Ruthie, still eating her eggs. "What is it?" she asks. "Legal emergency? Did Josie try to convince someone to rough up a rival psychic?"

"No," I say, my mind working fast.

I wanted to spend the morning with Ruthie and go to Danny's with her later. That seemed important. Because if I don't tell him the truth now, I'll go another day without telling him, and then another, and it'll only get harder to do the decent thing.

Maybe that's why I say what I say next, which I'm probably going to regret within half an hour.

"I've got to go to my mom's house to help her with something. Want to come with me? We can go straight to Danny's afterward."

She glances down at the shirt she's wearing. I wish I could tell her to keep it on. I'd like her to wear it all day, but I can see her unspoken point. It's probably not a great idea to announce to my mother and Danny that she spent last night in my bed, however much I might like the rest of the world to know.

"We can stop at your apartment so you can change."

I can see her thinking the obvious—it would be quicker for us to go our separate ways and reconnect at Danny's. But she meets my gaze and smiles, beaming in a way that I feel in my chest. It pulses outward, to the rest of me, and I'll be fucked if I don't feel my heart growing two sizes like the Grinch. "Okay, but I'm keeping the shirt as a souvenir of my victory."

"I wouldn't expect anything less," I say, because I wouldn't. And also because I'm glad she wants it.

twenty-seven

RUTHIE

SHANE PARKS in his mother's driveway, then steals a glance at me. I'm already staring at him and don't pretend to have been doing otherwise. He's wearing jeans—*jeans*—and a long-sleeved thermal shirt. Knowing him, he just did it because he wanted to prove to me that he's had these clothes all along and has chosen not wear them because he wanted to deprive the world of the sight. I don't care why he chose to do it, though—I'm happy to reap the rewards. I was also more than happy to let him keep Mrs. Longhorn busy when we dropped by my apartment so I could change. Judging by the speed with which she swung her door open, she probably noticed what I was wearing and had plenty to say about it.

But I got inside before I had to do anything more than shout, "Hello, Mrs. Longhorn!" Shane followed me in, but it took him a few minutes to make it into the living room, so he probably had to tell her another story about urinary incontinence.

As for why we're here at his mom's place...

I don't understand why he brought me here.

Shane's always been so careful to keep every part of his life in its proper place—and I know this isn't mine.

I'd like to think this is his way of telling me I'm becoming important to him, but I don't want to rely on it.

"We'd better go in," he says with a tap to the wheel that suggests nerves. "The sound's probably driven her half-crazy by now."

"You didn't need to wait for me," I say, a little annoyed by the supposition that he would have already been here if he hadn't needed to stop at my place. No, I'm not annoyed. I'm...on edge. I'm going to meet Shane's mother.

I've never met her before, not in all of the years he and Danny have been friends.

My parents weren't the kind of people who befriended our friends' parents and baked cookies for them—in fact, we were the kids parents worried about. Because there was always accessible alcohol and drugs. Because no one would notice if some of the stash was taken. Danny never took advantage of that, or saw it as an advantage, but I did for a while when I was a teenager.

Before I have time to fall too deeply into my head, Shane is opening my car door. He looks...human. Deeply, beautifully human in his long-sleeved shirt and coat. His jeans. He holds out a hand I don't need, and I take it. "Thank you for bringing me here," I say as I get out and shut the door behind me.

"Don't be too grateful. You haven't gone inside yet," he teases. But I am. I know it means something to him, especially after what he told me yesterday.

It's an unremarkable house. Large but not new. When I was a kid, I would have thought it looked like a castle, with the single turret.

"You grew up here?"

He puts an arm around me, surprising me. "I did. So obviously there'll be tour buses coming around here someday. I keep trying to emotionally prepare my mother for that."

"Very funny."

"I thought so." He gives me a half smile that doesn't meet his eyes, and I see it again. He's nervous. He doesn't know what he's going to find in there. I think back on all the years I've known Shane. For so much of that time he was holding this worry in his chest, and I never saw a hint of it.

We make it to the door, and he unweaves his arm from me. But it opens a second before he can knock. His mother has green eyes and stark white hair cut in a short pixie style. She's dressed in pajamas, although not pajamas that are in your face about their night-time status, like the ones I got for Danny.

"Oh, honey." She drops a hand to her flannel pants. "I didn't know you were bringing a friend. I would have changed."

"It's okay," I insist, stepping forward. "I wear pajama pants to school drop-off all the time. They're comfortable."

And I'm always late.

She smiles at me, then squints and angles her head. "You're Ruthie, aren't you? Danny's sister."

I'm taken aback.

"Yes, but how did you—"

The alarm bleeps loudly enough to wake the dead, and Mrs. Royce puts her hands over her ears and shakes her head. "Honestly. Did you hide the ladder, Shane?"

"I can't hear you," he says, steering me inside. I'm pretty sure he's lying. His mother follows us in and shuts the door behind us.

Shane is already following the source of the sound like a bloodhound. The determination with which he approaches every task makes me smile, especially since he just dropped everything on a Saturday morning so he could go to his mother's house and change the fire alarm battery.

It's...surprising, to be honest. Although I never would have accused him of being the kind of guy who'd ignore a distress call from his mother, I would have thought he'd send someone else. Give the task to an underling.

My hand rises to my chest, where I'm once again wearing the ring on the chain under my sweater.

"Would you like to have a cup of coffee while he deals with that racket?" Mrs. Royce asks.

"Yes, please," I tell her, "and while you're at it, I'd *very much* like to see any childhood albums you might have lying around. If you have embarrassing stories, all the better."

She gives me a bright smile. "There's nothing I'd like better."

I'll bet Shane won't approve. He doesn't seem like he'd be into the recitation of stories about how he used to eat his own buggers or stripped naked in the middle of a ballgame. Then again, he brought me here. So maybe this *is* what he wanted.

I follow her through the hall, walking slowly because the walls are lined with dozens of framed photos of the Royce family.

This is the Shane I remember. Lanky Shane. Zitty Shane. Dungeons & Dragons Shane. There's even a shot of Shane and Danny with Mr. Royce, each of them carting a bicycle. Other photos show all three Royces, smiling for the camera. Mr. Royce had Shane's hazel eyes, and his hair was the same dark brown. It hadn't been given enough time to turn white or do more than take on a couple of grey hairs, a thought that puts a lump in my throat. So does the trip down memory lane, which is awakening more emotions I'd thought I'd killed.

Mrs. Royce leads me into the dining room, where there's an old craft table surrounded by four chairs. A line in the middle suggests a leaf has been removed. It's not a messy house, but everywhere I look, there is...*stuff* is probably the best word. A pile of cozy-looking blankets. A stand full of magazines so old I see Prince William with hair on one of them. Novels stacked on top of novels on shelves. Doo-dads lined up on the windowsills.

It hits me that this is the room where it must have happened. This is where Shane's father collapsed. The thought is like a punch to the chest, because I can imagine it better now that I'm here. This is a warm home, a place where a family lived, and their lives were torn from them. I'm not surprised it still hurts.

The alarm stops assailing our ears, and Mrs. Royce gives a sigh of relief as she waves me toward the table. "Take a seat, honey. I'm glad to finally meet you." She glances back in the direction of the front door, looking a little befuddled now. "But where's Danny? I haven't seen him in a while, but Shane tells me he's got himself a girl. Your brother has always been such a sweet boy."

I can't help but smile at the thought of Shane telling his mother such a thing. "He does have a girlfriend," I confirm. "But Danny's not here with us this morning. I..."

Well, shit. What am I supposed to tell her?

I'm your son's wife. Surprise!

I'm in a fake relationship with Shane. Sort of. We really did get married, and we really are sleeping together, so I'm not sure where that leaves us. All I know is that I'm softening toward him, and that's always ended badly for me with other men.

I clear my throat. "Your son was helping me with something when he got your message."

She gives a fond smile, holding the top of one of the chairs, and I see it again in my head—Mr. Royce walking in and dropping the sauce pot. Mr. Royce collapsing while Shane and his mother could do nothing but watch. "My boy is so good to me. I'm lucky to have him."

Again, I have a sense of left-is-right and up-is-down. Then again, most people's mothers like them, mine being the obvious exception. Is it really so surprising that Shane's mom thinks he's the second coming? He had to pick up that attitude from somewhere.

That's unfair, though. He has some grandiose ideas, but there's more to him than that, and he's been showing it to me. I've seen that the boy in those photos is still a part of Shane—a buried part. A part he's taught himself to be ashamed of.

I think again of how she greeted me. "How'd you know I'm Danny's sister?"

"Oh," she says with a smile. "Shane's always after me to update the photos. He says it's not healthy to surround myself with them. Last year he brought in one of you and Danny and your sweet little girl and put it up in his room. He stays here sometimes, you know."

Well, crack my heart open and fry it like an egg. I feel like someone fed me that egg, actually, and I'm choking on it. He put up a photo of me in his bedroom? Months ago? This man is as transparent as concrete. Leave it to me to choose such a complicated man, one I need a lexicon to understand.

"He stays here?" I ask, thinking of that empty, clean-freak house of his.

"It's hard for me to be alone in this big house," she says, her tone soft. "He'll stay for a night or two when he knows I'm struggling." She pauses, studying me, then says, "I know you were married to Rand Callaghan for a while. His parents live in the neighborhood. They're..."

She seems at a loss for words, so I help her out. "They're not very nice, are they?"

"Goodness, no," she says, shaking her head. "That boy could have murdered someone, and they would have dug a shallow grave and paid off anyone who found it."

Sounds about right.

Sighing, I say, "Well, I don't have anything to do with them anymore."

"Neither do I," she says. "Not after he and my son got into that scuffle several years back."

"*What?*" I ask, immediately on high alert. I'd never heard about any scuffle. I'd known about their mutual dislike, but that hadn't come as a surprise. Rand hadn't appreciated any of the men in my life, my brother included. And, from Shane's point of view, Rand was a silver spoon kid, guilty of being successful without having earned it. At the time, I'd thought it was sour grapes, but go figure, he'd been right. For a while, I'd resented him for that, for warning me about something he'd been right about. Now, though...

"Oh, honey, I thought you knew." She seems flustered, like she knows she shouldn't have said anything. I don't want to push her... okay, I absolutely want to push her...but I don't want to upset her.

"I didn't," I say, choosing my words carefully. "This was before Rand left town?"

"Yes," she says. "It happened around Christmas. I remember because everyone had their lights up. He moved away not long afterward, and good riddance, although it hurts my heart that he abandoned you to raise your baby by yourself." Her lips firm. "No real man would do that. Not on purpose."

"You're right." I'm desperate for more information, but I let it drop. I'll ask Shane, and this time he'll have to tell me.

She looks away before meeting my eyes again, hers shining. "Shane was older when we lost his father, but I didn't take it well. It's not an easy thing, finding yourself alone when you weren't expecting it. I'm afraid I wasn't much of a mother to him after that."

"Oh, no," I say, even though I'm guessing she's probably right. "I'm sure you did the best you could. And, look, he's doing so well."

Or at least she thinks so.

I think so, too, actually, because if you ask me Mr. Freeman is a step up from his old job.

"Yes," she says with a put-upon smile. "Partner at thirty-three. His father would have been proud, but I wish he didn't feel like he has to work so hard all the time. I worry his life is passing him by." Her smile drops. "Look at me talking about anyone else letting life pass them by. I spend most of mine in this house, and it's still a mess."

"Have you ever considered adopting a dog?" I ask, because I

265

don't like the thought of her being alone in here. The rooms practically sing with the way things used to be, from the photos on the walls to those old magazines.

"You're not off-loading Flower on my mother," Shane says, strolling into the room easily on his long legs.

"I wasn't planning on it," I say, annoyance leaking into my tone. Mostly because we never did get to that photo album, and I'm dying to see more photos of young Shane. "Flower is a valued member of my family circle."

He approaches me, coming to a stop beside my chair, and I'm deeply aware of his presence, which ignites the memory of lying in his bed last night after he made me come. Again.

"You have a dog named Flower?" Mrs. Royce says. Being that she's Shane's mother, I half expect the question to be sarcastic, but she seems legitimately delighted. Then she lifts her fingers to her lips. "Oh, I didn't get the coffee." She seems shaken by it, like her forgetfulness about the coffee is a deep character flaw. I'm tempted to tell her to forget about it, or to pretend I don't even like coffee and was just going to drink some to be polite—something anyone who knows me would recognize as a blatant falsehood. Anything to soothe her.

"It's okay, I'll get it, Mom," Shane tells her. Wonders never cease, because he bends and kisses the top of my head before stalking off to the kitchen.

Mrs. Royce's eyes widen, and she studies me with renewed interest. Emotion wells in my chest, but I also feel like laughing, because Shane basically set off a bomb and then hightailed it from the room. Typical.

It's a snarky thought, though not without fondness.

"You and my son..."

"We've been spending some time together," I hedge, because it's the best explanation I can offer her right now.

She instantly brightens, like she has one of those dimmer

switches Poe was hoping to find last night, and someone just shifted her to high. "How *wonderful*," she says. "You know, he's been telling me for years about your van. What is it you call it?"

"Vanny," I say, my lips numb. Because, seriously, what the fuck?

"*Vanny*. He knows I like to hear stories about what you young people are up to. Sometimes I feel so closed-off from the world now that I'm retired."

"What did you do?" I ask.

"I was a teacher, and my husband was the principal." She gives an easy laugh. "I'll bet you're wondering how we came by this house on two teachers' salaries. Well, my husband grew up here. His parents left it to him. It caused a big to-do with his brother, but we needed it and they didn't, and there you have it."

This woman is a font of information. That's when it hits me. I know exactly how I can prove to Shane that his life outlook needs as much of a facelift as this house does. I know what to do...and dammit, I'm going to do it.

"Mrs. Royce, would it be possible to get your email address?" I ask, watching that door, because there's no way I want Shane to figure out what I'm up to. He'd tell me to stop or insist it's unnecessary, but my gut tells me it's *very* necessary.

She gives me the information, and then Shane brings out the coffee. We have a very nice hour or so together, drinking coffee while I coax Mrs. Royce into telling stories about Shane. Which slip into stories about Mr. Royce. I do get to see that photo album, but I regret it when I catch the look in Mrs. Royce's eyes—like she'd prefer to slip into the world of those photos and stay there. If Shane's problem is that he's trying to push the past away, hers is that she's hugging it too close.

We say our goodbyes, and Mrs. Royce surprises me by pulling me into a hug. "You'll bring your little girl around and visit sometime, won't you?"

"Of course," I say. Maybe I should have talked it over with

Shane first, but I don't see any harm in agreeing. I can visit her, with or without him. She needs more visitors. Besides, it wouldn't hurt Izzy to meet someone lovely like Mrs. Royce. Both of her blood grandmothers are ugly on the inside, but I suspect Mrs. Royce's soul is as nourishing as plate of pancakes with maple syrup.

twenty-eight

RUTHIE

WE GET INTO THE CAR, and we're both silent for a minute, though I catch Shane watching the house retreat in his rearview mirror as he drives away.

"*Shane*," I finally say.

"Uh-oh, here it comes," he intones, a glint of humor in his eyes, trained out the windshield.

"Your mom told me you got into a scuffle with Rand before he left town. What happened, and why didn't I know about it?"

Shane's flinch suggests he wasn't expecting this line of questioning. "Yeah, Danny told me he was giving you some trouble. So I went and had a talk with him."

"With your fists?" I ask in disbelief. "Does Danny know?"

"Not about that part. I didn't expect it to happen."

"Why didn't Rand or his parents try to have you arrested?" His parents are what you'd call the litigious type. They once sued a landscaping company because Mrs. Callaghan thought they'd purposefully pruned three of their bushes to look like a dick and balls. Knowing how difficult Mrs. Callaghan is, I'm guessing that they did, in fact, do exactly that, but that's neither here nor there.

Shane's lips twitch. "Because I gave him a good reason not to."

"You know, you're terrible at telling stories. I hope you're better at this in the courtroom, or Josie's screwed."

His mouth works, then he says, "Danny didn't want him to give you a hard time." A second of silence stretches between us, then he pulls the car over at the curb in front of someone's house, parks, and turns to face me. "Neither did I. I'd just started at Myles & Lee, so I had a P.I. from the office follow him around. He got some photos of him buying coke off a college kid. I told him to give you what you wanted and then leave you the fuck alone, that's it, I swear to Christ."

"So why'd you hit him?" I ask, my heart thumping hard. This would have happened years ago, before Izzy was even born. Shane and I were on particularly bad terms back then, especially after he'd gone to the trouble of telling me my future husband was a piece of shit before my wedding, then doubling down on that affirmation on the night of the rehearsal dinner.

He grips the wheel, then releases it. "He accused me of being Izzy's father. He said no man would care about you that much unless he was..."

"Fucking me," I say flatly. Emotion batters my insides, both because Shane cared enough about me five and a half years ago to bother with any of that, even though I'd made it clear how disinterested I was in his opinion, and because my ex-husband cared so little. There's anger too. Anger at all of them. Look at these men, thinking they could sort it all out behind my back. That it could be settled between them without involving me.

He swallows audibly before continuing. "Then he said he figured there were a lot of possible fathers since you were always hanging around with some other guy." He waves a hand. "I guess he was probably talking about the G.I. Joe. Rand's an idiot."

"I won't disagree with you there," I say. "But so are you. *And* Danny. You didn't need to do any of that. I signed a prenup, so it was already established what would happen when we got divorced.

And if it happened around the holidays, like your mother remembers, then he'd already signed the relinquishment of paternal rights. He didn't care whether Izzy was his daughter. He didn't want anything to do with having a kid."

He clenches his hand, then unclenches it. "I didn't trust him to do the right thing. He's not a good person."

"You're right. Is that what you wanted to hear? He's never once asked to talk to Izzy or see a photo of her." I pause, watching him. "Maybe he's really convinced himself she's *your* daughter."

He looks stricken, as if he'd never considered this possibility before. "I told him—"

I lift a hand. "I know. If he's convinced himself of that it's because he wants to believe he's a good guy. That he wasn't in the wrong. I don't care what Rand thinks. But I want *you* to care what *I* think. If we're going to try this, you need to have more respect for my opinion than he did. I don't need someone trying to steamroll me all the time."

Maybe his mother feels the same way, if he's tried to get her to move or pack away the photos. The situation might require a lighter touch—someone who will listen instead of trying to solve.

He nods, his eyes on me. "You're right."

I pause, my mind working furiously, hung up on this image of Shane confronting Rand. Of Shane hanging a photo of me and my family in his room.

I place my hand on his leg. "Your mom told me that you have a photo of me in your room."

"It sounds kind of messed up when you put it that way," he says with a soft laugh. "But it was a photo of you and Danny and Izzy. Danny's like a brother to me."

"I know," I say, my voice catching, because I know he's scared of losing my brother. He's scared, but he still wants to tell him about us, because I mean something to him. Maybe I have for a while.

"Don't worry," he says, his tone teasing. "I've never once

thought of you as a little sister. The dog act convinced me of that. No sister of mine would be so poorly behaved."

I lift my hand to give his arm a shove, then decide to keep it there, curled around his bicep.

A beat passes, then he says, "I'm not going to pretend I just put it up because of Danny, or because Izzy's the only kid in the world who's ever liked me enough to call me uncle. I liked having you in that room too. Because even though I didn't understand why yet, I knew you were important to me." He give me a half-smile. "A lot of people go around telling other people what they want to hear. Especially in the circles I used to run in. Most of the women I've dated have liked my suits, my car, my money. The way I look."

"Whoa, boy," I say, rolling my eyes. But I keep my hand on his arm. I can't seem to drop it.

"But you've never cared about any of that," he says. "You've always been straight with me, and I know you'll never tell me something just because you think I want to hear it." His half smile falls. "You said I was your little devil, but you've been my conscience. Pointing out whenever I fall short, which I know I do. A lot. So maybe a part of me needed you there, in my mother's home, where I feel like I've fallen short most of all."

Stunned tears fill my eyes. Because no one's ever said anything like that to me before, certainly not the man he confronted while defending my honor. I had no idea he thought these things about me. "You're a good son," I insist. "Your mother said so."

"She's hardly impartial," he says with a self-deprecating smile that doesn't quite hide the hurt he feels.

"You stay with her, when she needs someone around. That's more than most grown sons would do."

"It's not enough," he says darkly.

"Well, I'm not perfect either," I say, my voice hitching, my hand still on his arm. "I'm kind of a jerk. Only a jerk would say that thing about the little devil. If you're going to like me for seeing you as you are, I want you to see me as I am."

His lips twitch upward again. "Well, you always say I'm in love with myself, so I guess I like jerks."

"Shane... I...you make me want to do better too. What you said about me and Vanny... Maybe you didn't say it in a way your super sweet mother would have approved of, but you forced me to open my eyes and take a hard look at what I'd been doing with my life. At all of the time I'd been wasting. I'm grateful for that. And I..." I feel a couple of tears slide free, and my breath whooshes out of my chest when Shane reaches over and swipes them away, leaning in to kiss my cheek. "I'm so grateful for how kind you've been to Izzy. I'm a jerk for telling her not to call you her uncle. Because you've been like one to her. I mean...hell...you even remembered her argument with Goldie. You've been—

"I don't want her to call me uncle either," he says. "Like I said, you've never been anything like a sister to me."

My heartrate accelerates in my chest.

"But I'm not going to tell your daughter what she can and can't call me. I'm damn lucky she wants to claim me at all."

"She loves you," I say, feeling my voice catch again. The hope I didn't want to foster, that I'm so fucking afraid of, blooms in my chest. It's a little flame—brave and strong—trying to burn up a well of hurt and shame and disappointment. I want it to survive, but if I let it, there's a good chance it will burn me alive. I don't know how many heartbreaks and disappointments one soul can take. If it happens this time, though, I know it will be worse. I know it down to the roots of my soul.

"You've been more to her than her own father ever cared to be," I breathe out. It's a piece of goodness in him I've always noticed, even when I was inclined to focus on his faults.

He meets my gaze and holds it, his hand lifting to my cheek

again. "I meant what I said last night, Ruthie. I want to explore what's going on between us."

"I do too," I admit, the words wrenching free from that flame within me. "But I'm so fucking scared."

"So am I," he says, and then he gives me the sweetest kiss, a kiss that soothes even as it claims. And as I kiss him back, I reach with my other hand for the ring at my chest. Because I have to admit something to myself, even if I'm not ready to tell anyone else.

I want to believe there's a chance I can have it all for real.

twenty-nine

SHANE

I DRIVE us to Danny's apartment, my mind racing. I screwed up by not telling her about Rand. It could have ruined everything. I'm going to make other mistakes like that, ruinous ones, because I've never been good at letting people in. Telling them about my plans before I execute them. But she's still with me. And here we are in front of another hurdle.

This might be the one that destroys me.

Danny buzzes Ruthie in, and we hold hands as we walk up the stairs.

I can't seem to make myself let go of her. If I do, it feels like someone might tug her away from me.

I'm not a good man, but I want to believe I can be for her. For Izzy.

That's what I'll tell Danny, I decide, but I still feel like I'm an accused murderer walking into a sentencing. No, an actual murderer—because I committed the crime. I fucked his sister. I dared to do that, to ask her to be mine, when I know that I'm not good enough for her. I may be better than Rand Callaghan, but most things are better than a sack stuffed with shit.

We reach the door before I'd like to, and she looks at me and says, "It's going to be okay. He loves you."

I squeeze her hand, trying to internalize the way it feels in mine, then release it and knock on the door. The little dog immediately starts barking, making Ruthie wince. "She's still getting used to apartment living."

"Something tells me she'll always be getting used to apartment living," I say, but it's not without fondness.

She shoves me with her shoulder, smiling, and releases my hand just before Mira opens the door with a flourish.

The little dog launches out past her, straight toward Ruthie, dancing around her feet, its little legs pawing at her knees, as if she's a goddess to worship. Smart dog.

"I see you found some Twix bars," Mira says.

"What?" I ask, even as Ruthie hustles me inside, the dog following us. Izzy's on the couch with Danny, who's reading her one of those unicorn books she's so hot on.

"Oh, thank goodness you're here, Uncle Shane," she says, getting to her feet. "Uncle Danny tried, but he's no good with the voices. He made Mr. Rumptwinkle sound like an old woman."

Danny shrugs, the line of his mouth amused, but the expression drops as he gets to his feet, glancing back and forth between Ruthie and me. "Didn't know you were stopping by, Shane."

"I'll just be a minute," I say, my heart thumping harder. Was this how it was for my father? Did his heart start racing before it happened? It's a foolish thought—telling my friend something he doesn't want to hear isn't going to make my heart stop—but for a second it feels like it. "Can we talk out on the balcony?"

"God, that balcony is such a hotspot," Mira says, clucking her tongue. "I'm half-tempted to get Deacon to wire it so I can find out what you all talk about out there."

"I don't trust him to put in a wire. If you're really curious, I'll do it for you," Danny says. He's kidding in that dry way of his that some people don't pick up on. But Mira laughs.

Danny catches my eye and nods toward the door. "Let's go."

"But who's going to read my book?" Izzy asks with a pout.

"I will," Ruthie says, putting an arm around her shoulder. "But first, there's something I want to talk to you and Mira about." We decided that she'd talk to them while I talk to Danny; divide and conquer.

"Are you finally going to share the Twix bars?" Mira asks with plenty of insinuation.

"You have candy?" Izzy exclaims with excitement.

"I now realize that was a regrettable metaphor," Mira says. I'm guessing it has something to do with sex, and the fact that Ruthie and I have been having a lot of it, but at the moment I honestly could care less. Because my heart is still beating out of my chest, and now I'm following Danny out onto the balcony.

Danny really is a brother to me. The other guys are close friends, family in a way, but he's the one who held me together when everything else felt like using Elmer's glue to fix a shattered glass. He's the one who still goes on those bike rides through the Blue Ridge with me, because my dad used to bring us. Danny's the one other person, besides my mother and me, who really remembers my dad. Who honors him.

And he might be about to tell me to go fuck myself.

I close the door behind us, then sit down next to him in one of the chairs. He turns on the space heater, but there's a breeze in the air that makes it less effective than usual.

For a second I let the silence hang, because I'm very aware that I'm coming to him for the second time in as many weeks to share that I've taken liberties.

"You got something to say to me?" he finally asks. "Or did you just want to come out here to look at this view you've seen a thousand times in the cold?"

It's funny, and normally I'd laugh. But I decide it's time for me to confess.

Turning in my chair, I say, "I'm...interested in your sister, and I'm lucky enough that she feels the same way. I want to date her, but you need to know that I didn't plan on any of this when I asked Ruthie to help me out. I wasn't...I wasn't ever going to go there."

His face gives nothing away. He just watches me for a moment, then shifts his attention to the overlook again. Steepling his fingers, elbows on his chair, he asks, "Have you changed your mind about marriage?"

I flinch. "What do you mean?"

"You've always been dead set against marriage. *Real* marriage. You've told all of us hundreds of times. Hell, at one point you wanted us to make a pledge never to get married."

I think about lying to him and throw out the possibility. "I don't know," I finally admit.

I still don't like the institution of marriage. It brings the law into something that's supposed to be about feelings. It can be abused, the way Ruthie and I have abused it. And it often does not last. But my aversion to it has lessened.

His gaze meets mine again, sharp and not at all friendly. "So you want to date Ruthie, but you don't want it to go anywhere."

"No," I say, sitting up straighter and sliding to the end of my chair. "It's not like that. I really care about her."

He lifts his eyebrows. "That's news to me. You're always poking at her, wanting to know what she's planning with her van. Treating her like she's an obnoxious kid even though she's almost thirty. Is that what caring about someone looks like for you?"

He's not wrong, and the picture he painted doesn't look good for me. "I'm an asshole," I say, really and truly feeling it. "I think... I guess part of me was always drawn to her, and I figured I could make it stop if—"

"I'm not okay with this," Danny interrupts. "Although it's not as if you asked. You're not asking me now, either, are you?"

My heart thumps some more in my chest. I consider it. But no, I can't give her up. Not even for Danny. And if I did, I can't imagine I'd be redeeming myself in his eyes.

"No," I grind out. "I'm not. But you deserve to know."

"*Thank you,*" he says. "That's maybe the one honest thing you've said to me in weeks."

Anger flashes in his eyes, and he nods to the door without getting up. "You can see yourself out."

"So that's it," I say, flexing my hands on the arms of the chair. I didn't expect him to react differently, but it feels awful, like I'm being sawed in half. "You don't want to talk this through?"

"You shouldn't be running around with my sister unless you're serious about it," he says flatly, his gaze on mine. Cold, like it's never been before. "You know what she went through with those assholes."

"But I didn't say I wasn't serious. I...I think I'm..."

Falling in love with her. But the words won't come. Because it would be ludicrous to say it, to think it. A month ago, I would have sworn up and down that Ruthie Traeger was the most irritating woman alive. I would have almost meant it. But even then, her voice was a part of me. My conscience. My guiding light.

Five and a half years ago, I cared enough to pay Deacon to do that surveillance work, and back then, I had plenty of school debt. I cared about her enough to put that photo of her and Danny and Izzy in my room and be cheered by it, whenever I looked its way.

Still. I can't bring myself to say that to him—because it would feel like an excuse. He's asking me if I love his sister, and I can't give him a truthful answer. Either yes or no would only be a partial truth. And I know that what he is saying is categorically true. You shouldn't fuck your best friend's sister unless you're ready to marry her.

Yes, I *did* marry her, but he wouldn't be impressed if I chose this moment to point that out.

"I don't want to see you, I don't want to hear from you. Not until you're sure," he says.

He might as well have punched me in the solar plexus, and a part of me wishes he would. It might have made me feel better. He's looking out at the view as if I've ceased to exist, and Ruthie would probably be happy to hear that I don't feel particularly vain at all. I feel like shit on the bottom of Satan's shoe. I feel like the worst friend since Benedict Arnold.

"Okay," I say, nodding and lifting from my chair. "I'm sorry, man..." I turn back to face him before I open the door. "But I'm not sorry for wanting to be with her. I want to take care of her and Izzy. Both of them."

"They don't need anyone to take care of them," he says, meeting my gaze one more time. "And if they did, they have me. If they need anything, it's someone who loves them."

His words stick to me like a burr, the way only hard truths do.

I've always thought taking care of people was the same as loving them. I've thought it with my mother. I've thought it with Danny, even. Because you're supposed to take care of the people you love. That's what my father always said to me.

But the way Danny just said it now, it's different...

Maybe taking care of them is part of loving them, but it's only part.

And, what do you know? Here's further proof that I don't know everything.

I stumble out into the living room of the apartment, closing the door behind me, because I know Danny, even if he'd rather not know me right now. He needs to be alone and sit with this.

Ruthie looks up sharply from the couch, where she's sitting with Mira and Izzy. "Are we leaving?"

The little dog, who was lying by the couch, runs up and sits at my feet, her tail thwapping. Emotion rises in my chest, over a damn dog. Although maybe it's not this dog at all, but my childhood dog, who used to go hiking with my dad and me. She held out only a month longer than him.

"*I'm* leaving," I say firmly. "You don't have to."

Because Danny's message was clear and fair—this is my fault, not Ruthie's.

Mira's gaze instantly darts to the door. I don't have to glance over to know Danny's still staring out at the view. He probably doesn't look like he wants to kill me, but appearances can be deceiving.

"Well, we do actually," Ruthie says. "I have Izzy's car seat in your car, and my car is at your place."

Shit, she's right. I was hoping that I'd have time to think things through too. Because part of me feels like I've been selfish again, wanting her, and maybe this time it's going to ruin both of our lives.

thirty

RUTHIE

"DOES this mean I get to see Uncle Shane's house?" Izzy asks.

Oh, to be five again. I'd love to be able to ignore the silent tension filling the apartment, my brother's stoic form outside the glass door to the balcony, and Shane's pale, drawn expression—like someone just told him the fluctuations in the economy had wiped out his 401-K.

Low blow. It's just...

It's obvious that didn't go well.

Danny isn't happy. I didn't expect him to crack a bottle of champagne, not yet, but I didn't think he'd be *this* upset.

Shane's his best friend. Shouldn't he, on some level, want us to be together?

"Not right now, sweetheart," I say distantly, my gaze still on Danny through that door. Mira's watching him too, and as if he can feel our collective gaze, he turns to look at us. "I'm going out there to talk to him."

"No," Shane and Mira say at the same time. They exchange a glance, Mira laughing a little, but her laughter dries up when she sees the expression on his face.

282

"Give him some time to process it," she says, looking back at me. "Trust me, it's hard as hell—" Her eyes widen, and she glances at Izzy, who's heard much worse. "Oops, sorry. I was going to say it's hard for me, too. Waiting and me are never going to be friends. But it would be better if you do. I'm going to talk to him too, obviously. He'll get sick of all the talking I'm going to do."

Shit. They're right. I *know* they're right. But it would feel weak as hell to leave without saying anything to him. He's still peering through the window, so I tap two fingers to my heart—the sign Danny made up for *I love you* when we were kids. He'd do it in the middle of our parents' fights to let me know he was there for me. He immediately replicates the gesture, putting tears in my eyes, and then turns back toward the view.

It's not me he's mad at, but somehow that doesn't make it better. I just got back from seeing everything Shane's already lost, and what it's done to him.

They can't lose each other, and they definitely can't lose each other because of me. I'd never forgive myself.

"Okay," I say with a shaky breath. "I guess we'll go. Thanks, Mira."

I don't know what I'm thanking her for, exactly, other than being happy to hear news that obviously gave my brother no pleasure.

"Something weird is happening," Izzy says, glancing around at all of us. "And I don't like it."

"Let's go, honey," Shane tells her, calling her the same word I teased him for, before I heard his mother calling him that. "Let's go do something fun. What's the most fun thing you can think of?"

"Shopping!" Izzy says as she gets off the couch and runs over to him, hugging her little arms around his leg. My chest feels too tight suddenly. "Because then you can bring the fun things home with you, and the fun doesn't have to end."

"Ah," he says, mussing her hair with his big hand. "A budding capitalist. I approve."

He says this last comment with a little smirk at me. There's a hint of mischief in his eyes, but I know he's acting. Moreover, I know he's doing it for Izzy and me. He's crushed by whatever Danny said to him, and I know my brother well enough to know he feels the same.

I'm going to make this right for them. Whatever it takes.

We drop Flower off at the apartment and go shopping. Shane insists on bringing Izzy to a toy store and buying her the biggest Polly Pocket he can find, even though we agree it's ironic that a toy that was originally designed to fit in a pocket is now the size of a backpack. Then he helps me find more collapsible book cases and table for my bookmobile project.

Through it all, I sense his humming unease. But I can't ask him about it in front of Izzy, who loves both of her "uncles" and shouldn't be in the middle.

The way I am.

Izzy has asked us dozens of questions about this bizarre situation we're in—married and dating—but she seems happy about it. That's a gift, but it's one I'm afraid of keeping, because if she's happy about it, it stands to figure she might one day be sad about it. But I'm trying not to dwell on that possibility—on the what-ifs that lead to dark places.

After the store, Shane suggests a movie, and we go. Izzy insists on sitting next to him, and he covers her ears, at her request, during all the scary parts. It's a G-rated cartoon, but she asks him a lot. It's his attention she likes, and I can't blame her.

Despite what happened with Danny, I don't regret that Shane's with us. And I don't want him to leave. If he leaves, it feels like the magic will go with him. This beautiful thing blooming between us will shrivel, and I'll be left with nothing but the cold ring hanging around my neck. Maybe he feels the same way, because he stays, and stays. When it's time for dinner, he follows us back to the apartment and orders pizza.

He volunteers to read to Izzy, and I sit at the kitchen table, tears in my eyes, as I listen to them laugh and talk in her bedroom. Even though I'm worried about what the future will hold, it's been one of the best days of my life. I want this. I want it for me, and I want it for Izzy, and I wish I didn't, because the wanting might turn me back into that broken woman who had coffee with her mother.

Shane comes out with a smile on his face, but it drops when he sees me sitting there crying, or just about. Stalking over to me, he gathers me in his arms and carries me to the couch, Flower following at his heels. Then he holds me in his arms, his hand soothing down my back, and it hits me hard that his heart broke today, but he's the one comforting *me*.

"I should be the one making you feel better," I say through tears. It's almost an accusation, although I don't mean it that way.

"I can pretend to cry, if it'll restore your sense of justice."

I run my hand down his face, then lean in and kiss him. A sigh escapes him, so I kiss him again. Two times. Three.

"I haven't cried since before my father died," he admits after a beat.

I gasp. "That's not—"

"No, it's probably not good, and the therapist my mother sent me to after Dad died had plenty to say about it. So did the school counselor. But I've never done well in therapy. It always feels like the person's either talking at me or agreeing with everything I say."

"I figured you'd like that part."

"Very funny," he says with a smile, still rubbing my back.

I consider my next words carefully, because I know this man buries emotion like he's a dog hiding a bone he won't come back to. "Shane, it seems like there's still a lot you haven't processed from losing your dad."

"I know," he says. "But maybe there are things that happen to us that we can never fully accept or process. Things that defy the mind. This might be mine."

Maybe, or maybe he just needs to realize that his father *did* leave an impact—and that impact was good.

"I need to ask you what happened with Danny," I say quietly.

"He's thrilled by our news." He sighs again. "He doesn't want to talk to me again until I can tell him that I'm in love with you, that I want our marriage to be real."

"Oh," I breathe out, stricken. Obviously, it's too early to decide any of those things, but that little light of hope inside of me, which has been flaring all day long, is eager for those things. It wants to know, at least, that they're possible.

His hand keeps rubbing my back as he looks into my eyes. "I understand his position, Ruthie. He thinks I'm a man who can't give you want you want, and you're his sister. He wants you to have everything you deserve."

"Leave it to two men to decide what I want," I say, sounding braver than I feel. "*Again.*"

His lips tip upward. "Are you saying you're using me for sex?"

"Maybe."

"That's too bad," he says, his hand moving to my waist and tracing my side. "Because I want more for us. I just... We need time to figure it out. I never really wanted to get married. To me, it always seemed like something the law shouldn't touch."

"You're blowing my mind right now. You think there's something the law shouldn't touch?"

"I know, right?" he says, looking into my eyes as he tucks a stray lock of hair behind my ear. It seems like he's always doing that lately. Cleaning up my messes. "But I think you're forgetting something important. Josie the Great told you that everything was going to be okay for you. We should hinge all of our decisions on that assurance."

I smile, because it's funny, but I feel like he's trying to bury what he just said: he doesn't believe in marriage, and he's not sure he'll change his mind.

"She also told me I'd be getting married a third time."

"Not going to happen. I'd steal you from the altar."

I raise my eyebrows. "You don't get to steal me, Shane, I'm a person, not a candy bar."

"That's not what Mira seemed to think earlier. I know code words when I hear them."

A surprised laugh bubbles out of me. "*You* were the candy bar, not me."

"Are you going to take a bite?" he asks, his eyes sparkling. But it's still there, all the heaviness, all the baggage. All the emotion, packed down deep with six feet of dirt over it. He's hidden so much of himself, and not just from other people. I'm guessing he doesn't even know what's down there.

I pretend to go in for a bite, then kiss his jaw, but when he goes for my mouth, I pull back slightly. "If you don't believe in marriage, do you believe every relationship has an expiration date?"

He holds my gaze for a moment, one of his hands still settled at my lower back as I sit in his lap, my legs around him. The position is strangely natural, like we've been doing this for years instead of dancing around it. "I used to," he finally says. I don't know anymore." His brow knits, and I don't have to ask why. Not knowing something will always send him into a tailspin. "But I want us to spend more time together. I want to try."

And I kiss him, because I worshipped the boy he was. Because I'm drawn to the man I sense inside of him, beneath his ambition and unreasonable expectations for himself. The man he is at his core. Maybe I can reach him there if I kiss him deeply enough, long enough.

"I'd like you to stay for a while," I say, pulling back slightly.

"Thank God." He smiles at me, and this time it does meet his eyes. He nearly glows with it. "Because I had no intention of leaving, and it might have gotten awkward."

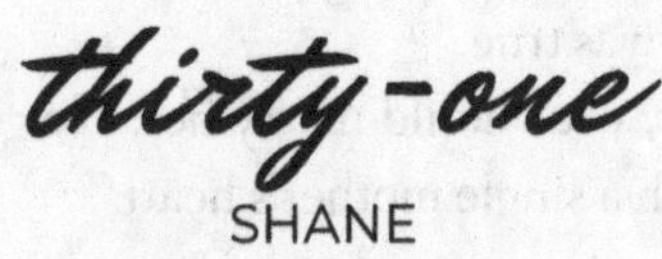

MY ALARM BLEEPS to life early in the morning on Saturday. Ruthie groans beside me.

"Smash the phone," she says into her pillow.

I'm smiling as I turn it off. I want to stay. I'd like nothing better than to burrow into her warmth and hold her and forget anything but now, here. This apartment that seemed like such a dump to me a week ago is...well, still a dump, but more inviting than my place. But Ruthie and I agreed last night that I'd leave early so Izzy won't see me. I don't know who the ruse is for, because we've already explained the situation for her. Change is best undertaken in stages, though, and I need time to process everything, too. I'm feeling raw in a way I didn't expect.

Before leaving the room, I let myself admire Ruthie for a moment, from the dark hair covering her forehead to the ruby shining from her neck. *My wife.* It's a thought I didn't ask for, but it's factual, at least, so I let it rest. I bend to kiss her forehead and then bring Flower out for a walk around the neighborhood. I'm not at all surprised to see Mrs. Longhorn peeking out of her door when I return.

"Good morning, Mrs. Longhorn," I say, barely holding back a *how's the peeping?*

"Is it?" she says with a sniff. "It's cold and dank. Makes my knees squeak." She lifts a finger to the door. "You said you were just a friend."

"At the time, it was true."

"If you like her, you should marry her. No good can come from playing around with a single mother's heart."

Well, I'll be...

This woman has always struck me as nosy as hell with little actual affection for Ruthie, but I suppose people can be complicated, capable of being snoops and actually giving a shit.

I'm tempted to tell her that I *did* marry her, thank you very much, but that would undoubtedly lead to twenty more questions, and I'd prefer not to be mired in this conversation for the indefinite future.

"You're right about that," I say.

She gives the harumph of someone who enjoys being right—a feeling I understand perfectly well.

"A man was over here yesterday, you know. The dog was barking. *Loudly.*"

My pulse picks up. "Oh?"

"I looked out of my spyglass."

"Naturally."

"He was fumbling around with a package—" she releases a loud sniff, "—and you know there are plenty of package thieves around these parts. Someone needs to keep an eye."

With her around to watch the stoops, it's surprising anyone gets away with anything. Still, I nod.

"I opened the door to ask him what in tarnation he was doing, and he said he'd come to deliver it. So, naturally, I took it from him. Didn't want any funny business. That girl over there's had enough of it, what with you and that dog and those cameras."

She hands over an Amazon package from a table just inside the door. I'm surprised there are no signs of tampering, but this woman runs a tight ship. She probably owns a steam machine that allowed her to open and then reseal it.

"She gets a lot of these packages, you know," Mrs. Longhorn says, the snoop overtaking the caring neighbor.

"Most people do. It's why they're taking over the world."

Her lips pucker. "She told me she has some secret admirers. They buy her stuff off some kind of wishlist. Are you okay with that?"

I'm okay with Ruthie getting the things she needs without feeling the compunction to send them back, absolutely.

"Yes, I'm okay with that."

She gives a harumph. "My father would never have allowed another man to see to my mother."

"Who says it's a man?" I say. Then, "I'll make sure she gets it."

"You do that," she tells me. "She's been avoiding me, your girl. I asked her to come see me, and I've barely seen hide nor hair of her."

"I doubt she's avoiding you," I lie. "But I'll let her know you're concerned."

"Thank you, and consider what I said, son." She taps her ring finger knowingly.

I return both the Amazon package and the dog to the apartment and leave a note telling Ruthie her favorite neighbor has been asking after her.

I go home, expecting regret to kick in.

I go home, expecting myself to start to freak the fuck out.

But it doesn't happen.

If anything, I miss Ruthie and Izzy. I wonder what they're getting into, and if that little dog of theirs is causing any trouble.

~

On Sunday afternoon, Ruthie calls to let me know Izzy has popped a fever. Another ear infection, she thinks. The doctor's office is closed, so I offer to drive them to the urgent care. "You don't need to do that," she insists over the phone. "I have the insurance card. I can bring her."

"I need to," I say, my hands shaking a little. I know it's just an ear infection, nothing major—she's had a hundred of them, to hear Ruthie tell it—but there's a worry in the back of my head. A feeling of...

I'm not superstitious, but I watched my father, a seemingly healthy man, collapse in front of me. I'd like to see Izzy with my own two eyes, is all. When I pick them up, Ruthie meets me at the door, Flower at her heels.

Alarm ripples through me. "What is it? Did she get worse?"

"No, nothing like that," she says, taking my arm. "Her fever went down with medicine. It's just...I wouldn't have been able to do this without the insurance, Shane. I would have had to treat her at home and wait for her doctor's office to open tomorrow morning to get her started on the antibiotics. My co-pay for the emergency room was, like, over a thousand bucks."

"Well, you don't have to worry about that anymore," I say, feeling like a knight. Maybe Danny's right and caring about someone isn't the same as taking care of them, but right now, it feels like I'm doing both. Right now, I could kiss Monty Freeman's feet.

I kiss Ruthie softly, and then we find Izzy, who's made a "sick fort" in her bedroom with five unicorn stuffies and a stack of Unicorn Diaries books. She brightens when she sees me, and I feel the rest of my anxiety fade. Not only is she okay, but she sees it as good news that I'm here.

In the car, Izzy announces, "You know, Uncle Shane, I'm going to get a surgery soon so we can make sure this never happens again. Mom says it's not supposed to hurt much, but I'm pretty scared. Do you think it'll be okay?"

"Yes," I say without hesitation. "I think it'll be just fine. And I bet your mom will let you eat as much ice cream as you want."

"Will you take us to the ice cream shop like last time?"

I glance at Ruthie, sitting beside me in the car, and put my hand on her leg. She covers it with hers. "Yes, I will. And I'll read you Unicorn Diaries too. As much as you can stand." A memory hooks into me, and I add, "You know, when I was a bit older than you, I had to get my tonsils out, and my dad set up the living room for a sleepover so my whole family slept out there, my mom, my dad, and me, because he knew I didn't want to be alone."

"Can we do that after my surgery?" she asks, an inevitable question that I hadn't considered when I'd shared what was in my head.

I take another peek at Ruthie, who smiles and shrugs. *Your move, Vain.*

"Yeah," I say, feeling emotion unfurling in my gut. Uncomfortable yet comfortable. "I'd like that."

I'd like it more if it were at my house, not the apartment, but that's a discussion for another time. We get Izzy's prescription, and I drop them off. And later, when Izzy's asleep, Ruthie sends me a photo of her in a in a slinky red teddy. *What do you think? Do you like this better than the flannel pajamas?*

Me: *I might need to come over to inspect it in person. I don't believe in signing off on something I haven't seen.*

Ruthie: *I'd expect you to be thorough.*

Me: *I'm already out the door.*

When I get there, I can practically feel Mrs. Longhorn's heavy breathing through her door, but my attention is fixed on the apartment across from her. The door cracks open, and Flower has either decided to take pity on my libido or is in her crate, because the only thing I see is the curve of Ruthie's silhouette in that red teddy, which hugs all the parts of her I've felt and worshipped. I'd like to do some more worshipping tonight.

"I'm ready for my inspection, Mr. Royce," she says in a sultry whisper designed to drive me crazy.

"Good," I say, pushing my way in. Ruthie's watching me from the side of the door, her lips parted, her eyes done up with smoky makeup. She's wearing spiky black heels.

I shut the door and turn toward her, backing her into the wall, falling to my knees as I do it. "I think I'll start here."

I slide up the bottom of the silky teddy and say, "Yes, I like how little it covers." A groan escapes me when I realize she's wearing nothing under it. Her legs are smooth and warm, and there's something even more exquisite between them.

"But you're making me cold," she says, looking down at my head with a sly smile. "So why don't you put your mouth on it?"

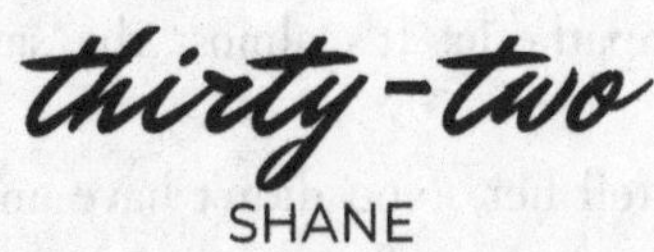

SHANE

"HAS your family moved in with you yet?" Josie asks.

It's Thursday, and we're in my office at Freeman & Daniels. I've spent a good chunk of the week working on Josie's case and digging into a few others. And, yes, I've spent plenty of time with Ruthie and Izzy. Burke and Leonard also came over my place with a bottle of scotch the other night. Turns out Burke's set a date for his wedding—April 19th, the day of his parents' trial. As *fuck yous* go, it's a pretty elegant one.

They let me know I have their support, for which I was grateful, but I felt Danny's absence, his continued silence.

"Well," Josie asks, increasing her volume as if I might have avoided her question just because I didn't hear it, "have they?"

"No, and can you be more discreet?" I eye the closed door.

"No," she says. "It's bad for my aura to restrain myself." She gives me a pointed look. "It's bad for yours too, you know. But you were finally honest with your friend Danny, so that's something."

Sighing, I say, "I happen to know that Mira talks to you occasionally for some godforsaken reason. There's no reason for you to perform for me. I'm not the one we have to convince about your talents."

295

"How are the witness interviews going?" she asks with a sniff, tossing her dark hair over her shoulder.

"Fine, although I'm not sure your old boss from the tea shop is the best witness, given she thinks she can read a person's future at the bottom of a teacup."

"She's very empathetic. It's almost the same thing as being psychic."

"You know," I tell her, "you didn't have an appointment here today, but I do bill by the hour."

She gives me a defiant look. "Not at the rate you used to charge."

Did she come in here just because she felt like pissing someone off?

"No," I agree, "but it's still not cheap. A therapist would be cheaper. Or a psychic. I've heard they come at a bargain rate these days."

"Not after this trial is over. I'm going to raise my rates. I might even have to hire staff."

"For your fictional TV show?"

She gives the sniff of a lady offended. "Everything that's real starts out fictional."

I sigh heavily. "That's one of those things people say to sound intelligent that doesn't actually make any sense. Can you explain why you're here?"

"We're not going to lose, are we?" she asks, and for the first time I see what I should have picked up on when she first shoved my door open, upending the potted plant Izzy picked out for me earlier this week. Josie's not here to taunt or annoy me. She's nervous.

"I don't like to speculate, but the chances of us losing are very low," I say. "Like I told you, it's a superfluous lawsuit. He's angry, and a person should never file suit out of anger. It would be extremely rare for a judge to award the plaintiff money in an alienation of affection case, particularly since the person the defendant is suing is not the man who alienated his ex's affection." I smile at her. "Besides, you have me. I'm good at what I do."

She studies me, perhaps looking for some fluctuation in my face or aura that will tell her I'm a liar. But, in this, I'm not. It's not vain to know you're capable.

She nods. "How do I get the most out of this? I feel like this is my big break. Maybe it's yours too."

"Don't talk to the press. It would look bad, and you could get into trouble with the judge." I think for a moment, then add, "But you could hardly be blamed if you have some friends who are alarmed for you. Friends who choose to talk."

"You're saying I should have my friends contact the press?"

"No," I insist. "Just that it wouldn't be your fault if they do. No one could blame you, so long as you keep quiet."

She gives me an overdramatic wink that almost has me believing she's psychic, if only because she's a shitty liar.

"Thank you," she says. "What's your address? I'm going to send you a housewarming present."

"That's not necessary. I've lived in the same house for years."

She leans back in her chair and smiles at me. "The present is because your family is moving in."

Sighing, I rub my temples. "It's Thursday. I'd know by now if they were moving in this week."

"If you've lived there for that long, I can find your address by myself. Damien showed me how."

"Is Damien one of the voices in your head?" I ask. It's easily the most unprofessional question I've ever asked a client, but she basically just admitted to wanting to stalk me, so there you are.

"He's a private investigator," she says, looking into my eyes and holding my gaze. It's a little uncanny, to be stared at by this psychic, and I feel that *a goose walked over my grave* sensation. "You'll be meeting him soon."

I swear to Christ, it's at that exact moment my phone buzzes. I'm not a superstitious man, but I flinch.

"You'd better get that," Josie says knowingly. So maybe she didn't come here because she's afraid. Maybe she's up to something.

When I check my phone screen, I see Danny's number. My heart thumps at a faster pace. I lift up a hand to Josie in a *please wait* gesture and answer it.

"Danny?"

"Yeah," he says, his voice agitated. "Ruthie asked me to call you, because she's too shaken up to talk right now. Someone vandalized her van." A beat passes. "It's bad. We're here at Tank's shop."

"Is she hurt?" I blurt, my voice loud in the small office. "Is she okay?"

"She hasn't been harmed, but I wouldn't say she's okay. The van's really messed up."

Fuck, *fuck*. Ruthie's been pouring her soul into her project, preparing for this weekend. She must be devastated. It must feel like the failure she's feared is happening. But that's not the only thing that worries me....

That van didn't mess itself up. Someone did it on purpose, and I doubt it was a random crime. Someone did this because they know how important Vanny is to Ruthie.

"Have you called the police?"

"Yes. They're on their way, and I also called those P.I.s Burke knows. I have a feeling they might be more helpful for something like this. There's property damage, obviously, but whoever did it didn't take anything. The cops are more interested when something's been stolen."

"Could your mother be responsible?"

"I'm hoping that's what they can tell us," he says, a low rumble of anger beneath his voice.

"Can we fix it?" I ask. "Or do we have to buy new stuff?" I think again of how much effort Ruthie's been pouring in, only for the cup to be broken.

"Maybe a mixture of both."

"I'll be right there," I say, already getting up and grabbing my coat from the tree.

"Thanks." Silence hangs over the line for a moment before he adds, "I didn't just call you for Ruthie. I wanted your take on this, man." Then the line goes dead. Maybe he's still mad at me, but he hasn't lost all faith in me.

"Where are we going?" Josie asks eagerly.

I'd forgotten she was there, which is ridiculous given she's sitting right in front of my desk, but my focus is now on getting to Ruthie. Helping Ruthie. Showing Danny...whatever it is he needs to see.

My gaze narrows on her. "Ruthie's van was vandalized. Did you have something to do with this?"

"I've been here with you for over an hour."

Yes, she has. I can't seem to get her to leave, but I will be billing her.

"What about your boyfriend?"

"He's at a mindfulness retreat. This lawsuit has caused a regression in his spiritual development. Just yesterday, he suggested we open a Roth IRA account."

"Not a bad idea."

She lifts her chin. "It was *beneath* him."

"I don't believe in coincidences," I say.

"Neither do I," she says. "This wasn't a coincidence. I knew something was going to happen today. Didn't I tell you that you'd be meeting Damien?"

I give her a look that's probably as annoyed as I feel, because I'm not inclined to try for a filter at the moment. "Yes, and that's precisely why I'm suspicious."

She rolls her eyes. "Oh, don't waste time having the police look into me. I only break the law when it's stupid, or when it directly benefits me. What benefit would I get from destroying your wife's van?"

My wife. My wife needs me.

"I have to go."

"Of course you do," she says, waving me off. "I'll just pop around and talk to Mr. Freeman. He needs to know that Mercury's in retrograde."

And she needs to ensure she tightens her hold on him prior to the trial. Fine. Right now I couldn't give a shit. I'll mention my interview with her to the police and the private investigators, but I can't deny she has a point. Why would she do something guaranteed to piss me off when she's relying on me to get her out of a bind?

I don't know. At the moment, I don't care. I need to get to Ruthie.

thirty-three

RUTHIE

I CAN'T STOP CRYING.

Tank wanted to throw a couple of sheets over Vanny so I couldn't see the damage, but Danny wouldn't let him in case it disturbs the scene. I'll never forget what it looks like—disemboweled books everywhere, along with debris from the destroyed book-making kits, assembled with such care and stored here because there was no room in the apartment. The mural painted on Vanny destroyed by random bursts of spray paint, like ugly fireworks. The sides keyed and scraped. The tires popped. The shelves broken.

There's an ache inside of me that won't ease, as if someone destroyed me and not my van. I want Shane. Something deep inside of me needs him. It's alarming, how quickly I've come to rely on his support.

He's coming. Danny called him.

I'd asked my brother to meet me here this morning so I could show him the updates I'd made to the "Vanny experience." I'd hoped he'd soften after seeing how much Shane has been helping me prepare for the party this weekend.

I've tried to talk to Danny about Shane a few times this week, but the conversation always hits a brick wall.

He knows what I need from him, Danny will say—and then he'll clam up. No one knows how to be stubborn like my brother, except for me I suppose. And Shane.

He's coming, I repeat in my head. And then, because I'm a fool, I remind myself, *Josie said it was all going to be okay. The police will take care of this. They'll figure it out in no time.*

Two officers do show up, but they don't seem particularly interested in processing the scene. They take several photos, ask Danny and me a few questions. And then they ask Tank to come down to the station for further questioning.

"Why?" I ask, pissed and still crying, tears coursing down my cheeks.

Danny, Tank, and I are sitting in the garage on a few folding chairs—the guts of Vanny exposed and raw next to us. Tank brought out a couple of chairs for the officers, too, but they've ignored them and turned down the offer of coffee.

The more talkative officer, Officer Loomis, rolls on his feet. "That's classified, ma'am." His partner stands beside him chewing something. It's probably gum but looks like one of those Hi-Chew candies. She hasn't said a single thing, so I've nicknamed her Officer Gumshoe in my head.

"Because it's my shop, and I'm the one with the keys," Tank says with a huff of air. He's wearing a long-sleeve shirt, but even though it's freezing in here, he's rolled up the sleeves. Then again, Tank always has run hot, ever since we were kids. "They think I did it."

"The vandal broke the lock," I say, incredulous, getting unsteadily to my feet. "And Tank's been my best friend since Kindergarten. He obviously didn't do it. Why would he?"

Tank looks away as the officer glances at the wreckage of Vanny and does the feet rolling thing again. "Thing like this...looks to me like a crime of passion. This was done by someone you know, ma'am. If the shoe fits..."

"I'm guessing it would fit *my mother*," I say. "She approached my daughter at school a few weeks ago, and when I confronted her about it, she was upset."

But they know this. I've told them several times by now. Danny, too.

"We're going to explore that avenue," Loomis says. "Surely will. But we intend to put in a thorough investigation."

"Is that why you took prints?" Danny asks, eyebrows raised, his tone caustic.

The door finally creaks open, and it's him, it's Shane. More tears flood my eyes as I get up and run to him. Actually, it's more of a stumble, because I can't get my legs to work properly.

"Oh, honey," he says, wrapping me up, and this time, I don't have the slightest urge to laugh. It feels like he's coating the broken parts of me in bubble wrap. "We're going to fix this, Ruthie. I promise. And we'll find the person who did it and stop them."

I believe him.

"Where's Izzy?" he asks. "She's not still at school, is she?"

"No," I say through tears, my face buried into his shoulder. "Mira picked her up. We were worried my mother might..."

"Good," he says. "That was good thinking. I'm glad she's safe. The guys are on the way. Leonard and Burke are coming. And Michael. It might take them an hour or two, but they'll be here."

"Your assistant?" I ask, shocked.

He runs a hand over my hair, then wraps his arm around me. "He wants to help. Freeman gave us the day off. We're going to make it work, Ruthie. We'll get Vanny ready for Sunday. Everything's going to be okay." He lifts his gaze to the officers. "Unless you're classifying this as a crime scene."

"We have what we need," Officer Gumshoe says, her first words. I can't imagine that's true, since they only took half a dozen photos, but I guess there are worse crimes than the dismantling of my dream.

"Are you coming with us?" Officer Loomis asks Tank, obviously itchy to leave.

"Why?" Shane asks sharply. Then, to Tank, "You must be Tank. I'm Shane." Turning to the officers, he adds, "Ruthie's husband."

A gasp escapes me, because it's the first time I've heard him call himself that, and he had no need to. I'm also surprised he remembers Tank's name is something other than G.I. Joe. Danny's watching Shane, and so is Tank. My friend's gaze settles on Shane's arm, wrapped around me. He looks upset, and I see Officer Loomis glancing between him and Shane and making inferences he has no business making. The next thing I know, he'll say Tank was driven to do this by jealousy.

"They want to take me in for questioning," Tank says after a moment, "since it happened at my place of business."

"Have you taken prints?" Shane asks the officers.

"No," Officer Loomis confirms.

"If you do, you can rule out Ruthie's mother. She's had more than one arrest." He glances at Tank, his gaze lingering, and then says, "And if this guy did it, he'd have cuts all over his arms and hands. He's clean."

The two officers exchange a glance, and Gumshoe slowly nods. "No one approach the van until I get back," she says, then heads outside, presumably to her car.

"I'm his lawyer," Shane says, nodding toward Tank. "If you want him down at the station, I'm coming with him, or you could talk to him here and save us all the trip."

"You just introduced yourself to him," Officer Loomis objects. "We all heard you."

"I'm just that efficient."

Again, I'm shocked. No, I'm blown over. Shane has acted dismissive or jealous of Tank in the past, like Rand. But he's a better man than Rand, in every single way, and here is my proof. He's putting me first. My friends. My happiness.

The door swings open, announcing Officer Gumshoe's return, but she's not alone. A woman with neon pink hair and a leather jacket with rivets is with her, and behind them is a tall, very good-looking man in an overcoat. The pink-haired woman's stare trains on me. "Don't worry, crying woman—"

"Ruthie," the man supplies.

"We can probably solve this in five minutes. This situation has nothing on the shit we've been dealing with over the past six months."

"And you are?" asks the chatty cop, his expression bored, or maybe annoyed.

"Your worst nightmare," the woman replies.

"I'm Damien, and this is Nicole," the man says. "Pleased to meet you."

"Oh, shit, I've heard about you," Loomis says, hitching his belt up and straightening his posture. "They don't much like you down at the station."

"See," she says, preening, "I told you."

"Can we please get back to figuring out who mauled my van?" I ask, although I'm happy they're here. They must be the husband-and-wife private investigators my brother called in. According to him, they get results—and I need to know who did this. If it was my mother, or if there's someone else who's decided they hate me.

"Get back to it?" Nicole asks smugly. "We're just getting started."

RUTHIE

THE POLICE OFFICERS took prints from the van, snapped a few more photos, and then asked Tank some questions inside the shop with Shane. They're gone now, and the rest of us are sitting around on the folding chairs in the garage.

"So," Nicole says, "now that they've left, tell us the real scoop. Other than your mother, who could have done this? Anyone acting weird?"

Shane stirs in the chair beside me but leaves his hand on my thigh, where it's been since we first sat down.

"Her neighbor," he says. "Mrs. Longhorn. She's taken an interest in Ruthie's goings-on." He lifts his other hand to his chin, rubs. "I don't think she'd be physically capable of it, though. And she's shown some fondness for Ruthie."

"Are you serious?" I ask in disbelief.

He nods. "Actually, she might have noticed something useful. She's always poking her head out the door, watching what's going on."

That, I have no objection to.

"What about your daughter's father?" Damien asks. He studies

306

me—probably looking for a reaction. "Could he be mixed up in this?"

"Yeah," Nicole says, picking up the thread. "You think he'd have a problem with you boning your brother's friend?"

Danny coughs, or maybe chokes.

"Is that necessary?" Tank says tightly, scowling at her. I feel a pulse of contrition, because I know this mustn't be easy for him. When I explained that I didn't feel *that way* about him, he claimed he was going to move on, but he probably didn't think *I'd* move on. I've gone years without being serious about anyone and now...

Now I'm falling in love with the man I married for convenience. No one's more surprised than I am.

"Surely is, Muscles," Nicole says. "If the ex has a problem with their situationship, he could have chosen to take it out on the van."

"I mean—" But Tank cuts himself off, his brow furrowing. His gaze shifts to me. "What about your secret admirer?"

"What's this now?" Nicole asks.

"She has a secret admirer, someone who's been buying her items from her online wishlist. It's gone on for years. I mean...maybe it's not just one person, but it's so regular..."

Nicole snaps her fingers and then points at me. "Maybe you have a stalker on your hands. This might be more than a five-minute case after all."

She sounds almost happy about it, but it feels like my heart has dropped out of my chest. For years, my secret helper has been making me feel less alone. Could it have been some weird psychopath playing a long game?

Shane clears his throat, and the room's collective attention shifts to him. "That's not going to lead anywhere."

"Don't you think that's for me and my ridiculously handsome husband to decide?" Nicole asks with arched eyebrows.

Shane meets my gaze, his hand still on my thigh, and I can see it in his eyes before he says a word. They're warm and deep, and *knowing.* A sense of wonder fills me. "It was *you.* All this time, it was you."

A corner of his mouth twitches up, and he nods. His gaze averts to my brother, who's watching us. Danny gives a slight inclination of his head, and my heart lifts, because I know without asking that this has done it. This revelation has given Danny the information he needed. And that means he believes Shane really loves me.

Despite what's happened today, I experience a moment of pure happiness.

Looking back at me, Shane says, "Not just me. I know Danny started doing it too, and probably some of your other friends. But... yeah. I guess it's mostly been me. I wanted to help make sure you and Izzy didn't want for anything. I know it wasn't easy for my mom after my dad died, and I was so much older than Izzy. It wasn't... I just—"

"You did that for me?"

I can see him thinking it through, trying to find a glib remark or a joke. Trying to stuff down what he's feeling the way he usually does. Or tell me he did it for my brother. And then I can see him deciding not to do any of those things. He turns in his seat, fully facing me, and lifts a hand to cup the side of my face. "Yes, Ruthie, I did it for you."

My heart is brimming with pride and love. That flame inside of me, the one that's refused to gutter and die through so many disappointments, flares brighter as I lean in and kiss Shane, in front of my brother. In front of Tank. In front of everyone. And I couldn't care less about making an exhibition of myself.

Distantly, through the haze of Shane, of love, which is blanketing every other disappointment and fear, I hear someone come in, and then Leonard's distinctive voice. "Ho-ly shit. I heard y'all were back to torture us some more. Whatcha been up to, anyway?"

"Well, now," Nicole says. "*That's* a story."

~

Later that day, Nicole and I pull into the parking lot of my apartment building. The guys are hard at work on Vanny—Tank, Burke, and Leonard are all working together to fix the interior while Danny, Shane, and Michael make runs around town to pick up the other things I need, the ones that can't be fixed. They're doing it together, friends again, and I'm as over the moon about that as both of them are. Leonard's girlfriend and Burke's fiancée have joined Mira at my brother's apartment, and Mira called to say they'd like to take Izzy out for a spa afternoon. When she put Izzy on the phone, she sounded so excited I nearly started crying all over again.

My heart is full. All of those times I felt alone, like the whole weight of my world was resting on my shoulders, it wasn't. I had support. I had a scaffolding. I still can't fully comprehend that Shane was my wishlist admirer all this time, helping me in a way that didn't make me feel ashamed or condescended to. Shane, who didn't want to be thanked or acknowledged. Who did it just to make sure that I was getting by, even though I thought the worst of him.

Shane, who has been suffering in his own way, and needs someone to look out for him the way he's been looking out for me. I've been trying—all this past week, I've been working on my secret project for him right alongside the work I've done for Vanny.

Damien, I guess, is out looking for my mother. He says the police will be doing the same, but he clearly agrees with Nicole that they can find her faster. Cases like mine aren't a priority for the overloaded department.

That's also why Nicole and I are here to talk to Mrs. Longhorn. "You'd be surprised," Nicole says. "Old people notice shit. Most of them don't have much else to do but notice things."

We get out of the car, and I lead the way, but then I stagger to a stop.

My front door is hanging open, the latch broken. The camera

sags from where it was mounted above the door. My whole body is rigid, my gaze fixed on the door. Terror trails the adrenaline rush, followed by rage.

"Oh my God, someone broke into my apartment," I call out, running toward it. Because Flower. My little Flower—

Nicole pulls me back, hard enough that I almost fall off my feet.

"Don't be a fucking idiot," she hisses into my ear. "You don't just go charging in there. What if the perp's lying in wait?"

"So what do we do?" I ask in an undertone, feeling another tremble work through my body. What if I adopted that little dog only for something horrible to happen to her?

"*I'm* going to charge in there, obviously."

"Do you have a weapon?" I ask, nervous. I don't know how I'll feel about her answer either way. I don't like guns, but I don't want to find myself on the business end of one.

"I *am* a weapon," Nicole intones, her gaze on the door. "But if you talk to Damien about this, maybe don't mention that I went in alone."

"I don't think—" I start, but then a familiar, deeply loud bark rents the air, even as I hear the telltale sound of the door behind us cracking open.

"Flower!" I shout as the little dog runs to me. I gather her up in my arms and hold her to my chest, getting a sloppy face-lick for my efforts. "Mrs. Longhorn," I say, turning to look at my neighbor, Flower still squirming in my arms. "You *saved* her." Because surely my dog must have come from my neighbor's apartment.

"*Oh*," she says in her raspy voice. "So I suppose you'll deign to talk to me now."

"You're Mrs. Longhorn?" Nicole asks, her gaze pinging between my neighbor and the broken door behind me, as if she still kind of wants to dart in there in the hopes she might catch someone raiding my refrigerator or stealing my underwear.

"Yes," Mrs. Longhorn says with a sniff. "And I saw *everything*."

Nicole nods in her direction. "I can tell this is an exciting moment for you. I'm just going to pop into Rachel here's apartment, and then—"

"No one's in *Ruthie's* place," Mrs. Longhorn says. "And the man didn't get very far before this little dog started biting him in the shins."

"Did you call the police?" I ask, breathless.

She makes a little noise, half laugh, half tobacco. "Yes. The officer gave me a card for you, but I wouldn't hold out much hope. The thief didn't take anything other than a hairbrush."

"Excuse me?" I ask, nearly fumbling Flower, because honestly, what the fuck?

"A hairbrush," she says with a tight nod. "The little girl's, I'm guessing, unless you're one of those Disney adults."

"God forbid," Nicole says with a theatrical shudder.

"This is awful," I say, anxiety prickling at me. "Was it some kind of weirdo pervert who's after Izzy?"

"Or maybe the perp grabbed the first thing they saw to take a swing at the dog," Nicole says. "Either way, it's obvious they arranged for a distraction so no one would be at the apartment. That means at least two people are involved."

With the theft of a hair brush?

Turning to my neighbor, Nicole says, "Can we come in and ask you a few questions?"

Mrs. Longhorn looks like she orgasmed for the first time in a decade, and I feel a rush of guilt. All she wanted was to feel important, like her opinion and observations matter. I understand that, and yet I've done my best to avoid her.

"Yes," she says, "come in, come in. And Ruthie, you can put the dog down once you're in here. I don't mind her none."

Wonders never cease. But I hold on to Flower, because I need to hold on to something. If someone's after Izzy...

I'll cut off their balls, obviously, but even so...

We settle onto Mrs. Longhorn's couch, a velvet upholstered piece with clawed feet, in front of a long coffee table. For a woman who always seems to have a cigarette, her home doesn't smell of smoke, so it must be a habit she relegates to the great outdoors.

"I have tea," she says, her voice harsh. "Bourbon."

"Oh, that's fun," Nicole says. "My friend here will take some of that. She needs to loosen up. You can hold the tea. But I'm good. I've got an emergency flask."

I give her a sidelong glance, and when Mrs. Longhorn disappears into the kitchen, I ask in an undertone, "Are you sure I should drink it? What if she's, like..."

"What if she's the woman who broke into your apartment, fucked up your van, and stole your child's hairbrush?" Nicole scratches her head, her eyes roaming. "It would make for an interesting twist, but I don't think it's likely. Besides, you don't have to drink it. I was just hoping to get a look at the room without her noticing. Seems pretty standard old lady stuff, though." She smirks at a little pile of doilies arranged on the side table by the door.

Mrs. Longhorn comes back with a serving tray that has two glasses on it, each filled with a couple of inches of bourbon. She sets it on the coffee table, then slugs back one of them before pushing the other toward me.

I finally set Flower down and pick the cup up, but I don't drink the contents. Maybe she didn't poison me, but I'm on edge. Other than myself, the only person I trust in this room is Flower.

"So," Nicole says slowly, her gaze settling on my neighbor. "This pervert was a man?"

Mrs. Longhorn nods. "I'd never seen him before. An individual was lingering outside Ruthie's door a few days ago with an Amazon package, but it wasn't the same man."

"Was the Amazon guy out there long enough for him to take photos?" Nicole asks. "And did he have anything around his face?"

"A hat pulled low," Mrs. Longhorn says. "And I suppose he

would've had time to take photos. He was as slow as molasses in January."

"Could've been an Amazon guy, could've been the perv's friend," Nicole says. "I feel you. And you said the little dog seemed to have gotten in a few bites?"

"Yes," says Mrs. Longhorn. "I was...indisposed when I first heard noise across the way."

"Indisposed how?" Nicole asks. "It may be important to the case."

Or to her curiosity, but I'm curious too, so I don't say so.

"If you must know, I ate too many prunes." Mrs. Longhorn snaps. "When I finally got to the door, the man was running out, Flower nipping at his leg. There was a hole in his pants, and he was shouting and trying to hit the little dog with the hairbrush."

Nicole gives me a look. *See, it's only probably a pervert.*

Her lips thin. "I went out there immediately, but the scoundrel kicked Flower and ran. I wanted to pursue him. It chapped my hide to give up, but my hip wasn't up to the task, so I checked on the dog."

"He kicked her?" I ask, my heart hurting. I reach down to where she settled at my feet, and she licks my hand.

"He did," Mrs. Longhorn says disapprovingly. "It takes a cowardly man to kick a dog." She waves a finger at me, as if remembering she disapproves of me in addition to the coward. "You haven't come to see me the way I asked."

"I've been...busy," I say, my hand still petting Flower, looking for hurts.

"Oh, I know what's been keeping you so busy. It's that big strong man. He may not be able to hold his water, but he's no harm to the eyes."

Nicole chuckles. I do not, because the reminder makes me ache for Shane.

"I've been busy with trying to relaunch my bookmobile, Mrs. Longhorn, but someone vandalized my van today."

Nicole gives me a look people reserve for idiots, which surprises me because she just got done telling me she doesn't see Mrs. Longhorn as a feasible suspect. I guess she probably goes through life thinking everyone is a feasible suspect until they prove otherwise. It sounds exhausting.

"Oh dear," Mrs. Longhorn says, lifting her fingers to her lips. I'm surprised by how genuinely upset she appears, because most of the time it seems she loves nothing better than seeing me fail. I'm tempted to say so. Instead, I give in and take a sip of the bourbon. It settles warm and deep in my stomach.

"Ruthie, that bookmobile was why I wanted to speak with you," Mrs. Longhorn says. "I used to work in a bookstore, back in the day, and it went out of business. I couldn't bear to see them throw out books, so I brought most of them home with me. I have hundreds. Thousands. They're all on shelves in the spare bedroom."

"You'd sell them to me?" I ask in surprise.

That surprise turns to shock when she frowns at me, her whole face creasing into familiar lines, and says, "Why in tarnation would I do that? They're in there gathering dust and not being read, which is the one thing that's supposed to happen with a book. I'm telling you to take them, girl. I've been trying to tell you for weeks."

For a second, I can't find any words. She has never once shown the slightest interest in helping me, or in the van, or in books in general. Not around me. But I realize now, sitting here on her claw-footed couch, that I never gave her the chance. I formed my impression early on, and everything she's said and done has fed into that impression.

I did the same thing to Shane.

What an awful thing, to think the worst of someone and be wrong.

"Thank you," I choke out through the tears in my eyes. I didn't used to be a crier, but lately I'm the mother who turns on the water-works over Hallmark commercials. "Thank you, Mrs. Longhorn. You know, today I found out Shane's the one who's been buying my wishlist packages. You know, the ones you thought random men were getting for me? He's been doing it all along. I believed he hated me. I believed *you* hated me. But you've both been helping me all this time, and I—"

She starts laughing and lifts a hand to her mouth again. "No wonder that fool boy didn't seem bothered when I told him you were getting presents from other men."

"Yeah, he's got this sexy stalker thing going on," Nicole says reflectively. "I don't hate it for you. Now, Mrs. Neighbor, can you give me a description of the jackass who got bitten and the guy with the Amazon package? As detailed as you can. I have a friend of a friend who's a sketch artist."

She makes a dismissive sound. "What's the point of those cameras if you're depending on my memory?"

"If he was wearing a hat, I'm guessing he knew he was being a recorded. Maybe his buddy showed up the other day to check things out. It's possible he knew where to stand and where not to as well. We need all the information we can get, and you're the woman who can give it to us."

Mrs. Longhorn has that *I just orgasmed* look again.

thirty-five

SHANE

"I WANT Ruthie and Izzy to come stay with me," I tell Danny as I load another collapsible bookcase into the shopping cart. Michael volunteered to go pick up floor pillows in another section of the store, because two of Ruthie's were slashed and defaced with spray paint.

I'm painfully aware that I'm giving Josie what she wants, or what she predicted anyway. Could it really be a coincidence? I made some calls to look into her boyfriend's whereabouts this morning. She was telling the truth, which doesn't mean she couldn't have hired someone to trash Ruthie's van. But why would she bother? I don't know, but I did mention her to the police officers before they left. They were so interested they didn't bother making a record of the information.

I sigh internally, then add, "It's not safe for them to be at the apartment until we have a better idea of what's going on."

"And the little dog, too?" Danny quips, raising an eyebrow.

I sigh as I nod. "Yes, the little dog too." Flower will probably wreak terror on my house and look adorable doing it, but I'm a resigned man. Ruthie and Izzy need to be safe. They need to be with *me*.

Danny claps me on the back. "It's not me you have to convince."

But it is, or at least it was. This past week has been half excruciating, half exultant—because I had her, but I'd lost him.

"You're not pissed anymore?"

"I'm starting to think I should have figured this out years ago. Maybe I would've if I weren't..." He shrugs, and I feel like a real fucker. I hate being the one to give Danny this thought—that if he were different, more typical, life would be easier for everyone.

"*I* didn't figure it out," I point out. I'd told myself I was helping her because it was the same as helping Danny. Because my mother had become a single mother unexpectedly, and if more people had helped her, she might be doing better now. But I'd also wanted to help Ruthie without shifting the dynamic between us, which I both enjoyed and drove me insane.

Even now, the thought of being in a relationship without an end date makes my skin prickle. It makes me think of losing my father.

"Well, you defended her to her ex, and you've gone out of your way to make sure she has what she needs without having to actually ask anyone for it..." He gives me a wry look. "I'd say you understand her, and it's obvious you're serious... I'm not going to say this isn't weird for me, or that it won't continue to be weird for me. But I love you, and I love my sister, and if you make each other happy, I have no objection. There's every chance I'll eventually be happy about it."

I laugh, feeling a wash of relief so profound it almost makes me stagger. "Thank God. I've missed you, man."

"I've missed you, too," he says and hugs me. From the way he's saying it, I get the sense that he's not just talking about this last week, but the fullness of this time when I haven't quite been myself. The past months of unemployment, plus the last couple of years at Myles & Lee, when I felt myself getting sucked into the machine and reshaped to be the weapon they needed.

I was on a path then, though, and now...

I don't know where I'm going, but I'm enjoying the journey. Ruthie's right about Freeman. He's a good man, and there's a chance that we can work together to push the firm to the next level. Maybe that would be enough to satisfy this thirst I feel. Maybe not. Either way, I've realized there's something else I've been missing.

And that's when Ruthie calls to tell us someone broke into her apartment to steal Izzy's brush.

~

There are a couple of scuffed suitcases in my living room, a cardboard box full of toys, and a very excited dog who just peed right next to the door.

At least she tried?

Either that or she's purposefully taunting me for the fun of it, just like her owner does.

It's official—Ruthie and Izzy *are* temporarily moving in with me.

"Uncle Shane," Izzy hollers. "Flower needs to pee."

"That's old news, buttercup," Ruthie says, already dipping into the kitchen for the paper towels and cleaner.

They're not the only ones here. My house, usually so empty it echoes, is stuffed full. Damien is still off searching for Rita, but Nicole, Danny, Leonard, and Burke are gathered around the now-too-small kitchen table, trading theories about what this all means. We've checked out the footage from this afternoon from the camera at Ruthie's door, and the results are unimpressive. The only thing it captured was the top of a man's head, verifying nothing but his shitty taste in hats.

Mira's also here, along with Burke's fiancée, Delia, and Leonard's girlfriend, Shauna. It's a full house.

My friends have come over a few times in the past, but my house has never hosted a gathering this big or loud. It feels surprisingly nice.

"Who wants pizza?" Leonard calls out, and most of the people present raise their hands.

"Yes, yes, yes," Izzy cries in response, jumping. Her little pigtails fly in the air, and I think again of that brush. That fucking brush. Unless it's solid gold, a ready explanation isn't coming to me. Nicole says the intruder might have picked it up to fight off Flower, but Flower's such a little thing. Sure, she's got a jaw you don't want latched around your body parts, but would a thief determined enough to set up this whole charade be so easily deterred?

Because this was a complicated job. The perp took out the camera at the apartment before breaking in and almost certainly arranged for the van to be destroyed. And then there's the suspicious type Mrs. Longhorn saw delivering the Amazon package the other day. He managed to do it without showing his face on camera.

Also, not to be a dick, but what else could the thief have been after? Ruthie's apartment isn't exactly a goldmine. A point that earned me a shoulder shove when I made it earlier. I stand by its validity. If you're going to go to such trouble to rob a place, wouldn't you want it to be a place you'd walk away from with something other than a fifteen-year-old TV?

Did they do it just to scare her? To show her they could break in at any time?

Either way, I agree with the cops who came by earlier: it's obviously personal, but how?

I don't like this situation one bit. The only thing I like about it is that Ruthie and Izzy are here where I can look out for them. Even if it means getting some piss on the floor.

Ruthie tries to sweep past me to get to the piss, but I put an arm around her waist. "I'll get it. Why don't you sit down?"

She barely has, all day. She's buzzed around, propelled by nervous energy and the need to fix things. It's a need that animates me too—we're both fixers, doers—but this situation won't be resolved in one day, and Ruthie's going to burn herself out if she keeps running on fumes.

"I can clean up a mess," she gripes.

"Your apartment would argue otherwise." Not a nice comment, but she's not the kind of person who wants to be coddled. I want her to know that I'm still going to treat her like she's herself.

Her lips tug upward. "You're the worst."

"No, he's not," Izzy says, darting forward and wrapping her arms around my waist. "He's the best. I really love him a lot."

Well, fuck. I lean down to kiss her head. "I love you a lot too. Why don't you go check out your bedroom, Izz? Fill it up with toys."

"Is it really going to be mine, Uncle Shane?" she asks, practically dancing on her feet. Mira and her friends brought her to the spa earlier, and her fingers and toenails are painted a bright, sparkly purple that she claims is a "unicorn" shade. Given they're fictional animals, no one can dissent—but I suspect Izzy would give them a hell of a good argument if they tried.

"Yes, honey," I say. "It's yours."

I can feel Ruthie watching me as Izzy grabs the box of toys, nearly as big as she is, and heads toward the room in the back of the house. When I look at her, there are tears in her eyes again. "Oh, Ruthie," I say, lifting a hand up to stroke her cheek.

"You said it was her bedroom," she tells me in an undertone. The others are far enough that they probably can't hear, buried in loud conversation as they are. I half expect Ruthie to tear into me for creating expectations that can't be fulfilled. But she doesn't. Instead, she lifts onto her toes and wraps her arms around me, the spray bottle and towels still in her hands.

"It is," I say into her hair, letting her presence calm me. Because she's safe, and she's going to stay that way. "I want you to be here. I've been wanting you here."

"Because my apartment complex is a dump," she teases.

"Whenever you're there, you look like you're cataloguing a honey-do list in your head."

"Yes," I agree, because I like it when she calls me out. "But it's also because I want you both here. I want you staying in my house, my bed. And I do want Izzy to make that bedroom hers."

I mean it. I feel at peace, even as I'm aching to fix this situation for her. I keep reminding myself of how far we've come on that front. Vanny's facelift is well underway, waiting only on a new mural, which Shauna, who knows an abundance of painters, is taking care of. Thanks to Mrs. Longhorn, we have hundreds of new books to add to Ruthie's collection and bundle for sale. Tomorrow, we'll focus on recreating the bundles that were ruined.

We'll make her project shine for her.

We'll make damn sure to erase her doubts and write a new script over them, so fear will never make her hesitate to let some quack read her fortune again.

We eat the pizza when it comes, then play a couple of rounds of Apples to Apples because it's a game Izzy can play with the help of a dedicated reader. But Nicole keeps making every round into a different dirty reference, some of them so obvious even a five-year-old might be in danger of figuring them out, and it's not long before Ruthie breaks off to put Izzy to bed.

Twenty minutes later, she comes out with a half-smile on her mouth. I rise without anyone telling me to. I feel compelled to as surely as if there were a hook in my lip and she just gave it a tug. Ruthie grins at this bit of telepathy. "She requires the great and powerful Oz to come read Mr. Rumptwinkle to her."

"Glad to hear you agree about the great and powerful thing," I say.

Danny groans, and Leonard starts laughing.

I ignore them both and get up, giving Ruthie a quick kiss on the temple as I make my way to Izzy's room.

"Uncle Shane," she says brightly when I open the door, much

too chipper for a kid who's supposedly on the verge of sleep. She frowns as I close the door. "I shouldn't call you that anymore, should I, if you're married to my mom?"

I come over to the bed and sit on the ground beside it, putting my head about level with hers. "You can call me whatever you'd like, sweetheart."

It occurs to me after the fact that giving a child an open invitation like that is as good as asking to be called Captain Fuckface.

"What if I called you dad?" she asks softly, the words carving a hole into my chest. "I know it's mostly pretend, but I've never had a dad. Mom said he moved away before I was born. She told me we don't need him, and she's right. My mom is a very strong woman."

A smile lifts my lips. "That she is. And you're shaping up to be another one."

Izzy's lips tremble. "Don't tell mom, but I've still thought about having a dad. I think I'd like to pretend."

That hole in my chest seems to stretch wider. Part of me wants to tell her no, because I don't know what the future holds.

It's indescribably painful to have a father and lose him. To watch the life be ripped from him. I won't give her that and then take it away—I *can't*.

But even if I don't get what I want, even if I don't get Ruthie, maybe I can still be that person for Izzy. Maybe I can still stand up for her and give her what she deserves.

I clear my throat, trying not to show her what a loop she's thrown me for. "I'd be very honored, Izz, but that's not a decision we should make tonight. Let's sit on it for a while, and I'll also talk to your mom."

"Okay," she says, "I think I'd want to take it slow, anyway, to see what it feels like. It would be a pretty big change. Can you read the Unicorn Diaries to me now? I know you're probably sick of them, but I don't think I'll ever get tired of them."

"How could a person ever get sick of Mr. Rumptwinkle?" I ask with a wink, ignoring the sudden sweatiness of my palms.

Dad. I never thought I'd be one. That wasn't the path I'd chosen—because that path was the path that led to annihilation. To being snuffed out and remembered only by the people who mourned you most. The ones who couldn't let go, no matter how hard they tried.

Sadness gathers in my chest, but it's not the only emotion there. There's also a deep kernel of love, growing brighter, stronger. It grows when I'm with this little girl, with Ruthie. It grows and grows. I only hope it won't prove to be a cancer, blotting everything else out.

"Shane?" Izzy asks, looking up at me.

"Yes, honey," I say, trying not to look like I'm having an existential moment.

"What are you going to do for my mother for Valentine's Day? It's coming up on Monday, you know."

"I was going to get her roses," I say. A play on her story to Mrs. Freeman.

Izzy makes a face that scrunches her little nose. "That's so basic."

A laugh rips from me. "What wouldn't be, Izz?"

"Something with a deeper meaning. Flowers just get dry and die when they're not in the ground, and that's sad."

From the mouths of babes.

"I'll give it some thought," I say, and I'm sure I will. I have a feeling I'll be up all night, giving thought to any number of things, including who thought it would be fun to mess up Ruthie's dream. Because when I find them, I *will* make them pay.

After Izzy's eyes flutter shut, I leave the room and shut the door behind me. I pad into the living and find it empty, other than Ruthie curled up on the couch, her dark hair loose at her shoulders, and Flower lying at her feet. There's not even much of a mess, other than those suitcases, still sitting out, because the trash from the pizza has been cleaned up.

She rises from the couch, and I feel my heart thumping in my chest as if it's a wild animal stuck in there.

"I need to thank you for today," she tells me.

"No, you don't," I say, stalking toward her. I consider telling her what Izzy said, then throw out the idea. I'm not ready to talk about it yet, and after the day she's had, I'm guessing she's not either.

"Don't tell me what I do and don't need to do," she says, her lips lifting slightly.

"But I enjoy telling you what to do," I respond as I reach her, my hands finding her shoulders. "Plus, it gives you the chance to tell me to go fuck myself, which both of us enjoy. I feel like I should point out that you like ordering me around too."

"I do. And *thank you*. I can't believe....all this time you were the one who was ordering that stuff for me. You don't know how much hope you gave me."

"You don't need to thank me," I repeat. "I did it because I wanted to. Because I couldn't stand the thought of you needing those things and not wanting to ask. It was nothing for me."

Her bottom lip trembles, and her eyes shine and blaze at the same time. "But it was everything for me."

She's made herself vulnerable, and I can see the silent question in her eyes. She's asking me to do the same. I already feel vulnerable. They're here. They're *here*. And she knows my secrets, all of them. But I understand. She's laid her cards out and wants to see mine.

I run my finger over her bottom lip before giving in to the impulse to capture it in my mouth and suck. A little moan escapes her. She lifts up onto her toes, and suddenly I'm lost in the kiss—my hand weaving through her hair to bring her closer as our mouths strain against each other. Her lips are so soft, so lush, but there's nothing delicate about the way she kisses. Because Ruthie's not a delicate woman. She's strong, the way Izzy said, and she's forceful. I love that about her. I always have, even when all of her forcefulness was turned against me.

I tear myself away, panting, because suddenly it's not enough to consume her mouth.

"I need you in my bed," I say. "I need to prove to myself that you're okay. To kiss every last inch of you."

Her hand flies up to my jaw. "*Yes.*"

The little dog takes one look at us, decides we'll both be preoccupied for some time, and takes the bold step of launching onto my couch. I don't attempt to stop her. I like my women bold.

This time I do carry Ruthie like she's a princess, and the smirk on her face tells me she notices. "You're not going to throw me over your shoulder this time?"

"Not this time," I say, kicking the door to my room open and carrying her in. I turn and close it behind me with my foot, press the lock. "But there will be other times, when the mood strikes."

"*Good.*"

I lay her down, and she instantly pulls off her sweater, making me smile. "I was going to do that."

"I figured I'd prove to you that I'm capable of undressing myself."

"I believe you're capable of anything you set your mind to," I say, and her red lips part. I lean in and capture them, and then I go about proving that I meant what I said. I take off the rest of her clothes slowly, kissing and licking my way to a greater knowledge of my wife's body. Of the dips and curves of her, of the places that tickle her and the ones that make her moan. And by the time she's fully naked, she's begging me for more.

And by begging, I mean she's swearing at me.

"You want my cock?" I ask.

"I think I've made that very clear," she says with a gusty moan, reaching for it through my pants. "You're wearing way too much clothing."

"Let it never be said I'm not a generous man." I undress quickly and roll on the condom, feeling Ruthie's hot gaze beating into me, watching every single fluctuation of my hand. She reaches down and starts touching herself, and I instantly get harder—my need a selfish thing that has caught hold of me and doesn't care to release its grip.

I take her hand and suck her fingers, then hold both of her hands over her head. Her eyes get wider, hotter. "Are you going to take me now?"

"Yes," I say, thrusting into her, but it doesn't end up going that way, not totally, because we're staring into each other's eyes the whole time, and I can't stop kissing her. Her lips, her face, her sweaty, sweet-smelling neck. As we come together, I realize, in a frighting burst of clarity, that this is what people mean when they talk about making love.

It's only later, as I lay awake sleepless, that another revelation hits me.

The hairbrush.

Why would someone with a personal gripe against Ruthie go out of their way to steal one? The pervert explanation doesn't hold water, because as far as I know, there aren't many people with a kink for shed hair....

Well, shit. They wanted it for a reason that had nothing to do with flogging Flower on the ass. And it might be all my fault.

RUTHIE

CONVERSATION WITH TANK

I didn't want to ask you in front of everyone, but you're really with that guy now?

I thought you hated him.

I was wrong.

Were you?

He defended you. Those cops wanted to take you down to the station.

He only did it to impress you.

Ruthie, this is a mistake, and I'm not just saying that because of what happened between us a few months ago.

I'm saying it as a friend.

You need to think this through. This guy's a self-important prick. Just like Rand. Just like Jarrod Travis.

> He's nothing like them. I'm sorry. I HAVE thought it through. Shane's not the man I thought he was.

> He is. And you're not going to see it until it's too late.

YESTERDAY WAS the worst and best day of my life.

It started with my dream being ruined, but my friends banded together to lift me up. Even Mrs. Longhorn has proven herself a friend. Then there's Shane...

Shane who gave me my wishes, one at a time, read my daughter to sleep, made love to me, and *asked me to stay*.

So I lost one dream but gained another.

Of course, dreams can be tugged away from you, no matter how tightly you try to hold on.

I think that's why I've been touching Shane all morning, ever since he shared his theory with me. The edge of his hand. His pants, which are—shockingly—not part of a suit. His shoe. I need the physical reality of him against me, because it's the only way I can confirm this is happening.

Shane's been my husband in name for two weeks now, and it's starting to feel real. That's dangerous. It's flat-out stupid, but it's also true. Still, my nerves are raw, both from the break-in and Tank's text messages, which keep repeating in my head.

This is a mistake.

I'm not used to disagreeing with Tank or being at odds with him. I don't like it. But I have to believe he only feels that way about Shane because he's angry and jealous.

Danny and Mira come over with breakfast, and at around ten, Nicole and Damien show up. Nicole has a serious case of bedhead and the sour look of someone who doesn't enjoy mornings. I understand. I see a similar look in the mirror every day.

A few minutes after they arrive, Shane, Danny, Nicole, Damien, and I settle in around the table in Shane's kitchen. Mira is playing spa with Izzy in her room so we can talk. All of us agree this conversation shouldn't be for Izzy's ears.

Once we're gathered, Shane shares his theory with the private investigators. He believes someone stole Izz's brush on purpose, because they want to test her hair follicles and verify that she is, unfortunately, Rand's daughter.

"You know, goddamn it," Nicole says, thwapping the table. "You fucked up my big reveal. I live for them."

Damien gives her a fond look and nods. "She really does."

"So it *was* him," Shane says, his hand fisting around the lip of the table like he wants to flip it over.

"No, actually," Damien says. Sighing, he glances at me. "I found your mother last night."

Dread crawls over me like a wave of many-footed insects. My gaze shifts to Danny, and I can tell he feels the same way. He has a far-off look in his eyes, like he's staring into the past and doesn't like what he sees. I clear my throat. "And..."

"And he pretended to pick her up at a bar," Nicole says. "He's *very* charming."

I'll bet. I'm not surprised to hear she was drawn in—or that she was hanging out at a bar despite her protestations that she's sober.

"She's been in touch with Rand's folks," Damien says. "They reached out to her."

Anger ignites in my gut, and I'm a lit match of a person. "Why?"

He glances around the table. "Your *husband* here is right. They wanted to verify whether she's actually their son's daughter."

"After he blew town, he told them someone else knocked you up," Nicole finishes. "This guy." She points a thumb at Shane with an amused look on her face.

He squeezes the table again, looking about ready to hop into a car and drive for hours just so he can beat Rand up again. Part of me would like to go with him and take a shot of my own. Then again, *of course* Rand told his parents that...

They wouldn't have been okay with him walking away from his own child, from their blood. Especially once they realized he didn't intend to go make babies with someone more appropriate.

"Well, we always knew Rand was stupid," Danny says practically, ruffling a hand through his hair. "Stupid people do stupid things."

"He knew the truth," I say thinly. "He just didn't think it made him look good."

I place a hand on Shane's arm before nodding to Damien. "Go on."

Damien clears his throat. "I guess Rand's mother has noticed a family resemblance, but they knew you weren't likely to be receptive—"

I snort. "Because she called me a gold-digging whore?"

"Precisely, so they sought out your mother to see if she could help them. They figured she could figure out a way to get to you."

"They'll *never* have access to my daughter," I say, feeling a shiver work down my back as I remember the things that woman did and said to me.

Shane layers his hand over mine. "No, they damn well won't," he promises. "Rand signed those papers. And we've caught them in the act, or we will. They're guilty of plenty of things. Breaking and entering. Theft. Hell, we might even be able to get them on attempted kidnapping."

I'm grateful for him, again. Grateful that he knows the law and can use it as both defense and weapon.

Damien gives us a second before continuing. "When your mother tried picking Izzy up at school, I'm guessing she intended to bring her to the Callaghans. Or obtain some sort of sample from her." I hear Danny swearing, but Damien continues, "But it obviously didn't work out."

"So she decided to ruin my van," I say, trying to keep my voice steady, "and give them a chance to break into my apartment."

"She didn't tell me that," Damien says, lifting up a broad palm. "In fact, she gave me a big sob story about her unfeeling daughter cutting off both her and her in-laws. But I get the sense your mother has a casual relationship with the truth." He withdraws a drawing from the bag he carried in and sets it in front of me. "This guy look familiar?"

"No."

"This is a near perfect likeness of a petty thief we've gotten to know pretty well. Our friend the sketch artist based it off Mrs. Longhorn's description. I've already gotten in touch with the perp. He claims he had nothing to do with the break-in, but I'll tell him we got him on camera. Which we do. He cased the place early in the morning a few days before the break-in. Probably to look at the cameras. He's only on there for a second, but a second's enough. He'll talk."

"To you?" I ask, dubious.

"To *us*," Nicole says. "We can get anyone to talk."

Shane's jaw tightens again, and I hold back the desire to run my fingers over it. "Good. We haven't heard from the police yet."

"You will," Damien says to him, then shifts his gaze to me. "There were prints on the scene. That's to be expected. Your prints would be all over it, but I have a contact at the station who told me your mother's prints are in the van too. She's going to get called in for questioning. Maybe she's already been called in. That means she'll be running scared. She might ask the DA to cut her a deal if she turns in the people who pushed her to do it." He lifts his eyebrows. "She might reach out to *you*."

"She'll regret it if she tries," I snap. I can feel Shane and Danny both watching me.

"So you're not inclined to give her a break?" Damien asks.

"No," Danny, Shane, and I all say at the same time, as if we practiced it.

Danny looks at me; I look at Danny. "She doesn't deserve any more chances," my brother says, his voice firm. "She's done enough."

I take his hand and squeeze it. "I agree." My voice doesn't quaver either. Shane puts his hand on my thigh under the table—his way of telling me that he agrees with us and we're making the right decision.

Damien leans back in his chair. "Mind, I wasn't implying you should."

Nicole waves a Twizzler she got from who-knows-where through the air like it's a magic wand. "We wanted to know if we were dealing with stupid people. No one wants to waste their time on stupid."

I laugh. I can't help it. It's nervous and loud, and this is mine too—the ability to laugh when all life gives you is lemons, and you don't have any sugar but the kind that comes from appreciating the absurdity. "That's fair."

Nicole nods in approval. "Family shit can be heavy. I only found out I have a half-sister when my old man kicked it and left us his house. It felt like I should have known about her, but Damien and I never tried to look for my dad. If we had, it would have been as easy as that—" She tries to snap, fumbles it, and scowls.

"There's more than one of you?" Shane quips.

"I don't think she'd appreciate the comparison," Nicole says with a movie villain laugh.

"I don't know," Damien puts in, "she seems to be learning the way of things."

I'm guessing she didn't have much choice.

"Speaking of parents," he adds. "What would you like to do about your ex's?"

"Press charges," I say, holding the side of the table.

If they cared about Izzy, they never would have sent someone—a criminal—to break into our apartment. The only thing they care about is her DNA. They don't deserve her.

"Thank God," Shane says, miming wiping sweat off his brow. Or maybe it's real sweat; he seems genuinely relieved. "I was worried you wouldn't want to get litigious." Then he surprises me by adding, "I'll ask Freeman to handle it. I'm too close to the situation."

"So you trust the legal beagle?" I ask, the world narrowing to us. This feels like a change in him. A blossoming awareness that power isn't the only thing that matters in a person. I'm hoping my special project will help with that.

"I do," he says. His gaze holds mine, something like an entreaty in them. "It wasn't ever about a lack of trust, Ruthie."

No, it was more a lack of respect, and it would seem he's gained some. For the legal beagle and for me.

"Say," Nicole says, pausing in her attack on the Twizzler. "I hear you're representing our associate Josie in her court case."

Shane heaves a weary sigh. "No comment."

Nicole winks at him. "Sure, *you* have no comment. But she's been making plenty. She says you have the aura of a corrupt politician."

"She probably meant that as an insult, but I take it as compliment," he says, prompting me to roll my eyes.

"Well, we're going to be in the peanut gallery," Nicole says with a laugh. "Along with half the town, probably." The cackle gets louder. "I have it on good authority that there's going to be an article about the case in the local paper today."

"I don't know anything about that," Shane says. I'm surprised, because he's obviously lying.

"You told her to talk to the press?" I ask.

"No comment." But he smiles at me as he delivers the rote words.

He's changing before my eyes—becoming less rigid and more human. I'd like to think I'm part of it.

Still, in the back of my head, I can see Tank's messages.

You're making a mistake.

~

It's Sunday, and Loving is full for the first time in years. It puts tears in my eyes to see so many people here, snacking on the appetizers and drinks Charlie keeps bringing out from the kitchen. There's no ordering today, just special plates inspired by their decades in business.

I'm touched for Eden, but I hurt for her too, because if all of these people cared so much, they could have kept the diner open. Then again, she and Charlie seem excited about their plans for the future.

Shane brought Izzy and me here early, and Charlie made her a milkshake. While she sucked it down, Shane helped me set up my mobile bookcases and book bundles in the back of the diner, along with the puffs, floor pillows, and oversized stuffed animals for sitting. There's a book-making station, too, plus an informational pamphlet about my partnership with Dog is Love, featuring Izzy reading to Flower, and Charlie put together a hot cocoa bar.

This is it. This is the dry run for the new and improved version of my bookmobile.

Vanny is parked out front so everyone can see her restored glory. The front and center parking job has a second advantage: if anyone tries to mess with her, there will be dozens of witnesses.

Several of those witnesses will be the very people who helped me, because they all showed up—my brother; Shane's friends and their partners; Tank, even though I felt sure he'd skip the party after his texts yesterday; and Shane's assistant, Michael. Ralph came, and it must be a Goldilocks day, because he pronounces his coffee just right. Mr. and Mrs. Freeman are also here, along with a couple of other staffers from Freeman & Daniels.

When Josie shows up with her boyfriend, Shane and I are talking to the Freeman & Daniels crew while Izzy plays in the book area at the back of the restaurant. No one invited them, but that doesn't ever seem to be an impediment for Josie. Eden zeroes in on her. "Want some chocolate cake?" she asks, lifting her brows.

"You're being sarcastic," Josie says with an upturn of her nose. "Sarcasm is the lowest form of—"

"I'd like some, actually." Poe wraps an arm around the maybe-psychic. "I love chocolate cake."

Josie the Great gapes at him, and I can feel Shane laughing beside me. I lean into him, letting myself absorb the feeling of his laughter, and he looks down and murmurs, "Do you want some chocolate cake, Ruthie, or are you worried about your chakras? I'll feed it to you if you ask nicely."

I step on his foot. Mrs. Freeman, who clearly missed that, heaves a happy sigh and says something about young lovers to Mr. Freeman. They head off. Someone taps me on the shoulder, making me jump. I turn and see Mrs. Longhorn. She looks smaller here, as if she shrunk when she left the apartment complex.

"I see you put those books to use," she says, and I'm so bad at reading her, I honestly can't tell whether or not it's a complaint.

"Well..." I hedge. "Yes."

"Good." She gives a wave of her hand, then pulls out a pack of cigarettes she obviously cannot smoke in here.

"You can't smoke those in here," I tell her.

She gives me a look that would wither a lesser person. "I'm eighty-seven years old, Ruthie, I know where I can and can't smoke. If I decide not to care, that's my business."

The laundry room at the apartment complex would beg to differ, but she *did* give me those books.

"Thank you," I say, meaning every bit. "You made this happen for me."

"Don't be foolish," she says dismissively, waving her pack of cigarettes. "When you've done something, good or bad, don't be so quick to give away the credit."

"A woman after my own heart," Shane says, smirking at me, but I know he's trying to lighten my mood. To reassure me that everything will continue to go well today, even though we're both expecting a less-than-welcome guest.

"It's *her* heart you're after," Mrs. Longhorn tells him with a sniff. "I hope you have more patience than most young men."

"You think he needs patience to put up with me?" I ask. And here I was starting to think she likes me.

"All worthwhile pursuits require patience," she says loftily, as if she just added *dense* to her internal list of my failings. "So yes, Ruthie, I should say so."

She wanders off, presumably to get her nicotine fix, but I continue to think about what she said as Shane and I make our rounds. As I speak with Mr. Freeman's event planner friend, newly arrived, and lead him through all of the updates I've made to Vanny.

He's interested, and Shane and Eden are like my own personal sales staff. They talk me up as if my bookmobile is a real, viable business, not just something I pieced together with scraps of construction paper and glue sticks. Then Izzy runs over from the book setup and hugs me around the waist. "Mom, this is the best project you've ever done."

I'm feeling good. I'm feeling giddy, so of course that's when I see my mother at the door.

I tighten my arms around Izzy. Shane follows my gaze to the front of the diner, and everything about him sharpens. I expect him to stomp over there and tell her to leave, or possibly inform her that we'll be pressing charges.

I'll have to hold him back. To tell him this is my battle to fight, and I'd like him to let me do it instead of treating me like a child.

But to my surprise he turns to me. *"How do you want to handle this, Ruthie?"* his eyes silently ask.

Although he doesn't want to alarm Izz by saying anything out loud, it's all there in his eyes. Warmth floods me, filling me with strength that doesn't feel borrowed. He's letting me handle this my way.

In that moment, with him so surprisingly agreeable, I'm tempted to let him take over. If he ushers her out, I won't need to speak to her or look at her face. But that would be the coward's way, and I don't want to be a coward anymore. I want to be the woman I've been these last weeks, brave and hopeful.

"Why don't you and Izz work on creating a book together, Shane?" I ask. "There's something I have to do."

"I was hoping you'd say that," he says, giving Izzy a big grin. A *salesman* grin, but I don't hold it against him. He's keeping it together for her, and I'm struggling.

I watch them head toward the table in the back, where a boy of nine or ten is standing with a red-haired woman and a big man who are beaming at him. The woman's holding a toddler who's watching the boy with interest.

All day, the kids have gone crazy over my setup—as if there were candy buried into the floor pillows and cushions, an idea Shane jokingly suggested the other day.

My mother is here.

I consider looking for Danny, but it hits me that I need to do this alone. I need to know that I can face her by myself, without a filter or a helper or anything but my own will.

So I take a big breath and push my way toward her. She's standing at the front of the restaurant, frowning at the crowd as if it offended her. That frown deepens when she notices me. Life has worn her down, dulling her features and her hair, pressing her frown lines into permanence, but she's tried to fight back by dying her hair and using too much makeup.

I can't help but wonder what she sees when she looks at me. Can she tell I'm happy? Is she hoping to ruin it?

When I get close, she says, "It's a free country. You can't keep me from coming in here."

"You said you'd stay away from Izzy," I remind her.

She gives me a sour look. "She's my *granddaughter*. You're my daughter. I have rights."

"You don't have the right to vandalize my property or break into my apartment," I say. "Last I heard, that was illegal for anyone."

Color leaks out of her face. "Who told you I did that?"

Not a denial, I note. "You left behind prints. Were you drunk when you did it?"

She glances around, her gaze lingering for a moment on Shane, who is watching us but hasn't come over. Danny, who's now standing with him and Izzy, only gets cursory notice from her.

"I need to talk to you privately," my mother says.

I direct her around the corner to the hallway leading to the single-occupancy bathroom. There are a couple of people waiting in line, and there probably will be the entire time we're here. It's private but not too private.

Her expression suggests she doesn't like it.

Good.

"Izzy's grandparents want to give her money," she says, trying to make it sound like she's delivering welcome news.

"Izzy doesn't have any grandparents," I insist.

If that hurts, it doesn't register on her face. "The Callaghans have a lot of money," she continues, "and they want to give her some of it. *As they should.* I was helping. I knew you'd be too stubborn to hear them out, so I did what I had to do for my granddaughter."

"What is it they want in return for all of this money, *Mother*?" I ask tightly.

"Shared custody." She waves toward the main part of the diner. "You're busy with all of this. It would be a relief for you. And *much* better for her. Think of that place you live in."

"What? So the person the Callaghans paid to break in didn't think much of it? Excuse me if I'm not impressed."

"I don't know anything about that," she insists with flat lips. "But I'm guessing you don't live anywhere nice. You've been working at *this* place for years. It would be better for her if she spent half her time with them. If you had the support to find a better situation."

"And I'm guessing it would also be better for you?"

"I wanted to help them because Isabella's my grandbaby," she insists. "They're going to let me see her too. We all want to help you, Ruthie, but you're too stubborn to accept help from anyone.

"How much money did they pay you?"

"It's not about the money," she lies.

"So, what? They paid you to help them make sure Izzy was their granddaughter instead of, I don't know, fucking asking me?"

"You're crude and stubborn," she says, her lips trembling. It's not from sadness, though. She looks angry, like I'm fucking up this awesome situation she wandered into. "They made the right choice. You never would have listened to reason."

"And you're going to jail. Maybe they'll only keep you for a few days. Maybe longer. But you're going, and I'm not going to do anything to save you. Them either. I'm going to see to it that they're prosecuted to the full extent of the law. Izzy is their granddaughter, but they'll never know her."

"You're a fool," she seethes, gripping my arm so tightly I can feel the bones in her fingers. Edging closer, she floods me with the scent of alcohol barely covered by cheap perfume. Her eyes are shrewd and cruel, her grip punishing. "You're nothing but a stupid little whore. The only thing you ever had talent at was spreading your legs."

I feel him coming before his hand descends on my arm, plucking hers away as if it's nothing, as if it didn't feel like a shackle made of bone seconds before.

I glance over to see Shane and Danny beside me. For a second I'm worried about Izzy—the Callaghans are after her, and they might know by now that she's related to them—but my fear settles because Shane and Danny value her safety as much as I do. They would never let harm come to her. *Never.*

Shane is giving my mother a look that rains fire. "You'd better watch how you to speak to *my wife.*"

My heart leaps in my throat and lodges there, growing so large that it threatens to choke the life out of me. Because he said that like it meant something to him.

"Your wife?" she asks, incredulous.

"*My wife,*" he repeats, with a possessiveness that instantly makes me want to back him into a wall. "And neither of us will allow you speak to her so disrespectfully again."

Her gaze shifts to me, shrewd. "Well-played, Ruthie. You know how to marry men who are better than you. Let's see if you can keep this one."

"I won't warn you again," Shane says in a growl. "You mess with her or Izzy, and I will make you suffer for it. I don't care why you're doing it, or what made you the way you are, or why you feel it's okay to torment the people you should value above anyone else. I will make you pay. And I will make you keep paying. I will *destroy* you."

"Stay away from all of us," Danny adds. "This is your last warning."

"I don't want anything to do with *you,*" our mother tells him. "I'm here for—"

"You're here for no one but yourself," Danny says, his hand rubbing the edge of his pocket, "and this is us telling you that we know it. Now, leave. If you don't feel like you can manage the twenty steps that will take you out the door, there are half a dozen people here who would be happy to carry you out. I'm just one of them."

It goes without saying Shane is another. But instead of piling on, he wraps his arm around me, and three of us walk away.

That slender flame inside of me has been fed kerosene.

I know I'll be replaying this moment in my head for a long time to come, maybe for the rest of my life. The first time when Shane called me *my wife* and meant it.

I hope to God it isn't the last.

SHANE

ON VALENTINE'S DAY, I leave a single rose on Ruthie's pillow, along with the storybook Izzy and I finished the previous night. It's about a superhero single mom and the van she uses to save the day.

I have another offering planned, but it'll take longer. It'll also take maneuvering—what Ruthie would probably call manipulation —but that's my specialty and I'm never put off by a challenge. Still, it might take months.

I head into the other room to get some work done, and am interrupted by her laughter a few minutes later. Ruthie and I both get up early—me, because it's my habit, and her because she needs to get Izzy ready for school. Smiling to myself, I keep sipping my coffee and answering emails until Ruthie walks into the dining room with a wrapped package.

"I got something for you too, stalker," she says.

"Oh?" I ask, oddly excited.

She walks up and hands the present over.

"Is this going to kill me?"

"Probably not, but it's hard to say. You're a difficult man to read."

I tear into the wrapping paper, laughing as I pull out a pair of flannel pajamas that's the same style as the ones in my drawer.

"What do you think?" I ask. "Should I wear them to work?"

"Mr. Freeman probably wouldn't care," she says with a twinkle in her eyes, like she knows how much I'd prefer for him to care about things like that. Then she leans in to kiss me. And I feel a buoyancy in my chest that I'm starting to recognize as happiness.

"Say, Ruthie," I start, my heart speeding up.

"Say, Shane."

"Izzy told me something I think we should discuss..."

And I tell her about our Dad talk the other night. Ruthie looks like she's on the verge of tears, so I feel like I made a mistake, probably a stupid one, but when I finish, she mutters, "Oh, my sweet little girl."

"What should I tell her?" I ask.

"I'll talk to her. It's..." She caresses my face and then kisses me. "It's too soon. But someday..."

"Someday," I say firmly, because I'd like to think of it as something that's on the horizon.

From the way she kisses me, she doesn't object.

At work, I explain the situation with the Callaghans to Freeman, who immediately agrees to represent Ruthie in civil court. Ruthie and I go to Mira's party at her bar that night, while Izzy stays in with Uncle Danny.

The week passes, days falling through the hourglass like sand, full of moments to remember. The dog pissing in my shoes. Ruthie and Izzy dancing to Taylor Swift and then laughing hysterically when I join them. I know the lyrics despite myself, since it's part of the soundtrack of their lives. *Our* lives. Having dinner with Danny and Mira. Visiting my mother with Izzy and seeing my mom's eyes light up. Working on some wills and a couple of property disputes at Freeman & Daniels while I wait for Josie's day in court. Attending a work reception with Ruthie and Izzy. We both wear our rings for it, and neither of us take them off afterward. It's not something we discuss, just something we do.

The police call us after they arrest Rita. And again when the perp who was paid to break into Ruthie's apartment confesses and asks for leniency for turning in the people who hired him. The Callaghans are arrested. I'm positive they'll get off without more than a scratch, because people like them—and the Burkes—usually do, but they'll have to pay for the privilege. Money that will go into Izzy's college fund.

Meanwhile, Ruthie has gotten at least half a dozen calls from potential clients who want Vanny events. The buzz will keep building, I think. She's already gotten around to setting up a website, and if we add an online store, it'll generate more business.

Another week passes, and I'm...happy. But I also feel like a teetering domino—with the potential to fall and take everything I've been building down with me.

This situation I'm in is supposed to be a placeholder.

My marriage, fake.

My job, temporary.

But I care about my wife and stepdaughter, and my job...

I'm employed by a firm that's middling to mediocre, a place that will never make legal magazines or history, but a voice in my head has been suggesting that maybe I could help them think bigger. It's been getting louder.

Perhaps it's a vain thought, a prideful one, but there's no denying I have more ambition than the other lawyers in the practice. I suspect I really can help amp up our profile.

Still...wouldn't I reach even higher if I worked somewhere else?

Then there's Izzy's surgery, fast approaching. I've done extensive research on the doctor Ruthie chose and also the surgery itself. There's no reason whatsoever to believe there will be complications, but I'm terrified.

Meanwhile, the interest in Josie's case has warmed up. There was an editorial in the paper about superfluous lawsuits, with her case as the example, and then a reporter from WLOS ran a piece about her, interviewing several past clients—some satisfied and others less so. The dissatisfied ones are hardly a nail in our coffin, because several of them are pissed that her predictions "came true," including Shauna's old friends, Colter and Bianca, the couple whose wedding Josie "ruined" because the cake ended up being destroyed, just like she'd predicted.

It's heating up to be a big deal.

If I lose, a huge deal, because I'm counting on a jury of Josie's peers to think it's possible that she can read the future. The more I think of it, the more I think I'm in for it. But I'm also excited, because it's a challenge, isn't it?

I'm going to give that pain-in-the-ass woman a defense that will make history.

The day comes in the way long-awaited days do, with little fanfare. When my alarm goes off absurdly early on Thursday, Josie's court date, Ruthie rolls over in bed and looks at me. "I'd wish you luck, but I don't think you need it. You're going to win this for her."

I kiss her softly. "Thanks for building up my ego the way you've always promised me you won't. I know it must have cost you."

When I get to court, Nicole and Damien are already present in the audience. When Nicole sees me, she points to her eyes and then points to me, which I take to mean she expects me to win. If I don't, I'll be on her shit list, which is probably an uncomfortable place to be.

I recognize a few of the other spectators as press. The tea lady, Josie's old boss, is also there. She's knitting a sweater, of all things, having managed to do the impossible and convince the security guards to allow her to bring in her knitting needles. She smiles and nods at me, and I nod back as I pass her.

I slide into my seat, Michael sitting down beside me. "Let the show begin," I say to him in an undertone.

"This is way more exciting than anything that ever happened in the jewelry store," he whispers back.

A couple of minutes later, Josie enters the court, wearing a kaftan embroidered with golden stars and an oversized golden hair ornament shaped like an open, staring eye. Well, good to see she listened to me when I advised her to dress conservatively. She looks like a quack, the kind of person you'd find if you went to the boardwalk at the beach—a particularly seedy one—and slipped into a tent with a sign reading "Psychic."

"Well, what do you think, Josie the Great?" I ask her with a smile as she lowers into the chair next to us. I could give her a hard time about the costume, but she's already wearing it, and I'm guessing she doesn't have a business casual suit stuffed in her bag. "Do you predict we're going to win this thing?"

She surprises me by pulling a Magic 8-Ball out of her bag and shaking it. Without speaking, she shows me the readout: *Prospects are murky*.

"Well, it's not a no," I tell her. "We'll take it. All the same, you should probably keep that in your bag. If you start flashing it around, people might get the wrong idea about your *abilities*."

"It's for you," she says, trying to hand it to me. "It's your house-warming present."

"Thanks," I say glibly, "but you'd better keep it in your bag right now all the same."

She tucks it back in before worrying her lip and saying, "There's a lot of press here."

"Good. All the better to report our win."

"I'm glad you're feeling optimistic," she says. "It's because of your wife, isn't it? She has a *much* sunnier aura than you do."

"You're right about that," I say, feeling a glow at the mention of Ruthie. It's like she's here with me, my own personal sunshine.

"I feel that way about my boyfriend too, but we figured it would be for the best if he didn't come after what happened between him and the plaintiff."

"Yes, I'm the one who told you that."

"But I already knew you were going to say it."

Seems I'm not the only one who enjoys having the last word.

It doesn't take long for us to get into the swing of it. Jury selection. Opening statements. I call witnesses. A woman who claims Josie saved her life because she predicted—correctly—that her house was in danger of burning down (the heating system was broken.) A man whom she'd helped find a lost relative. Plus a few more for good measure.

The opposing attorney cross-examines them, but even though he's adept at creating doubt, will it be enough? Because many of the predictions she's made have come to pass, more or less.

We break for the day, and in the morning, the wife whose affections were supposedly alienated goes on the stand, called by the opposition.

"Were you planning to divorce my client before you started getting psychic readings from the defendant?" he asks, giving her a sharp look.

"No," she says immediately.

I grit my teeth, because that's not good, but I have plans for a rebuttal. When it's my turn to question her, I ask if she ever told Josie about her husband's best friend or showed her photos from their wedding. No and no. And there were no official photos because the wedding photographer they'd hired had used their deposit to buy himself a plane ticket to Costa Rica. Her now-boyfriend isn't even on social media.

"She had no way of knowing," the woman says with the conviction of a proselyte.

Josie mouths, "No *other* way of knowing."

It's time for closing arguments. We're given a break first, and I excuse myself to the family restroom, which has the advantage of a locking door, because I feel a familiar urge to throw up.

This is it. Make or break. If I lose, then I'm sunk. Buried in the sands of obscurity. But if I win...

When I'm done, I look at myself in the mirror. This is my usual dance, but I find myself taking out my phone, giving in to the urge to pull up the photo of Ruthie, Izzy, and me from the day we played that game. There's a text waiting for me, though. Ruthie:

If anyone can sell a roomful of skeptics on the possibility of the supernatural, it's 100% you. You've got this. Your girls are rooting for you.

It's accompanied by a snap of Ruthie and Izzy—Flower photobombing them with someone's shoe in her mouth. Probably *my* shoe. Warmth and conviction thread through my limbs, and I head back into the courtroom to make my closing argument.

Two hours later, the jury returns a not-guilty verdict, and the judge follows my suggestion and confirms that the dumbass who started this whole thing will be paying my bills.

I turn to Josie with a grin, the victory lifting me up as surely as if someone had given me a boost onto their shoulders.

"Congratulations, you're officially psychic, Josie the Great."

"Of course I am," she says, but she's obviously pleased. "Should I offer to give everyone readings as a thank you?"

"Yeah, that's a no."

Before we leave the courtroom, I text the good news to Ruthie and my friends. As soon as Josie and I get outside, we're pulled aside by four different reporters who want to hear all about the win. I play my part, but I know what I need, and it isn't here.

I want to be home with my family.

A half hour, I finally open the door, and Ruthie's waiting for me in a blue sweater dress that hugs her ass. Her eyes are alight, and the way she looks at me...

She puts her arms around my neck and squeals right into my ear. "You're going to make me deaf," I say, swinging her around.

"Don't make promises you don't intend on keeping."

It's only then that I notice all of the people gathered in my living room, my buddies and their partners. Izzy's watching a show with Danny that's put a constipated look on his face, but he gives me a tortured smile when I look over.

"Were you going to invite me to our party?" I ask Ruthie.

She grins. "I told them to park around the corner so you wouldn't know."

"What were you going to do if I lost?" I ask.

"You weren't going to lose," she says, then shrugs. "And if you did, I figured you could use the company."

No, what I've always done after a loss is get blind drunk and spend the night considering what I could have done differently to make the loss a win. But maybe her way is better.

"I'm making everyone cocktails," Mira says, getting up. "You look like a man who could use a Psychic and Tonic."

I catch sight of the ring on her finger, and my gaze shifts back to Danny, whose smile widens. "Yeah. That happened too."

"Are you hijacking my victory party?"

"Seems only right. You hijacked my engagement."

Damn right, I did.

thirty-eight

SHANE

BY THE TIME EVERYONE LEAVES, Ruthie is giving big, jaw-cracking yawns, so I carry her to bed, literally, and tell her I'm cleaning up.

"But it's your party. You can't clean up after your own party," she complains.

"I won't say anything if you don't," I tease, feeling a wave of deep contentment as I tuck her under the covers.

"You don't have to tuck me in."

"Like hell I don't," I kiss her forehead and then her lips. "Thank you for tonight."

She smiles up at me. "I knew you were going to win."

"You know, I feel like saying something sentimental."

"Do it," she says, propping up on her elbows to look at me, her eyes gleaming.

"I feel like I'd already won because I have you," I tell her.

"Oooh, yup, that was almost unforgivably cheesy." I pretend to lift my hands and walk off, but she grabs my tie and pulls me back. "And I loved it."

She gives me another soft kiss, sweet enough that I consider staying until I notice how heavy her eyes still are.

"Get some sleep, honey," I say, then I head into the living room to clean up.

Flower thwaps her tail on her dog bed, and I give her a quick pet before cleaning up the plates and cups we left out. I find myself humming as I work, then laugh at my own absurdity. I'm flying high, feeling good.

When I'm done, I stop by Izzy's room on a whim, opening the door and peeking inside to check on her. She's curled up, her dark hair splayed on the pillow, and she looks so much like Ruthie it makes me smile.

I'm brushing my teeth, getting ready for bed, when my phone buzzes. I'm half tempted to turn it off without checking—surely I've done my work for the day—but then I see something interesting on the screen. An email from one of the many people I interviewed with prior to finding a job with Freeman. I spit out the toothpaste and check it out.

I listened to your closing argument today. If you're still interested in a future at Beckett Brothers, come see me on Monday. 7 a.m.
-Lance Beckett

It's ballsy of him, all things considered. Two months ago, he told me I was interesting, but not interesting enough to tempt *him*. Apparently, he'd only asked me in for an interview to find out if I'd really called Fred Myles a withered dick in a bad suit.

I didn't, but regrets are a real thing.

I don't answer the email, because an answer isn't required.

It's a challenge he's handed me, and my choices are thus: *Go, don't go.*

Two months ago, when I left Beckett's office and immediately showed myself to the closest bar, I would have been ecstatic to receive a rude email from him. I would have bought everyone in the bar a top-shelf drink, but now I don't feel anything approaching relief. In fact, the peace and happiness I've felt all evening have disappeared like vapor, and I'm so conflicted, I consider pulling out a coin.

Freeman let me handle this case the way I wanted to. He didn't interfere, even though my approach should have been a loser's choice. He believed I could pull it off.

I like Freeman. But loyalty to him isn't my main hesitation.

There are two problems, as I see them: the interview time and day. Izzy's getting her surgery on Monday. Not until noon, but she's scared, and I want to be there holding her hand. Reassuring Ruthie. Then there's my knowledge of what life is like at Beckett's firm. The hours are on par with what we had at Myles & Lee. If I take a job there, I'll be working around the clock again, living at the office. I'll hardly ever see Ruthie and Izzy, a thought that fills me with something like panic.

But you'll be able to provide for them, I tell myself.

And if I work there, I can build a name for myself. A legacy. The kind of thing that can't easily be washed away by waves.

I'm distracted and pissed off all weekend. It's no one's fault but mine, but my mind is stuck on that interview and what it might mean, not on the victory that closed out my week. The only other thoughts that intrude are about Izzy's surgery, and they're dark ones. *What if you lose her? What if it's all been for nothing, and it would be better if she didn't get the surgery? What if something happens to her and it's your fault for suggesting this whole thing?*

I get her floor pillows and enough ice pops to stuff the freezer.

"You've been a real dick, you know," Ruthie says to me on Sunday night. It's late, and we're standing in the bedroom after arguing for five minutes about nothing. I've gotten this far without telling her about the interview, and I know it's time to make the decision I've been dancing around since Friday.

"I'm sorry," I say, running a hand through my hair and looking off. I feel my jaw working.

She raises her eyebrows. "How about you finally get around to telling me what's wrong with you?"

Leave it to her to put it so succinctly.

"You've always said I'm a dick. Is it really news that I've been acting like one?"

She puts a hand on my chest, whether to caress me or push me, I couldn't say. "Shane. What's going on?"

Sighing, I sit on the bed and put my head in my hands. And I tell her.

"You're going, aren't you?" she asks when I finish. She's still standing, looking down at me as if she's my confessor and I fucked up bad. There's a hard edge to her now, as if the Ruthie of the past few weeks just pulled on armor.

"Yes. This is what I've wanted. This is what I need."

Even as I say the words, they don't feel quite right, because I can sense the distance they're putting between us. But this *is* the opportunity I've been hoping for, and it would be foolish to turn it away as if it doesn't matter.

She gives me a tight nod. "Will you be back in time for the surgery?"

I swear under my breath and reach for her. She lets me pull her onto the bed next to me, but I feel that distance between us even with her thigh pressing against mine. Flower, who's been resting on the floor at our feet, looks up with an accusatory glance that makes me feel even more like a screwup. "Is that what you think of me?" I ask, holding Ruthie closer, like I can keep her from slipping away. "I promised Izzy. I promised *you*. Of course I'll be back."

"Okay," she says, her voice coming out shaky. "And the job....what'll it be like?"

"It'll be busier. More like it was at Myles & Lee."

"You'll always be at the office." She doesn't look at me as she says it. "You'll forget you have clothes other than suits."

"Hey, you like my suits," I joke, trying to lighten the mood, even though I feel my own gut tightening. Telling me she's right.

She turns her head, and her eyes look almost shiny, as if...

She lifts a hand to my throat, caresses where my tie would be if I'd had one on. "I don't want you to become a stuffed one."

"It'll never happen. Unless you're the one who stuffs me, and then you'd only have yourself to blame."

Staring into my eyes, she says, "We've been giving this a try, and it's been good, hasn't it? Really good." Her voice shakes on those last words.

I lift my hand to her cheek, tracing it with the pads of my fingers, needing to feel that she's here. That she's with me. "It's been the best part of my life."

"We've been wearing the rings," she adds, "but we haven't talked about what it means. If you've changed your mind..."

"I haven't changed my mind. I want you here."

I need you...

"You said this arrangement would only last until Izzy got a surgery and you got a new job. There's no real reason for Izzy and me to keep living here. The locks were changed at the apartment, and we caught the people who did it. We'd be safe there."

No. No. No.

"Things have changed," I insist, staring into her eyes, my hand still on her cheek. Because I need her to see I mean it. That if she leaves me, I'll be a hollow man, left only with my ambition, which cares so little about me it might incinerate me from the inside out. "*Everything* has changed. You're my wife." I kiss her softly. Then I kiss her again, harder, wanting to show her what I can't say in words. Wanting to erase the doubt I see in her eyes. The worry that she was right in the first place, and it's only in the last month that she's gotten it wrong.

I love her, I love her so fucking much, but I can't bring myself to say it.

Because love is a weakness.
Love is a curse.
And I always lose the things I love.

RUTHIE

THE SURGERY STARTS IN AN HOUR, and we have to leave for the doctor's office.

Shane's not here.

I'm pissed, because I'm already worried about Izzy, and now I'm worried about him too. Was he in some kind of accident, or is he just making the wrong decision and doubling down on it like the all-or-nothing person he is? I have no way of knowing, but my gut tells me he's still at that meeting. He's there, and I'm here, waiting for him like a chump.

Maybe Tank was right all along.

This is a mistake, he'd said. He's kept saying it too, like a song refrain no one wants to listen to.

I'm worried about you.

He's going to take advantage of you.

He's not trustworthy.

"Dad's still not here," Izzy says, peering out the front window. We've both been pacing the house like caged things, Flower tracking our footsteps with pacing of her own.

"What did you call him?" I ask, stopping in my tracks. After Shane told me about their conversation, I had a sit-down talk with her and told her it would be better to wait to call him that.

"I want to, Mom," she tells me. "I've put a lot of thought into it. Shane treats me like a dad would."

It's what I've dared to hope for, but hearing her say that about him now, when he's possibly choosing a job over us, might very well kill me.

I get down on my knees next to her. "Izz, he's not your father or your uncle."

She rolls her eyes like she's suddenly morphed into a teenager. "I know that, Mom. That man with the crazy parents is my dad, but *he* doesn't care about me. Shane does. I want him to be my dad."

Tears press at my eyes, because goddammit. How dare Shane make her feel that way if he wasn't sure...

"Okay, honey," I tell her, because I won't be the person to crush her, and especially not right now. "But we have to leave. We can't be late."

"But he said he'd be here," she says, her gaze trained out the window. "He's going to be here."

I can feel her heart breaking. Or maybe it's my own heart that's breaking, because how many times have I let myself believe I'm more important to a man than I actually am? How many times have I peered out of a window, waiting for someone who will never come? Who never *intended* to come.

There was Rand of course, and Jarrod Travis. But they weren't the first men to let me down. Maybe, in a fucked up way, *Shane* was the first. Because my parents never had enough of a hold on my heart to break it. But Shane did, asking Danny why his sister always had to hang around. Making me feel like I meant nothing to the boy who meant the world to me.

Why is my heart like this? Why does it only want what it can never have?

In my head, I can hear Shane telling my mother that he will destroy her if she so much as breathes wrong when it comes to Izzy and me. I can hear him calling me *my wife*. And I can see all those tidy little Amazon boxes lined up, filled with my wishes, and a jewelry box with a red ring...

My heart is stupid, because I'm in love with him, of course. Desperately, horribly, irretrievably.

I feel so messed up inside, like a science experiment gone wrong, but I need to keep it together for my daughter. "We have to leave, sweetheart," I say, hugging Izzy to me. "I'll tell Shane where he can meet us. If he doesn't get there in time, I bet he'll make it up to you later. And he'll have a really funny story about whatever he was doing."

Or at least he'd better make one up.

"I'm scared, Mom," she says, her lower lip trembling. And I don't know whether she's scared about the surgery, or about whatever's taking Shane away from something that's supposedly so important to him.

"It's okay to be scared, and I never want you to be afraid to tell me how you're feeling, but this is going to be good, Izzy. It's going to help you, and we're going to have so much fun tonight, just like we've been planning."

"With Shane?"

Hating that I might be lying for him, I say, "With Shane."

It's not until we're in her hospital room that he finally texts me back. My first reaction is relief—*he's not dead, he's okay*—and then dread as I click through.

I'm so sorry, Ruthie. There was no clock in the conference room, and my phone wouldn't turn on until I did a hard restart. Shit. Is Izzy okay? I'm on my way.

She asked if her dad was coming. You can imagine my surprise. We're already in the room at the hospital. I don't know if you'll make it.

I'm coming.

But by the time he arrives in the waiting room, panting, wearing a suit with a red tie, I'm back in there. The anesthesiologist has already come and gone with Izzy.

His face falls when he sees me. "I'm too late," he says in an almost a whisper, his voice harsh. When he crosses to me, he reaches for my hand. I let him take it, but it's like a dead fish in his grip. "I'm so sorry."

"Do you know how many people have apologized to me?" I ask, my voice like sandpaper. "I don't give a single fuck if you're sorry."

"It was a test, Ruthie," he says, looking down like he can't bear to meet my eyes. "Beckett left me sitting in there for a long time before he came in. He wanted to see how I'd react. I had to act like I didn't care. But you've got to believe that I wouldn't have stayed so long if I'd realized...I thought there was still plenty of time."

"So he treated you disrespectfully, again, and made you miss Izzy's appointment. And you want to work there?" I laugh, not caring that people are watching us. "Maybe this was a test too. And you failed it. I could have had Danny come with us, and then I wouldn't have been alone."

Because it wasn't just the disappointment to Izzy that hurt. I've been sitting here with my own fear for her, with no one by my side except a man who smells like mayonnaise and is wearing a Christmas sweater in March.

Shane looks wrecked, and right then I'm glad for it.

"I'm going to make it up to both of you. I have big plans for tonight."

"Until this Beckett guy asks you to do something for him? Is this what it'll be like if you take the job? Every time he says jump, you'll ask how high? I didn't think you were the kind of guy who liked being told what to do."

"I don't," he says, his jaw flexing. "Which is why I don't like what you're trying to do right now. It was like this at Myles & Lee in the beginning too, and I made partner there. I know what I'm doing."

"Do you?" I ask, getting up. I can feel mayonnaise guy watching me, so I throw him a salute as I tug Shane out into the hallway where there are a couple of poorly stocked vending machines full of melted chocolate and stale salty things. "Don't get excited," I say. "I don't have any stupid ideas this time. I just want somewhere private to yell at you."

"Why bother? You've never seemed to care before."

"Because I never felt on the verge of crying before," I lie, feeling the tears pressing against my eyes, hot and angry and devastated. "You've made it pretty clear where we rank for you."

"It benefits all of us if I have a better job," he insists, but I can tell he's upset, maybe even angry. "You didn't ask how the interview went. For all you know, I don't have a chance."

"I know he made you an offer. Nothing else would have kept you that long."

"You knew I wasn't going to stay at Freeman & Daniels forever."

"Because they care about making sure the people who work there can have lives? Yeah, what a horror show. I can see why you'd want to put that place in your back mirror."

He wraps a hand around my shoulder, and I don't shrug it off. I can't bring myself to because I want the heat of it too badly. "You know why I need this, Ruthie. I told you."

About his dad. About his desire to make a legacy. I could tell him about the project I've finally finished, but I'd rather show him than tell him. And right now I'm not done having my say.

"But what kind of legacy do you want to make, Shane? Is being great more important to you than being good?"

"Why should I have to give up one to be the other?"

"You don't." I let myself lift my hand to his face. "I see the goodness in you. I'd let myself think it wasn't there anymore for a while, but it's never left, even if you want to stuff it into a box. I'll be damned if I'm going to keep sitting at the window and waiting for you to come back to me and Izzy. I might have accepted that for myself, but I won't do it for her."

He releases my shoulder and smooths his tie, his face barely registering the mess I know is going on underneath. "This morning was a mistake, a fuckup, but I *am* going to have to work long hours, Ruthie. You know that."

"There's a difference between long hours and living at the office. I understand one, but I don't understand the other."

He watches me for a long moment, his eyes sad.

"I'm worried you're going to lose yourself again," I tell him. "It's already happening. I can't just stand by and watch."

"Please don't do this, Ruthie," he says, as if I'm the one who's doing it. "Let me make it up to her."

"You will," I say. "But I don't think it's a good idea for us to keep staying with you."

"That's not what I want," he says, reaching for me again. I let him, because I want him to keep reaching for me. For us.

"No," I say. "But for right now, that's how it's got to be. I have to protect her."

And I have to protect myself.

Because Tank's not right, but I know he's not altogether wrong either. If I let myself keep playing house with Shane, pretending that our life together is real, it's going to hurt even more if he chooses to leave us behind. If he decides he's more interested in what he'll look like after he's dead than about being alive.

"Are you saying we're through?" he says, his voice rough. "Just like that?" His eyes are pleading, and I'm tempted to tell him to forget it. We'll stay. We'll see what happens together. But I *can't.*

My hand finds his tie, and I give it a tug for old time's sake, my fingers shaking. "I don't know, but maybe it's time for us both to think through what we really want. And it'll be easier to do that if we're not living together."

"I don't want you to go," he says. I know how much it costs him, I do, but it doesn't matter.

He still plans on taking that job for all the wrong reasons, and it'll still be a mistake—maybe the kind of mistake that will ruin him.

I can't bear to have a front-row seat to that. I won't.

But I haven't given up yet.

I have one last play, and I'm hoping—I'm praying—it will win the game.

SHANE

I'M AT WORK, but I'm only physically present.

Izzy's surgery went off without any complications, thank fuck, but I could tell Ruthie wasn't the only one I'd disappointed. I talked up the sleepover plan, but Izzy insisted she didn't feel like doing it anymore. We went out for ice cream, and I overcompensated by getting her three pints to take home, but everything felt off. Tainted. Poisoned.

I was the only one who ended up sleeping in the living room. By myself. Even Flower left me for the bedroom.

Then, this morning Ruthie told me she was going to take some of their stuff back to the apartment. Starting tonight.

I'm going to lose them.

It's a thought that makes everything inside of me quail. Because I *can't* lose them.

I'm so fucked up that when Freeman calls me into his office, I don't so much as flinch. Even though I'm pretty sure I know what it's about.

"Take a seat," he says when I enter the room, but his chair is swiveled around to face the singular window. I feel like kids probably did when they were called into my father's office back when he was a high school principal, a thought that makes me flinch. I shut the door and then lower down into the hot seat in front of Freeman's desk.

"I heard from Lance Beckett, Royce," he says, then finally turns his chair to face me. I can't read his expression, but he's obviously not pleased. Why would he be?

Ruthie was right. It's a shitty thing I'm doing, thinking about walking out this soon. It's not something you should do to a man you respect. I can feel her standing on my shoulder, poking me, telling me to shape up. My heart twists in my chest, feeling like a withered thing.

"Yes, sir," I say, my tone coming out flat and wrong.

"I'm not surprised to hear that he offered you a job, son. I expected you'd be getting offers after you won that case for us."

"I haven't given him an answer yet," I hedge, even though I'm ready to. Or at least I think I am. I've picked up my phone to call him half a dozen times over the last fifteen hours, but I can't quite bring myself to do it.

"There's something I should tell you," I sputter, surprising myself because I know where those words will lead. There's no point in telling him the truth. I can leave, move onward and upward, and the truth won't matter. He'll go on thinking Ruthie and I were married for years before I ever met him, and I'll go on thinking he's a nice man but too much of a putz to really make it. That's how it should go down. But even though Ruthie left, she's still in my head, giving me *that look*. Telling me that I don't have to be an asshole—it's just a choice I keep making.

"Go on," Freeman says, his gaze lingering on me.

"When you met..." My brain supplies *my* wife. I let myself say it, because for now, at least, it's true. "She...wasn't my wife yet, sir."

He cocks his head. "Oh?"

Has my duplicity robbed him of any other vocabulary?

I still have the chance to lie. I could say that Ruthie and I were already been engaged, and it was just the timeline he got wrong, but shouldn't he know who I really am? Then he won't regret it when I prove to him, as I've proven to Ruthie, that I'm not a man who can be relied on to do the right thing.

"No," I say, swallowing. "It was a misunderstanding, sir. You thought she was my wife, and when it became clear to me that you were only looking to hire a family man, one who'd fit in with the team, I let it stand. Because I needed a job. Myles had poisoned everyone in town against me."

He meets my gaze. "She's on your insurance. Wendy cleared the paperwork through me. Did you include all of us in your lie?"

This is where I'm going to look like a psychopath, but in for a penny...

"We're married now," I say. "Izzy needed health insurance so she could get her surgery. So Ruthie and I really got married."

He makes a *hm* sound and leans back in his chair. "Why are you telling me all of this now, son?" he asks after an excruciating moment that has me sweating.

I don't know.

But that's not strictly true. I'm getting better at reading the emotions before I stuff them down.

"I respect you," I admit through a dry mouth. Like my father, he's someone who does the right things the right way. He cares about what he does—and does what he cares about. I may think it's naïve to live that way, like a Pollyanna handing out lollipops and talking about world peace, but I'll be damned if I don't admire it.

"You didn't." He lifts his eyebrows. It's a challenge I recognize—and accept.

"I didn't," I admit. "I thought..."

"You thought this job was beneath you," he says, finishing my thought as if we're an old married couple.

I nod, feeling a rare burst of shame. Remembering when my father sat me down the day after I talked Danny into giving me his favorite toy. *Just because we have the power to convince someone of something doesn't mean we should.*

"Certainly we have different values than Myles & Lee. And Beckett Brothers, for that matter. But you're wrong if you think I don't see the value in bringing on people who do things differently and reach higher. Why do you think I hired you?"

"Because Ruthie..."

He lifts a hand. "Ruthie is a delightful young woman, and I think very highly of her. But she's not the person I hired, even though I'd heard around town, from many people, that you weren't a team player."

It's my turn to settle for "Oh."

He rubs a hand over his face, and it strikes me that he looks tired and a little sad. "But I saw something in you."

I half think he's going to say, "I saw myself in you," but we both know that wouldn't be true, and instead he says, "You're ambitious, and we need a bit of that energy around here. I thought you could make waves with us, Royce. Hell, you already have. You probably made history last week." He lifts his caterpillar brows. "You think Beckett would have allowed you to represent that woman the way you did?"

"No," I say, because he's right.

"We like to play by our own rulebook around here."

My mind feels like it's a thousand-piece puzzle with the pieces all shaped the same. I don't know how to solve it, or if it can be solved.

"You may have noticed that Daniels never came back from his vacation."

"Yes," I say. Truthfully, it's become something of a joke between Michael and me—the invisible Daniels of Freeman & Daniels. "I'd wondered about that."

"A couple of weeks into the New Year, he told me he'd decided to retire. That's why I brought you on, Royce. I need new blood in this practice, maybe a new partner someday."

"Sir," I say after a moment of silence. "I lied to you. Surely you'd be happy to get rid of me."

"You may have lied to me, son," Freeman says, pushing back in his chair, "but I think the person you lied to most is yourself. I saw something between you and your wife that day. There was already a connection. You were looking for an excuse to pursue it, and I was the man who gave it to you. Now, I won't tell you not to consider Beckett's offer. You need to do what's right for you, same as any of us. But know that we have something else to offer you here. Creativity. Time for your family. You go on home and give it a thought. But don't think too long."

For a second, I feel my mood lifting, because here he is, offering me what I need for the second time in less than two months. A fulfilling job, and Ruthie and Izzy. But then dread wraps around me and makes me its bitch, because it's probably too late.

I stumble back to my office, and Michael whistles and then grabs something from his drawer and follows me inside, shutting the door behind him.

Once it's closed, he shows me the flask.

"I should probably yell at you for having that," I say as I motion it over.

"But you're not going to," he says as he gives it to me. "I should probably yell at you for not telling me about your interview."

"Christ." I shake my head after taking a gulp of the whiskey. "What, you got a wire in Freeman's office or something?"

"You're not nearly as quiet or subtle as you think you are. I brought coffee over to his assistant so I could figure out what was up with you. I take it things aren't going well with Ruthie of the ruby?"

"I fucked up, big surprise." I hand the flask back over, and he waves it off.

"Your need is greater."

Fine by me. I set it on my desk. He studies me for a second, his eyes surprisingly piercing for someone who's so mild-mannered, and I flinch. "What?"

"I'm trying to decide whether I should tell you something."

"Go for it. My day couldn't get much worse."

He lifts his eyebrows, his mouth scrunching to the side. "It's just...you know how I told you in the beginning that I could tell your friend was in love but you weren't?"

"I changed my mind," I say. "Maybe I don't want you to continue."

He winks at me. "I think you already know what I was going to say, boss. So am I going to lose this job just after I started getting comfortable here?"

"If I decide to go to the other firm, I'll find a position for you."

"I don't know about that, boss man. I like the way things are here."

My first thought is: so do I. My second one is less generous: He's leaving me too.

I just nod—a *please get the fuck out right now* nod—and Michael, being the body-language wizard he is, understands it and goes.

I leave the office early, because I can't seem to function anymore. No one seems to look down at me for it, and Wendy at the front desk tries to get me to accept a lollipop.

On the road, I skip the turn that would take me back to my house. Instead, I find myself weaving up into the mountains, taking in the stark trees that look like hands lifted in supplication. I don't have a plan at the forefront of my mind, but it turns out one was forming anyway, because I find myself parking in a spot that's familiar to me. I cut through the trees, and a few minutes later, I find it.

The safe space. I feel almost feverish as I run my hands over the wooden bench, and then I find it, the crooked heart with our initials inside, carved by Ruthie when she was ten. She thought I was worthy then. She thought I was worthy last week.

But I keep proving myself otherwise.

Maybe I came here to torture myself more. If so, it's working. I return to the car and head home, my mind busy and ill at ease. When I get back, I'm not surprised to see Ruthie and Izzy and even Flower are gone. They didn't take all of their stuff, but I know that will come next. Their stuff will follow them out of my life, and soon there will be no sign left of them other than the blankness they've left behind and the persistent smell of piss in the foyer rug.

Then I find it, lying open on my bed where she should be. It's a scrapbook, and after I glance at the first page, I sink onto the mattress. Because I don't know if my legs could have held me anymore.

I keep flipping.

Each page begins,

I remember Edward Royce.

RUTHIE

I'M at Mrs. Longhorn's apartment drinking tea laced with bourbon.

Izzy wanted to go to school today, and since the doctor had assured me it would be fine, I took her. Then I spent half the morning pacing around Shane's house, trying to convince myself my plan would work and this wouldn't be the end. When pacing didn't improve my mood, I headed over to my apartment.

As soon as I deposited Flower inside, Mrs. Longhorn swooped her door open and asked me over for tea. Which is how I ended up telling her the whole story, or near enough.

"So it was all fake in the beginning," I finish.

She sniffs and takes a long sip of her tea, then says, "It wasn't all fake. The ring's real."

"What?" I ask in disbelief, because it's one of the last things I'd expected her to say.

She holds out her hand, and I give her the ring, feeling a little pang as I slip it off my finger. She lifts it to the light, hems and haws, and then nods. "Honestly, girl, I'm surprised at you. Getting to your age and not knowing a fine ruby when you see it. My daddy taught me to tell real from fake when I was ten."

"Why?" I ask, gaping.

370

She shrugs. "He was a jeweler."

Shit, so she actually knows what she's talking about.

She chuckles at the look on my face. "What'd you think it was made of, rock candy? You may not be happy with your fellow, but he doesn't seem like the kind of man who'd buy a woman a fake rock."

No, he really doesn't. But he bought that ring for me before we'd even kissed. Why go to so much trouble and expense? I know he didn't want anyone to think he was cheap, but for God's sake, there are good fakes.

"I'm...I'm speechless," I say. "I was so sure—"

She heaves a nicotine-laced sigh. "That man's in love with you. Any fool could read between the lines. And he supports your work. You know, a very wealthy man fell in love with me once." She snorts at the surprised look on my face. "I didn't always have a face like a raisin. I was with him, and he said he loved me better than anything, but he tried to get me to quit the bookstore. I said any man who loves me wouldn't expect me to quit my job."

Well, crap. When she puts it that way...

Shane's supported my dream, and I haven't supported his. It's just...it's not his career I object to, or even the long hours. It's his belief that only work will give him the kind of legacy worth having, and that only working for an *asshole* will be challenging enough to help him achieve that. I can't let him operate on that premise.

"Life's complicated," I say with a sigh, taking another sip of the bourbon tea.

"It's not that complicated," she says, giving me one of her patented *you're too stupid to live* looks. "The boy loves you, and you love him. What you're doing back here confounds me, to be frank. Your apartment's a heap of cheap bricks, same as mine, and you're lonely in there. I saw it the first day we met. I kept trying to invite you around for some company, but you're very stubborn."

Huh. I didn't see it that way. I figured she was asking me around so she could show me that list of my flaws, or subject me to a lecture about motherhood and being a woman, but I've come to realize she's just a thorny person. A thorny person with a kind heart.

"Guilty as charged," I mumble.

"And then you got that dog without telling a soul, and I *knew* someone was going to catch you. I wanted to warn you, but you kept lying to me."

I sigh again, this time at myself. "You knew it wasn't an animatronic doll?"

"Do I look like was born yesterday?"

I'm tempted to remind her that she's the one who said she bore a resemblance to a raisin, not me, but she saves me the effort by continuing. "Anyway, I figured you'd be smart and take your escape with that *very* fine man when you were offered it."

I fiddle with my teacup. "I haven't given up on him. Haven't you heard that proverb about letting something go if you love it?"

"That's just plain dumb," she says with a sniff. "If you love something, you hold on tight."

It's with those words ringing in my ears that I head back over to my sad, over-stuffed apartment. Then, a couple of hours later, I pick Izzy up at school.

She assures me that she feels great and is full of stories, until I tell her that we're heading back to the apartment for a while.

"But I like my room at Shane's house."

"I know, honey," I say, glancing back at a red light. "But we have to spend a little time at home. The apartment might fall apart if we're not there to hold it together."

"Mom, it's falling apart anyway," she says in a huff. "A few weeks ago, a piece of plaster fell off the ceiling. Did you forget?"

Honestly, can a person forget a thing like that?

"This probably isn't forever," I say, hoping it's true. "We just need to give Shane a little time to figure some things out."

She pauses for a second and then says, "Okay, Mom."

"That's it?" I ask, surprised to have been let off so easily.

"I know you love him, and he loves you. It always works out in the movies when that happens. I think it'll work out for us too."

If only I had my child's optimism.

But when we get back to the apartment, Shane is waiting outside our door. It's a gray suit today. A gray suit and *the* green tie. He's looking at me so intensely, I feel his gaze in every nerve ending and pulse point in my body.

"Oh, good. Dad's here. That didn't take as long as I thought," Izzy says, giving him a hug. He hugs her back hard, and then she glances up at me. "Mom, can I go inside and watch *My Little Pony?*" I open the door with a quivering hand, the keys making a percussive sound, very aware that he hasn't said anything to me yet.

Izzy slips inside, and if she weren't just five, I'd suspect her of giving us a chance to talk. As is, I'm guessing she really wants to see what those pastel ponies are getting into.

When the door closes, he finally says my name, pouring so much love into it, I nearly start crying.

"You found the book," I say, my voice shaking. And he takes both of my hands. When he looks me in the eyes, I don't look away. The warmth in his gaze nearly burns me.

"I found the book. Ruthie, I can't tell you what it means to me. I..." To my shock, I see tears welling in his eyes. "I didn't know. *I didn't know.* They never talked about him to me. Or to my mom. I thought..." The tears start falling down his cheeks.

I start crying too, because it's impossible for me to see him like this without crying. I trace his tears, and he looks at my wet fingers with wonder.

"Is that from... Fuck, I barely remember what it feels like to cry. It's horrible. No wonder I waited so long."

"And it's wonderful too. You probably have twenty years' worth of tears buried inside of you."

"Oh God, let's hope not."

I cup his face. I kiss his wet cheek. I give into my need and kiss his lips, and he kisses me back hard. The feeling of him is a relief so profound I'd happily drown in it.

"They remembered him," I say, tugging away, "of course they remembered him. I met so many people who loved him, Shane. They *still* love him. They were so happy to talk to me and your mom. She says it really helped her."

"You've done more for her than I ever could," he says. "I...I can't believe you did this for us. Ruthie, there are no words."

I'm torn between giving him a shove and throwing myself at him out here in the open. Because this man is impossible and beautiful, and so complicated it would take twenty encyclopedias to figure him out. "Yes, I did this for you. And you...you were my wish list angel, and you helped me achieve my dream, and you stood up for me. And that's not even mentioning the fact that you bought me a real ring, you dumbass." I do give him a little shove then.

He smiles at me through his tears. "I couldn't let my wife have a fake ring." He pauses, and then corrects himself. "I couldn't let *you* have a fake ring. I...I want you to know that I've decided to stay with Freeman. You're right. There's nothing that other job could have given me that matters more than what I already have. Freeman will let me grow the way I want to grow. And I told him the truth about everything, Ruthie."

"You did?" I ask, shocked.

"I did. I wanted it to be out in the open. And he and Michael both told me what I already knew. What an idiot would know."

"What's that?"

"That I'm in love with you. I'm so in love with you. I...if I lose you and Izzy, my life will mean nothing."

"I love you too," I say, more tears coursing down my cheeks. "I think part of me has loved you since I was a kid."

He laughs and traces my face, his arms wrapping around me. "No, I think you really hated me. But I don't give a shit, as long as you've made the horrible decision to love me now. I'm going to do what I can to make sure you don't regret it, Ruthie. I never want you to regret it. I want to make damn sure you feel as lucky as I do right now."

"I do," I insist, laughing and crying and wrapping my arms around him tightly, because I don't want to let anything or anyone take him away. "I already do."

He kisses me again, his lips claiming and consuming mine, and I give it back to him just as good, holding on to his back, his tie—to every little bit of him I can touch. Then he touches the ring around my neck, and asks, "Can I borrow this for a minute?"

A gasp escapes me, then I reach up to unclasp the necklace with shaking hands. He takes it from me, his grip on the ring steady and uncompromising, not shaking at all.

Then he gets down on one knee, one hand holding mine, the other holding the ring. "Ruthie Traeger," he says, looking up at me. "Will you marry me again? I love you more than I thought I was capable of loving anyone. You light me up inside. You make me feel like a different man, a better one, and I never want to spend a night apart from you."

"Yes, obviously yes," I say, crying more. It's a wonder where all the tears are coming from, only I guess I must have had a well of them inside of me too. Waiting. I pull him up and kiss him again, and again, and then he slips the ring on my finger.

Distantly, I hear the door crack open. "I have a bottle of champagne," Mrs. Longhorn says with an indulgent smile. "And some sparkling grape juice for the little one. Why don't you come on over, and then you can leave the girl over here to watch some shows so you can fornicate in private instead of out here on the open where God and all of his angels can see you."

Damn, I'm not even mad she was spying on us.

"Thank you, Mrs. Longhorn," I say, beaming. "I think we just might take you up on that. We need to go in and get Izzy."

I take Shane's hand, beaming at him, and we go inside to tell Izzy the news that we're getting married again.

"Wait," I say as we step inside, swinging the door shut behind us. "You do realize this means Josie the Great was right again, don't you?"

He laughs, his eyes twinkling at me. "I'd prefer to pretend I'm just that good of a lawyer."

SHANE

"LEAVE it to you to be the first of us to get married and also the last," Leonard says, thumping me on the back of my summer-weight suit. It's a warm balmy day, a year and a half after I took the job at Freeman & Daniels, and we're standing in one of the sitting rooms in the house Ruthie and I rented for the weekend for our re-wedding. It's a rambling place, just outside of town, with extensive gardens and room for everyone to spend the night.

Since Ruthie and I were, technically speaking, already married, we weren't in a hurry to race back to the altar. It felt important to do it right this time, which isn't to say we're doing it big. We only invited our closest friends and family—my mom, my friends and their wives, Ruthie's friend Tank, who has moved past the hatred and resentment stage of our relationship and actually helps me with my car, Eden and Charlie, Freeman and his wife, Michael and his new boyfriend, Josie the Great and Poe, and Nicole and Damien. Of course, no party would be complete without the imitable Mrs. Longhorn, who has agreed to officiate our vow-renewal ceremony. Or Flower, who's going to be taking up flower girl duties with Izzy.

"He likes to get the last word," Danny says, giving me a long look and a nod. I return the gesture, feeling a knot in my throat.

377

Shit, last year my body chose to remember it's capable of falling apart, of crying, and it's as if it developed a taste for it. I'm not about to advertise it to my buddies, but I cried last night, when I asked Izzy if she'd be okay with me submitting adoption paperwork after Ruthie and I were married, and she said, "Of course, Dad. If you didn't say anything, I was going to email it to you."

"I do like getting the last word," I admit. "I'm glad I could do it with all of you here."

"So are we," Burke tells me. He was the second one to get married, technically, and true to his word, he did it the day his parents' case went to trial. He and Delia got married at the Rolf Estate, where they'd first met.

The Burkes were convicted. They've lost their fortune, or the bulk of it, and they're going to spend ten years each in prison, give or take. I heard the news from my old assistant with immense satisfaction, which only had a little to do with the fact that they were represented by the man who'd tried to ruin me.

Because he may have tried to break me—but he was the making of me instead.

"But why'd you invite Nicole, man?" Burke says. "She's out there trying to get your mother to do shots."

I laugh at the image. "Maybe she should take one."

My mom's doing a lot better these days. I credit Ruthie and Izzy. Ruthie's special project too. If it helped me to know that people still remembered my father, it helped my mother tenfold. I'd thought it would be best for her if we didn't keep talking about him and poring over photos, and in some ways I was right. In the more important ways I was wrong. She needed to know her memories were safe before she could move on. These days, she's trying, largely because she's so happy about Ruthie and Izzy and me.

We're selling my house, and after several nightmare rounds of home renovation, we're moving in with my mother. She couldn't be happier about it. Izzy might as well be the ruler of the known universe as far as she's concerned.

"We figured Nicole should be here," I continue. "She's one of the people who helped us. And Burke."

"And Josie the Great?"

"That's obvious," Danny says with a grin. "She's the one who made Shane famous. He's not going to fail to see the value in that."

"She also predicted we'd have another wedding," I tell him. "It would have felt gauche not to invite her."

"And yet we would have thanked you for it," quips Leonard, even though he and Shauna also invited her to their wedding, held at a flower farm this spring.

"I don't know," says Drew, who flew in last night from Puerto Rico. He's still living there. He and his now-wife moved out there with her grandmother, who'd been given a few months to live and wanted to spend it in her ancestral home. But the warm air must have preserved her, because that happened two years ago, and she's still kicking. "Josie's not so bad. Her ego hasn't changed much considering how well she's doing."

"Because she already had an enormous ego," Danny says. "I'm not sure it could have gotten any bigger."

Josie the Great didn't get that TV show she wanted, but never say never. She has a staff now, and an office with a neon sign. I begrudgingly like her, although we don't make a habit of running into each other.

My mother peeks her head into the room, a huge smile on her face. "They're ready for you, dear."

I get a round of back pats from the guys, then I head out into the gardens to stand next to Mrs. Longhorn, who's decked out in an intricate black lace dress. This woman. She's full of mysteries, and she only lets one slip every three months or so. Ruthie says it's so she can keep us hooked. If so, tip of the hat, Mrs. Longhorn. We've all become fond of her, and Ruthie is so invested in keeping her around that she's tried to learn hypnosis from Josie so she can convince our elderly friend to stop smoking. I'm not holding my breath.

"About time, boy," Mrs. Longhorn says, tapping her watch. It doesn't work, but only a fool would risk saying so.

"I'd have married her a year ago."

She snorts. "You *did*."

I look down the aisle, taking in my friends' faces. Nicole does the *I'm watching you* thing, so I salute her. Then I grin as Izzy and Flower come down the aisle, my little girl dropping petals as she goes. She's wearing fairy wings, because this year she's decided she's a fairy. When they reach the front, Izz stops for long enough that I get to drop a kiss on her head—and receive a sloppy lick from Flower—before my mother ushers them over to sit with her.

And then Danny walks Ruthie down the aisle to me, and fuck, I feel it again—tears welling in my eyes. At my request, she's wearing the same dress she wore at the courthouse a year and a half ago. She's the most beautiful sight I've ever seen, and she's my wife. It's not something I deserve, but I'm not going to turn my back on good fortune.

Danny grins as they reach me, and I feel another surge of gratitude so strong it nearly bowls me over. It hits me that he's remembering what I am—a different wedding, a different day, watching him walk her down the aisle to a man I hated. I'm grateful we're here in this day and not that one. So is he, I think.

"Look at you being a softie," Ruthie says, smiling as she lifts onto her toes and kisses me.

"Come now," says Mrs. Longhorn. "I know how you two are. No getting carried away before I have a chance to work my magic."

So we let her do what she does best—act completely disinterested while being the opposite. We exchange vows, and everyone cheers as we kiss in front of Mrs. Longhorn in an "obscene display." Our friends get up to mob the bar, and I know this is the moment

I've been waiting for—my chance to whisk Ruthie away and show her the offering I've been working on.

"We can't leave our own reception," Ruthie hisses to me when I pull her aside and tell her it's time for us to go.

"*You can,*" Izzy tells her, hugging her around the waist. "Dad has it all planned. Everyone knows you're going to be gone for a little while. Aunt Mira said she'd dance with me."

"Aunt Mira likes dancing with everyone," I say with a laugh. She even got Danny to dance with her for a solid hour at their wedding, which is both definitive proof of his love for her and the transformative power of hard liquor.

"So you can go, Mom. Don't worry. We'll make sure everyone behaves."

Ruthie shoots a disbelieving look at Josie, who's cleared a table of appetizers, setting them all on the ground for the squirrels, and seems to have every intention of setting up her crystal ball. I could care less. Her predictions have done me a world of good, ultimately, and if she wants to tell everyone at this party they're going to get food poisoning, so be it.

"How long will it take?" Ruthie asks me in an undertone.

I glance at my watch. "An hour. Maybe longer."

"You're being very mysterious."

"Let him have his moment, Mom," Izzy says, jumping a little on her feet. She has Flower on a leash beside her, and the little dog looks like she's about to start jumping too.

Ruthie rolls her eyes, but I can tell she's loving this. She's always liked being surprised. I'm happy to oblige, because the look on her face when I get it right will always be worth it. "Okay, let's do it."

So I take her hand and sweep her into my car. As we head up the mountain, I slide my hand onto her thigh. "You look amazing, Ruthie. So indescribably amazing. I'm a lucky man."

"Yes, you are," she says, making me laugh. "And I'm a lucky

woman. No one could take their eyes off you today. Mrs. Longhorn looked positively jealous."

"It was the tears that did it. No one can resist a weeping man. I should pull that card in court sometime."

"You do that. So where are we going?"

"You'll see."

I park at the outcropping when I reach it, and she gives me a surprised glance, because she knows this place, of course. We both do. It's her safe place.

"You told me you've already seen the initials on the bench," she says slowly.

"That's not why we're here," I insist, going around to open her door. She laughs when I pull her up into my arms, princess style.

"You're my wife. Indulge me."

"Oh, I've got no problem with being carried."

So I carry her to the spot, hoping Izzy and Danny were right when they gave me the green light, and this isn't a total screw up that will ruin our new wedding day.

When she sees it, her eyes fly wide and she looks at me. "*Shane.*"

I set her down on it—the new bench with the plaque reading

Donated by Shane and Ruthie Royce

"Where's the old one?" she asks, her voice breathy as she traces our names on the plaque. I wasn't so vain as to assume she wanted to take my name. She's the one who suggested it a while back. She told me she'd carried around the name of a man who didn't love her for long enough, and she'd prefer to have mine.

"I asked them if we could keep it," I say, sitting down beside her. "I thought we could put it in the garden. I don't want to ever forget how I let you down. If I can't forget, I won't do it again."

She turns my face to her. "I love this, Shane. It's...it's like a fresh start for this place. But that's a terrible reason for keeping the old bench. Let's keep it because it's a reminder that I've always loved you, and you finally saw sense and started to love me back."

"If I'd loved you when you were ten, it would have been pretty screwed up."

"True," she says with a half-smile. "But you still have some lost time to make up for." she pulls me to her. "I suggest you start now."

And, because I've finally smartened up, that's exactly what I do.

ANGELA CASELLA is a romcom fanatic. Writing them, reading them, watching them—she's greedy, and she does it all. In addition to her solo releases, she's lucky enough to collaborate with Denise Grover Swank. They have three complete series and more co-written projects to come.

She lives in Asheville, NC. Her hobbies include herding her daughter toward less dangerous activities, the aforementioned romcom addiction, and dreaming of having someone else clean her house.

Visit her website at www.angelacasella.com or Angela and Denise's shared website at www.arcdgs.com.